WINCHESTER AFFIDAVIT

WINCHESTER AFFIDAVIT

G. G. Boyer

GUNSMOKE

This hardback edition 2010
by BBC Audiobooks Ltd
by arrangement with
Golden West Literary Agency

Copyright © 1997 by Glenn G. Boyer.
All rights reserved.

ISBN 978 1 408 46281 2

British Library Cataloguing in Publication Data available.

LIBRARIES N.I.	
C900130274	
AudioGO	30.09.10
F	£9.95
MOY	

Printed and bound in Great Britain by
CPI Antony Rowe, Chippenham and Eastbourne

WINCHESTER AFFIDAVIT

Part One

The Bandeliers

Chapter One

Cleve Bandelier was on the alert as soon as his terrier, Maggie, cold-nosed him. When lightning illuminated the room, he saw his tomcat, Pedro, sitting up on the bed, ears pricked, looking toward the window. Something threatening was disturbing both animals. He'd been uneasy since the previous evening when his two hounds hadn't come in for their usual handouts at the supper table. Sometimes they stayed out hunting, but never before for two days. He had a hunch that they were in trouble this time, and his hunches were usually dependable.

He got up and edged to the window, six-shooter in hand, listening intently, but heard only distant thunder and thrashing cottonwoods, stirred by gusts of wind preceding the storm. Occasional lightning lit the front yard, but nothing unusual was visible. Nonetheless, Maggie's continued agitation told him that her keener senses detected something alien, something dangerous. He pulled on his Levi's and went to the next room to waken young Cleve.

At fourteen Junior was almost a man, inured to the hard knocks of the frontier in a country that had been ravaged for centuries by raiding Apaches and Comanches and by neighborhood feuds among the original Mexican settlers, dating back to the 1600s — and now a range war was brewing. Cleve shook Junior, and the boy awoke, clear-headed, and asked: "Is Nellie startin' to foal?"

"Somebody outside, prowlin' around, I think," Cleve said, low-voiced. "After we take a gander out the windows from up here, I aim to go downstairs."

Both avoided standing in front of the windows, aware that lightning could reveal them as targets if they stood too close. They made a circuit of all the upstairs windows but couldn't be sure if anyone was skulking out back, even though the area was sharply illuminated when lightning flashed. The creek bottom there was bushy and heavily sheltered by dense cottonwoods. The front yard was empty, but the stone barn was big enough, either inside or behind, to hide a small army.

"Can't see a damn thing," Cleve complained. "Someone could even be on the front porch."

"Maybe a coyote after the kittens," Junior suggested.

Cleve shook his head. "Their ma'd have raised hell before now." Then he added: "Wake up your sister and be sure to keep her away from the windows. Tell her what's goin' on, but try not to scare her. I'm goin' downstairs for a while. If I yell up the stairs, it'll be time to put your little plan to work."

Long-range shots in the past month had sent bullets whizzing past both him and Junior, most likely from a buffalo gun, judging from the big boom and the range it carried. The heavy slugs had come close enough to convince him the ambusher wasn't simply trying to scare them. And twice in the past month Cleve had found notes tacked to his corral gate. They both read: **Pull Out — Or Else** and were signed: **The Regulators.** Obviously someone had been able to sneak up on the place at night, even with the hounds on patrol. Then he'd also gotten a letter that read:

You ain't got long to run, Bandelier, unless you leave the country!

Cleve edged his way down the steps, barefoot, Maggie at his heels. His hair prickled when she rubbed against him. Downstairs, he felt his way across the kitchen and fumbled left-handed in the alcove behind the door, fishing in the dark for his double-barrel shotgun. His right hand clutched his .45, thumb hooked over the hammer. Feeling the shotgun barrel, he grasped it and quietly lifted it out. In the dark a scatter-gun had the edge over a pistol, so he shoved his six-shooter under his belt as a backup and shifted the scatter-gun into the business position.

Next he rechecked the shutters all around, then held his ear against the kitchen door but heard nothing, even when he held his breath. He thought: *If the Regulators are out there, it probably wasn't an accident they picked a night when the boys are all gone. They've probably been watching the place.* Normally, some of his men would have been around, but they were all with the herd of beeves he'd sent to market early to avoid overgrazing. Two dry years in a row had hurt the range badly.

Whatever was around had to be outside. No intruder could have gotten into his stone ranch house. The first floor had heavy, iron-reinforced shutters carefully secured by bars. The front and back doors were constructed the same. Louvered, plank ventilation ports were located high in the walls, but they were too small to let in even a cat. In this violent country he never left the shutters open at night, since ranchers had been shot right in their homes.

The first heavy rain drops hit the metal porch roof, which scotched his chance of hearing anything. He decided to get a look at the porch, which he couldn't see from upstairs, and slipped to the window closest to the door, cracked the shutter to the end of its short retaining chain, and then waited for the next lightning flash. It highlighted a man, wearing a slicker and Mexican bell-crowned sombrero, hugging the wall near the door. He thought there was another beyond the first, similarly garbed, holding a gun. The next flash confirmed that there were definitely two of them, holding either rifles or shotguns ready. Since they hadn't announced themselves by knocking or hallooing in the usual frontier fashion, they were out there for one reason only.

His stomach tensed as it always had during the war just before a battle. That happened no matter how many battles a man had survived; there was always the unhappy chance that the next one might be the last. Cleve wondered how many others were outside.

They obviously planned to sucker him into opening the door, then cut him down. He figured they'd have someone ride in and pretend he needed a place to put up for the night. He was a prophet. In a few minutes he heard a call outside.

"Hello, the house."

He didn't answer, waiting for another flash of lightning to reveal the caller. A rider was sitting his horse close to the porch, appearing as though politely waiting to be recognized and invited to get down. He wasn't anyone familiar, and Cleve hadn't expected him to be.

The call came again, louder. "Hello! Is anybody home?"

In view of the two men in ambush outside the door, he didn't see any point in answering. He knew what this rider was there for and debated cutting him down. He allowed a few more minutes to go by, not moving or making a sound. He was betting there were a lot of others with these three and intended to smoke them out. The next time he could see, the rider had moved toward the barn. Another joined him. They were obviously having a confab, perhaps trying to decide whether he was home or not. If they'd come here by prearrangement, they knew he was home earlier but might be wondering if he'd pulled out after dark. Under the circumstances he wished he had. He'd had a premonition of trouble coming and had thought of taking the kids to town and boarding them with the schoolteacher as he did during the school term.

The two riders disappeared, and Cleve rechecked to see if the two on the porch had left. They hadn't. He wondered what the other two were doing, then froze as a file of a dozen riders, wearing slickers and white hoods, entered the yard. This was the first time he'd seen the ghostly Whitecaps, a bunch obviously imitating the Ku Klux Klan. Their eerie garb had its effect here as well as in the South after the war, scaring off some of his more timid neighbors without firing a shot.

They didn't wear the hoods primarily to scare people, or as badges as the Klan did, but because some of them were locals; they would be recognized if they showed their faces. The Regulators were composed of both imported gunmen and these locals who had gained title to their land from the syndicate in return for their loyalty. The Regulators had dragged other ranchers and farmers out of their houses and beaten them half to death, and Cleve knew they wouldn't stop with a beating in his case. He was the recognized leader of the resistance to the syndicate's land-grabbing scheme. The Regulators were their enforcers, like Brigham Young's Destroying Angels.

Cleve had come into the Amarillo Grant country years before, a discharged sergeant-major of cavalry stationed at Fort Garland. His neighbors had soon learned he couldn't be bullied or bluffed. A few had found out to their sorrow that he could scrap with his fists and hit what he shot at. In the past few months he'd run off some of the Dutch syndicate's men with his Sharps buffalo gun, playing their own game of dropping a long shot or two in their vicinity. Everyone knew the syndicate was the money behind both the Regulators and the local law. When Cleve arrived in the Amarillo country, no one realized there was going to be a problem over the grant, which then was a few thousand acres in extent as the original deed had intended. Since then the syndicate had expanded it to nearly two million acres by manipulating both the law and politicians. The idea of his neighbors' doing the dirty work of the rich foreigners who controlled the syndicate turned his stomach. Regardless, "neighbors" undoubtedly accounted for the pedigree of some of his visitors.

Despite the violence he'd survived, he still felt queasy over this crew here to kill him. With heavy odds against him, they just might do it if he was simple enough to try to bargain with them. They aimed to get him to open the door to jaw with them in the hope of saving his skin, then gun him down. And they'd kill Junior and Amy, too, leaving no witnesses.

Cleve annoyed himself by jumping sharply when a loud voice brayed: "Hey, Bandelier! We want to talk! We know you're in there!" The voice wasn't familiar.

Cleve told himself: *There's only one kind of talk'll keep us alive now.* It was in his hands. He closed the shutter and moved to the base of the stairs.

"Hey, Junior," he called.

"Yeah, Pa." The boy's voice came from the head of the stairs. His son had stayed right where he wanted him.

Cleve said: "Cut loose with your little plan."

He returned to the window, slipped the shutter open a crack, and peeked out. The two on the porch were still there.

The braying voice sounded off again. "Hey Bandelier! We just want to talk this time."

Some fools, now dead, had believed that sort of proposition. With a little luck Cleve aimed to give them something to talk about for a long time. It was the moment to bring this toe-dancing to a close. If it was going to come to a war anyhow, why not get in the first lick? Those fellows out there weren't exactly a peace commission. They could only be Pancho Wingfield's Texas gunmen and probably several of his local hardcases, judging from their numbers. He knew their type and figured he could drive them off with a dose of the right medicine. *They weren't aiming to warn me if I went out that door, so I reckon I don't have to warn them,* he reasoned.

Junior was taking so long he was about to go upstairs and see what the boy was doing, then with the next lightning flash an added torch of light arched across the yard, and another. Junior didn't miss once with his fire arrows. Their Jicarilla Apache cowboy, José, had taught him well. A long windrow of grease-soaked hay leaped aflame, and he was glad he hadn't discouraged Junior from what he'd first thought of as a hair-brained idea. The kid had even sheltered the hay with scrap tin roofing in case it was raining when they needed shooting light.

The riders spun their horses to look at the growing line of fire behind them. One of them yelled: "What the hell! We're sittin' ducks out here!"

Another howled: "Let's get the hell out of here!"

The more wary had already hung steel to their mounts and streaked for the darkness. One horse skidded and fell in the mud. Its rider threw himself clear, scrambled up, and tried to remount as the horse regained its feet, but couldn't manage it on the run, and grabbed its tail as it darted away. He was practically flying behind the frightened animal. Cleve snorted involuntarily, then checked himself, thinking: *This is when those two on the porch will skedaddle, too.*

He'd unchained the shutter, and, when the first of the two panicked and ran, he pulled down on the runner. "Damn fool!" he muttered as he drew a bead. He gave himself the split second that made the difference between a hit and a miss, then squeezed off. The second ambusher, no cooler than the other, legged it frantically behind his buddy, slowed to help his fallen partner, and gave Cleve an easy shot with the second barrel.

Then he slammed and latched the shutter almost before the second man hit the ground, expecting a volley at the house.

None came. He stepped out of the powder smoke.

Must have really surprised the bastards, he thought. *Maybe they were so busy saving their own necks, they didn't even see me beef those two.*

He reloaded the scatter-gun before he went back up the stairs. Junior was at the window from which he'd shot his arrows, now grasping his Winchester.

"Where's your sister?" Cleve asked.

"Here I am," Amy quavered.

"I got her sittin' against the wall," Junior said.

"Good boy!" Cleve knew even the heaviest rifle rounds wouldn't penetrate the thick stone walls. Then he cautioned her: "You be sure to stay where you are, honey."

He peeked out at the two bodies he'd dropped, clearly highlighted by the fires. He wanted to make sure neither of those two lived to tell a bunch of lies later. The Mexicans had a saying about that — *los muertos no hablan.* Cleve was already looking ahead, sure he'd have to account for this night's business in court or else run away. Even though what he'd done was self-defense to any frontiersman's way of thinking, he was in for it now. In an unbiased community such an affair wouldn't go beyond a coroner's hearing. Here, where the syndicate's money was talking, it would be different. In one syndicate case a Supreme Court justice had even exercised his prerogative to convene a hearing in Colorado. Cleve was in no small-time, local fight. Even the Army might stick its paddle in for the Santa Fé Ring as it had in Lincoln County.

The Amarillo Grant was not the only place in the West where the terms of the Treaty of Guadalupe Hidalgo were bent to permit such robbery. Those with the most to lose were former Mexican citizens who had been absorbed by the United States after the Mexican War. Aware of the stacked deck that he and his neighbors were playing against, Cleve would not have hesitated to finish off either of the desperadoes lying in the yard, if they showed signs of stirring. He'd killed before and had never doubted he'd do it again in a case like this. It was what they aimed to do to him, and they'd get the two kids afterwards.

Junior was close beside him looking out.

"Both dead, I reckon," Cleve said. "Now let's get away from the window. When they get organized, they'll pepper us for sure."

The first shots came almost as he spoke. Amy let out a stifled moan, and the sound angered Cleve even more. Several shots followed, muzzle flashes blazing from the barn.

Junior jumped to the window, rifle half-raised, and Cleve jerked him back. "Stay undercover," he growled. "Some devil might get in a lucky shot."

"Hell, Pa," Junior protested, "let me pepper 'em back. They won't hit nuthin' in this light."

Cleve said: "What makes you think *you'll* hit anything in this light?"

"Can see 'em when lightning flashes," Junior said.

Just then a slug took out the upper window pane, spraying glass on the floor. "They can see you when lightning flashes, too," Cleve observed dryly. "A lucky shot will kill you just as quick as any other kind."

More slugs splattered sharply against the stone house. One whined through the open lower panel of the window and smashed through the far wall with a tearing noise. Plaster trickled on the floor.

The voice Cleve had first heard yelled: "We'll git you fer this, you son of a bitch!"

Cleve yelled back: "Why don't you fellows come in for a little confab? I only want to talk this time, like you did." This earned another volley.

The storm was slacking off, and he could hear better. He

listened intently, but other than his own breathing, the receding thunder, and rain dripping from the roof, he heard nothing. Amy sobbed a little. He went to her, lifted her to her feet, and held her close. After a few more gasping sobs, she asked: "Are they going to kill us, Pa?"

"Not if I can help it," he reassured her. "Besides, I think they're gone." She stopped crying and snuffled instead. Cleve released her and gave her his bandanna to dry her eyes, which she did, then blew her nose several times — loudly.

Junior said: "What do we do now, Pa?"

There was a tremor in his son's voice for the first time. Junior had been steady as a rock when it counted, but even veteran soldiers got shaky after the fighting was over. Cleve wasn't feeling too steady himself. He'd never liked to kill and still didn't. "We'll stay under cover till daylight in case those *hombres* ain't gone, then, if the coast is clear, we'll get rid of those two out there."

"You figure they might be someone we know?" Junior asked.

"Maybe. Some of the crowd were, that's for sure."

"What do we do if they are?"

"Same thing we do if they ain't. Hide 'em where they'll never be found before Sheriff Butler comes sashayin' out here." Then he added as an afterthought: "If he wasn't out there with that bunch."

"You think he was?" Junior asked.

"He's likely a little too careful for that, but he's swillin' at the syndicate's trough." Cleve wasn't entirely sure, either way. He didn't know enough about the man and didn't want to, not if it involved being his guest.

Junior was silent for a while. Then he said: "Old Butler will be here, all right. Word's bound to leak out. Some of those guys out there'll spill the beans, even if they ain't supposed to."

Cleve smiled, pleased at his son's understanding of human

behavior, but the smile had little humor in it. His Indian-like face was drawn tight over his lean, high cheekbones. Junior made out that look in the reflected light of the dying fire and was almost afraid of his father. He thought he looked like a wolf in a trap.

Cleve finally spoke. "I reckon you're dead right, son. It's plain those skunks planned to beef us, but they'll lie about it to git the law on us. Let 'em. We can't stop 'em anyhow. At least then we'll know who some of the others were . . . once they have to do their lyin' in court. When it gets light, we'll find out who the only two *good* ones in that outfit are." He laughed grimly.

Amy had been listening and thinking hard about what happened. She blinked away more tears, scarcely able to believe that her warm-hearted pa had just killed two men and seemed to be making a joke of it. *You'd do it, too,* a little voice inside her spoke. *When you love somebody, you can be as brave as you have to be.* She figured maybe her pa laughed because he needed relief from the same sort of strain she was suffering, not because he was cold-hearted. Like her brother, she spent a lot of time observing people and trying to understand what made them tick.

Amy had learned a lot in short order after her mother died. The main thing was that out here women might suddenly be called on to fight just like men — the surviving kind of men, anyhow. Some men rolled over and yelled "uncle" as soon as they were punched in the snoot. She'd only half understood before tonight that her pa was the exact opposite of those yellow bellies. Weaker men in situations like this had tried to talk to save their necks, when they should have been shooting. She was thankful her pa wasn't like that. *If he was, I guess I'd be dead now,* she reflected. She wondered what it felt like to be killed, and shuddered.

Junior asked: "Think they'll really come to arrest you, Pa?"

Amy recognized that Junior was trying to conceal the same fears she had and was comforted to know she wasn't the only one feeling pretty shaky.

Cleve said: "It's a dead moral certainty they'll try to pull me in, but I don't aim to be around when they come. I'd stand about as much chance on the way to jail as a jackrabbit with coyotes. I'll come in and give myself up, if and when I figure it's safe to stand trial."

"What about us?" Amy and Junior said almost in one voice.

Cleve knew there was no way in the world they could stay at home, even if his cowboys came back and ran the place while he was on the dodge. "You'll have to stay in town, I reckon. No one will bother you there. The schoolteacher wants to take Amy anyhow so she can curry her."

Amy made a face. She thought the teacher, Gloria Peabody, was dumb. Besides, she hated school as much as Junior did but never let on because she knew her pa was courting the schoolteacher — sort of. He was also seeing Dolores Zamora pretty often. Amy loved Dolores and knew Junior did, too. Dolores tried to mother them both when they went visiting at Zamora Plaza.

"Why can't we go up to Dolores's place?" she asked.

Cleve wasn't about to mention his real reason, which was that Dolores couldn't read or write. He might have agreed to let the kids go there if someone could teach them something out of books, even if they weren't real teachers. Schooling was hard to come by, and like his neighbors Cleve placed a high value on it, even if it was pretty poor. It never occurred to him that a year's vacation from books, with Dolores and her brothers, might teach his kids a lot more that they needed to go through life than any school could. Their Mexican friends had the priceless knack of making-do and appearing happy all the time in the bargain. None of them was afraid of back-breaking work. It was all they'd ever known. But they knew how to play, too. Probably that was why they were seldom sick and lived a long time. If Cleve had told Amy his real objection to the kids' going up to stay with Dolores, his daughter would have countered: "So? We can teach Dolores to read and write." That would have been a real stumper.

The otherwise self-reliant Mexicans were like children in the *gringo* world. The Anglo laws that were clamped down on their formerly happy homes confused and frightened them. They knew nothing of the world except their own simple lives, and now they discovered that maybe they didn't even own the land on which their ancestors had lived for centuries. Most of them understood only that the Anglos could get away with almost anything, and they were all afraid.

Cleve was afraid, too, but he wasn't confused about what was going on. None of it was legal. His fear was that his neighbors were apt to dodge a fight as long as they could. They still had a chance, but time was running out. Sooner or later crooked courts would put them in the wrong about land titles. The Santa Fé Ring run by Tomás Pringle had a finger in the local pie, as it did in everything in the territory, and its influence reached into the capital at Washington. It was obvious that the syndicate had bought the ring's support. Now was the time to spill some more blood, if need be, in a Winchester court with quick decisions, appealable only in the hereafter. He'd thought of simply pulling out, but building a ranch for his kids had been his whole reason for living since their mother had died when Amy was six. Amy was now twelve, two years younger than Junior who was going on about thirty. Cleve sometimes talked to the kids' mother by her grave on the hillside and, whether she could hear him or not, had vowed to her: "I'll be damned if I'm goin' to lose everything without a fight, especially to a bunch of foreigners."

The Amarillo Grant had been purchased by a Dutch syndicate and, worse yet, had an English manager, Lord Montague Ransom. In their hands the grant had grown miraculously, cultivated by some of the most crooked schemers and manipulators who had ever drawn a breath. Locals knew what was happening, but it was so monstrous they couldn't believe it. Washington obviously was looking the other way. Why try to fight the people who controlled the courts on their own ground? Cleve figured maybe he'd go up to Santa Fé, if he went on the dodge, and submit a Winchester affidavit to the ring's leader, Tomás Pringle himself. Until now the syndicate's killers had stayed out of Cleve's country at the head of the Rio Aguila, but he was the natural leader of the growing opposition, and some of Cleve's neighbors were ex-soldiers who would fight under his leadership, if it came down to it. So would the Mexicans, if they had the right *jefe,* and probably even the Jicarillas on the sly, but they had to be wary of being caught at something that would call in the Army. He aimed to be that right leader, but first he had to unite something to lead. He grinned in the dark, thinking that after tonight he'd have to do his leading from the rimrock.

They'd been standing to one side of the window, talking quietly in the darkness. Now Cleve took a quick gander to see if anybody was in sight. Junior's fire was no longer much help, and the storm had moved away. Seeing was a hit or miss affair. A gust of air blew in, faintly smoky but delicious with the fragrance of damp sage and the soaked grasses and shrubs of the high country. A rising wind stirred the cottonwoods along Musica Creek. Frogs were croaking loudly, happy over the renewal of their habitat. On the horizon more storm clouds, silhouetted by intermittent lightning, were moving in, their thunder growing louder.

Cleve loved the summer rainy season, especially now after a couple of dry years. He hoped they'd get a whole raft of hen drowners like the one that had just gone over. In this country rain was the key to survival, the more the better since there was barely enough in the best of years. What survived here was hardy, and the people who survived had to be the same. The weak pulled out or died, usually quickly.

His thoughts returned to their predicament, and he said: "I hope them skunks are gone, but it's not quite light enough to tell. I'm goin' down and recheck all the shutters, then we'll fix breakfast."

Amy was surprised that it was breakfast time, even though they always rose before sunup. Her father had kept her away from the windows, so she hadn't noticed that the sky beneath the low clouds was paling to the east.

Junior wondered if his pa was apt to stick his nose outside but was afraid to warn him not to. He was almost sure he wasn't that rash, but before tonight he'd been almost sure his pa wouldn't load two men with buckshot, except in a real pinch — then he realized that tonight had been a real pinch.

Amy wasn't sure she could eat breakfast. In fact, she was pretty sure she couldn't and wondered how her pa could think of eating after killing two men. She didn't understand that the Civil War had inured men like him to deadly violence. Her pa had eaten gratefully, if he was lucky enough to have something to eat with a lot of dead soldiers lying around.

Amy had been cook since her ma died because someone had to be. Her brother and father helped, and so did the cowboys, but they were mostly outside, working often far away on the range, returning famished at meal time. Her pa had called her "a dern good cook" more than once, and she vowed she'd cook for him if it killed her.

Cleve rechecked the shutters downstairs, comforted that

he'd had the foresight not to underestimate the danger of this land. Not everyone could afford the luxury of iron-plated shutters like his, but most wouldn't have installed them, anyhow. Cleve had made considerable money here. Almost everyone recognized him as the best and thriftiest cattleman in the country — although an envious few wrote him off as lucky. He laughed at that and told himself: *I don't give a hoot whether I'm lucky or damned good at what I do, it amounts to the same thing — money in the bank.* He pitied those who didn't thrive and knew that it was usually due to either ignorance, laziness, or both.

Some of those not cut out for this country were planted permanently on the homesteads where they'd stayed too long. Their widows and kids had salvaged maybe a wagon and team, if they were lucky, carried as much as they could and abandoned the rest, occasionally most of a lifetime's accumulation. He pitied them, regardless, and had helped some, knowing it was wasted effort. Those still hanging on were the surviving kind, but he wondered if even they would back him. Probably only a few. The rest would hang back and see how he made out, fighting their battle. In any case he knew that tonight he'd started a war. Now it would be: choose sides or get out.

Chapter Two

As he ate breakfast, Cleve mulled over his toughest problem. He had to hide those incriminating bodies where they'd never be found. It was the only way to combat the lies he knew would be told by Wingfield and his crew. Men were seldom convicted of murder if the body of the deceased couldn't be produced by the prosecution. Hiding the bodies successfully would eliminate the legal threat to his neck in an honest trial. A rigged jury might find him guilty anyhow, based on circumstantial evidence, or in the syndicate's bailiwick no evidence at all, which raised the question of whether he would ever submit to arrest voluntarily. Had he condemned himself to be always a fugitive?

If he went on the dodge and was captured later, everyone would know that the corpses had disappeared, thus diminishing the chances of hanging him legally and a good reason for him to suspect the infamous Mexican *ley fuga* would be his fate on the way to jail. The ring's newspapers would report that Bandelier, realizing he would be convicted and hung if brought to the bar of justice, had made a desperate break for freedom and had been shot down like the mad dog he was.

His kids recognized that he was deep in thought and kept quiet. It wasn't their usual happy morning meal with Cleve pleasantly joshing them, or talking about his plans for the day and what he'd like each of them to do. Finally he realized that the kids probably needed cheering up and dropped his somber line of thought. "Everything is going to work out in the long run," he said, smiling at them, "provided we all stick together and don't lose our nerve. First of all we have to get rid of those two outside."

Junior had his ideas about how to do that but held his tongue to hear what his father had to say. He knew where there was a deep prospect hole not too far from the ranch. The fact that he thought of it indicated how far last night's experience had brought him down the path toward desperation. He knew that, if need be, he could hustle the bodies there himself and dump them in. Unlike his father, he hadn't considered the telltale trail he'd leave in wet ground.

Cleve said: "First, I'm goin' out and check to see that none of that crowd from last night is still around. I want you two to cover me from the upstairs windows. Amy, you can handle a Winchester, and Junior, I want you to have my Sharps in addition to your Winchester, just in case someone is back on the rise and takes a shot at me. You can pepper 'em. I want Amy at the back windows and you out front. The trickiest part will be if some of 'em are in the barn."

"You'll be a sittin' duck, goin' across the yard," Junior said. "Why not slip out the back way and work around to the barn by goin' down the creek, then up one of them gullies?"

Cleve had thought of that and explained: "It's just as risky that way. I'd have to work down from behind the ridge in plain sight all the way to the barn, anyhow. And there's no tellin' who may be up on the other side of the ridge. I'm bettin' that crew didn't go far . . . probably sent for the sheriff so they can come back in here, all legal and proper. Maybe, if our big dogs were around, I could risk goin' that way. They'd sniff out the ground ahead of me."

Amy was worried about the two dogs. She loved them as she loved all living things, except maybe poisonous snakes. "What do you suppose happened to Dash and Jack?" she asked.

Cleve was pretty sure what had happened to them but to

avoid hurting her said: "I don't know. Maybe got on the track of a lion and stuck with it."

"I sure hope so," Amy said.

Junior figured the same as Cleve and thought someday they'd come across their skeletons. It was another score to hold against the syndicate. Junior was discovering he had an unsuspected capacity for hatred. He hoped someone would stick out his damned head and try to ambush his pa and give him a chance to blow it off. He was sure he wouldn't get buck fever, if the time came, and knew he was a quick, dead shot and didn't freeze up in a tight spot.

Cleve made a last survey of the area with field glasses before sallying out to investigate. Just before he let himself out the door, he said: "If either of you see anyone coming while I'm out there, fire a shot. I'll hustle back in. If you see someone skulking that I don't, either shoot them, or let out a holler, and it don't make any difference to me who they are if they're strangers."

Besides the Winchester Cleve had armed Amy with a full box of shells in her apron pocket, and she gritted her teeth, wondering if she could live up to his confidence in her. That little voice spoke to her again, reminding: *If you love someone, you can be as brave as you have to be.* She sure loved her pa and her brother, too, and aimed to fight for them.

Cleve read what was going on in her mind and gently patted her cheek. He clapped Junior on the shoulder, looked them both in the eyes for what they all realized might be the last time, and headed downstairs, calling back: "I'm depending on you two. If they get me, stand them off." He stopped and came back to the head of the stairs and said: "Above all, never let them sweet-talk you into giving up unless it's the sheriff . . . I don't think Butler would let anybody kill a couple of kids. Otherwise, after last night you gotta remember that any of that crowd that was here will likely kill you so you can't testify for me . . . or against them. Those are real mean snakes. They'll kill you sure if they get a-hold of you. But they'll play hell, bustin' in here with a couple of Winchesters working them over."

Amy knew she could shoot a Winchester. She'd fired one for the first time when her ma was still alive, killing a rabid skunk in the front yard when her ma had been too sick to get out of bed. The dogs had been circling it, and one of them might have gotten bit.

Cleve, too, was confident both kids would shoot in a pinch, regardless of how they might feel about it. *Shoot straight, too,* he thought. He'd made sure, over the years, that they all had target practice together and worked at it often enough to be familiar with how the guns worked, as well as how to hit what they shot at. Nonetheless, he fought off a queasy feeling as he stepped out the door. He hated to risk leaving it unbarred but needed it that way, in case he had to dive back in.

Junior called from the upstairs window: "I don't see anything stirring out there yet. If someone pokes a rifle out of the barn, I'll pour it into 'em."

Cleve carried his double barrel at the ready, with two six-shooters shoved in his belt, and had Maggie along. Once inside the barn her sensitive nose would sniff out danger. The barn was his big worry. He kept his eyes swiveling between its windows as he walked. He recognized that he'd hardly been breathing and inhaled a deep breath, then another. His back muscles had also tensed, and his palms were sweaty. *Relax!* he impatiently commanded himself. Easier said than done.

When they got to the first body, Maggie sniffed it cautiously and growled, hackles raised. "It's O K," he reassured her. "Those kind can't hurt you."

The two bodies were about six feet apart, both lying on their backs, knees drawn up, eyes staring. Flies were crawling on their eyes and in their noses. Neither was Mexican, despite the sombreros they'd worn. Cleve said: "Well, Maggie, I reckon they thought those sombreros would put us on a false lead in case we saw them and somehow got away."

Junior heard him and called down: "Did you say something, Pa?"

"Talkin' to Maggie. Keep your eyes peeled and don't mind me."

He continued his steady stalk toward the barn door. Once there, he heaved a big sigh. *So far, so good.* He jerked the door open. Only Nellie, waiting to foal, was in sight. She nickered softly, telling him it was past time to be fed.

"In a little while," he said to her.

He and Maggie went down the alley, checking every stall. His palms were sweating again, and he wiped them on his jeans. He felt a little foolish, since it wasn't likely anyone would wait for him to get inside. Nonetheless, he was taking no unnecessary chances. He had to stay alive, at least till he got the kids out of this scrape.

Best check the hay loft, too, he told himself and, having put down the scatter-gun, started up the ladder one-handed, holding a six-shooter in the other. When a quick check of the loft showed no one, he stepped out onto the resilient hay and crossed to the loading window to view the blind spot behind the barn. Only the night horse, Dave, was out in the small corral attached to the rear of the barn, looking up as though to say: "Now, where the hell did you come from?"

He threw down an armful of hay, thankful they hadn't run Dave off. Then, after picking up the scatter-gun, he headed back toward the house, stopping to check the bodies a little more closely. He opened the slicker of one and said: "Oh, oh. Real trouble." The man was wearing a U. S. deputy marshal's badge. A bullet buzzed just over his head, and shortly he heard the mellow boom of a heavy rifle. He legged it for the house and heard Junior's return fire.

Inside, he barred the door and took the stairs two at a time, joining Junior at the window. "How many out there?" he asked.

"Just one, as near as I could tell. He was on the run when I cut loose. I think maybe I hit him. Might have tripped on a rock, though. He must have been a quarter of a mile back."

Amy yelled: "What's happening? Can I come over there now?"

Junior yelled back: "I told you! Keep at your post!"

Cleve was tickled but didn't show it. Junior sounded just like a tough noncom. "Let her come," he said. "We don't need her there right now."

"Hey," Amy yelled, "better come back here and look. There's a whole passel of men comin' this way on horses."

Cleve left Junior at his post, grabbed the glasses from Amy, and trained them on the riders. "Too far away to tell who they are," he muttered, then yelled to Junior: "We've got to get those bodies out of sight. Come on!" To Amy he said: "You stay here and keep an eye on those galoots."

It took only a couple of minutes to carry the two bodies, and their hats and rifles, into the house. "Best we can do," Cleve said. "No time to wipe out our tracks." He barred the door again. "Let's take 'em back to the bunk room."

He was glad Amy hadn't seen any part of it. She was still at her post like a real trooper. "Gettin' mighty close," she said. "They look like our cowboys."

"They can't be back so soon." Cleve trotted over to take a look. "Give me the glasses." He laid the glasses on the six men. "It's them all right. Something must have happened."

Whatever it was, he didn't expect it to be good news. They

must have lost the herd. His mind sorted out reasons why that might have happened. Only one cause made sense. The syndicate. If they had attacked him, they wouldn't hesitate to attack his men. If the herd was gone, his loss was more than he could afford, and he needed money to fight the syndicate. Before he went back down to meet his men, he posted Junior and Amy again as look-outs.

Nimbly he took the steps and opened the front door, carefully scanning the porch both ways, not forgetting that someone could sneak up from around back. Leading his cowhands was his *segundo,* Jesús Sandoval, followed by big black Sam Buchanan, an ex-slave and his best and most dependable man after Jesús. Two other ex-slaves who'd come to work when Sam did, Lawrence and Thomas, followed and then José, a Jicarilla, known only by that single name, and Jeff Mills, one of two Wisconsin farm boys Cleve had been making into hands. Jeff's sidekick, Johnny Evans, was missing. The men dismounted wearily at the porch. Cleve noted their solemn faces, but he waited for Jesús to report.

The latter hesitated, registering pain and embarrassment. Finally he said: "Plenty trouble, *patrón.*" They had been close for years, and Jesús usually called him *jefe* or Cleve, reserving the formal address for touchy matters where Jesús expected blame. He continued: "A bunch of gunmen jumped us near Tres Huérfanos at sundown yesterday. Maybe twenty of 'em, maybe thirty. They pumped a lot of lead and holed us up in the stock pens. We stood 'em off O K, but they ran off the herd and the remuda. We got most of the horses back."

"Where's Johnny?" Cleve asked.

Jesús hesitated. Johnny's sidekick, Jeff, answered for him. "He's shot up bad. I'll get the sonsabitches that done it!" Tears were running down his cheeks. "Now I gotta write his ma . . . worse yet, she was just like a ma to both of us."

Jesús said: "He'll pull through. He's tough. We put him on the train to town."

"I should 'a' gone with him," Jeff said.

Jesús objected. "I need you here. You couldn't do anything for him. That woman lookin' after him was a regular nurse. He'll be O K."

"Where is he hit?" Cleve asked.

"Clipped him good in his collarbone and went clean through."

"I'm sorry as hell." Cleve stepped over and put his hand on Jeff's shoulder.

"You ain't half as sorry as me. His folks only let him come out here 'cause I promised to take keer of him."

Cleve said: "I reckon we'll have plenty chance to get even before we're done." He asked Jesús: "Did you recognize any of 'em?"

Jesús caught his eye and swung his head almost imperceptibly, indicating he'd like a private word.

Before that, Cleve thought he'd better explain what happened during the night. He did briefly. To Junior, whom he'd called down to join them, he said: "Saddle Dave and run up the hosses. Be sure Star comes in with the bunch. You go with him, Jeff." He figured Jeff needed something to take his mind off his trouble. Then he added: "Sam, take Lawry and Tom on a little circle for sign, and see where those *hombres* went but don't go so far you can't hear us, if we fire a warning shot. If we do, look good before you come in. You might wanta run for it instead. If you have to hide out a while, get word to us where you are, if you can."

He realized, as he was saying this, how rapidly disaster had overtaken his life — here he was telling his cowhands to hide out, which amounted to admitting he might be driven out of business. Regardless, the first thing to do was get the horse herd up, so they could pack those bodies off the ranch and run the herd across the yard to wipe out the sign of what had happened. He had kept José behind because he wanted him along when he left with the bodies. If anyone knew of a place to hide a couple of dead ones, it would be José.

When they were alone except for José, Jesús said: "Pancho Wingfield was in charge. There's no mistakin' his horse. They all had those damn' white hoods on, so the only other one I know was there for sure was Devil Ed. He was yelling like the loco fool he is. No mistakin' his voice."

"Did any of the others recognize anyone?"

"I don't think so. I was the only one close enough, coverin' our rear. If they did, they'd have mentioned it."

"Good," Cleve said, "we don't want Jeff goin' gunning for either of those two. He wouldn't have a chance, especially with Pancho." Wingfield reputedly had a dozen gunfights behind him. With that in mind Cleve added: "Somebody is gonna have to take Pancho out, sooner or later."

"You're dead right," Jesús agreed. "I tried to get a bead on him when he ran down Johnny, but some damn' tourists on a train were in the way."

"Too bad," Cleve said.

Wingfield was the number two local man for the syndicate, right under Lord Ransom, the English resident manager. Cleve always wondered how a proud Texan like Wingfield could stomach an English boss. Not very well, he guessed, but Pancho knew how to bide his time. Cleve suspected he was probably after Ransom's job. The name Pancho, hung on Wingfield by locals, was misleading since he wasn't a Mexican. His given name was Frank, the equivalent of the Mexican Francisco, which carried the nickname Pancho among Mexicans. The community knew he hated his nickname, and no one used it to his face.

"So he's the son of a bitch that ran off my cows," Cleve muttered.

A thousand head at maybe thirty dollars a head. He wrote that off for sure unless they could go after them damned quick. The rest of his stock would go the same way if he let it. He decided right then to strip his range, sell, and restock after the trouble blew over. He was relieved to think: *They'll play hell, stealing gold buried under some fencepost.* The added thought wasn't so comforting. *What makes me so damned sure the trouble will blow over?*

It would take a lot of manpower to outgun the syndicate under the likes of Wingfield. At the very least he could count on his own men under the strong leadership of Jesús. The latter was a rare bird, captured young by the Jicarillas, then sold to Comanches, and bought back by Comancheros who returned him to civilization where Archbishop Lamy had adopted him, as he had several others. Lamy, out of the kindness of his heart and depth of incomprehension of what he thought of as *his* Mexicans, sent Jesús East to be educated. Jesús would rather have returned to the Comanches. At best, he came back from the East sort of schooled. For example, he'd picked up the American game of craps, which was not played much in the West, but deep inside he was more Indian than anything else. No school could change that.

He spoke good English as a result of his schooling and had spoken fluent Spanish, Apache, and Comanche before he left. His only loyalties were to himself, Cleve and the kids, and their land. Like all of his breed he never questioned that he and the land were one. Unlike most cowboys, he had no objections to gardening, raising hay, irrigating, and the drudgery that went with cultivating the land; on the contrary, he loved it. He and Sam Buchanan did the farming and gardening between them.

After the others had departed on their chores, Cleve showed

Jesús and José the bodies. It was the first chance he'd had to take a close look at them. He pulled open the slicker of the first one and showed Jesús the badge on his vest. He discovered that the second sported a similar one.

"Some of Wingfield's gunmen, probably," he mused. "Maybe fixed up with badges by the ring. The U. S. marshal plays their game, if he wants to keep his job. Well, I ain't in any worse trouble for killin' a lawman than for killin' anyone else under the circumstances."

José, who had ears like Cleve's cat, broke in and said: "Somebody comin'."

Amy, who was still upstairs on look-out, yelled down: "Junior is bringing up the horses."

In a short while he had them corralled — some two dozen in all.

"Rope out a couple of those we use for packin' dead game," Cleve told him. "They shouldn't balk at carryin' dead men."

With several men on the job they quickly had the two corpses lashed on pack saddles with tarps tied around them. Cleve and José were ready when Sam Buchanan and his boys returned at a run.

"The sheriff and a posse are about a mile out, just over the ridge!" Sam yelled.

Cleve had been about to congratulate himself that the worst was over. Now he figured his chances of being far enough out on the trail to keep ahead of the sheriff with two loaded pack horses weren't too good. And if Wingfield was along, the kids would be at his mercy.

"Let's get those bodies back inside quick. Me and the kids are going to hide up in the attic," he said. "Jesús, try to convince the sheriff that when you and the boys pulled in, no one was here. If he knows what I think he does, he's apt to buy that story . . . at least for now . . . and circle to pick up our trail because he'll think I'm makin' a run for it to hide the bodies."

"Suppose he decides to search the place?"

"Run the horses in the barn and put the men in there to hold it. You and me and the kids will hold the house. Tonight we'll all make a run for it."

Junior protested: "Why don't you just dig out on Star? He can outrun anything in the country. We can take care of ourselves." Star was Cleve's Thoroughbred gelding.

José interrupted them. "I can get those dead ones out of here without being seen maybe, I think. I know where I can dump them for now, and we'll move them later."

Cleve had so many things being thrown at him, he was at a loss for a choice. He decided to gamble on José. "Do it," he said. At least they wouldn't find them on the place.

José led the two pack horses behind the house at a fast trot and down into Musica Creek. He was soon out of sight.

Junior pleaded: "You head out the other way, Pa. It's your best chance. You can let us know where you are."

Cleve read the desperation in his voice. Much as he hated to desert them, it was best all around. If he stayed here, he'd have either to give up and run the risk of being killed on the way to jail, or fight and put his kids' lives in danger. He knew his hands would fight to the death for him, but why put them to it?

He was well up a draw on the opposite side of the creek when the sheriff rode into the yard alone. There, Cleve ran across a sight he hated to look at: his two hounds dead, a few feet apart, their mouths open, fangs showing, having died in agony. "Poisoned," he muttered, "and coming to get me to help them. Only they didn't make it."

He pressed on to the top of the ridge and looked back to see if he was apt to be seen crossing. The thought occurred to him that he was home free if they hadn't sent someone to circle the place. When he turned, Devil Ed Targee was sitting his horse directly in front of him, rifle trained. Star shied violently just as Targee fired, which kept Cleve from being gut-shot. The Winchester slug hit him just above his right hip joint.

Hit bad! he thought. Shock prevented him from doing more than hanging on as the horse leaped into a run and almost ran down Targee. It took Devil Ed a while to settle down and fire after Cleve. Several bullets whined past.

"I can't pass out now," he mumbled into Star's mane. "Got to keep goin'."

A hard run of a couple of miles left Targee behind but nearly used up Cleve's last reserve of strength. He slowed the horse down to a lope, and finally a walk. Targee was no longer in sight, and Cleve slumped over, panting and seeing stars. If he could only hold on, he might make it to the Zamoras'. They would hide him, care for him, and fight for him. It was a long way. Thirty miles, at least.

After he got his breath back, he stripped off his shirt, rolled it up as best he could, and strapped it over the entrance and exit wounds with his belt. Doing it hurt like hell. If the bullet had cut his intestine, the smell would be unmistakable, so he sniffed the blood on his hand and decided it hadn't. This gave him the lift he needed.

Targee probably was part of Sheriff Butler's posse, in which case he would go back and fetch a lot more men who would soon be trailing him. Cleve tried to think where he should go to find ground that would make trailing him slow work, if not impossible. Thinking was hard. Sometimes he thought he was back in the war.

After going up a rocky draw for a mile or more, the horizon turned topsy-turvy and something hit him hard on the side of his head. He didn't realize it was the impact of falling off Star onto the rocky ground.

Chapter Three

Cleve left a scene of confusion behind him. He remembered, too late, that he'd forgotten to tell Jesús to hide the kids in the attic. He needn't have worried. That was the first thing that occurred to his *segundo.*

"We're gonna make it look like we just pulled in and no one was here," Jesús said. "You two kids hide up in the attic and keep still. If the sheriff does find you and starts asking questions, tell him you were both scared out of your wits last night when somebody shot the place up, kept under cover, and didn't see a thing. Sam, you help 'em up through the hole and get the ladder out of sight."

Junior said: "We don't need any help, and the best thing to do is pull the ladder up after us. I can handle that. But suppose the sheriff finds us and asks where Pa is, or if we saw two dead men out in the yard?"

"Say your pa pulled out before daylight and told you to lock yourself in the house, and you didn't see a thing in the yard after it got light. Now git!"

Amy wondered if she could tell whoppers like that without looking guilty as sin. The idea of having to try scared her. She felt like crying and wished someone was there whom she could ask: "Why is this happening to us? We didn't do anything?" She made a silent prayer: *Please, God, don't let the sheriff find us . . . and please, please take care of Pa, wherever he is.*

Jesús watched the kids haul up the ladder, then turned to the cowboys who were gathered around him. "Butler knows we lost that herd, I'd bet, so we have to look like we came in to get Cleve and some more cartridges and supplies and aim to go back and round up those cows. That's what we're gonna do anyhow, with or without Cleve. Wingfield didn't have time to do any more'n scatter the herd, so get to work. And let me do the talking when Butler comes."

"What do you aim to tell him about losin' the herd and Johnny gittin' shot?" Sam asked.

"Nothing. Like I said, I'd bet he already knows."

"Won't he get suspicious if we don't mention it?" Jeff Mills asked. He was still enough of an Easterner to believe that you always reported killings and robberies to the sheriff.

Sensing this, Jesús said: "If you let out one peep about all that unless Butler asks you, I'll drown you in the horse trough as soon as he skins out. He's already damned suspicious, and he knows we've got no use for him and wouldn't tell him if Christ rode by on a burro. Let him bring it up if he wants to. He's probably here because Wingfield was coming on his own hook after he hit our herd, got in over his head, and yelled for the law. You can bet he lied like hell about how it happened. The sheriff wants those bodies, and he naturally wants Cleve because Wingfield told him he killed them."

That was as much as he had time to cover before the sheriff rode into the yard.

In the attic Junior soundlessly lifted a section of the overhanging eave up on hinges. "We can shoot down in the yard real good from here," he whispered to Amy.

She didn't feel much like shooting, or even thinking about it, and was wondering how Junior had pried up the board without making any noise. She couldn't see the sheriff, so she whispered back: "How'd you get that board out of there?"

"Easy," he whispered back. "Pa and me put in a bunch of these on hinges all around the house. We done it when you was in town so you wouldn't get scared thinkin' about the

Regulators maybe raiding us."

She was impressed but still didn't feel like shooting out of those slots, especially at the sheriff. She knew her pa thought Butler was in with the night riders, but she wasn't so sure. The one time she'd seen him in town, he had passed on the sidewalk, touched the brim of his hat, and said: "Howdy, young lady." She thought he had a nice face and hoped her brother didn't go off half-cocked and shoot the sheriff. Sometimes Junior scared her with the crazy look he got in his eyes when his dander was up.

Sheriff Clint Butler was a good lawman who knew the business from years of experience. He'd been a constable in Mississippi before the war, marshal in a tough riverboat town afterward, and a sergeant in the Texas Rangers — twenty-five years in a tough business. He'd handled a lot of hard ones, never been shot, though he'd been shot at plenty, and, if he had scar tissue, it was where it didn't show, perhaps only in his tough mind. Until recently he'd been graveled at the need to be the "performing bear" for Lord Montague Ransom. A few days before he'd decided to tell them all to go to hell. He had a small nest egg, not much but enough to buy a small spread. The people he had to deal with decided him to turn to something else, even if he had to do it on a shoestring.

Ransom and Pancho Wingfield, both in Butler's posse, would normally have bulldozed him with orders about what to do. They were perplexed by Butler's changed attitude and afraid to object strongly without knowing what new ground they might be treading. When they tried to issue their usual orders, Butler had told them brusquely: "I'll run this my way."

The sound of authority in Butler's voice told Wingfield he'd better lie low for the time being. Butler wasn't a man to fool with, and shooting a sheriff was no laughing matter even in violent New Mexico Territory. Therefore, the confrontation at

Cleve's ranch was Butler's show.

Butler had only one man with him. He left him at the edge of the yard and rode up to Jesús who greeted him formally with a touch of sarcasm: *"Buenas días, Señor* Shereef. *¿Com' esta?"*

"Tol'able," Butler answered, ignoring Jesús's snide pronunciation of sheriff. He knew all the Mexicans up in that country hated him because he was the syndicate's man. Finally, since Jesús didn't offer the customary invitation to "light and jaw a while," he said: "Mind if I get down?"

Jesús shrugged.

Butler dismounted stiffly and stretched. "Ahh," he sighed loudly. "Gittin' too old and stoved up for this business."

Jesús knew it was an act. He'd seen Butler move lightning-fast while disarming one of Wingfield's drunk young toughs who was shooting up a saloon in town.

"Cleve around?" Butler asked.

Jesús shook his head. "Probably took the kids to town. Leastways, there wasn't anybody here when we pulled in."

"Oh," Butler said, "when was that?"

"About an hour back."

Butler pulled out his tobacco sack and papers and slowly built a cigarette, occasionally cutting his eyes toward Jesús. The latter looked everywhere but at Butler. He passed the makings to Jesús who said: *"Gracias"* and built his own cigarette, moving deliberately, as though nothing in the world were on his mind but that little task. Both now lit up and took a drag, blowing the first puff out their noses. Butler was doing a good job, pretending that the fresh lead-stained bullet marks weren't in plain sight on the wall of the stone house next to them. Earlier Cleve had had Amy collect a couple of dozen flattened slugs from the porch where they had dropped. Whatever the sheriff was thinking, he kept to himself, and he ignored the other men who were carrying supplies out to their pack horses. Finally he said: "Well, tell Cleve I'd like to talk to him . . . real soon."

Jesús admired Butler's cool handling of a situation where he knew a wrong move could start a shooting. Cleve could just as well be somewhere around with a rifle trained on his gizzard. He nodded. "*Sí*, I'll tell him that when I see him."

Butler saw no need to push. He wanted to find out more about what he was riding into before he decided to bring it to a showdown. He had enough men to lay siege to the place and starve them out, if need be. He rode back and joined his undersheriff, Dave Ralls.

"I have a notion that Cleve isn't here from the way they act," he said to Ralls. "Jesús told me there wasn't anybody here when him and the boys rode in to get some more supplies. It looks to me like that's what they're doin'. We'll take their word for it. I don't expect those bodies are still on the place, either. I notice they ran a lot of horses over the yard and churned hell out of it. There's only one reason they'd do that."

"See any signs of blood?" Ralls asked.

"Nary. Probably shoveled it up and buried it."

They headed back the way they had come at a trot, pretending to be in no hurry, but once out of sight they touched their mounts into a lope and rejoined the rest of the posse.

Lord Ransom and Wingfield moved out to meet them. Butler didn't particularly like Englishmen, this one especially. He wore a pith helmet of the India army variety, wide-flapping English riding pants, and flat-heeled boots with blunt cavalry spurs.

"Here comes the Prince of Wales on his damn' postage stamp saddle," Butler muttered, and Ralls guffawed.

"Well?" Ransom inquired, pulling up short.

Butler grunted.

"What does that mean?" Ransom asked.

"Bandelier ain't home."

"How can we be sure?"

"We can't without starting a shooting war we don't need."

Ransom thought about that. He didn't think Grut Voerbeck, the big boss in Holland, would appreciate it if news of a huge foreign syndicate shooting up poor, hard-working American settlers on contested public land reached all the newspapers — at least not yet.

"Where the hell is Bandelier, if he ain't home?" Wingfield put in.

"His *segundo* thought he went to town with the kids."

"I wouldn't believe that greaser on a stack of Bibles," Wingfield said.

"Neither would I in this case," Butler agreed. The sheriff knew Pancho was perfectly aware that he himself was married to a Mexican woman but remained outwardly unruffled. He was used to racial slurs.

"What do you aim to do?"

"Wait'll the boys we sent out circling for tracks come back and tell us something."

The first of them came in at a hard lope a few minutes later. He rode straight toward the sheriff, waving his arm toward the San Juans to the west and yelled: "A guy with two pack horses is headed that way."

"Could you tell if it was Bandelier?"

"Too far away, but I don't think so."

"Well," Butler said, "we'll cut him off. Wingfield, how about takin' a few of your boys and circling around to do that?"

That's what the Texan wanted to hear. He picked a half dozen to go with him, including Harmony Dabney, his best rifle shot.

Like an Indian, José sensed he was being followed before his eyes or ears told him. He tethered the two pack horses to a juniper and rode up a rise to look. Two of Wingfield's men were in sight, coming fast, and José decided to make a run for it, untying the pack horses and driving them ahead of him. He hoped he'd make it to the Aguila gorge so he could dump the bodies into the rapids. Instead, he rode directly into Dabney and Wingfield who were still over a hundred yards away. Unlike a white man, José, as soon as he recognized he was going to lose the pack horses and perhaps get killed in the bargain, abandoned them and cut away, spurring his horse into a run to get over the nearest hill. The pack horses tried to follow, and Dabney cut one of them down with a single rifle shot before he turned loose at José. By then the Jicarilla was far away and swerving his horse violently. He heard a couple of big slugs sing uncomfortably close but got over the hill unhit. He hoped they'd stop to take in those two bodies before trying to follow him. Regardless, he kept at a run for more than a mile, before pulling in to let his mount blow.

He dismounted and left his horse on dropped reins, making his way on foot to the rimrock to look over his back trail. He wasn't concerned about keeping the horse in case someone was close on his trail. His best bet to get away was on foot up in the cliffs because he wouldn't leave tracks as a shod horse would. His horse, which he'd picked because it was sure-footed in the mountains, was too slow to outdistance his pursuers.

No one was in sight, so he cautiously returned to his mount and decided to work back toward the ranch, figuring the posse would expect him to head for the high peaks. His Indian mind held a map of the country as accurately as if drawn on paper. He knew exactly where the rocky ridges were that would make it slow work, if not impossible, to track him. He had gone a couple of miles when he saw Cleve's black Thoroughbred in the brush ahead of him.

He turned into a depression and again left his horse, so he

could search the area without being seen. Finally he saw Cleve, sprawled on the ground. José carefully circled with such stealth that even Star didn't see or hear him until he came upwind where the horse scented him and threw up his head, looking directly toward him.

He stepped out slowly and called: "Easy, Star. You know José." He kept talking. A long look and a familiar voice satisfied Star. The big horse nickered softly, put his nose down, and nudged Cleve.

José knelt beside him and checked his breathing. The bloody, improvised bandage told him where he'd been shot. The question in his mind was the whereabouts of whoever did the shooting. Had Cleve got him? Or was he circling around to finish the job? Whichever the case, he knew he had to hide Cleve until he could be moved farther away without killing him. He ran to his horse and, when he returned, unslung his canteen from the saddle horn and poured some water on Cleve's forehead to see if this would bring him around.

Devil Ed had ridden rapidly back to Butler, told what he'd done, and where he figured Cleve was apt to be. The blood all along Cleve's trail assured him his shot had tagged Cleve or his horse.

"O K," Butler said, deciding on a definite strategy. He pointed to a couple of men. "You two keep an eye on the place. If Cleve's cowboys down there leave, follow 'em. If they don't, I want to know. They might just wait around for Bandelier to come back."

As Butler prepared to follow Cleve's trail, one of Wingfield's men came in at a gallop. "We got the bodies," he yelled. "Dabney shot one of the horses. Maybe winged the bastard leading them, but we got both horses and the bodies. Wingfield's bringing them in."

"Bully!" Ransom exclaimed, which irritated Butler more than it should have. He was glad to see one of the men from the Amarillo ranch attract Ransom's attention and take him away in earnest conversation.

This new development changed Butler's plans. He said to Devil Ed: "I'm sending some men with you to trail Cleve. I'll be camped right here until I know more about what's going on. Let me know if you get Cleve. If I'm not here, I'll be down at his place."

So far his plans had all paid off because he'd looked before he leaped. He aimed to keep it that way. He sent a man into Dorado for the coroner. There were enough witnesses for a hearing. Wingfield's men had been at the ranch the night before and could testify. He figured they'd lie like hell, but it was enough to get a coroner's hearing on the record. If they brought Cleve in alive, they could thrash the rest out in court.

That reminded him that Devil Ed needed watching. He might simply finish Cleve, if they caught him, and it was a sure bet none of Wingfield's men would stop him. Butler called over Dave Ralls and drew him out of hearing of the others. "I want Bandelier kept alive. Wingfield's whole story about what happened at the ranch last night doesn't hold water. What the hell did he go there for in the first place?"

Ralls shrugged. "To kill Bandelier, I reckon."

"He said they went with two U. S. deputy marshals who had a warrant to deliver, and Cleve beefed them when they tried to serve it."

"I wouldn't have gone to Cleve's place at night on a bet the way this country is," Ralls said. "Why didn't they wait till morning?"

Butler shrugged. "That's what I mean. Their story doesn't hold water. Anyhow, I want you to find Devil Ed and keep a close eye on the crazy son of a bitch. Shoot him, if you have to. I want Cleve alive. When Wingfield comes in, I'll keep him with me so he doesn't come up there and horn in."

Butler was relieved that Ransom hadn't decided to go with Devil Ed. He'd underestimated his man and didn't realize why the Englishman preferred to stay with him, but Ransom was smart enough to steer clear of a possible murder. He had lived in New Mexico long enough to know that was what to expect if Devil Ed caught Cleve.

Shortly after they'd crawled into the attic, Junior heard Devil Ed's rifle shots. Amy thought she might have heard them, too, but her hearing wasn't as good as her brother's.

As soon as the coast was clear, Jesús called them back down from the attic, and Junior asked him right away: "Did you hear shooting up there where Pa went?"

"When?"

"About the time the sheriff rode in."

Jesús hadn't. "Are you sure?"

"Sure, I'm sure. I'm surprised you didn't hear it."

Jesús shrugged. "Sounds carry funny. I don't think the sheriff heard anything, either. At least he didn't show it."

"I heard what might have been shooting," Sam Buchanan said. "But I couldn't be sure it was over there. You know how sounds echo around here."

"Hadn't we better go up and check?" Junior asked.

Jesús thought about that. "I don't think so. The sheriff isn't dumb. He's bound to have someone watching us through field glasses. I would in his place, and I'd go around and check on them every once in a while. So, if what you heard wasn't shooting, and we go looking, we'll lead Butler right onto your pa's trail for no good reason." He read Junior's rebellious look and added: "I know what you're thinking. Forget it. *You* especially can't go up and look, that's for sure, because if either you or Amy go outside, whoever is watching'll see you, and Butler will find out you're still around and know we lied to him. In that case he'll likely be right back down here to pull you two in as witnesses. How'd you like to sit in the *juzgado* for a while?"

"I don't give a damn about that," Junior protested. "I know shooting when I hear it. Suppose somebody shot Pa, and he needs help bad?"

"Whether it was shooting or not, we'll have to risk it," Jesús said.

That didn't satisfy Junior. He felt himself almost hating the *segundo* for being so damned calm. He had a feeling that shooting signified exactly what had happened. It was a strong hunch, and, like his pa's hunches, his were usually right. However, he recognized that further argument with Jesús would get him nothing.

Jesús said: "You're gonna do what I say, or I'll see that your pa wears you out when he comes back."

Junior snapped: "If he needs help, and we don't go up there, he might not come back."

Jesús ignored that and said: "Regardless, you and Amy are going to stay in here till after dark, then head for town. Me and the boys are going to go back and try to round up the herd again. If we hadn't shot up most of our ammunition, I'd have stayed out there."

Junior said: "The sheriff'll probably come back down here anyhow. I'll bet he'll want to snoop around as soon as you leave."

"Chance we have to take."

Junior was losing his temper again. "What do you mean *we* have to take? What the hell do me and Amy do if he does?"

"Get arrested. He won't hurt you. He'll take you to town. I reckon that's where your pa wants you to go anyhow."

Junior only managed to curb his temper because he'd formed a plan that suited him. "O K," he said. "I hope you aim to leave us a couple of horses to get to town on." The sarcasm didn't escape Jesús.

"In the barn. Both fast. That green-broke bay, Dynamite, and Dave for Amy. Let out Nellie before you leave. She'll have to foal on the prairie like all the rest."

Amy hated that idea. Nellie was her pa's prize mare. She knew her pa wouldn't like it, either, but what else could they do so the mare could get food and water? She didn't know when they'd be back. Maybe never. Her little voice said: *Don't ever think that. It might really happen if you don't keep thinking on the bright side.*

Junior and Amy watched from an upstairs window as their cowboys left. They were cooped up in the locked house again, and Junior fidgeted at the delay. He bet that Jesús would watch until he was out of sight to make sure they weren't trying something foolish.

Junior told Amy: "Get together a pack of grub for the trail."

"We got plenty of time," she said.

"No, we haven't. I aim to pull out of here as soon as Jesús is where he can't see us doing it. I'll give him ten minutes after he's out of sight, because he's just sneaky enough to slip back and watch a while."

"If you pull out, I'm going along," Amy said.

"I didn't expect you wouldn't."

"Where're we goin'?"

"On Pa's trail."

"Suppose the old sheriff sees us and follows?"

"Suppose he doesn't? I'll worry about that if it happens. I'd as soon shoot a sheriff as look at him, especially this one."

He sounded like he meant it. He scared her worse than she already was. *Look on the bright side,* she told herself again, then wondered: *Just where is that from here?* She had a pain in her chest like you got after you almost stepped on a rattlesnake and just managed to jump out of the way. She'd felt like that a lot since she'd heard her pa fire those first two shots the night before.

Chapter Four

Amy stood at a second-story window, Winchester ready, while Junior ran to the barn to saddle their horses. Once inside, he worked fast, pressed by the need for speed in case he'd been seen by a look-out in the hills as he crossed the yard. If the sheriff had someone watching, he'd be on them like a duck on a June bug.

Amy had their packs ready in the house. While he saddled, he reviewed their contents. Were they forgetting something? — blankets, slickers, extra ammunition, food, and matches, all rolled in tarps, ready to tie behind their saddles as soon as he brought up the horses.

He rode Dynamite and led Dave to the house at a fast trot, jumping off onto the porch. Amy carried out their rifles and canteens, while he tied on the packs, then went back, and padlocked the door. He slipped Amy's Winchester into its saddle boot after she was mounted.

"Remember, this ain't no ornament," he warned. "I expect you to use it if we have to."

"What makes you think I won't?"

"Because you're only a girl."

She stuck out her tongue. Her little voice whispered: *We'll show him when the time comes,* but she wasn't so sure. She hoped the time would never come.

They couldn't leave Maggie behind, so the little terrier ran alongside. "If she can't keep up, I'll take her up here with me," Junior assured.

Amy thought her brother looked formidable with a six-shooter and Bowie knife slung to his cartridge belt, hat pulled low over his eyes. He led the way down into Musica Creek at a fast trot.

"We'll stay in the creek to cover our tracks as long as we can," he called back without turning his head. He was busy scanning their path and keeping a good watch on the creekbank as well to be sure he didn't miss the spot where Cleve and Star had left the water. He expected it would be on one of the rocky shelves, but Cleve had left the creek on a sand bar.

Pointing to the plain tracks, Junior said: "Pa must have wanted to lead the sheriff away in case they saw him dig out, so's to lead him off José's trail. I sure hope old José got away with them two bodies."

"Me, too," said Amy.

Junior looked back to see if Maggie was keeping up and was surprised that she was right on his horse's hoofs.

Star's tracks led up a shallow, sandy arroyo. When they neared the crest, Junior ordered: "You stay here, Amy, while I take a look over the top."

She didn't like Junior pulling so far ahead. Dave fidgeted, wanting to follow. Junior stopped to study something on the ground. It looked to her like Maggie was sniffing at the same place. Then Junior rode back.

"I think we might be sittin' ducks, comin' out of the arroyo the way Pa went. We better pull out a ways where we can see ahead of us."

Amy suspected whatever he'd been looking at was something he didn't want her to see. She asked: "What were you lookin' at so long on the ground up there?"

"Where Pa got down and tightened his cinch," he lied. "Might not be a bad idea for us."

He hopped down and handed her his reins, quickly taking up both their cinches. He was nursing a renewed desire to kill someone after he'd found their two hounds, ghastly and pitiful in death.

Amy said: "You're lyin' to me. Somebody shot Pa, and he's layin' up there dead, isn't he?" Her face was already breaking in anguish.

Junior was exasperated. "I swear I ain't lyin' to you. Now, stop wasting time."

Before he could remount, she kicked her horse into a lope up the arroyo to see for herself. When she found the lifeless bodies of Dash and Jack, it was almost as bad as if it had been Cleve. Junior was right on her heels. "I tried to keep it from you," he said, "but you had to be a danged interferin' girl about it, didn't you?"

She hardly heard him. "Those two never done a thing to anybody," she gulped, blinded by tears, recalling their friendly brown eyes, shining in anticipation of a pat or of treats handed to them at the supper table, tails always happily wagging.

Junior said: "I swear I'm goin' to gut-shoot whoever done this if I find out for sure."

His savage glare, when he said it, frightened Amy. She felt as badly as he did but didn't think she could gut-shoot anyone in cold blood. She was almost convinced that her brother could. She wondered if he'd gone out of his mind over all the recent violence.

"C'mon," he said. "Cryin' won't do any good."

She bet he felt like crying himself, and her pa had probably felt the same way when he saw the dogs. They'd been members of the family.

On the crest she stopped briefly and looked back at the only home she'd ever known. *I wonder if I'll ever get back?* she asked herself. Then she remembered about looking on the bright side. She set her jaw and brushed away her tears.

She'd ridden up here often in the carefree old days, just to watch the sun set over the mountains. Passing this way while helping out with the range work, she had always stopped to admire the San Juans, jutting skyward with glistening white heads. Her whole heart was wrapped around this once-happy place. Looking down at her mother's grave on the opposite hillside, she said aloud: "Good bye, Mama." Tears came again.

"C'mon," Junior's said, reining close.

"I was lookin' at Mama's grave and sayin' good bye."

"So was I," he said, gripping her hand and squeezing it.

He circled to pick up Star's trail where it came out of the arroyo and found the spot where the horse had leaped into his long-running stride. A couple of rods beyond he saw Devil Ed's empty cartridge cases, lying on the ground. He stopped and pointed. "Those were probably from the shooting we heard. Pa ran right into someone here, and they shot at him."

Amy could read the sign for herself. "Star almost ran down whoever did the shootin'," she said.

They followed the trail and shortly came to the first splashes of blood on the ground. Amy quavered. "Whoever was back there shot Pa. I wonder if he's bad hurt?"

"I don't think so, or he couldn't have stuck on Star at a run," Junior said. "Maybe they pinked Star and not Pa, but whoever it was took out after them."

The trail led through clumps of juniper where Cleve had zigzagged before he'd lined out. Shortly the trail of many horses joined Cleve's. The hoof prints only told them that a lot more men had taken up the chase. "Now who the hell are these guys?" Junior muttered.

"Must be Sheriff Butler's posse," Amy answered.

"I know that," Junior said. "I was talkin' to myself."

Amy knew he sounded gruff because he wasn't sure what to do, was probably as scared as she was.

Junior weighed the risk of sticking on this trail where they might run into a hostile posse. Finally he said: "Let's git up in the hills where there's less chance of us being seen."

Devil Ed possessed the cunning and cruelty of a predator and was almost an animal when after prey. Unerringly he led the posse on Star's tracks until where they played out on a rocky plateau. In this sort of ground tracking was a problem even for Indian trailers. They could take days to unscramble a trail on rocky ground, sometimes losing it completely despite their reputations. Devil Ed wished they had some bloodhounds. He decided to slip away from the posse, most of whom couldn't track a herd of buffalo, and go it alone, circling for sign. To facilitate getting away unseen he said: "Split up boys and look around for his tracks."

If Dave Ralls had overtaken the posse before they got to that point, he'd have been keeping an eye on Devil Ed and following him when he ditched the others, but he was still far behind.

Cunning, half mad, Ed knew by instinct what he had to do and knew the area well. He planned to ride completely around the entire five-mile-wide rocky plateau to see if Star's tracks left it. If he found no tracks leaving the area, he'd know that Cleve had holed up or played out, in which case he'd find him, one way or another. It was just a matter of time. He was half way around his circuit when he saw Junior and Amy.

He concealed his horse, then stealthy as a mountain lion slipped back afoot, Winchester in hand. Even Maggie didn't detect him in ambush since she was panting along behind Junior's horse, having a hard time keeping up.

Devil Ed leveled his rifle and yelled: "Pull up!"

Junior started to reach for his pistol, then remembering Cleve's caution — *always respect the drop, play for time* — thought better of it. He wanted to tell Amy to make a run for it but recognized Devil Ed, and he was reputed to be a crack rifle shot and the kind who wouldn't hesitate to shoot his grandmother.

Maggie circled Devil Ed, growling. Ed ignored her but read Junior's intent and warned: "I don't aim to hurt you kids unless you make me."

Amy's heart was in her mouth as soon as she recognized the bearded ogre. She thought of making a run but wasn't about to leave Junior alone. She didn't believe Devil Ed when he said he wouldn't hurt them.

"Unstrap that six-shooter and let it drop," Devil Ed ordered.

Junior had no choice. He debated slipping out his Bowie knife and throwing it but didn't think he'd be fast enough, and Devil Ed was watching him like a hawk.

"No tricks, kid," he warned. It seemed to Junior like this man was reading his mind, which was unsettling.

Devil Ed calculated that these two kids would be bait to draw Cleve into a trap. He wanted Cleve alive until he himself had the pleasure of killing him. His grudge stemmed from the fact that, years before, he'd filed on the Bandelier ranch but lost it because his neighbors soon learned his ways. He used the sheep and goats of his Mexican and Jicarilla neighbors for target practice, treated their owners with contempt, and openly lusted after their women. They had no objections to Anglos who married into their families, but it was clear that wasn't Devil Ed's intent. Besides, he was so ugly that no woman wanted him. Before he had done more than build a stone foundation for his house, he was interviewed one dark night by his neighbors, a hundred or more strong. It took three swings into the air at the end of a rope tossed over a cottonwood branch to give him a convincing taste of what strangling was like before he agreed to pull out.

When Cleve filed on his abandoned claim a few years later,

Devil Ed decided the newcomer was stealing his property. He made threatening visits and finally was soundly thrashed by Cleve. Later, he forced a gun play in town in which Cleve disabled him with a .45 slug in his arm. Devil Ed saw none of this as trouble he'd brought on himself; he simply wished to get revenge. He'd come from the feuding Tennessee mountains and never forgot an injury, real or imagined. He made up his mind that Cleve had to die and was mortally certain his chance to kill him would come. Now it had. If he held the Bandelier kids, Cleve would come after them sooner or later, if he was still alive.

Chapter Five

Clint Butler thought Cleve Bandelier's ranch was located in one of the prime spots in that country. Musica Creek had a fair amount of water running in it, even after a few dry years, and the valley was sheltered by grassy slopes dotted with juniper and *chamiso,* gradually rising to broad table lands that, in good seasons, were covered with lush grass. In the distance, dominating the horizon to the northwest, were the San Juans, crowned with snow. Butler had stationed himself at the head of the valley where the pines mingled with spruce and fir. He'd instructed his searching parties to send someone back to keep him posted, and he was expecting Wingfield and his men to return with the two bodies they'd taken from José. Wingfield's return created a stir among the men who were still in camp.

Wingfield delivered the two bodies, proud as a kid back from his first hunt. "Where do you want me to dump these trophies?" he asked Butler.

The sheriff didn't like this disrespect for the dead, regardless of who they were, and replied in the same callous manner: "Put them bodies downwind somewhere. I sent for Doc Ewing, but Lord knows when he'll show up."

Wingfield laughed, followed the sheriff's suggestion, and was shortly drawn aside by Ransom. Butler saw them in earnest conversation, apparently arguing about something.

The sheriff had nothing to do but wait to hear from the men out with Devil Ed after Bandelier and wait for the coroner. He stretched out, snoozing, his saddle for a pillow, hat over his eyes. He'd been half serious when he told Jesús he was getting too old for this business. Physically, he was in prime shape for a man who'd seen forty-seven hard summers, but he didn't relish sleeping on the ground, cooking over a smoky fire if he were lucky enough to have anything to cook, and all the other inconvenience that went with it. He was glad to be roused by the arrival of Bud Henessey with his camp wagon. It was a chuck wagon converted into a sheep herder's home on wheels, except that it retained the outside kitchen layout in back. Butler had the wagon follow him because his comfortable bed was inside. He didn't care if Wingfield and his crew starved or froze. The wagon was his personal property, used for hunting and prospecting trips whenever town got on his nerves. He looked forward to retiring to a ranch somewhere in these hills. He knew, if he could play the syndicate's game, he could get clear title to a small piece of the grant, possibly even Bandelier's home ranch and some ground, but he wasn't built right to do that — in fact the idea turned his stomach.

He thought it was a pity Cleve had been in the way of the syndicate's ambitions, and he wished all of the foreign dudes would stay to hell home and eat, drink, dance, and ride themselves to death, which, it seemed to him, they had tried to do since they had come to New Mexico. When Bud stopped, he walked over to the wagon, put one foot on the wheel, and spit.

"Did the guy I sent after Doc Ewing pass you?" Butler asked.

"Yup. It'll probably be a while before Doc gits out here, though. I heard he went out in the country to take care of some damn' fool kid who accidentally shot himself."

"That's O K. He can do more for the kid than he can for the two over there. Was the old bastard sober?"

"Lord knows. Where do you want me to set up this shebang?"

"Suit yourself."

Bud drove well inside the clump of trees, set the brake, and slowly climbed down. Butler followed him and helped unharness the team.

"You can water 'em down at the creek. Bandelier's whole crew pulled out, so you won't run into any of them. Besides, they ain't hostile."

"Got water in the barrels. For now I'll water with a bucket. How about I make us some coffee?" He knew Clint was a lot happier after he had his coffee, and Bud made a study of repaying Butler for making him a deputy when he was too stoved up to cowboy any more. Bud thought the badge was a joke, but he liked the easy money. "You didn't ketch Bandelier yet, I see."

"Not yet. Devil Ed pinked him with his Winchester, but Cleve outrun him, so I figure he wasn't hit too bad. I got a bunch out on his trail. Wingfield run down a guy packin' out them two dead ones, which is why I sent for Doc."

"With them two stiffs for evidence, I reckon old Cleve will do a long stretch, even if his neck doesn't." Bud snorted at his little joke.

"Maybe. We gotta catch him first. If Devil Ed didn't finish him, we may never see him again. In his place I'd dust for Canada or South America and send back for the kids."

"Where're they?"

"Don't know. I was down an' talked to Cleve's *segundo* but didn't get anything out of him. He claimed they came back in for supplies, and nobody was down at the ranch when they got in. I took his word for it. He really didn't act like he knew what went on there last night, and I didn't bring it up under the circumstances. Figured he might lead me to something if he was putting on. I'm havin' 'em trailed when they pull out to see if they're really rounding up cows or meeting Cleve somewhere."

"I'd have played it dumb, too, in his boots," Bud said,

“ ’specially if I knew what happened. It figures, if he did, he knows where Cleve went.”

“Jesús is a smart one, all right,” Butler conceded. He was one cowboy that Butler had never had to run in for getting drunk and causing trouble in town. “There’s a chance he helped Cleve pack out them bodies. It’s a cinch it wasn’t Cleve that was leadin’ the pack horses that Wingfield ran down.”

“Who was?”

“We don’t know. He got away.”

“Maybe Cleve’s boy.”

“I don’t think so. Cleve wouldn’t let him run a risk like that. He’d have done it himself before he let the kid do it. Probably one of his cowboys.”

Bud got a fire going and put on the coffee pot. “You want I should feed that crew over there?” He nodded at them and looked disgusted.

“I guess we’ll have to.” Butler didn’t sound any more enthusiastic than Bud looked and added: “Let’s have some of that coffee first.”

Butler got out his folding canvas chair, sank into it, then rolled and lit a cigarette. He wished he was out hunting something besides people.

“What you aim to do, now?” Bud asked.

Butler grinned. “I kind of like it here. I aim to park till we know how that crew went after Bandelier makes out . . . be here overnight at least. Don’t let word get out, but to tell the gawd’s truth I hope he gets away. I ain’t tryin’ to prove anything any more, if I ever was. He’s a hell of a sight better man than the bunch lookin’ fer him.”

“That’s a fact. An’ you know I never blab.”

That reminded Butler of what was bothering him. He wasn’t confident they’d bring Cleve in alive, even if he tried to give up, especially if Devil Ed got another bead on him. Dave Ralls was a good man, but maybe he wouldn't be right on hand with the bunch that got Bandelier. He said: "I have a notion to mosey along after that crew on Bandelier's trail."

Bud sensed the uneasiness in Butler's voice and looked at him questioningly. When the sheriff remained silent, Bud asked: "Any special reason to be in a hurry?"

"I want Bandelier alive. He deserves his day in court. What the hell was this bunch doing around his place in the middle of the night, anyhow?"

"Tryin' to kill him, I reckon."

"That's what Ralls said. Hell, in his place I'd have done exactly what he did. It wasn't only his neck, he was protecting his kids. He's too good a man to check out without a chance."

With that, he got up and saddled his horse, then said to Bud: "When Doc shows up, tell him I'll be back by sundown, most likely."

Wingfield's men silently watched the sheriff leave, but none said anything. Lord Ransom had returned to the Amarillo ranch, for which Butler was thankful. He wanted to ride alone.

Distant thunder, rebounding off the mountains, forecast rain. The sheriff's horse pricked his ears, listening to the long rumble, and trotted faster. Butler said to the animal: "Gittin' rain perks up everything out here, don't it?" Then he thought soberly: *I'll bet old Cleve ain't feelin' too perky, though, if he got hit bad.* He knew that he was siding with a man, who, according to the letter of the law, he should be hunting. "To hell with the letter of the law," he muttered and urged his mount into an easy lope. *Christ,* he thought, *that crew might even string up old Cleve out of plain orneriness if I don't git up there in time.* He had the strong feeling his only mistake so far had been sending out a wild man like Devil Ed in charge of the crew on Cleve's trail, but he couldn't recall ever having a posse as sorry as this one. *Can't trust any of 'em but Dave and Bud,* he thought sourly.

The urge was on him to go faster, but he wasn't about to wind his horse just because he was feeling nervous.

He easily followed the broad trail of Devil Ed's posse to the place where Cleve was shot. They had churned up the ground, so he had to circle to find where Cleve had come up the arroyo. He found the poisoned dogs. *Those bastards got rid of the dogs so they could sneak up on the place. Probably Devil Ed's work.* He owned a pair of hounds himself and would have savored killing anyone he was sure had poisoned either of them.

Two new sets of tracks joined Cleve's at the top of the arroyo, which puzzled him. *Who would this be?* He set out along that trail with a sense of urgency. He had just ridden inside the tree line, walking his horse a while to let it catch its wind, when he heard a rifle shot. Cautiously, Indian-like, intending to see before he was seen, he worked closer, tethered his horse in a dense clump of junipers and, taking his rifle, moved slowly ahead on foot.

Chapter Six

Everyone who looked Devil Ed Targee in the eyes suspected he was crazy, but it didn't pay to look him in the eyes for long because, like many Tennessee mountain men, he took it as an affront. Bloody tradition and madness ruled him. When he led the posse after Cleve, he spurred and quirted frantically to stay in the lead. The only man who drew abreast of him turned and saw his bearded face twisted into a glassy-eyed leer, teeth showing like a snarling dog. Animal growls issued from deep in his throat. He drooled tobacco juice into his ragged, reddish-gray beard, flecks of it blowing into the wind. It was too much for the man, hardened though he was to frontier coarseness. He looked away and quickly pulled back again. To no one in particular he said: "No wonder they call that crazy son of a bitch Devil Ed."

Now, after capturing Junior and Amy and looping Junior's gun belt over his arm, Devil Ed ordered: "Git down off'n that horse and don't make any funny moves." To Amy he called: "Now you, missy, come up here'n do the same." Then he started mumbling to himself, "Gotta figger out what to do with these two. I guess I'll jist let 'em walk an' come back for their horses later." He eyed their horses, which were a lot fresher than his, and said to Junior: "I reckon I'll jist ride that big bronc' of yours. Bring him over here."

Junior's heart skipped at this rare opportunity to have the tables turned. Dynamite was a one-person horse — *his*.

Ed looped Junior's gun belt around the saddle horn, led the horse away a few yards, and, slinging his arm holding the rifle over the cantle, put his foot into the stirrup. He bounced on the other foot once and had partially heaved himself into the saddle, when the horse bogged its head and bucked viciously. Ed went flying off straight ahead, lit on his knees and, when the horse bucked right over him, was kicked flat, the wind completely knocked out of him. Unable to draw air, he gave a series of uncontrollable gasps: "*Ah! Ah! Ah! Ah!*"

Junior snatched Amy's rifle from its saddle boot and covered Devil Ed, waiting for him to get his wind. When he tried to get on his feet, Junior ordered: "Hold it right there! I'd mortally love to perforate your ugly carcass, mister. Keep your hands on the ground and don't move."

"I ain't movin'," Devil Ed said, knowing a scared kid would kill a man quicker than anyone.

His gun hadn't spilled from its scabbard when he was bucked off, though the scabbard had been twisted around behind him. Junior, knowing he was dangerous as a rattler as long as he had a gun, ordered Amy: "Work up behind him careful and take his six-shooter."

She didn't want to get anywhere near the frightful-looking brute who smelled like a bear den, but she did as she was told. Both she and Junior were astonished by the speed with which Devil Ed raised an arm and grabbed Amy, jerking her between him and Junior's rifle.

Junior couldn't risk shooting without getting closer, then decided it would be even safer if he could brain Devil Ed with the rifle barrel. Ed had his eyes on him and was trying to get to his hide-out Bowie knife, which hung behind on a thong beneath his shirt. He was in the wrong position for that but managed to grab the barrel of Junior's rifle. He turned Amy loose and hung onto the rifle, forcing its muzzle away from him, then jerked Junior off-balance long enough to get to his feet.

A deadly tug of war started, Junior being flung off his feet and into the air as Devil Ed swung him to make him let go. Both were gasping for breath and churning up the ground like a couple of battling bulls.

"For Christ's . . . sake!" Junior yelled raggedly at Amy. "Grab one o' them . . . guns . . . and shoot . . . this son of a bitch!"

She'd already tried to get the rifle off Junior's horse, but the animal danced away, spooked by the fight. Blinded by panic, it took her a long time to find Devil Ed's rifle, but finally she snatched it up, only to be confronted with the same problem Junior had. If she shot, she could hit her brother. Desperate, Junior yelled: "Shoot, god damn it!"

She aimed at Devil Ed's feet, knowing, if she missed and hit her brother, at least she wouldn't kill him, and Devil Ed's howl informed her she'd hit her target, even before she saw the blood flying. He let go of the rifle, and Junior spun away, still holding it, but tripped and fell. He rolled and came up with it leveled, gasping for breath and shaking from the strain.

Devil Ed jumped around, holding his torn and bleeding foot, then sat down. "Gaw damn you two!" he howled.

He still had his six-shooter around behind him, but Junior had no intention of making the same mistake twice. "Unbuckle that gun belt and throw it away from you," he demanded when he got his breath.

Targee complied.

Then Junior said: "Now, you mean son of a bitch, I aim to blow your worthless head off, so we don't have any more trouble with you."

He was paying him back for the fright he'd just suffered, blowing out his anger with no intention of actually shooting him. Mistaking the look in her brother's eyes as he drew a careful bead, Amy yelled: "You just can't shoot him like that," and, rushing in, thrust up his rifle.

"Git out of my way!" Junior pushed her away harder than he intended, so that she tripped and fell into Devil Ed's arms. He kept her in front of him, desperate fear in his black eyes, but also determination to play every card he had in a frantic try for survival. He jerked his Bowie knife and whipped it to Amy's throat in one continuous motion.

"Put down that rifle, sonny, or I'll slit her throat," he growled.

Amy was petrified, as much over the sudden desperate expression that came over her brother's face as over the knife.

"I ain't putting the rifle down, mister," Junior bluffed. "You aim to cut her throat anyhow, and you know it. Go ahead. The damn' fool brought it on herself. Git it over with. Then I'll blow your head off."

Amy prepared to die but wished she didn't have to. She couldn't make a sound and almost wanted to die after what her brother had just said.

Junior knew how to look deadly, the animal cunning of a natural born fighter. Devil Ed had never before seen a look in anyone's eyes to match his own madness. Junior's did, his light blue eyes turned transparent like those of a mortally wounded cat. A terrible fear palsied Ed, and the fleeting thought that he was going to be killed in a fight with a couple of kids further demoralized him. Nonetheless, he knew his only chance was to keep up the stand-off. Finally, Junior lowered the rifle slowly and laid it on the ground. Devil Ed felt an indescribable sense of relief. When he could manage a fairly steady voice, he said: "Step away from that rifle now, kid."

Junior stepped back, and Devil Ed crawfished across the ground for the rifle, awkwardly hanging onto both Amy and his knife. He let Amy go and grabbed the rifle at the same time. Junior made a dive for it and got a grip on it.

Amy rolled away and sprang to her feet, seeing Junior and Devil Ed on the ground, locked in another deadly battle, this time with a Bowie knife ready to come down into Junior's heart. Devil Ed said: "Let go of the rifle, kid, or you'll make me do it."

Amy grabbed the biggest rock she could heft and brought it down as hard as she could on Devil Ed's head. The arm with the knife went limp, and the knife fell to the ground. It took Junior a few seconds to realize that Amy had knocked Devil Ed out cold.

He said: "I take back everything I said about you bein' only a girl."

Amy's knees were wobbling. In a faint voice she said: "I've got to sit down." Then she turned white and started to fall. Junior grabbed her and let her down easy, dragging her a good distance away from the unconscious man.

He debated shooting the lunatic who had caused the Bandeliers so much trouble over the years. He'd have bet a hundred dollars that Devil Ed had done the long-range shooting at them the past couple of months, probably had shot his pa today, and, if it wasn't he, Junior knew he'd have ridden a five-hundred-dollar horse to death for a chance to do it, poisoned their hounds, and most likely was the one who'd fired the long shot at Cleve that morning in the ranch yard.

Why not get rid of the son of a bitch? he asked himself. A happier thought was that he might be dead already from the blow on the head. Taking his pulse involved the risk of getting near him, so he settled for the wish.

Chapter Seven

José had to get Cleve away, hiding him quickly, but do it very carefully to prevent more bleeding. He couldn't tell how much blood Cleve had lost, but it looked like a lot. The improvised bandage was soaked, and a little blood still oozed out.

José knew exactly where he wanted to move Cleve. In the caprock a few miles away was the secret Jicarilla hide-out where Chief Don Alonzo had retreated whenever the Army or the Utes had made it hot for his little band. José recalled his fear as a child, while they were running, and how secure he felt after the band reached this secret haven. Even the Utes had never been able to discover its location. Its entrance, behind a rock shelf, was invisible from more than a few yards away, hidden by a dense growth of trees and brush, and was reached only after climbing steeply over a half mile of broken rock.

There was only one way to move Cleve, since no material for a travois existed in that vicinity. José would have to hoist him onto a horse like a sack of meal and tie him on. If Cleve regained consciousness, perhaps he could be tied upright with less chance of bleeding, but he hadn't stirred. José had no way of knowing that Cleve had suffered a concussion in falling from Star onto the rocks.

He decided it would be easier to get Cleve on his own horse, which was a hand and a half shorter than Star, and had been used before for packing. Mustering all the wiry strength in his broad body, he crawled under Cleve, heaved himself to his feet, and pushed and shoved him over the saddle, then tied him securely with his riata. Cleve's bleeding had been started again by the inescapable roughness of manhandling him into the saddle. José thought: *Not hard to follow us if that keeps up.* But he had no choice. To stay was to wait for certain discovery and capture, probably the outright killing of Cleve, if Wingfield's men got him. José vowed they'd do that over his dead body.

He had his foot in the stirrup, ready to mount Star, when the horse threw up his head, listening, then stared intently toward something concealed by the junipers. In a while José made out voices, then a laugh. If these were men hunting Cleve, they certainly didn't care if they found him. José pulled the horses' heads close together, ready to stifle a whinny, and prayed that such heedless possemen were also blind and would blunder past. If discovered, he would have to shoot it out. The gunfire would draw others, but by then he would have a chance to hide some place.

After what seemed too long, the voices receded and finally could be heard no more. José mounted Star and led out, looking back to see if they were leaving a trail of blood. He was relieved to find the bleeding had stopped, at least for a while.

After leaving Amy and Junior at the ranch, Jesús was plagued by an oppressive sense of uneasiness, as though he'd left something important undone. He turned over the possibilities in his mind. It wasn't any concern that the sheriff might come down and find the kids; he sort of hoped he would. That would prevent Junior from doing something rash. But what if Wingfield or some of his men came to the ranch? Junior and Amy would have sense enough to fort up and start shooting, which would bring the sheriff on the run, so that wasn't a problem. Although the sheriff was a tool of the syndicate, he wouldn't let anything happen to a couple of kids. Then the real problem occurred to Jesús. What if Junior decided to pull out and hunt his father? It would be just like him. He was of a mind to return to the ranch. The scattered cattle could wait. He pulled up, and the others drew up beside him.

"I'm not sure we should have left those kids alone," Jesús told them.

"Want me to go back and bring 'em along?" Sam asked.

Jesús considered. He could have brought them along in the first place but had been afraid they'd be seen by some of the posse and draw in the sheriff again. He wondered why he hadn't admitted to Butler that the kids were there and placed them under his protection. That had its negative side — they'd have been grilled about what had happened the night before, but they probably would be sooner or later, anyhow. Things had simply been happening too fast to think out every move ahead of time. Jesús decided that what was really bothering him was that Junior's rashness would lead to exactly what he was doing at that moment — pulling out to follow his father's trail.

He made up his mind and said: "Sam, I want you to go back and see that the kids stay under cover till dark, then make sure they get to town. Cleve always leaves them with the schoolteacher. She'll keep 'em out of trouble. You'll have to look around to find us when you come back because I don't know where we'll be exactly."

Sam agreed. Without asking any questions, he turned his horse and hit the back trail at a fast trot.

When he reached the ranch, it took only the sight of the padlocked door to tell him that the kids were not there. *Can't be more'n a half hour ahead of me at the most, if I cut out after 'em right now,* he thought. He had no sensible alternative except to follow. Most likely Junior had pulled out on Cleve's trail. Sam had heard Junior's argument with Jesús, and it figured he'd do that. No way would Junior go to town of his own volition. He didn't like the schoolteacher, and Sam didn't blame him. He wondered why the *segundo* had trusted Junior not to dig out after Cleve as soon as they were out of sight. He'd have done the same. He thought: *Jesús hasn't been around him lately as much as me. Must think he's still a kid.*

Sam picked up the hoof prints of Dynamite and Dave where they followed Star out of Musica Creek and didn't miss a print all the way up the arroyo to the dead dogs.

"Son of a bitch!" he grated under his breath. Sam loved all animals and had loved the two hounds especially. He knew how Amy must have felt, seeing these trusting animals, pitiable in death, and his heart ached for her. He loved Amy, too, and looked out for her as much as he could.

When Sam topped out of the arroyo, the puzzling mosaic of many tracks confronted him. Finally he unscrambled them to his satisfaction and followed, almost immediately seeing the empty cartridge cases. That could spell bad trouble, but for whom? This proved Junior had actually heard shots up here, just as he insisted, and fired at that time they had something to do with Cleve — either he'd been shot at or fired at someone else, maybe both. Sam's trained eyes picked up a few of the blood spatters, even though dozens of hoofs had disturbed the ground. It all added up to bad news.

He followed the broad trail and saw where someone had cut in on it. These were Butler's tracks. Had someone seen the kids leave and followed them? Whoever made them could only be an added danger. He kept his horse at a fast trot, alert to discover some spot at which Junior and Amy had recognized their danger and headed away. He cursed Junior for being a reckless young fool, inviting disaster by blindly following the trail of this posse. When he finally found two sets of tracks headed for the timber and the high ground, he breathed easier.

Amy's rifle shot, far ahead, raised Sam's apprehension for the kids even more. He slowed his horse to a walk, then stopped to listen. He knew that Junior and Amy and some unknown were ahead of him, and possibly a great number of others, any of whom might have set an ambush. He expected more shooting. None followed. Nonetheless, the kids might be in trouble. He had a hard time restraining his pace, but rushing into an ambush himself wouldn't help them.

He moved closer at a walk, then decided to dismount and lead his horse. After moving several hundred yards, he saw Sheriff Butler's tethered horse. Like all seasoned cowboys, he carried in his memory an inventory of most of the well-known horses in the country. He froze in position, looking all around and listening. He could hear only flies, buzzing nearby, but far ahead jays called alarm, telling him that someone, most likely Butler, was moving ahead of him.

Sam wondered why the sheriff was up there by himself. No ready answer occurred, and there was always the possibility that the posse was with him and had spread out. In any case he knew he must not be seen and decided to hide his horse and proceed on foot.

Sam stood a while, thinking hard, then decided to move his horse back to rocky ground and conceal it. He had to retreat at least a half mile to do that.

José also heard the shot that Sheriff Butler and Sam Buchanan heard, only he was much closer to its source. He had reached Chief Don Alonzo's cave earlier, hidden Cleve and the horses, then retraced their back trail afoot to expunge any signs of blood. He was returning to the cave when he heard Amy shoot.

The fight was over by the time he reached the scene, and Devil Ed was lying on the ground, out cold. José gave a low call as he got close. "Hey, Junior, Amy, it's me, José."

Junior whirled, rifle ready. Recognizing José, he said: "Christ am I glad to see you. What're you doin' here? Did you get rid of them dead ones?"

José's face fell. "I got jumped and had to run for it."

"What about the bodies?"

"They got them."

"I guess Pa will have to go on the run," Junior said. "I wonder where he is."

"I have him where he's safe for now. You two can help me get him away. Maybe tomorrow. He's shot up a little bit."

Amy's heart sank into her boots. She knew how these Indians, like the Mexicans they'd rubbed elbows with for centuries, evaded coming right out with bad news by using phrases like "a little bit."

"Bad?" she asked, feeling the familiar strangling compression returning to her chest again, rendering her unable to breathe for a few seconds.

José shrugged. "Bad enough. He's not gonna die. But he might if we move him too soon."

"Where is he?" Junior asked.

"I'll show you. Bring your horses. We'd better get out of here. Someone may have heard that shot."

Junior said: "They probably did. There's a posse ridin' around. If any of 'em heard that shot, they'll be over here. They'll track our horses, sure as hell."

"Not where I'm goin'. Even José couldn't track where I'm goin'," he said, pointing to himself. "We won't leave any more track than a rabbit."

"What'll we do about Devil Ed?" Junior asked.

José looked at him and spat. "Leave him here."

"How about his horse?"

"Leave it here, too."

José led the way, Junior following. Amy, coming behind, was anxious to see her pa. She told herself: *I'll nurse him and make him well.*

They had been gone only a few minutes when Sheriff Butler arrived. He recognized Devil Ed's horse from a distance and wondered where its owner was. As he drew closer, he saw Devil Ed, lying on the ground. The sheriff moved in and studied the signs of a struggle but couldn't figure them out. Whoever Devil Ed had been fighting had obviously won. Butler saw the bleeding foot immediately, but it took him a while to discover the huge egg on Ed's head from the rock. He thought: *Maybe he ran down Cleve and came out second best.*

He pondered what to do next. It wouldn't do to leave Devil Ed here in the shape he was in, and he wasn't pressed for time. He rolled a cigarette, lit it, then squatted down beside the unconscious man, checked his pulse, and found it steady enough. "He'll keep," Butler muttered. "I'll be damned if I'm gonna mess up my clothes trying to pack him out on his horse."

That decision was reinforced by the fact that the sheriff couldn't stand the billy-goat smell of him. *I'll send someone back for him,* he decided.

After finishing his cigarette, he remounted and headed directly toward the Bandelier ranch rather than following the half circle he made coming in.

Sam Buchanan was afraid to slip close enough to spy on the sheriff but kept a watch on his horse to see if he returned. When he did, Sam wondered where he'd been, and, as he departed again, that posed an even more puzzling question. Why was he leaving when he should have stayed on the kids' tracks? One troubling possibility was that some others of his posse had caught them and were bringing them in by the direct route.

After he was absolutely sure that the sheriff was gone, he decided to get his horse and try to find the kids before dark.

Chapter Eight

Amy felt a chill as they led the horses down the dark passage into Chief Don Alonzo's cave. The low ceiling she'd expected was as high as a cathedral, not quite distinct through a hazy, yellow light. Somewhere, high above, fissures penetrated the sheer cliff and admitted light. She wondered if someone could get in that way and shoot down at them, or if snakes might crawl in and fall on them as they sometimes did down abandoned mine shafts. A cool, dank draft swept past them from inside. The entire place was disquieting, not threatening but awesome.

"Where's Pa?" she asked.

"Up ahead," José pointed. "This place is *muy grande*. Our whole tribe stayed here once."

Their horses caught the familiar odor of the other two, nickered, and were answered almost at once.

"The horses are up by the water," José told her. It was now possible to make out things a little better so that his horse and Star were visible, tethered beneath a low ledge, jutting into the cave. A grotto met the ledge, lit by a flickering candle. "Your father is up there," José said, pointing.

"I'll unsaddle later," Junior said. "We want to see Pa."

He left his horse on dropped reins. Amy followed suit, scrambling up behind her brother. Amy could only see a buffalo robe spread out at first, then realized her father was under it, and lying on another. Feeling totally helpless, just as she'd felt on the long vigils when they'd watched her mother slowly die, powerless to help her, Amy prayed: *Please, God, don't let Pa die, too.*

Cleve drew in a deep breath and exhaled raggedly. Candlelight emphasized the deeply etched lines of pain on his face.

José reassured them. "He ain't gonna die. Just needs lots of sleep and something to eat when he wakes up."

Amy put her hand on her father's forehead as her mother used to do with her, to see if she had a fever. How good and reassuring it had always felt. She tried to will her father to feel the same way, to pour her strength into him. "He's got a high fever," she said.

Junior pushed her aside and said: "Let me feel," as though a girl couldn't know. She forgave him, knowing that he was scared and didn't want their father to have a high fever, trying to make it go away by denying it. Finally he said: "You'd have a fever, too, if you got shot." And to José: "Where is he hit?"

"It got him through the side just above his right hip. At least he ain't gut-shot, but he lost a lot of blood."

Junior looked relieved. Amy knew her brother had tried to look tough and unconcerned. She thought: *He's as scared as me. He loves Pa something fierce, too.* She pitied men who weren't supposed to act scared and never were allowed to cry. She placed her hand on Cleve's forehead again and left it there. In a while his face became calmer. He sighed again.

"Good medicine," José said, grinning.

Cleve's lips moved, but Amy couldn't catch the words. She placed her ear right above his lips, and this time caught what he said. "Leave the light on, Ma."

"I will," she said. "And I'll stay right here." She leaned down and gently kissed the ravaged face. His lips curved briefly into a smile. After a while he pulled one arm from under the robe and fidgeted around, as though feeling for something. Amy took his hand into both of hers and squeezed, then held on, feeling him relax.

She wondered where José had found such soft, prime buffalo

robes. Later she would learn that the Jicarilla kept this secret place well supplied, a refuge for their tribesmen, some of whom were — even yet — harassed into becoming what whites termed renegades.

José said: "I've got to go back out for a little while."

"What for?" Junior asked. "Someone might see you. The country's crawling with Wingfield's killers."

"They won't see José," he assured him.

Junior didn't look so sure but merely shrugged. "Want me to cover you with a Winchester?" he asked.

José didn't reply at once, considering, then said: "O K." He turned to Amy and said: "We'll be right back."

Amy wanted to ask how soon that meant but didn't want to cause them any unnecessary worry. She sensed that they'd just as soon not have a female around and were very conscious of the need to protect her.

When she was alone with Cleve, and just Maggie and the horses for company, she wondered aloud to Maggie: "What should we do if they don't come back?" Maggie looked at her but didn't move. She'd come in, sniffed Cleve, sensed he was sick, and lay down beside him, head on her paws, on guard. She looked like she was praying. Who could say she wasn't?

Amy was very conscious that she didn't know where anything was that she might need, just the supplies that she and Junior had brought. She'd need more candles if there were any, especially when her father's bandage needed changing.

Suppose he has to go? she thought. She remembered that when her ma had finally been unable to get out of bed, Doc Ewing had brought them a pan. She was sure there wasn't one of those here. *Maybe Pa'll go in his pants like a baby. Well, if he does, we'll just have to clean him up and make the best of it.*

Her ignorance and inadequacy oppressed her. She tried to remember what *The Doctor Book* said about this and couldn't remember a thing except onion poultices for chest colds.

In a while she smelled smoke and wondered what was burning. There was nothing in the cavern that would burn except a big pile of firewood, stacked along the wall. Shortly she heard the men returning. Maggie's ears pricked up, told her who it was, then lowered. She never moved from her guard post. "What's burning?" she asked Junior when he joined her.

"José set the grass on fire down the hill."

"What for?"

"So we can build a fire in here and nobody outside will get suspicious if they smell smoke. They'll think lightning started a fire. Pretty smart."

Amy could see the sense of that. After a grass fire the vicinity smelled of smoke for days.

A little later Junior and José fixed a meal. She couldn't eat. The thought repelled her, and she wondered how they got down their food, then topped it off with coffee. Both rolled cigarettes to savor with their coffee, and for the moment looked like they didn't have a care in the world. Like most boys in that country Junior had smoked since he was twelve, and she thought little of it, being glad, however, that he didn't chew.

While the men ate, she held Cleve's hand, Maggie in place beside them. He still had a fever but was breathing easily.

From deep in the grotto José produced additional buffalo robes for the rest of them and laid them out. He touched her gently on the shoulder and said: "Better get some sleep, *chiquita*."

"I'm all right," she said. "When I get sleepy, I'll turn in."

He shrugged and disappeared to the rear of the grotto, returning with a wood box full of fat candles. Then he rolled into his robe.

"I'm turning in, too," Junior said. "I'll be right here if you need me."

Her senses sharpened as the deep stillness descended. Even the horses were quiet, patiently enduring hunger, only occasionally stamping and shaking themselves. She heard water dripping that she hadn't noticed before. The flickering fire reflected on the walls and even reached the cave's dome. An owl hooted suddenly, causing her to jump a little. She could see it circling up near the top of the cave and wondered how it got in.

Later she dozed off and started awake, not knowing where she was, or even who she was. Ghostly light played across the ceiling, then disappeared, increasing her terror and loneliness. The fire had burned down, so she knew what she'd seen hadn't been a reflection. There were a few glowing embers left, and she put some wood on it, then lit another candle. Her heart was beating painfully against her ribs as she waited to see if the lights returned. She thought of waking Junior, but before she did the distant rumble of thunder came to her. That ghostly light had been lightning, reflecting into the cave. Her heart was still pounding, but gradually subsided. She grinned weakly, then almost jumped out of her skin at a sudden shout — "Rebels! Rebels! Rebels! Grab your guns, boys!" — before she realized that the cries were made by her father. She felt his forehead again. He was still feverish. The shouts aroused both Junior and José.

"What's the matter?" Junior asked, raising up on one elbow.

"Delirious, I guess."

José had heard the "get your guns" part and appeared with a six-shooter in his hand. He heard Amy's remark and lowered it.

"Pa's out of his head," Junior said to José. "I'll stay here with Amy."

José rolled a cigarette and smoked it, contemplating Cleve fixedly, as though trying to divine his condition. Finally he flipped the butt into the fire and said: "He's all right."

Cleve's cries had disturbed Maggie, who got up and shivered, looking at Amy for reassurance that wasn't forthcoming. She sniffed Cleve and, apparently satisfied, curled up again, on guard, never taking her eyes off of him.

Cleve raised up on one elbow and stared wildly around, eyes open for the first time. The heavy clap of thunder broke in on them. He cocked his head. "That's the gunboats down on the Tennessee." That seemed to satisfy him, and he settled back down and went to sleep.

In a few minutes Cleve again sat upright, startling them all with his quickness. "Wingfield!" he yelled this time. "He's out there with the Whitecaps! Grab your Winchesters!" Large drops of sweat popped out on his forehead.

Junior touched his shoulder and said: "It's O K, Pa. They're gone."

Cleve looked at him, puzzled, trying to figure out who he was. "Junior?" he said. "Where's Amy?"

"I'm right here, Pa."

He recognized her. His face relaxed, and he said softly — "Thank God, the kids are all right" — then went back to sleep.

They all remained close for several minutes, not talking, watching Cleve. He stirred again, turning his head back and forth, staring wildly. "Where am I?" he asked in a low, confused voice.

"It's all right, Pa. I'm right here," Amy said.

For several more seconds Cleve stared around. Gradually his eyes lost their feverish glow, his gaze settling on Amy. He worked his mouth a while and then said: "Amy? Where did you come from?"

She said: "Just stay there, Pa. You're safe, and we're all here. You got shot."

"Yeah, I know," he said. "I ran smack into Devil Ed at the

top of the hill." He put his hand down to his bandage, throwing off the robe to do so. "Outran him finally. I'm about tuckered out." Then he closed his eyes and inhaled once deeply, exhaled gustily, and went into a healthy sleep.

Amy tenderly covered him again with the buffalo robe, then felt his damp forehead. "Fever's broke," she said, a smile trembling across her face. "Let's hope it doesn't come back." For the first time she was satisfied he'd really live. While her hand was on his head, she discovered a big bump. "He's got a big goose egg here."

"He must have passed out and fell off Star where I found him." José guessed. "Hit his head on the rocks, prob'ly."

Junior, who'd caught his share of lumps from falls, said: "I hope he didn't crack his skull like I did when Dynamite pitched me off. I didn't know which end was up for a couple of weeks."

A light went on in Amy's mind. That could explain why Junior was acting so crazy lately. Their pa had been kidding at the time when he said — "Junior maybe cracked his marbles." — but it might be true. Now she had something else to add to her worries. After all, only a few hours before Junior had been itching to shoot the sheriff. It was all too hard. Suddenly she was tired, barely able to hold her eyes open. "I've got to lie down," she said.

"Go ahead," Junior said. "I'll stay up with Pa."

Chapter Nine

Amy woke up to the mouth-watering smell of coffee and frying bacon, surprised she was hungry after the way she'd felt the night before. She rose and joined Junior and José at the fire. To Junior she whispered, "Where do you suppose I can pee?"

"Back there anywhere," he pointed with his thumb. "Injuns don't use back houses."

José, getting the drift, laughed. "We got a couple of poles you can sit across. You'll find 'em. The chief got too old to squat without falling over." He laughed some more.

After breakfast José said: "We gotta get these horses on grass pretty soon."

"They can last another day," Junior replied. "Maybe Pa'll be in shape to move by then."

Cleve had been awake, trying to decide if he could hold down food. "I'm fit to move now, if I have to. I gotta move pretty soon or fill my pants."

They all laughed.

Junior said: "I'll give you a hand."

"Help me sit up first," Cleve cautioned. "I think I can walk. Give me one of those long sticks of firewood for a cane."

He hobbled back into the cave, and Junior followed, careful to see he didn't stumble or fall. When Cleve came back, the strain of it showed on his face. He settled back on his robe, breathing hard. "Maybe I ain't as pert as I thought," he allowed. "I'm a little dizzy."

Junior said: "I don't think you should try to move out of here very soon unless you have to. Wingfield and the sheriff will still have their posse sneakin' around."

Cleve tried to think clearly and had trouble focusing his mind. He felt more like going back to sleep for a long while, but he knew he couldn't give in. They needed to convince that posse that he'd escaped. He got an idea, risky but worth a try. "José, what do you think about riding Star out of here and making a plain trail . . . there's bound to be some in that posse that can recognize his tracks, especially Devil Ed. If they spot you, so much the better. Star can outrun them."

"I don't think Devil Ed will be doin' a whole lot of trackin' for a while," Junior interrupted.

"Why not?" Cleve asked.

"Amy brained him with a big rock." He told the story of their fight.

Cleve laughed, then wished he hadn't. "Ouch." After a while he said: "It serves the son of a bitch right for shooting me. What are the chances you killed him?"

Junior said: "Not as good as I wish they were. I guess he was alive when we left him, layin' out there. I should have put a big pill between his eyes."

José asked Cleve: "Where should I take Star?"

"Up to the Zamoras'. Maybe the Zamora brothers will come down here. Wingfield wants a fight. It's time to give him one."

If only the Zamora brothers came, it would be almost enough with eleven of them, ranging from eighteen to forty-five years old. Dolores was the only girl in the family.

"I can get a lot more than them," José said. "*Padre* Maldonado can raise a hundred against that *Tejano cabrón,* Wingfield. He shot the *padre's* dog and ran off his sheep."

"Let me go," Junior interrupted. "I'm thirty pounds lighter than José, and Star hasn't had anything to eat."

Cleve was about to protest that it was too risky, then held his tongue. The boy was as apt to do the job as José, and the way he'd fought Devil Ed showed it. Cleve, after hearing of her part in the fight, would have trusted Amy to make the run if he'd had to. Junior was expecting to be told no, and his face lit up with elation when Cleve said: "O K, Junior, you go."

José didn't protest, perfectly aware of Junior's feelings, those of a young warrior on his first war party. Besides, José was as confident as Cleve that the kid could get the job done and hold his own against almost anyone, if he got an even break. It was best for him to stay there, anyhow, since he knew where everything was and where they could hide and fort up deep in the cave, if they had to.

Sam Buchanan had finished a very light breakfast of berries and water, saddled up, and was trying to make up his mind what to do. He decided to ride to the highest point around and glass the country. He saw a rider on a big black, refocused his glasses, and squinted. *Star?* He was sure of it and elated that Cleve had gotten away and hidden out successfully overnight. Sam mounted and rode to cut him off. When he reached level open ground, he saw Star running, a half dozen riders trying to overtake him, dropping farther behind at every jump.

Even in this tense situation he enjoyed watching the long, piston-like stride of the big black. Sam held his breath as he saw the horse falling, wondering if Cleve could pick him back up with the reins. At this distance the sound of rifle fire took a couple of seconds to reach him. None of the pursuers had a gun out so far as he could tell, yet a shot had cut the horse down. The pursuers appeared as puzzled as Sam and apparently decided to pull up and figure out what was going on. Sam looked back where Star had fallen and saw two new riders break from the brush, carrying rifles. Cleve had ridden straight into an ambush.

When Star fell, Junior hit the ground hard and blacked out

but regained his senses before anyone reached him. Blood gushed from Star's nose, and Junior realized he'd been shot through the lungs. The horse fought to regain his feet, biting and tearing the ground with his teeth in a desperate effort to rise, as though he expected to survive, if only he could get up. Suddenly he stiffened and whimpered like a baby, a sound that wrenched Junior's heart. Then the bright, fighting spirit ebbed away, and his eyes dulled and glazed in death. Tears blinded Junior. He remembered Star as the prettiest and friskiest little colt he'd ever seen. Now he was gone.

"Bastards!" he shouted. "Bastards!" He brushed away tears with his sleeve so he could see to shoot. He started to get up and go for the rifle in his saddle scabbard and discovered his right leg wouldn't support him. As Wingfield and another rider approached, he reached for his six-shooter and found his scabbard empty.

Wingfield laughed. "Looking for your revolver, kid? It's over there." He pointed at the ground.

"Did you shoot my horse?" Junior demanded, his voice harsh.

"Happens I didn't," Wingfield said. "He did." He pointed at Harmony Dabney, who'd ridden up beside him, still holding his rifle in his hand.

Junior glared at Dabney. "Mister, I'll kill you someday, if it's the last thing I do."

Wingfield eyed him coldly, deliberately drawing his six-shooter and taking his time about aiming it. He said: "You'd better make it quick, kid, because the last thing you do ain't gonna happen very long from now."

"Ease off, Wingfield," a new voice said, "or I'll let a little daylight through your skull."

Sheriff Butler's rifle was pointed straight at Wingfield. The Texan's other gunmen arrived on the scene, and one of them said: "What the hell's goin' on?"

"Stay the hell out of this!" Butler ordered, while his under-sheriff, Dave Ralls swung his rifle back and forth, covering the new arrivals.

"Where the hell did you pop up from?" Wingfield asked, disgustedly sheathing his Colt. "I was only tryin' to scare the shit out of the kid."

Junior didn't think so. Neither did Butler, but he slowly lowered his Winchester and said: "If you say so, Frank."

He and Dave Ralls had been shadowing Wingfield at a distance ever since he'd left camp. Butler didn't intend to have another crazy like Devil Ed running around, trying to murder the Bandeliers, and, besides, the more he saw of the syndicate crowd, the better he liked Cleve's outfit.

"You aimin' to stay in office?" Wingfield asked.

Butler ignored him and dismounted to help Junior, who pointed his finger at Dabney. "He killed the best damn' horse in New Mexico You ain't got long to run, mister."

Dabney laughed.

Under his breath Junior said, "The dirty son of a bitch. His day is comin'."

"You're pretty feisty for the shape you're in, kid," Butler said. He helped Junior mount behind Dave Ralls and added: "I don't know if Doc Ewing has showed up yet, but, if he has, he'll set that busted pin for you." The sheriff thought: *If I'd had a kid, that's the way I'd want him. He didn't even peep when I boosted him up, and it must have hurt like hell.* He asked Junior: "Was you down at your ranch night before last?"

Junior thought fast. He knew they'd find out different if he claimed they were in town, so he said: "The ranch hosses strayed off, or somebody run 'em off." He looked at Wingfield. "We was all lookin' for 'em and got caught out overnight." He laughed and added, to sound convincing: "Got soaked, too."

"Who was we?" Butler asked.

"Pa and me and my sister. The rest of the boys are out, makin' a gather."

Butler said: "I don't suppose you'd care to tell us where your pa is."

"Wouldn't if I knew, since you guys seem so all fired hot to find him. Anyhow, the last I saw of him, we split up, and he pulled out to join the boys, drivin' the hosses we rounded up."

"How come you're ridin' his horse?" Butler asked.

"He told me to take him home, and he rode Babe . . . she's been runnin' wild since she foaled . . . needed a few wet blankets to settle her down."

Butler hadn't asked Devil Ed what horse Cleve was riding when he shot him, or he could trip the kid up on that. In the shape Devil Ed was in, it would be a while before he made much sense. He didn't even know his own name. "If that's so, how come you took so long to get back to this neck of the woods? And where's your sister?"

"I took my sis up to Zamora Plaza and come back down." Junior knew they couldn't check up on that lie. The sheriff wouldn't be apt to go up there without taking along a small army. Even if he did, they wouldn't tell him a damned thing. "What did these sons of bitches shoot at me for?"

Wingfield said: "We thought you were your pa. He killed a couple of men down at your place, and you damn' well know it. You're lyin' like a rug."

Butler cut Wingfield off. "Let me ask the questions. Is what he claims so, kid?"

Junior said: "I sure as hell wouldn't be apt to tell you if it was, now, would I? What're you plannin' to do with me?"

"Get the doc to fix your leg, like I said."

"And after that?"

"That's up to you. You won't be gittin' around so right smart for a while. You can stay with me and the missus, if you want."

"I'll make out," Junior said.

Butler thought: *Maybe the kid is telling the truth and really doesn't know his pa got shot.*

"You aim to give me back my guns?" Junior asked.

"I reckon you might need 'em."

Wingfield, riding within hearing, said: "Ain't you gonna arrest the kid?"

"What for?" Butler asked.

"As a witness."

"To what?"

"Murder. He was probably down there when his old man beefed them two marshals."

Junior said: "My pa never killed any marshals."

Wingfield looked exasperated. He snapped: "You might get a chance to tell that to a judge and jury, kid."

Junior gave him a killing look. "If somebody doesn't shoot me in the back first, you mean?"

Wingfield flushed, then spurred ahead. Looking back, he said to Butler: "Remember what I said about the next election."

"I'm not runnin'," Butler called after him.

After Wingfield was out of hearing, Dave Ralls said: "You'll have to keep your eyes open for him from now on."

"I always did," Butler said.

The sheriff was pleased. Wingfield and the syndicate would play hell, pinning anything on the Bandeliers, if they all stuck to the kid's story. No one had seen Cleve or the kids during the shooting. A few claimed they recognized his voice. Just because Devil Ed shot him up on the hill above his ranch didn't prove he'd been down at the ranch before that. He could have been coming back, trying to find his men who'd obviously come back in for supplies. The kid's story could hold up, and Devil Ed would be the one in trouble. With such flimsy evidence to the contrary, a good lawyer could get Cleve off on the double killing. Saddle tramps might have taken over his ranch while he was gone and shot a couple of threatening men who came to the door at night — a far-fetched story but one a *friendly* jury could buy.

Junior was convinced he needed to get back to the cave and let them know what was going on as soon as he could beg, borrow, or steal a horse and slip away. He wished he could tell whether or not the sheriff knew his pa had been shot. It made a big difference. Maybe Devil Ed had been out on his own hook when he did the shooting. In that case the sheriff might not know his pa was shot, and, if he didn't know it and believed Junior's cooked-up story, maybe he'd gather his posse and go look for his pa out on roundup. That obviously was where Jesús and the boys were heading after the sheriff talked to them at the ranch.

Part Two

The Syndicate

Chapter Ten

The seed of the trouble with the Amarillo Grant had been planted a world away some years before, when Lord Montague Ransom first saw Mariposa Voerbeck in London. They were riding in Rotten Row where people of their class rode to be seen, to show off their horses and equipages, and less often for the simple pleasure of riding. Rotten Row was a great deal more of a pleasure for the men when Mariposa rode there. Ransom's reaction to laying eyes on her the first time was: "My God, that's the most beautiful woman I've ever seen!" He was talking half to himself but also to Baron Percy Waterford with whom he was riding and added: "Do you know who she is?"

"Not really. I wish I did. In fact, I will."

That his companion didn't know her surprised Ransom, since Percy had made a life work of knowing all the beautiful women in the world, but it didn't surprise him that under the circumstances Percy was certain he would know her.

Percy set directly about accomplishing that, saying: "Let's ride ahead of her and wait till she passes again."

Mariposa didn't notice their maneuver, but Lady Fetherstonhaugh, her companion and an old hand at this game as a former "official beauty," certainly did. She, of course, knew both Montague and Percy and expected them to do exactly what Percy had proposed. When they cantered past, she said to Mariposa: "Watch those two men who just passed. They'll park somewhere up the line and doff their hats when we go by them."

"How do you know?" Mariposa asked.

"It's part of the game."

"Do you know them?"

"Yes, unfortunately."

Mariposa was too polite to ask what that implied. It meant that Lady Fetherstonhaugh had desired an affair with Percy for some time — knew better than to aim for marriage, of course, because he was simply too busy with other women, and in the case of Lord Ransom their rôles were somewhat reversed. He had wanted an affair with her, but she had no time for him, although he was undoubtedly a very handsome fellow. If she had been a heiress, it might have been different, but neither she nor Ransom had enough money to live beyond what their set considered minimum luxury, so neither could afford to support the other.

Lady Fetherstonhaugh, or Daisy as her friends including Mariposa called her, regretted this tragedy which was rather common to her set. The regret that she was not an heiress set Daisy's gold-digging mind onto the happier case of Mariposa who was an heiress and one of the world's most fortunate. Her doting daddy, Grut Voerbeck, had as much money as the Rothschilds. This prompted Daisy to tell Mariposa: "You'll undoubtedly meet those two soon. At least Baron Waterford."

Mariposa had only got a look at their backs and wasn't sure she wanted to meet them. She asked: "How do you know?"

Daisy laughed. "Just a feeling I have. Be sure to ignore them when we pass."

Mariposa, although only twenty-two, understood what Daisy implied. The baron at least would be what the English and French called a *roué*. The English used the term pejoratively; the French as well as her Dutch countrymen thought of them — or at least *knowing* women did — as interesting. Mariposa had met a good many of them because of her beauty, a very non-Dutch, classical face with a straight, patrician nose, full lips made for laughing, which she did often, sky-blue eyes with an almost Oriental cast, and long, pale blonde hair, all crafted upon a perfect neck that arose above a tall, slender, hour-glass figure. Her whole appearance, beyond that of striking beauty, was of health and strength, and she radiated good nature, which was not misleading, although beauties were seldom noted for being friendly and approachable. This combination, of course, was too much for men of the *roué* class and a lot of others as well, some of them her father's old married cronies, although the Voerbeck fortune would have brought around droves of the same kind if she'd looked like a cow-faced peasant. She naturally had had a lot of experience, tactfully coping with these sorts. Her father, who recognized her effect on men, would have coped for her with anyone she couldn't handle, including having them drowned in the Zuider Zee, if need be. Nonetheless, she hadn't been raised prudishly, like English and American upper-class ladies. This was not due to spending her youth in Holland, since her mother had died when she was fourteen, and she'd been her widowed father's companion as he tended his business affairs all over the world. She was now perfecting her English in a London Academy. She understood that he intended her to take the reins of his financial empire when he died and perhaps sooner, and she savored the idea. A home and children didn't appeal to her; they were for her domestically inclined friends.

As Daisy and Mariposa rode past the two men, Mariposa ignored Daisy's advice and glanced at them. Ransom's appearance, especially his obvious good looks, prompted her to smile at him. She was more than normally immune to male beauty, but she admitted to herself that he was indeed handsome in a way that she admired — not delicate but attractively molded, like the statues of Roman warriors.

Just as Ransom had, she thought: *This is the most attractive member of the opposite sex I ever laid eyes on.* There was a significant difference. He knew that many women considered him irresistibly attractive. She was hardly aware she was good-looking, much less a beauty. She never thought of it and didn't regard looks as important, compared to brains. Brains were power because they taught one to make the money that inevitably brought power.

When she smiled at Ransom, Percy exclaimed: "You lucky devil! She smiled at you."

"Of course."

"Are you trying to be droll?"

"No, why do you ask?"

Ransom genuinely expected women to notice him, even if his slim purse held it to no more than that. The painful truth was that he couldn't afford to keep both polo ponies and a mistress, much less a wife. In fact, he couldn't afford any one of the three. The only reason he had the only one of those three that was really important to him — the ponies — was that Percy was fascinated by polo. As soon as he'd heard of it, he made himself one of the founders of the Hurlingham Polo Association. He was delighted to underwrite Ransom as the man who'd brought polo from India. The name Montague Ransom was famous as the captain and star player on the 9th Lancers team that played in the first polo match in the mother country.

Lord Ransom's sole source of income was Baron Waterford's generosity. Monty and Percy were like Damon and Pythias. Where one appeared on the social scene, if at all possible the other was along, Percy picking up the tabs. Monty had sold his commission in the army and quickly run through the money. The original purchase price had been his sole inheritance from his father, who'd been a lieutenant general with no fortune except what accrued from the usual plunder that thrifty types acquired in being stationed around the empire. Monty at least nominally supervised both Percy's horse-breeding and cattle-raising affairs on his estate in Suffolk.

Fortunately, the baron was not the jealous type. On the contrary, he was very generous in matters of love and took it upon himself to matchmake between his best friend and the unknown beauty they'd ogled on the bridle path. He had no trouble discovering her identity from Daisy. He dropped by Daisy's town house expressly for that purpose, appearing to be making one of his frequent informal visits. They were old and close friends. When he inquired about her riding companion, Daisy got right to the heart of the matter. "You nasty old man. She's a child. Besides you're after her money."

"I don't even know who she is. And I don't need any more money."

Daisy sighed. "I wish I could say that."

"How much do you need?" He'd made loans to her before, which they both knew were gifts.

She smiled. "Percy, you are a dear. But I'm all right just now, so you can't buy the girl's name from me."

"How about beg?"

"Maybe." She laughed. She really had no intention of keeping the name from him. "You'll swoon when you hear."

"Try me."

"She's old Grut Voerbeck's daughter and sole heir."

"My God! Crœsus. Wait'll Monty hears."

"Are you matchmaking for Adonis again?"

"Still. What luck! He needs the money."

"You got them married rather quickly. In any case, I hate you both. Women have to be subtle about trolling in the sea of matrimony."

"I'll find you an American millionaire, and you'll feel better and still be able to maintain appearances."

"Please. And soon. I can always hire an interpreter to tell me what he's saying."

They both laughed. "Who do you want, Daisy? An Astor? A Vanderbilt?"

"They're taken."

"Not all of them, but there are a lot more fish. I'll come up with somebody." He reached for his wallet.

She held up her hand. "I said I'm all right."

He appraised her seriously. "It's not a loan. I'd like you to have a party here for me."

"To which I invite the Voerbeck girl, right? And you and Monty will be here like a couple of your prize stud horses, I suppose?"

"There's no law against that, thank God."

"No. And I have no objections, so long as you don't forget to bring that American millionaire."

"A guarantee. Just the man comes to mind. He's traveling to get over the loss of his wife. He owns a railroad, or a steamship company, or something. And you be sure the Voerbeck girl is here. What's her name, by the way?"

"Mariposa."

"How precious. How about having her old man, too?

"Voerbeck *pére?* Why not? I've only met him once, but I like him. I'll invite him."

Lord Ransom was, as yet, unaware that he would find the principal rival for Mariposa's affections to be her father. His lordship had several distinct advantages over the small, bespectacled Dutch capitalist, however: his comparative youth — a respectable thirty-six but far from old — good looks, and the fact that he was a glamorous ex-military man from Her Majesty's Indian Army. In addition, he rode like a centaur, and, as was often the case with those with uncomplicated minds, he was brave as a lion. Notwithstanding all that, it was not Ransom's skill as a romancer, but Sir Walter Scott's, that would bid well to accomplish his heart's desire — to marry money and become comfortable. Mariposa was seduced before she ever saw Ransom by Sir Walter Scott's cavaliers. As soon as she became acquainted with Ransom — and their friendship, indeed, picked up immediately following Daisy's party — she saw his lordship in the mold of Brian De Bois Gilbert and Reginald Front De Boeuff, if not Rob Roy. Wistfully she wished he were more like the last, a crazy-brave leader of a wild clan, fighting against corrupt power. But, beyond that, there was polo. In due course the baron, not Monty, discovered that she'd become addicted to its thrill in Manipur, where Grut had taken her while he looked after his tea enterprises. There, she had enchanted the local polo crowd with her willingness to ride astraddle in jodhpurs.

Percy gave her the chance to do her stuff at Waterford Manor and was scared half out of his wits as she drove one of his ponies with suicidal aggressiveness, appearing to be a part of the animal's body. All of his ponies adored her at first acquaintance. He toyed with the notion of slipping her into the Hurlingham crowd, disguised as a young man, but even he wasn't willing to risk discovery and the disastrous consequence — the entire chauvinistic membership might sicken and die if they discovered that a woman had played on their sacred turf. So she was restricted to playing at Waterford Manor, long blonde hair streaming behind her like a flying Valkyrie. Monty, looking to the future that required her to survive, objected mildly and was politely invited by the lady to go to a warm climate. Percy privately put it a little more bluntly to him. "She isn't apt to kill herself, but, if you peeve that one, she may as well. You'll never see her again. Do you want to work for a living all your life?"

Monty did not. As a penniless aristocrat he'd been driven

to desperation by age thirty-six over the obviously unfair, pinching contradiction of loving luxury but being bone lazy. It was epidemic in his class. Since he loved luxury more than ease, he drove himself to hard work.

At Daisy Fetherstonhaugh's party Grut Voerbeck had read all of that in Lord Ransom as though his lordship carried a sign proclaiming his history in large capital letters. The old Dutchman recognized a potential threat but dismissed it, based on his confidence in Mariposa's good sense. Besides, he was busy with Lady Fetherstonhaugh whose mature beauty impressed him. He was a true Dutchman, which was to say at heart a wild man with an eye for women. If he hadn't kept both characteristics well in control, he wouldn't have been in a position to buy out the relatively affluent crowd in Daisy's house and still have several million pounds to spare.

The American millionaire didn't attract Lady Fetherstonhaugh so much as Grut Voerbeck, and it wasn't merely a matter of money. She managed to get him beside her on a couch. "You speak English well?" she said.

He recognized a question in that, and his eyes revealed restrained humor lurking behind them. He said: "I was with your 'Chinese' Gordon and the ever-victorious army at Shanghai, watching him wave his wand of victory and dodging bullets."

He didn't mention that his presence there had more to do with business than fighting and had put him in a commanding position in the opium trade, which had then financed the future ventures that had made him filthy rich.

"Oh, my!" she exclaimed. "That wonderful, eccentric man, Charles Gordon. I wish he were here. He's a holy fool, you know. I wonder where he is tonight."

"Probably a couple of thousand miles up the Nile, I'd guess." He had ample reason to agree that Gordon qualified as a holy fool, having watched him stroll through hails of bullets, waving his cane.

She wondered how he knew where Gordon might be, but realized it probably wouldn't be wise to ask. Voerbeck had various prospectors, many of them very strange people, such as Gordon, roaming the world on their own business with an eye out for their little, twinkly friend, Grut, who paid generously for information. At that moment he had one of them looking over the territories that the United States had plundered from Mexico, as a matter of fact in a place quaintly called New Mexico.

When Grut learned that Mariposa had accepted Lord Ransom's marriage proposal, he was shrewdly practical about it. Instead of putting his foot down, he merely arranged for a very long engagement. "Does this change your plan to run my affairs when I'm too old to carry on, and after I'm gone?" he asked.

She looked startled. "Of course not, Papa."

"Then you want to be sure Lord Ransom is prepared to help you. What can he do?"

"Well, he manages Baron Waterford's horse and cattle enterprise."

"Just exactly what does that mean?"

"He's breeding some of the finest horses in England. And he's improving the baron's beef cattle every year. He does know stock breeding."

She had no intention of withdrawing from her planned career as an entrepreneur since she wasn't driven by the heedless passion that herded some young women into marital chambers, as had been the case even with Queen Victoria's daughters. The world may not have noticed, as Mariposa had, that such admired women, though they might be intelligent and well schooled, were unworldly and doomed to suffer as a result. That, she vowed, was not for Mariposa Voerbeck. She didn't think that women came into the world to suffer. She intended to savor all that life offered to those strong and smart enough to grasp it.

This, then, was the background that led to Grut Voerbeck's sending Lord Montague Ransom to New Mexico. His lordship bore an introductory letter to Tomás Pringle, whom Voerbeck had heard was at the head of something called the Santa Fé Ring. He understood that group would be indispensable to acquiring a ranch. That had been in 1879. Three years would pass before Cleve Bandelier ran afoul of Voerbeck's schemes, and by then many others were involved.

Chapter Eleven

Grut Voerbeck's business sense would have warned him that something was wrong with the New Mexico syndicate's operations, even if its balance sheets didn't. He'd grilled Ransom at length about the matter on Ransom's last visit to Leyden in Holland, getting nothing but evasions. If he hadn't come to appreciate Ransom for his insouciance, he'd have fired him long before. He was quite happy with him so long as the wedding bells remained distant. Ransom wasn't entirely a court fool. Voerbeck appreciated his mad courage; in fact, in this he reminded him of "Chinese" Gordon. However, he would have wanted "Chinese" Gordon as a son-in-law perhaps even less than he wanted Ransom. Gordon would have been uncontrollable where his conscience prompted him to contrary notions, whereas Ransom had no such problem — not that he utterly lacked conscience, only that in his charming, typically English mercenary mind it always lost out in a contest with money.

Ransom's excuses boiled down to one recurring theme: the operation is just getting started. "But the operation has been just getting started for three years," Voerbeck had pointed out to him, "and so far it has been all expense and no income." Ransom had looked embarrassed when Voerbeck had said that.

"We must have patience," he had counseled, sounding impatient himself, so he had quickly added: "Besides, we're just about to remove the fly from the ointment."

Voerbeck had raised his eyebrows, inviting an explanation.

Ransom had responded: "An outlaw named Cleve Bandelier

has been agitating the settlers to steal our cattle and oppose us by illegal means when we try to reclaim what's legally yours."

"Why haven't I heard of this Bandelier before now?"

It wasn't a question that Ransom had anticipated, or he wouldn't have mentioned Bandelier. Ransom's mind had whirled rapidly, fumbling for an answer.

Grut then had decided to take him off the hook and asked: "Just how is this Bandelier illegally opposing us?"

"With Winchesters."

"Ah," Voerbeck had said. He knew what Winchesters were. They were not unfamiliar in the Orient as well. They shot rapidly, but he preferred double-barrel express rifles that shot a mile. Even if they only dispensed two pills rapidly, those two pills would kill an elephant. This preference sometimes paralleled his favored business tactics as well.

"This Bandelier must have a large band," he had supposed.

"Maybe a hundred or more."

"So many? How can they hide?"

Ransom had looked surprised. "They live in homes on your land."

"Why haven't the officers removed them?"

It had occurred to Ransom that he should have told Voerbeck all about the situation before now. Worse yet, he realized that Voerbeck was thinking the same thing. Despite this, the old man had decided not to press Ransom further. Instead he had made up his mind to visit New Mexico himself. He was especially persuaded to do so by hard-earned knowledge from other enterprises that, when settlers were aroused sufficiently to start shooting for what they considered their rights, there was another side to the dispute. In any case, he intended to stay in New Mexico long enough to set his investment on its feet or dispose of it.

Ransom had argued by letter, often and vehemently, against

a New Mexico visit by the syndicate's czar. His arguments ran from inadequate facilities at the ranch, through the possibly fatal effects of altitude on a man Voerbeck's age, to the hazards of life in a lawless land. The mention of age to Voerbeck was like waving a red flag at a bull, and the other matters didn't faze a man who'd grabbed a fortune in the East Indies, to say nothing of getting an education with "Chinese" Gordon's army.

Mariposa was enchanted at the prospect of adventure in a dangerous land and extracted from her father a promise to procure several riding horses for her after they arrived in New Mexico. When she had overheard Ransom's remark about Winchesters, she had started taking shooting lessons on the sly, not only with rifles but with pistols of various makes. Secretly stowed inside her trunks were her final choices of weapons, based on a thorough testing of many: a .44 caliber Winchester 1873 carbine and a .44 caliber Smith and Wesson Schofield pistol, both of which she could shoot with remarkable skill.

Voerbeck arranged a private car on the Denver & Rio Grande from Colorado Springs to the town of Dorado, New Mexico, which was the closest station to his Amarillo headquarters ranch. He enjoyed the scenery and wasn't appreciably affected by the altitude. The most noticeable changes in him, that Mariposa observed and approved, were that his appetite became hearty, and he slept like a log at night. Accompanying them for a visit to the American Wild West were Daisy Fetherstonhaugh, of whom Voerbeck had become more than fond, and Baron Percy Waterford, a staple in the Voerbeck social circle due to his uniform good humor that Grut relished — moreover, he had so much money himself that Grut needn't suspect him of sycophancy in the guise of friendship.

On the last leg of their rail journey, Voerbeck reviewed a letter he'd requested from the syndicate's attorney, Frank Carson, regarding the personalities of the locally influential people the lawyer had suggested that he meet. He realized that these people were the movers and shakers of the Santa Fé Ring and all manipulators. He intended to manipulate them instead, confident that he held the same advantage a professional gambler held over the average yokel. What he didn't suspect was that these men weren't yokels, but men who dealt from the bottom of the deck and who hesitated at nothing, including murder. They, of course, were the inner circle of the ring. Technically, Carson himself was a member through close association, though he never was admitted to the plenary — planning or, more accurately, scheming — sessions that took place. The group ran the territory to suit itself and that meant lining the pockets of its members who resented any such big-money incursions as that of the syndicate which they weren't equipped to resist or control.

Carson wrote:

> Tomás Pringle is the recognized head of this group. He has held numerous official offices in the territory and is a practicing attorney as well. He was an officer in the Confederate Army and an opportunist who came out here after the war to make his fortune, realized he'd have to become a Republican to do it, so switched political parties. Now he's the head of the Republican party in the territory. He's after as much land as he can grab and heavily in debt to get his hands on it. Any local who plans to do well here has to keep on the good side of him.
>
> His former partner, Slinkard, moved East some years back and married into an influential family. He's in the Senate in Washington but keeps his finger on things here where he still has large investments, probably financed by his father-in-law. He is the ring's fixer in Washington and is close to the powers there.

Voerbeck smiled when he read this. He had known the biggest power in Washington when he was Collector of Customs in New York and had his hand out, and he knew he could get almost anything he wanted from Chester, as he always thought of the President. In fact, he had stopped in Washington on his way West to assure himself that was still the case.

Carson's letter continued:

> Perhaps the most interesting, and certainly the most dangerous man you'll meet is Bill Laxelt, currently the U. S. attorney, who once shot the chief justice of the territory over a fancied slight and got away with it. Nonetheless, he's a good man to know and stay on the right side of.
>
> The current chief justice of the court is former governor, Sam Norton, who's a political hack and has held offices all over, even in Utah where he was also governor until Brother Brigham had him fired. He, of course, can be fixed for a price. So can all of them, for that matter. The current governor, Ben Walters, is a man that the Republican party often sends to troubled areas to resolve problems. He is absolutely incorruptible. You probably should meet him, but I am certain he can't be used in any except the most proper manner.

Voerbeck thought: *If he takes orders from Chester, I can use him any way I want, if he wants to keep his job.*

Carson's letter concluded:

> He was also a general in the Civil War and tramped on General Grant's toes at Shiloh through no fault of his own and effectively ruined his Army career. Bill Bissell

is Pringle's partner and probably is the straightest one of the bunch. He'll play square unless it tramps on his partner's toes, and he won't take work if it does.

These men can control the U. S. marshal whose services we may need. The Army is another factor to consider, but the ring can't control them directly. The current Department Commander is General Gryden, actually a colonel, but here they go by their honorary ranks earned in the war. He was a music teacher before the war, which is fairly typical of the democracy that this country prides itself on. I am reasonably sure he can't be bought at any price. He'll have to be controlled through Washington, if we need him.

Mariposa was seated at the window beside her father, watching the country but nonetheless curious over his obvious absorption in the letter in his hand. She knew better than to interrupt him. He concentrated intensely and resented interruptions. She knew that, if he wanted her to know what the letter was about, he'd tell her, and, if he didn't, prying wasn't wise. Instead of telling her, he handed her the letter and waited while she read it. When she finished, she looked at him for a clue regarding what she might be expected to say, if anything.

"Our hosts," he said. "I'll have to keep my hand on my watch."

She laughed. "And how about Mister Carson who wrote the letter? What do we know about him?"

Voerbeck said: "That, if he's in a meeting with those rare birds, he'll probably be keeping his hand on his watch, too."

She laughed again. "It should be interesting, at least."

He nodded. "At least."

Chapter Twelve

Tomás Pringle had one advantage in getting the touchy Pancho Wingfield to respect his orders: both were veterans of the Confederate Army. Pancho tolerated him for that reason, although he couldn't forget that Pringle had been a captain whereas Wingfield had only been a first lieutenant. Before he put on shoulder straps, he'd oscillated between high private and first sergeant in inverse relationship with his whiskey supply. Despite having finally joined their ranks, he disliked officers as most enlisted men and non-coms did on general principles — but, in his case, even more so because they were the class that had busted him to private several times for getting pig drunk and disorderly. It wasn't in his nature to reflect that they also had advanced him again because of his fighting qualities. Pancho wasn't the reflective sort.

In order to become an officer he'd deserted and migrated west of the Mississippi into Kirby Smith's confederacy. They were more guerrillas than regulars, involved in smuggling cotton to Matamoras for shipment in British and French ships that evaded the blockade by departing from a Mexican port. On return trips Pancho's outfit brought rustled Mexican beef and sold it to Kirby Smith's contracting officers. The latter business was so profitable that Wingfield remained in it for a couple of years following the war, the only difference being that now no less conveniently blind Union contracting officers bought the cheap stolen cattle.

After several years of freebooting about the West, Wingfield had learned the cattle business from the ground up and become an experienced trail driver. His drinking habits and pugnacious nature rendered it natural for him to become a "gun swift" as a matter of survival. Finally, he'd found his natural niche as foreman of the Amarillo ranch, providing Ransom both the expertise and strong arm the enterprise needed to survive. He also had a great deal to do with the fact that the enterprise didn't thrive, though it might have. In this matter Tomás Pringle exerted an important influence.

Wingfield had been called to Santa Fé for a business meeting with the ring's *jefe*. Grudgingly he faced the necessity of keeping Pringle happy because Pringle was the key to getting a cattle ranch of his own some day. On the syndicate's ranch he played second fiddle to Lord Ransom, which particularly graveled him because Ransom knew less about the range cattle business than Gloria Peabody, the schoolmarm from New England. Pancho knew why Pringle arranged these meetings after dark, even agreed it was necessary, but resented it anyhow. The ring's *jefe* never allowed anyone to know what he was up to or even whom he was meeting, especially if it were shady characters such as Pancho Wingfield whose reputation, like that of the late Billy the Kid's, was well known from Fort Bowie, Arizona to Tascosa in the Texas Panhandle as *un muy malo hombre*.

Pringle kept his home office for confidential meetings. If his downtown office were placed under surveillance, no evidence of his real sources of income could have been surmised from the nature of his clientele who were either solid, respectable citizens or poor people, both Mexican and Anglo. He also did a lot of charity work. He'd once been dirt poor himself and as a result gave everyone the benefit of the doubt and pitied all those who were in the same boat. Besides, he always played to the electorate. Charity helped his reputation, and his highest ambition, after getting rich and staying that way, was to be a senator when New Mexico became a state. The office wouldn't be elective at first, but voters elected the legislature that selected senators. However, he didn't want statehood too soon. A territory allowed him to throw a wider loop in his pursuit of wealth. First things first was his motto.

Wingfield was indispensable to Pringle whose first objective on the road to real wealth was to get title to the syndicate's Amarillo Grant. He'd had his eye on it for years and gritted his teeth when Voerbeck picked it up for a song while he was financially strapped. Pringle always tried to turn bad fortune to his own purposes. He helped Voerbeck buy the grant, figuring better a foreign absentee owner than some rich American who might be harder to fool and even live on the property to keep an eye on things. At that time he formulated a plan to assure that Voerbeck never realized a profit from his investment.

Now Pringle had freed enough collateral to swing a purchase, and he intended to intensify his campaign to convince Voerbeck he'd made a poor investment. However, the reason he'd called Wingfield down for this meeting was only indirectly related to this intention. Pancho was useful in other ways. He had few scruples about anything, including murder. Pringle wanted Cleve Bandelier put out of the way for two reasons, one of which had become pressing.

Flickering street lamps provided light for Wingfield to make his way up Palace Avenue where Santa Fé's aristocracy lived. Their *casas* were all located behind high walls so that the usual lamplight from windows was absent. Wingfield knew that there were impressive homes hidden behind those walls with spacious patios as well as carefully tended flower gardens whose fragrance perfumed the air where he walked. He hoped to own one himself some day. It was the reason he played Pringle's game. He dreamed of his own *rancho* and a home in Santa Fé that it would finance.

He let himself through a massive, carved door that had been

left unlocked for him. When Pringle had first escorted him here, he'd told him the door was over two centuries old. Inside, guided only by starlight, he walked carefully down a flower-and-shrub-bordered path. Unlike the preferred Santa Fé style, Pringle's house had two stories in the manner of California's Spanish architecture with balconies jutting from the second story. Pancho always felt that hostile eyes were staring down at him from those deeply shadowed perches. The only lighted room was Pringle's office, heavily shuttered inside, only a faint light seeping through the louvers.

At Wingfield's knock Pringle called: "Who is it?" He was careful to identify the voice before he opened the door. He had a lot of enemies. Someone had once taken a shot at him through his bedroom window.

Pancho wondered who the hell Pringle thought it would be and said: "Wingfield."

Pringle opened the door. "Come on in," he invited, wanting to add: *Quick!* He had felt like a target ever since being shot at in his own home, and he never went out at night unless armed and in the company of a good, dependable man. He closed and bolted the door, then moved behind his desk to emphasize that this was a business meeting. "Have a seat, Frank."

Pancho sank into a wide, leather-thonged chair directly in front of Pringle's carved desk and cast his eyes around the room lined with leather-bound books. Navajo rugs were strewn on the floors and hung on one wall, and Indian pots graced the library table. The high ceiling was supported by varnished, peeled-log *vigas*. Wingfield had been here when a fire was lit and was sensitive enough to wish it was now, for charm and fragrance. He imagined himself sitting in a room like this of his own some day and knew he could if he played his cards right.

Pringle offered him a cigar from a mahogany humidor and

passed him his brass desktop cutter with match box beneath. He was relieved when Pancho accepted the cigar, since he dreaded these ranch types, rolling their cigarettes and dribbling tobacco onto the furniture and rugs. Notwithstanding, he was not about to deny anyone the pleasure of smoking. He prepared and lit his own cigar, and they joined in the male ritual of luxuriating in that first fragrant puff, blowing a cloud of smoke toward the ceiling. Despite great personal differences, they felt the companionship that expensive cigars fostered, somewhat akin to Indian smoking rituals.

Pringle came directly to the point. "The time is here to get tough with the squatters on the grant. We've got about as much out of them in court as Frank Carson can get for the syndicate. Public opinion is swinging against us, and judges read the newspapers, too. We could lose our shirts in court if we push too far too fast. I ought to know . . . I've been a lawyer ever since the war." He dreaded the thought that the courts might reverse themselves due to an accidental infusion of honest judges and scale the grant back to its original size of 42,000 acres, a chance that still existed. He puffed his cigar thoughtfully as he continued: "Anyhow, it's time to take another tack. First on our list is this fellow, Bandelier."

Wingfield said: "If we get rid of him, we'll have to get someone else to blame the syndicate's rustling losses on. Ransom told me he's already convinced Voerbeck that Bandelier and his gang are robbing him blind."

Pringle wasn't surprised. He had given Ransom the idea to invent a gang and made a mental note to caution Ransom to be less forthcoming with Wingfield.

"Ransom is so damn' green he wouldn't notice we were missing cows if we wiped the range clean," Wingfield continued. "He'd miss a horse, though. He's like an Indian when it comes to horses. Can tell one of his own five miles away."

"We don't give a damn about horses," Pringle said. "At least not his lordship's."

So far he'd kept his personal dealings with Wingfield entirely secret. It was no one else's business, not even the rest of the ring. The two were in partnership to siphon off syndicate cattle, move them onto range in Colorado to rebrand, then push them north to market along the railroads, or drive them to Wyoming where Pringle had a ranch disguised as a corporation to conceal his ownership. His secrecy also extended to Wingfield who thought Ransom didn't know where syndicate cattle were disappearing. Pringle had early convinced Ransom that he could feather his own nest, and no one need be the wiser.

At first Ransom had balked, saying indignantly: "Do you mean stealing from my prospective father-in-law?"

"Nothing so crude," Pringle had assured him. "I know the parties who will do the stealing, and I'm willing to sell some of that stock to you cheap. You might consider it an investment."

Ransom had little trouble divining who would do the stealing. He already suspected Wingfield. Ransom had thought about that a while, then laughed boisterously. "You're a card," he had said. "How much do you want per cow?"

"Let's say I'll sell them to you at half price?"

"But you won't be paying anything for them."

"Exactly."

Ransom had laughed again. It had occurred to him that he was very likely not going to be able to cut the mustard with old Voerbeck and his prospects of getting fixed for life with an admirable marriage would fly out the window as a result. It had never occurred to him to court Mariposa passionately and marry her, whether her father approved or not. People who did that were common. When they weren't common, their independence always kicked up a scandal, and one was no longer accepted in proper circles. In fact the Prince of Wales had a lamentable habit of wielding the social scalpel in such cases.

Pringle had warned Ransom: "Just be certain that Wingfield doesn't learn what we're doing. He's not to be trusted and is a dangerous man. He'd hold it over our heads and bleed us."

It wasn't hard advice to follow, since Ransom had sized Wingfield up as capable of blackmail, and certainly as dangerous, though that didn't deter him. He'd been the finest pistol shot in India; and, although he hated to recall the incident, a duel had been at the root of his retirement from the Indian Service. The other poor fellow was buried there. He wasn't afraid of Wingfield.

Pringle had similar secret arrangements far and wide, and some nearer home, which explained his sudden interest in getting rid of Cleve Bandelier who had recently underbid him for a large cattle delivery to Fort Union where Pringle had previously held a monopoly. He didn't mention any of this to Wingfield. They made a complementary pair in that respect. Wingfield somehow never mentioned to him that he stole a second time a good many of their stolen cattle and located them on a ranch in Nebraska, jointly owned by him and his brother.

The vast, unfenced West in which law enforcement was non-existent or at best uncertain had made such deals common since the end of the war. Most of the cattle first driven from Texas to Kansas railroads had been of uncertain ownership. There were enough of them that no one cared. Pringle anticipated the end of this free and easy practice with the coming of barbed wire and cattle associations that hired brand inspectors. He gave himself three or four more years at the outside to clean up. Freebooters were on the way out, as evidenced by Pat Garrett's killing of Billy the Kid the year before, and the Earps' cleanup over in Arizona just this spring. Regardless of the latter's motives they'd wiped out a rustler combination by killing off the leadership.

Pringle asked: "What's going on up at Bandelier's ranch?" He knew Wingfield had the place under almost constant surveillance by Devil Ed Targee.

"They're rounding up a herd, for one thing."

"Why now?" He knew why. This would be the herd for Fort Union but asked the natural question because Wingfield would get suspicious if he didn't.

"Hard to say. The range is poor . . . maybe he's movin' them up into Colorado. Maybe selling off early."

"How many head?"

"They ain't through yet, but I'd say it'll run a thousand."

"That's a lot of cows. Maybe he aims to pull out and get out of all the trouble." He knew better.

"He ain't the kind. He'll be the last to go."

"Or maybe the first."

"You want him beefed?"

"Maybe, if it comes down to it. Right now, I want you to scatter that herd from hell to breakfast. It's probably too big to run off. You might be able to cut out a couple of hundred head, though. We're gonna start giving him the same treatment as the syndicate."

"He won't be as easy."

"Then he'll have to be put out of the way."

Wingfield asked: "You got any particular notion how you'd like Bandelier done up?"

Pringle stared at him with protruding eyes, unblinking in his fat, baby face, then averted his gaze toward the ceiling, taking a long, reflective puff on his cigar and blowing the smoke upward. Finally, returning his pop-eyed gaze to Wingfield, he said: "I'll leave that up to you when the time comes. Just don't move till I pass the word."

Since Pringle seemed to have a reason to want Bandelier alive for a while, Wingfield made a note to call off Targee who'd tried to drygulch Cleve a couple of times because he had a grudge against him.

Pringle was considering the consequences if Bandelier was disposed of. He'd been the most convincing scapegoat for the continued syndicate cattle losses in case Voerbeck found out the true extent of them and cracked down. So far he'd been indifferent, at least on the surface. Pringle didn't think the other squatters would serve as well as Bandelier to blame as the source of the wholesale rustling. Bandelier ran several thousand head of cattle and had built up herds quickly. It was easy to convince people that he was swinging a wide loop. A decision to dispose of Bandelier was, therefore, problematical. They might have to work on the syndicate's herds another couple of years before Voerbeck decided he'd made a bad investment. Beefing Bandelier was a case of balancing off immediate gain in getting rid of competition against his long term usefulness as a scapegoat. On the other hand, Voerbeck might never give in. He had a hell of a lot of money. In that case the continued rustling would be his only gain. Best keep Bandelier around a while.

Another tricky consideration was that delay would give the squatters a chance to upset his plans in court. They had a smart lawyer, Polocarpio Baca, or Polo as everyone called him. He'd become a political power in the entire territory and was related to the Zamoras up on the grant who themselves numbered in the hundreds, counting cousins that included the Bacas, of course, but also Maldonados, Perezes, Sandovals, Villanuevas, Vargas, Coronados, Huertas, Luceros, and a dozen more families, all of whom had lived there before the Spanish were driven out by the Indian revolt in the 1680s. Afterward they had returned, tenaciously reoccupied their land, and surely would fight for it again.

The Jicarilla Apaches could be a bigger obstacle to Pringle's hopes. They wanted a reservation carved from the grant. With the help of Eastern sympathizers who hadn't had a relative eviscerated or burned at the stake by Indians for a couple of centuries, the Jicarillas might convince Congress to slice off a piece for a reservation. Polo was representing them, too. A dangerous man in more ways than one, he carried two six-shooters and shot too fast and straight for comfort.

After their talk, as Pringle saw Pancho to the door, the latter assured him: "I'll run that herd into the mountains. They'll be a couple of weeks gathering it again. As for Bandelier, just say the word when you're ready."

After he was gone, Pringle sat at his desk, deep in thought. He mumbled aloud, "Rustling is one thing . . . murder is another cup of tea." He wondered how deeply he could get in with Wingfield without becoming his hostage. He certainly couldn't trust him.

Wingfield had similar thoughts about Pringle as he made his way back to his hotel. He suspected there was plenty that Pringle wasn't telling him. Obviously Pringle didn't trust him, but then he probably trusted no one. That was a two way street. He wondered why Pringle wanted to hold off pulling the trigger on Cleve Bandelier. He'd heard that Cleve was something of a shootist. To Wingfield's type that was a challenge. He'd met Cleve a couple of times and recognized that, unlike most, Cleve wasn't afraid of him. He thought: *Maybe I'll just brace him and push him into a fight. Why wait for that slippery bastard, Pringle, to give the word?*

That was pleasing to think about, but there were safer ways to get rid of a man. Like most gunmen, Wingfield liked to pick his victims carefully, preferring poor shots or unarmed ones. He'd fight anyone, if forced to it, but there could be a fellow who had a bullet in his six-shooter with his name on it. His final thought on the subject was: *Pringle hadn't better wait too damned long.*

He was passing the Poco Loma saloon when he remembered that Pringle hadn't even brought out a bottle. He turned in and swaggered to the bar, certain that someone was bound to recognize him and point him out. A half dozen shots of whiskey later he decided his reputation required him to shoot out the lights. He cleaned out the place and was at the bar, too drunk to realize that both his pistols were empty, when the marshal netted him with a double barrel. He was so pleased with himself that he went along cheerfully, having let off the steam Pringle's high-handed manner had built inside him.

In the morning U. S. Attorney Laxelt stopped in for his morning eye-opener with his old friend, Tomás.

"Mornin', Tom," he greeted Pringle.

The familiar bottle was produced, and they both performed the ritual locally known as *libating.* They toasted one another with their eyes before tossing them off, let out satisfied *Ahhhs,* and grinned. They'd known each other since right after the war when Pringle had arrived in the territory and found Laxelt already there, a veteran of General Carlton's California Column that had come to hold New Mexico against the Confederacy in 1862.

Finally Laxelt asked: "What's new?" He already knew what was new but wanted to find out if Pringle did, or, if he'd admit it, if he did.

"Nothing that I know of," Pringle said, blank-faced.

"Did you know Pancho Wingfield is down in the *juzgado* for shooting up the Poco Loma last night?"

Pringle kept his poker face. "I wonder what the hell he's doing in town."

"I thought maybe you knew."

Pringle laughed as he said: "I will when he sends somebody

up for me to bail him out . . . after he sleeps it off."

Later, as Laxelt was walking down the street to his own office, he thought: *I'll just bet old Tom didn't know Pancho was in town, or why! I wonder what the hell they're up to now?* Whatever it was, he hoped he'd never hear about it, a vain hope since, before it was over, even Europe would be reporting it in the newspapers.

Chapter Thirteen

Frank Wingfield was born November 29, 1841 on a cotton plantation along the Sabine River. Texas had recently won independence from Mexico but was not too certain it could keep it. By the time Frank was old enough to understand such things, the United States had annexed Texas, the Mexican War was won, and life for people in the circumstances of his family was fairly easy by the standards of the times. The Indian troubles were far to the west, and his family owned black slaves who relieved rich whites of all drudgery. Since before his earliest recollections young Frank had had his own body servant to do everything, from helping him get dressed to saddling his horses.

His man, Eustace, was the son of his mother's personal maid and was in his late teens when Frank was ten. Because he was much older and had more common sense, Eustace sometimes forgot himself and tried to be a big brother to his white charge. Although it was in Frank's best interest every time, he seldom appreciated it and sometimes cuffed Eustace. The latter only dodged, or put up his arms to fend off Frank, and laughed as a rule which drove Frank to insane fits of anger. Such instances didn't happen often, but, when they did, Frank sometimes went to get a gun to kill Eustace, and the latter headed for the piney woods to hide out till his master cooled down. It was the only life Eustace had ever known, and he made the best of it, unaware there was any other kind.

When Eustace's mother found out about the gun incidents, she reported them to Frank's mother, who passed word to Frank Wingfield, Sr., who laughed and said: "The boy won't hurt him. He's only bringin' him to heel. I told him that nigger is worth eight hundred dollars, and I'd wear him out if he killed him. Let the boy have his fun."

This precious sort of parental moral instruction was fairly common, cited by some social writers, even in the South, as a bad influence on developing good character. Whether a bad influence or not, tolerance of brutality was common, and certainly it had an impact on developing the violent character of the future Pancho Wingfield. When Frank, Junior, later came in contact with Mexicans, he considered them in the same inferior class as blacks. In the Amarillo Grant country of New Mexico this obvious contempt for the native majority, who considered it their land by virtue of centuries of residence, did nothing to smooth his path. Those he sneered at were people with the blood of *conquistadores* who'd conquered Mexico with Cortez, descendants of the original few hundred warriors who'd prevailed when outnumbered by hundreds of thousands. Pancho grudgingly hired them for the Amarillo ranch, because it was that or nothing, but barely tolerated them, though he had sense enough to realize that, if he cuffed them as he had Eustace, he was inviting a knife in the ribs some dark night or a shot from ambush out in the mountains.

Pancho was capable of projecting a veneer of good manners when it suited him. He'd attended Princeton for two years before the Civil War had interrupted his schooling. This enabled him to get on with Lord Ransom better than most frontiersmen. They also recognized in each other a reckless disregard of danger, although Pancho disliked having to admit the fact that during Ransom's three years in New Mexico he'd come to admire him for this as well as his ability to punish a bottle without visible signs of drunkenness. He'd first recognized Ransom's fearlessness in an odd manner. Polo. He'd watched with disgust as Ransom created two polo teams from among the local *vaqueros*. As the effort progressed, he had sometimes stopped to watch. Finally Ransom had invited him to try his hand at it.

"It looks like a pretty damn' idle waste of time to me," Wingfield had said. "We could use those men out on the range."

Ransom had looked surprised. "Hire some more."

It was Wingfield's turn to look surprised. He couldn't believe Ransom was serious. He had decided to take his lordship at his word and hire more men. If Ransom noticed, he didn't mention it. Finally Wingfield could stand it no longer. One day he had approached Ransom between chukkars and said: "Give me one of them hammers, and I'll try it."

"You'd better try a different saddle," Ransom had said. "And those 'hammers' are called mallets."

"This saddle will do for now," Wingfield had said. "Those postage stamps, with their damned dangling short stirrups that keep your knees under your chin, look to me like a good thing to fall off of and get dragged around in the bargain."

Ransom had merely shrugged. It was the same opinion the Mexican polo players had held when they first rode them. They had gripped the horse with their legs, as though riding bareback, until they had gotten the hang of it. It didn't take long, since they were natural riders. Most of them had straddled their first horse at about the age of two. Wingfield had been the same. He had learned the English seat in time and preferred it for polo. He had also turned out to be a remarkably good polo player.

Thus a common interest in the sport was the glue that bound together two very different men in grudging respect for one another. They also shared a common liking for the bottle and were frequently seen carousing together in the bar of the Santiago House in Dorado. Although Wingfield was the closest thing to an American friend that Ransom had, mostly he depended on trips to England or visits by English friends to break the grip of loneliness. He was also an avid hunter of grizzly bears and other large game such as elk. His final diversion was Carmen Peralta, the seventeen-year-old daughter of the ranch's housekeeper, Belen. Carmen was what kept Ransom out of Maud's house in Dorado that Wingfield patronized on a regular basis. Wingfield's departures for the congenial company at Maud's was what always broke up the drinking bouts with Ransom. The latter would either put up at the hotel or head home.

Wingfield always said: "Better come along and see the new talent."

And Ransom always declined: "You'll catch a cold down there . . . on the wrong end."

Carmen's obliging attitude toward Ransom, as well as her mother's, was based on the conviction that keeping Lord Ransom's bed warm, as well as making it, was their ticket to the softest life they'd ever known. If there was a sinful aspect to it, that's what Belen's cousin, *Padre* Maldonado, was for. Common knowledge had it that he kept his own bed-warmers in every one of the villages on his marriage and Mass circuit. In addition, it was rumored that he granted absolutions either before, during, or afterward. Probably this story was apocryphal. At least it was always told with a laugh.

Waldo Holmes was one of Tomás Pringle's silent partners and an important one as the attorney who conducted the business of Pringle's Wyoming cattle corporation. His fee was a twenty percent share of the operation. He seldom visited Santa Fé because neither he nor Pringle wished to provide people with a reason to remember them as having been together. He came now ostensibly because he'd learned some disquieting news from an old West Point classmate at Fort Leavenworth while he'd been there, posting performance bonds to qualify for long-term cattle contracts at military posts.

Holmes's classmate, Captain Anson Palmer, had no idea that Holmes was connected with Pringle. Palmer had once been commander of Fort Garland where his sergeant-major had been Cleve Bandelier. Bandelier had sent Captain Palmer a letter, containing allegations that most of the beef contracts filled by Tomás Pringle and the Santa Fé Ring consisted of rustled cattle. Bandelier also supplied information that Pringle was engaged in large-scale rustling of cattle from the Amarillo syndicate's ranch, driven out of New Mexico to an intermediate ranch on the Purgatoire River in Colorado, then to parts unknown. Holmes went directly to Pringle's office when he arrived in Santa Fé and unburdened himself of this information.

"Jesus Christ!" Pringle exploded. "Just what we needed. What's the Army doing about it?"

"For one thing, they've hired the Pinkertons who've hired range detectives."

"How much have they found out?"

"Plenty. They're bound to find out the whole thing, if they can connect syndicate cattle to our Wyoming operation."

Pringle thought that over. "It's a damn' good thing rustling isn't a federal offense. But that's not the point . . . if the Army poisons our well on beef contracts, it'll cost us a hell of a lot. How did that s o b, Bandelier, find out as much as he did?"

"One of his cowboys spotted a herd of syndicate cattle being driven out and followed it."

"Did you find out who?"

"Of course. His name is Buchanan."

"Can he be bought?"

"I have no idea, but it might be a good idea to find out."

"I've got a better idea."

"Such as?"

Pringle clammed up at that point, saying evasively: "I'll have to think it out. I'd rather not go off half-cocked."

Holmes laughed. "In other words, none of my damn' business. I don't blame you. I don't want to hear."

Pringle eyed him coldly. He didn't trust anyone and would just as soon have had Holmes leave town before someone saw them together. Besides, he wondered why Holmes hadn't sent him the information by letter. Did he have some other business in New Mexico? He thought of asking him but knew he wouldn't get a straight answer.

Reading his mind, Holmes said: "I'm on a little vacation junket to see the country, headed for the coast, so I thought I'd stop by. Besides, I want to look over Tombstone. Might buy some stock in the mines there. I hear George Hearst is looking it over."

"Where'd you hear that?" Pringle's ears always pricked up when someone as savvy as Hearst was thinking of investing in something.

"Some of the Wells Fargo crowd were in Chicago and mentioned it."

"Who?"

"I don't remember, to tell the God's truth. I think it was Hagen, but I can't be sure."

Pringle laughed. Holmes probably never told the God's truth in his life. Like most West Pointers he was full of hot air about duty, honor, and country until it came down to putting rhetoric into practice. "Can I put you up out at the house?"

"Nope. I'm staying at La Fonda and heading out tomorrow. I'm having dinner and a few snorts with some old Army friends over at the fort."

"You might try to find out what kind of baloney Bandelier may have been spreading over there. He just beat me out of a contract for beef at Fort Union."

"He's got one for Fort Garland, too, did you know that?"

Pringle's face answered for him.

"You've got a real burr under the saddle there, Tom," Holmes warned. "If you're not careful, he'll run you out of the business."

"What do you mean run *me?* We're in this together."

Holmes headed for the door. He'd just as soon not be overtly together in anything with Pringle when he decided to run over the competition. He'd heard too many stories about something known as the Whitecaps. He had his own ideas about who they really worked for, though their dirty work was blamed on the Dutch syndicate that owned the Amarillo Grant. He'd almost told Pringle that his friend at the fort was General Gryden, whose aide-de-camp he'd been for almost the entire Civil War. On reflection, he was glad he hadn't. No telling what Pringle may have asked him to try to wring out of the general.

As a direct result of Holmes's visit, Pringle made a definite decision about Cleve Bandelier. He was entirely too dangerous. He drafted a wire to Pancho Wingfield at Dorado that read:

The bear hunt is on. Am sending you two customers in a couple of days.

After dispatching that, he headed over to see the U. S. marshal about securing deputies' commissions for the two bear hunters he planned to recruit. He knew exactly who would fill the bill. Unfortunately, it would be these recruits who ended up draped across two of Cleve Bandelier's pack horses, like the bears they were ostensibly hunting.

Chapter Fourteen

Frank Wingfield debated the wisdom of letting Lord Ransom know the true purpose of the bear hunters employed by Pringle and concluded he'd better tell him. Heretofore, so far as Wingfield knew, Grut Voerbeck had never so much as hinted that he'd condone using force to advance the syndicate's aims. Nonetheless, Wingfield used it anyhow; it came naturally to him. He was sure that it was safe in cases of small game, where the facts, if they got out at all, wouldn't go beyond territorial newspapers. Disposing of Cleve Bandelier, a prominent rancher, would be a different story. Whether to ally himself exclusively with Pringle and rub out Bandelier, which was his natural preference, posed a problem for Wingfield, since he had his eggs in two baskets. He probably had more to gain in the long run by following Pringle's orders, but he hated to risk his soft job under Ransom, since it positioned him to make rustling syndicate cattle much easier than it would be if he were fired and a new, honest *segundo* were hired to replace him. The new man would probably be a real cattleman who wouldn't take long to figure out what had been going on. He'd tell Ransom and, in effect, Voerbeck. Wingfield, of course, had no idea that Ransom was already onto his game, thanks to Pringle. He wouldn't have cared, had he known, but there was no telling what a man with Voerbeck's money might do if he found out, as was bound to happen sooner or later. Voerbeck could financially afford to have Pringle's whole crowd hounded out of the country. Wingfield had no taste for going on the dodge, having been there before, so he decided to tell Ransom what was up in the case of Bandelier and the bear hunters. He hoped to cloak the affair under Ransom's authority, in case something went wrong.

He and Ransom were at their usual table in the Santiago House bar when Wingfield gave him the word. Ransom's eyebrows shot up high. "Say that again. Pringle is sending men to do what?" He couldn't believe he'd heard right.

"He wants to put Bandelier out of the way for good."

Ransom had no doubt that Voerbeck would approve of that objective, especially in view of what he'd told the old man about Bandelier, but he wasn't at all certain Voerbeck would approve of the means. If Ransom read him correctly, the old Dutchman was very conscious of the need to respect public opinion in the United States, particularly where a foreign investor was concerned. Everyone knew Americans were xenophobic, even if they didn't hold a monopoly on it. Ransom could imagine Voerbeck's horror if the New York newspapers were to publish an article along the lines of:

Giant Dutch syndicate hires assassins to kill the leader of poor, hard-working American homesteaders, trying to secure their lawful rights to small, subsistence plots of Public Land in New Mexico Territory. Night riders' reign of terror continues, financed by well-known international pirate, Grut Voerbeck.

It was the sort of news that would be picked up in places as far away as London and Berlin, and, in view of the nationality of the syndicate, surely in Amsterdam and Voerbeck's hometown, Leyden. "I don't think Voerbeck will like it." Ransom said. "In fact, I'd bet he'll raise hell if he hears about it."

"He won't hear about it," Wingfield argued. "None of the other rough stuff has got beyond the territorial papers, and nobody pays much attention to them. Everyone knows these jack-leg editors out here are always throwing rocks at each other. Besides, if we do this right, Bandelier is just going to disappear."

"From what I hear, he isn't apt to be quietly led out and knocked on the head like a duck," Ransom said.

"That ain't the way we have it planned. Two U. S. deputy marshals are going to serve papers on him and take him in. He won't raise a fuss with them, and nobody will know about them except him and us. Something happens to him on the way to Santa Fé, and he disappears."

"What about his men . . . and I understand he has a couple of kids? They'll know who took him away and inform the authorities."

"His men are out on a roundup. He'll be home alone with his two kids . . . one's a girl. They can't help him or put up much of a fuss. Besides, the marshals will take them along, too."

"But they'll tell who took their father away."

Wingfield laughed. "Hell, whole families disappear out here all the time. It can be made to look like the Injuns done it."

Ransom looked truly shocked. "Are you saying you plan to have the kids killed along with their father? Even a little girl?"

"Nits breed lice. Does Voerbeck want to get the squatters off his land or not? If Bandelier disappears, the rest of the squatters'll be packin' up and pullin' out the day they hear about it."

Ransom poured himself a water glass full of rye from the bottle in front of him and tossed off half of it at a gulp, silently stared at the rest, then downed it, too. He had no strong scruples against killing fighting men, having done his share of it as well as having ordered a lot of killing done. Punishment of the Sepoys in India by his own countrymen, only a generation before, had approached genocide in places. Mutineers had been strapped across the muzzles of cannons heavily charged with powder and blown to pieces. Whole villages — men, women and children — disappeared without the atrocities having been reported in newspapers. Still, this wasn't colonial India but a sovereign country where little people, like those who would be killed, were the sacred icons of a folk religion that worshipped human rights.

"You and Pringle are mad," Ransom concluded. "Out of your minds."

"It's too late to call it off now," Wingfield said.

Ransom read the purpose in his eyes. This brute was going to go ahead with his and Pringle's insanity, no matter what he said. And going to the sheriff would do little good, so far as he knew. Butler had been kept in office for years with the backing of the ring. Ransom concluded his best move was to distance himself, as far as possible, from the whole thing. He shrugged. "I don't want anything to do with it. As far as I'm concerned, I never heard of it. You can go ahead and do what you bloody well please . . . you will anyhow, but I don't want to hear any more about it."

Wingfield laughed. That was good enough for him. He considered himself a fool for having brought it up in the first place. "Forget I ever said anything," he suggested, pushing back his chair. "If those bear hunters pull in, lookin' for me, have 'em send Dick-Dick over to Maud's, and I'll meet 'em here."

Ransom had no desire to meet the bear hunters. As soon as Wingfield was gone, he sent Dick-Dick Grovelmost, as the saloon's swamper was known, over to the livery stable to have his horse saddled. When Dick-Dick returned, he scurried toward Ransom and said: "Your horse'll be ready as soon as you want. Should I bring him over?" He bowed and scraped to Ransom more than he did to most others in that subservient manner that had earned him his nickname.

"I'll go over myself in a little while," Ransom said, flipping a quarter to the swamper.

"Thankee, sir," he acknowledged the coin. "Thankee kindly, yer lordship."

"You're welcome, Dick-Dick."

Ransom rather liked the groveling, a reminder of the forelock-tugging respect still accorded nobility at home. For that reason he always felt kindly toward the pathetic swamper. He wouldn't have thought of kicking him as drunk cowboys sometimes did out of sheer orneriness. Dick-Dick bowed himself out of the noble presence, turned, and ran back to his mop.

Ransom downed another tumbler of whiskey neat and left. Dick-Dick by now was standing by, holding his mop at "present arms" without realizing it, and resumed going through the motions of cleaning the floor, as he did continually for fear of losing his job.

The bear hunters pulled in on the next train, made their way to the Santiago, bellied up to the bar, downed a shot apiece, and then asked the bartender the whereabouts of Wingfield. The bartender indicated the swamper with a nod.

"Dick-Dick over there will most likely know where he is and fetch him for two bits, I'd guess. I heard Wingfield mention you'd likely be looking for him."

Wingfield returned with Dick-Dick, picked up a bottle of whiskey, and took the two men upstairs. They were closeted for quite a while. Meanwhile, men Wingfield had called in earlier assembled in the Santiago bar, their horses hitched outside, all with Winchesters in saddle scabbards and bedrolls tied behind. They attracted no undue attention, since Wingfield often formed crews here before going out on the range. The Amarillo main ranch was only a few miles up the river from town. Some savvy townsmen, like Sheriff Butler, suspected Wingfield gathered his forces here when Ransom was at the ranch, to keep his comings and goings secret from his nominal boss.

Whenever such crews congregated, the Mexican denizens of Dorado took in their goats, pigs, and dogs, and warned their children off the streets, since almost anything might be used for target practice by Wingfield's hardcases, who customarily left town at a dead run, screaming rebel yells and shooting in all directions. This time the townsfolk were to be pleasantly surprised. Wingfield came downstairs shortly after his crew arrived, well before they got oiled, and said: "No shooting this time when we ride out. We might need all our ammunition."

He led the way quietly from town, assembled his men for instructions, then led them down the road north toward Tres Huérfanos. The two bear hunters rode beside him on horses he'd provided.

The bartender and Dick-Dick Grovelmost were alone after the crew pulled out. The former said: "I wonder what the hell devilment they're up to this time?"

Dick-Dick shrugged. He was afraid to say anything for fear Wingfield might hear he'd talked against him. Dick-Dick's days were filled with groundless fears, from the time he awoke till he went back to sleep. He reckoned they'd probably hear about some unfortunate homesteader who'd been burned out, but hardly dared think it for fear his mind would be read by a *bruja* and word would get around.

Chapter Fifteen

Grut Voerbeck had no trouble providing his party sumptuous travel accommodations *en route* to the Amarillo ranch. The D. & R. G. came right through the town of Dorado, which was three and a half miles from the ranch headquarters. Voerbeck had bought up half of the five-million-dollar bond issue of 1879 that had enabled the D. & R. G. expansion south through Dorado to Española and had invested substantially in other American railroads as well. Consequently, he had the use of private palace cars of various tycoons across the entire United States. General Palmer, president of the D. & R. G., provided Voerbeck with his own private car.

Voerbeck's excursion, aside from his business interests, had the appearance of a vacation trip. Baron Waterford had brought a dozen rifles and shotguns and intended to try his hand at hunting everything he could. Even Lady Daisy Fetherstonhaugh was known to shoot game birds and was a fair shot. Mariposa Voerbeck's sympathies were all with the game, but she was prepared to keep her hand in at target shooting. The baron had also brought his fly-fishing paraphernalia, having heard that Colorado and New Mexico streams were full of trout.

The train that carried them south toward Dorado was entirely private with even the conductor under Voerbeck's orders. Consequently, they sided at Tres Huérfanos, since Waterford had decided to try the nearby lake for ducks and had seen flights of doves in the vicinity of all the ponds they'd passed. He'd also noticed eagles perched in the tops of dead trees and hoped to bag a couple for his taxidermy collection. While Waterford was hunting, everyone else took pleasure in the scenery and mountain air during a leisurely day, walking outside the cars and stretching their legs.

Grut remarked to Mariposa: "I think I'll go in and take a nap before supper time."

"I might do that later myself," she said. "But its so pretty out here, I hate to miss anything."

Mariposa and Daisy continued to stroll, admiring flowers and wondering what the names were of the strange ones. Mariposa picked a bouquet for the dining table, took it in, placed it in a vase, then went back out and seated herself in a folding chair on the rear observation platform beside Daisy.

Baron Waterford returned from his hunt and joined them, bringing a full bag of doves and ducks.

"Jolly good hunting," he observed. "The fool birds don't know what a gun is. They just keep flying in." He looked toward the sun, approaching the western horizon, and said: "I suppose the doves come in to water in the evening."

The rumbling sound of thousands of running hoofs burst on them too suddenly to identify at once. It was punctuated by the sound of distant gunfire.

"What the devil?" Waterford said, looking perplexed.

The first of the stampeding herd thundered over the hill east of the railroad line and ran toward them. Hundreds more followed, riders visible among them for the first time. They all watched, fascinated.

"It must be a stampede," Waterford said. "I've read of them."

The shooting increased in frequency and volume, and, as they watched, they saw that the men were shooting at each other rather than attempting to turn the cattle.

"Whatever in the world are they doing?" Daisy wondered.

Mariposa, who had been in places where people fought and killed one another, wasn't confused. "They're trying to shoot each other," she said.

"Damned if they aren't. You ladies had better get inside!" Waterford ordered.

Mariposa had no intention of missing this show unless the shooters came a lot closer. Shortly, cattle were rushing all around them, and the riders had separated into two distinct groups, the smaller headed for cover with the others closing behind.

Waterford said, more urgently: "They're headed right over here. I believe they intend to take shelter on our cars, if they can reach us."

He wondered if he should try to drive them away, since their presence would endanger the ladies' lives. It never occurred to him that he was in danger. As an observer in the Franco-Prussian war, he'd gained a reputation for exposing himself as though he was unaware people were shooting all around him.

The smaller group of riders rushed past and dismounted, a couple, both blacks, firing repeatedly to hold off their pursuers while the rest corralled their mounts in the loading pens. Then all took position behind the heavy log fence, still firing rapidly. One of the riders who'd fallen behind was trying to overtake his friends, pursued closely by another. The pursuer provided Waterford a close view of the white hoods worn by the much larger attacking force.

"Get inside, ladies!" he insisted, replacing the bird shot in his eight-gauge double barrel with buck.

Mariposa's first thought was to get her own Winchester rifle from her trunk, and she rushed back into the car, almost running into her father. He looked sleepy and confused.

"What's that shooting about?" he inquired.

"I don't know," she said. "Some men are fighting each other

over a herd of cattle, I think."

He went to take a look for himself. She ran on after her rifle.

Waterford watched as a fleeing rider was shot off his horse and fell heavily on the embankment directly behind the car. His pursuer pulled up, taking no notice of Waterford. He walked his mount up to the fallen man, pistol in hand, and started to take deliberate aim. The baron had no idea what the fight was about, or who was right or wrong, but he knew cold-blooded murder when he saw it.

"Hold up there," he thundered, cocking his double barrel and taking dead aim at the horseman who noticed him for the first time.

The horseman hesitated, undecided, then said: "Who the hell are you?"

Waterford said nothing, merely kept the twin tunnels of his shotgun trained on his target. Obviously the fellow respected what a shotgun could do, especially at that range.

"This is none of your affair," he said, but he raised his pistol skyward just in case, careful not to move the muzzle of his gun toward either Waterford or on the helpless man on the ground.

"Murder is everyone's affair," Waterford said. "Put up that pistol, or I'll fire."

During this exchange the rest of the attacking crew had veered away, driven off by the heavy fire of the men inside the pens.

Very carefully the horseman uncocked, then lowered his pistol, and put it back into its holster. "I think I'll go now," he said.

It struck the baron as a strange thing to say. He'd have been astounded to know that the man was unnerved as much by his broad English accent as by the shotgun.

"Go right ahead," Waterford said. "Don't come back."

He noted the large A on the horse's flank, but had no idea what it signified. He also noted that the man's fancy black, carved leather boots bore an embossed W just below the pull straps at the top.

Inside the car Voerbeck restrained Mariposa from joining the baron on the rear platform. He noted her rifle, but decided this was no time to ask her where she'd got it. He was glad she had it, knowing he could use one expertly if need be, whether she could or not.

The man Waterford had driven off seemed to be the leader of the others, yelling at them when he was beyond range of Percy's shotgun. "Come on! Follow me!" He was obviously more interested in driving the cattle off than in fighting the other men.

Waterford hopped nimbly down the steps and off the observation platform, going to check on the downed man. Mariposa and her father joined him, followed by Daisy who had taken it all in, wide-eyed, but not particularly frightened. She wasn't the type to get frightened.

Mariposa knelt beside the body. "He's just a boy," she said.

Waterford checked for a pulse. "Alive," he announced.

He took out his penknife and cut the shirt from the bloody spot. "It looks to me like a ball came right through without hitting anything vital. I'd say it broke his collarbone. The fall is what knocked him out."

"Let me look," Mariposa said. Obviously the bullet had entered his back and exited through a larger hole in front. He was bleeding heavily. "I don't think it cut an artery, but we've got to get the bleeding stopped as quickly as we can."

Percy took out his handkerchief and wadded it in the hole in front. The boy moaned a little, then opened his eyes. The sight of Mariposa puzzled him.

"Don't move," she ordered. "I'm going to get something to bandage you up."

By the time she returned with first-aid material, a man had detached himself from the crew hidden inside the loading pens and approached.

"I am Jesús Sandoval," he introduced himself. He knelt beside the wounded man and told him: "Take it easy, kid. We'll take care of you." He looked up at Voerbeck's party who were watching him uncertainly and said: "This man works for me."

Wanting to reassure the man, Mariposa said: "I'm a trained nurse. Let me take care of him." She didn't wait for Jesús's permission but said to the wounded man: "Try to relax."

The boy let his head fall back, and he groaned. He was obviously very frightened. "Am I going to die?" he asked.

She place her hand reassuringly on his forehead. "No," she said. "You've been shot, but not too badly. The bullet went right on through." To Jesús she said: "Help me lift him up a little to get a compress bandage in back."

His right arm twisted at an unnatural angle when he was moved, and she straightened that out. The boy moaned, then said: "Stop. I can't stand it."

"Let him back down and keep him still."

By then the balance of Jesús's crew straggled up, still carrying their rifles just in case. Jeff Mills bent over his friend and asked Mariposa: "Oh, Lord! Is he going to live?"

"Yes. Now get out of the way." Then she said to Jesús: "We must get the bleeding stopped before I can splint his broken arm. You'll have to hold him in a sitting position so I can bind the wound on the back." As Jesús picked Johnny up, she noticed the unnatural movement of his shoulder. "The collarbone *is* broken, I'm sure. Daisy! Go in and rip a sheet into strips about six inches wide and bring them out here."

It took her a few minutes to bandage and bind the wound

and wrap the sheeting several times around Johnny's chest and shoulder to immobilize him as much as possible. She then splinted his broken arm. "There," she said.

The others had watched in amazement. Daisy, who'd taken nurse's training with her but had never got down into the actual dirty and bloody business of it, admired Mariposa's efficiency and grit. "I could never have done that," she said.

Mariposa let out a gusty breath, brushed her hair back with her arm to avoid touching it with her bloody hand, and replied: "You could have, if you had to." To Jesús she said: "Is there a doctor in Dorado?"

"Yes."

"We are going there. We'll take him on the train with us."

The rest of the Bandelier ranch hands had silently watched while she worked. Mariposa looked them over for the first time and was surprised to see three blacks and another Mexican or Indian among them.

Her patient stirred, opened his eyes, and asked: "Where am I?"

His young sidekick knelt beside him again and inquired urgently: "Are you all right, Johnny?"

Johnny nodded weakly. "I guess."

"Does it hurt bad?"

"Of course, you idjit! It hurts like hell." He had forgotten himself, but he added quickly: "Pardon me, ladies."

Mariposa smiled and squeezed his hand. "It's all right. We understand."

She did, indeed, having treated many painful injuries as part of her charity nursing work in London's slums.

Voerbeck spoke up for the first time. "What was all this shooting about?" he asked Jesús.

"Those men ran off our herd of cattle."

"Who were they?"

Jesús shrugged. It was none of these people's business. Finally he said: "How can we tell? They all wore hoods. In this country they call them the Whitecaps. You will find this a dangerous place, a good place to stay out of."

"Were those your cattle?" Voerbeck asked.

"No, *señor,* they are the cattle of my *patrón.*"

"And his name?"

"*Señor* Cleve Bandelier."

Maintaining a completely unreadable face, Voerbeck said nothing further until after they got Johnny Evans safely aboard and he gave the order to pull out. Johnny's young friend had wished to go with him, but the man, Jesús, had told him not to.

Out of the hearing of Johnny Evans, whom they'd placed in a spare bedroom with Daisy watching over him, Mariposa said to her father: "Isn't Bandelier the bandit that Lord Ransom has told us about?"

Her father appeared detached, answering almost idly: "Yes."

"Then the young man we have here is one of his brigands?"

Somehow he didn't fit her prior notion of what a brigand should look like. He looked more like a scared boy. It was what her father was thinking. He said: "We must take care of him no matter what he is."

Voerbeck remembered now how, decades before, he had hidden many frightened Sepoys from the vengeful British due to his natural sympathy for the underdog. This present situation would obviously need a lot of sorting out.

Chapter Sixteen

Pancho Wingfield imagined Percy Waterford's shotgun trained where his suspenders crossed and felt a chilly sensation there until he was sure that he was out of range. He'd experienced this feeling during the war when discretion became the better part of valor, and the *chivalry* found themselves running for it before the guns of the contemptible damyankee *shovelry*. Even cavaliers recognized the wisdom of living to fight another day.

Pancho rounded up his men and gathered them around him, well out of rifle range of Bandelier's crew. He'd been considering his next step, even as he rode away, and had already mentally selected some of the locals to do the least demanding work that had to be done. These were men he'd found were most apt to avoid danger. Pete Miller was the recognized head of the local group, all of whom had knuckled under to the syndicate to gain title to their small outfits, which told him all he needed to know about them.

He said: "Pete, take some of your boys and run these cows off into the hills. I want them scattered from hell to breakfast."

Pete took the men Pancho suggested and set them to work. It would take a couple of days, but they hastened to get as much done as they could before it got fully dark. At a minimum, it was necessary to get the herd as far away from Tres Huérfanos as possible before sunup.

Pancho watched them leave, then turned to the hard core of his Texas imports and local hardcases who included the two U. S. deputy marshals Pringle had sent. He had told none of the others that they were actually hired killers and saw no reason to do so. Another stalwart with him was Devil Ed Targee for whom he had a special job.

He faced the group and announced: "Now we're goin' over and pay Bandelier's ranch a visit. Ed here's been watching the place for a few days. The time is ripe to hit him. He's there alone with his two kids. These here two marshals will get him to come out, and we'll take it from there." He laughed. "If he's found hangin' to one of them big cottonwoods behind his house, plugged full of holes, the rest of the riffraff will pull out in a hurry. Now, let's ride."

As they set out, he called to Devil Ed and the two marshals to ride near him where they could talk. He told them: "There ain't gonna be any problem gettin' up to the house. We'll wait till after midnight, then I want you two to get up on the porch. Ed here will lead you around the back, so you can slip up without anyone hearing you. We'll trick Bandelier into coming out, then you can burn him down in his tracks."

Ed Mason, one of the marshals, asked: "How about dogs? I've tried this sort of thing before and got tripped up by a damn' dog."

Devil Ed laughed. "I took care of that. I babied up his dogs for days, so they trusted me, then fed 'em strychnine." He laughed again. "Pity, too. They was good'ns."

"Jesus, Ed," Wingfield cursed. He truly liked dogs and found it hard to stomach the mountaineer, through he recognized he was almost indispensable at this stage of his operations.

Mason asked: "Why don't we wait till morning, when me and Dave can ride up in the open? This guy, Bandelier, is more apt to come to the door that way. We might even serve the papers on him and get him to come along peaceful. That's the way Pringle figured it."

Pancho replied: "If we do it in daylight, we'll have to bump off his kids after we get rid of him. Pringle never thought about the kids, I'll bet. I don't mind knocking 'em off, if we have to, but I'd rather not. In the dark they won't see anybody, and we can ride away in the clear."

Dave Estes, the other deputy marshal, said: "It makes sense to me. I don't trust guys like Bandelier. They got second sight sometimes. He'll maybe read us like a book and won't open the door. Might even burn us down, if he's as tough as you say."

His partner said: "You gettin' cold feet?"

"Naw, I'm just talkin' good sense."

They rode on without any further discussion. Pancho assembled the whole group around him again when they were within a mile of the Bandelier buildings, where he told off the details. To Devil Ed he said: "You take these two marshals around back by the creek. They can sneak up onto the front porch from there. Be quick about it, before that storm gets here. Somebody might get up to take a leak and happen to look out about the time lightning shows you up like a sore thumb. The rest of you follow me. I aim to work down behind the barn. When Devil Ed lets us know you guys are on the porch, I'll have someone that Bandelier doesn't know ride up and halloo the house and ask to put up for the night."

"Suppose Bandelier says to put up in the barn and doesn't open thc door?" Mason questioned.

"In that case we work it the other way and wait till morning for you guys to serve your papers."

They hadn't figured their man right and thus failed to ask themselves what to do if Cleve wasn't suckered by the decoy. When that was what happened, Pancho decided he could at least give Cleve a good scare and then let the two marshals come back alone and get him some other time. That was a big mistake. When Junior's fire arrows ignited the hay piles and lit up the yard like a Christmas tree, Pancho was the first to recognize the danger and cut out, retreating behind the barn. He had survived the Civil War unscathed because of both quick thinking and callous disregard of anyone's neck but his own.

After their initial panic, Wingfield's men assembled again behind the barn. Someone said: "Who was shootin'?"

Another replied: "Bandelier cut down them two marshals. I saw the damn' fools run for it. They're a-layin' out there in the yard."

"God damn!" said Pancho. "I underestimated that son of a bitch. Why didn't those two damn' fools run back the way they came?" Presuming that he had answered his own question, he added: "We'd best stay out here behind the barn till this storm lets up. They're apt to pick somebody off, if lightning shows us up while we're makin' a run for it."

"I'd like to take my chances on that," someone muttered, low-voiced.

"Who the hell said that?" Pancho asked. When no one replied, Pancho growled: "I'll shoot any lily-livered damn' fool that tries to back out now. Some of you get in the barn and pepper the house through them front windows." No one seemed anxious to be the first to go inside the barn, so Wingfield threatened: "You think there's a boogie man in there? I'll go first. Best place to be while it's rainin', anyhow. Tie them horses and let's all get inside."

The whole crew went in and worked their way to the windows. Pancho poked the glass out of a window and waited. Others followed his example. After watching a while, Pancho was almost sure the lightning showed up someone at one of the second-story windows, probably Bandelier himself. He waited for another flash and put a shot through it, followed by a second the next time the night was lit up.

"Pepper the bastard good," he urged his men.

They poured in a volley. Pancho was thinking over his

options. None of them pleased him. They'd botched the deal. Although he had Bandelier holed up, he couldn't get at him. It was common knowledge that his house was a fortress. They could keep him trapped but with no chance of smoking him out before one of his neighbors stumbled onto them and recognized Bandelier's plight, then roused the whole country. The Mexicans from Zamora Plaza alone could bring a hundred or more by the next afternoon, and he knew they bitterly hated the syndicate. If he waited for that to happen, he'd find their positions reversed, himself surrounded and outnumbered. He had no doubt those small landholders would wipe out him and his crew with as little compunction as he felt about killing Bandelier and his kids.

His obvious move was to bring in the sheriff, much as he hated to have him involved. Butler was a syndicate man, but Wingfield always felt he was his own man first. Besides, he'd have to explain to him what he was doing here in the first place. He wished he'd had sense enough not to stick his nose in where it really wasn't needed. On the other hand, if he got the sheriff out soon enough, they'd catch Cleve with the bodies, and he'd be put out of the way legally — might even stretch hemp.

He had no idea how long it would take for the sheriff to get on the scene. Another unhappy thought was that he hadn't covered the back of the house. After yelling threats back and forth with Cleve, he'd pulled back. The Bandeliers might have gone out the back way and got away on foot by now. If even the boy left and had gone for help, he and his men could be in a hell of a pickle. Bandelier had scores of friends up in this country. He thought: *Much as I'd like to stay right here and keep the place surrounded, we can't take the chance.*

He decided to pull back a few miles, set up a camp, and wait for Sheriff Butler to show up. He even considered pulling out entirely and simply not mentioning the whole thing, but he feared that some of his men would blab, sooner or later. Pringle would surely raise holy hell when the truth came out.

As soon as the storm moved on, they left as quietly as possible. If the Bandeliers saw them, they didn't send any parting shots after them. Maybe they were gone. Probably not. In Bandelier's boots he'd try to get rid of those bodies before he left. Bandelier had a lot to lose if two killings were laid at his door. On the other hand, if he could get rid of the bodies, he could brazen it out and hang onto his ranch. His alternatives otherwise were to risk jail or go on the dodge.

Wingfield figured that at least Cleve was still in the house, and he wouldn't make his move until morning. This reasoning prompted him to leave Devil Ed behind, watching the place as he'd been doing for several days. If Cleve managed to pack out the bodies before the sheriff got there, Ed could follow and see where he took them.

Devil Ed had posted himself in a clump of junipers on the ridge above the ranch, hunkered beneath his slicker, his horse tethered out of sight behind the ridge. The next morning he saw Cleve emerge from the front door and cautiously make his way to the barn. He had a notion to take a shot at him but wanted to see what he was up to, so he waited. Maybe the kids would follow Cleve outside when they thought the coast was clear. Then he'd know for sure that neither of them had gone for help. He definitely didn't want to get caught by a mob of Mexicans and Indians who would savor an excuse to finish the job they'd started on him years before.

When no one followed Cleve outside, Devil Ed decided to take a shot at him when he came out of the barn. He might be able to finish Bandelier and earn a bonus, which he knew Wingfield would be glad to pay. His chance came once Cleve returned to the bodies and stopped to examine them. His shot only missed because Cleve bent over just as he fired. He started to reload the single-shot buffalo gun and was rudely surprised by a quick return shot. He cut out up the hill, slipped, recovered his footing, and was soon out of range.

Chapter Seventeen

About an hour after Johnny was shot, the Voerbeck entourage reached Dorado. Doc Ewing was sent for immediately, and, since he wasn't yet drunk, he showed up promptly. Ewing had received his early training as a Regimental Surgeon during the Civil War and, although he was a little deficient in bedside manner, had mastered the specialties of the military medical breed: he was an ace at gunshot wounds, treating venereal disease, and diagnosing malingering. He had no trouble determining that Johnny wasn't malingering.

Since the boy was in a lot of pain, Ewing performed a brief examination, then injected him with a large dose of morphine. He was sure the injury wouldn't prove fatal, unless it became badly infected. He inserted a drain in the wound on both sides and stitched the torn flesh together. His diagnosis was the same as Mariposa's: a broken collarbone due to entry by a bullet that went straight through and a broken arm that he reset and put in a cast.

When he was finished, aiming the question at whoever wanted to volunteer an answer, he asked: "How did this happen?"

Mariposa briefly told Ewing about the attack on the herd and drovers.

Ewing surmised who the attackers had been since he'd seen Wingfield and his crew leave town, headed toward Tres Huérfanos.

"Can we get the authorities here soon?" Mariposa asked.

Ewing thought that over and pretended to be making another inspection of his work while weighing an answer that would say just enough about the authorities in that part of the world. He recognized the Voerbeck name and wasn't about to tell them that they probably wouldn't want an investigation if they knew what was going on. In any case the syndicate owned the sheriff for all practical purposes, and, if they called him then or next week, it wouldn't really make a hell of a lot of difference. He compromised. "Out here this sort of thing happens pretty regular. I wouldn't bother the sheriff till morning. Nothing he can do, anyhow. Those fellows that did the shooting will be out of the country before he could take a posse up there."

"What an awful place!" Mariposa exclaimed.

"Good climate, though," the doctor countered.

Voerbeck decided to take charge. He thought he'd formed an accurate notion of what was going on. The crew he'd seen attacking Bandelier's men were probably his own, recovering stolen cattle. He knew syndicate influence assured that the sheriff wouldn't be too anxious to investigate the affair, and he wasn't sure he wanted him to — at least not until he knew more about the situation. After all, why did his men, who had the right on their side, have to conceal themselves behind hoods? Ransom had never mentioned hoods, and he'd have to ask him. Was it possible that Bandelier's bandits were so strong that syndicate men were afraid to expose their faces?

About calling in the sheriff he said: "We won't bother him tonight. Do you have a hospital where we can put this man to be properly cared for?"

Ewing snorted. "I wish I did. Dorado ain't that big. Wait'll you get a look at it in the morning. If people have something real bad, we get 'em up to Santa Fé, if they can stand the trip . . . the Army takes 'em in at Fort Marcy. If they have any money, the Army charges 'em for it, and, if they don't,

Uncle Sam foots the bill. Around here folks have to mend at home . . . if they ain't got a home, me and the missus take 'em in."

Voerbeck understood conditions like that. "We'll keep him here in our car for now. My daughter is a good nurse."

Ewing looked at Mariposa with respect. "I reckon it was you that bandaged him up then and put that temporary splint on his arm. I couldn't have done a better job myself."

She smiled. "Thank you. And I'll be glad to continue taking care of him."

Her father said: "We'll take him out to the ranch with us tomorrow, since there are no facilities in town." That, of course, would present an opportunity to interrogate one of Bandelier's outlaw crew. Thinking that, he added: "Maybe we can get the sheriff to come out there and talk to him."

"I'd guess so," the doctor agreed, but he thought: *This is really something. Wait'll Wingfield finds out one of Cleve's boys he shot up is convalescing out there at the ranch!* He wondered if Wingfield might not try to have Johnny finished off to keep him quiet. He wouldn't put it past him. He also wondered what the Voerbecks would do, if and when Wingfield concocted a story about who the wounded man was. Somehow these people didn't impress him as the kind who would throw out a helpless kid, regardless of what they were told. Ewing knew Cleve well and was one of the people who didn't believe the syndicate and ring propaganda about him. He knew Wingfield and Pringle, too, and sized them up for exactly what they were — ruthless men with unlimited ambition who would stop at nothing.

"I own a ranch near here and have never been there," Voerbeck told Ewing. "Can you suggest someone who might show me the way out to it?"

"I figured you must be *that* Voerbeck. I'd be glad to help you take this boy out there in the morning, and that'll take care of that. I'll bring what passes for our local ambulance and lead the way. Maybe you'd like me to get the livery stable to send over a carriage for you folks, since no one at the ranch knows you're here?"

"That would be good," Grut Voerbeck agreed.

Doc thought: *That old boy ain't anybody's fool. If I was in his shoes, I'd show up without any brass band and start snooping around on my own, too. Word about what's going on around here must've got back to him.*

Bright and early the next morning Doc Ewing showed up with his makeshift ambulance, a spring wagon with a bow top for rainy weather. The bed was filled with a thick layer of straw with a mattress on top. Due to the wagon's tendency occasionally to swerve crazily, as though exhibiting a mind of its own, Doc called it "The Lunatic."

When he stepped down, Mariposa met him and apologized since they were still at breakfast. "We didn't expect you so soon. Have you had anything to eat?"

"Yep, but I wouldn't mind a cup of coffee."

He comfortably seated himself at the immaculately appointed dining-room table. Percy Waterford offered him a cigar from his leather case.

"Don't mind if I do, thanks," Doc said.

The baron, a man of steel, was able to look perfectly cool while he watched Ewing cut about an inch off the end of the expensive cigar with his Barlow pocket knife, tamp it down into a corncob pipe, and shove the rest away in his vest pocket. He struck a match on the leg of his trousers and lit up, puffing contentedly. Grut Voerbeck enjoyed the performance immensely but appeared not to notice, looking at his daughter and winking when he was sure Doc wasn't looking. She smiled. Lady Fetherstonhaugh kept a poker face and almost choked on her coffee over the effort.

Before leaving, Doc gave Johnny another shot of morphine. With the help of the train crew he moved him into the wagon and then led the way. The Voerbecks followed in a livery stable surrey.

Grut Voerbeck didn't miss a thing on the way to the ranch. There were no cattle in sight, which might confirm what Ransom had told him about being rustled blind — but, of course, he was thinking in European terms, forgetting that the grant was over twenty-five miles wide by one hundred miles long. He liked the looks of the deep, wide valley with the small river winding through it. Cottonwoods and willows fringed the river's banks. Extensive orchards and irrigated hay and grain fields bordered it for the last mile before they reached the ranch buildings.

Those came as a shock to him, since Ransom had said one of the reasons he shouldn't visit was the inadequacy of the facilities. He'd seen châteaux that looked modest by comparison with the rambling adobe main dwelling, surrounded by deep verandahs with dozens of chimneys denoting fireplaces in each room. He savored the idea of confronting Lord Ransom about misleading him as soon as he could arrange a private meeting. He also took in the extensive outbuildings and corrals, recognizing that some must be stables, but was curious about the two neat rows of adobe houses that housed Ransom's polo teams.

Randy McCoy, Wingfield's straw boss for maintenance of the ranch area and farming operation, saw the Voerbeck cavalcade coming and angrily rode out to head off whoever had ignored the **No Hay Paso — No Trespassing** signs posted at the beginning of the long poplar-bordered entrance drive. He recognized Doc Ewing and stopped him.

"What the hell is going on?" he demanded, then looked in the wagon. "Who's that, one of our boys?"

"Nope," said Doc. "If I'm not mistaken, it's one of Cleve Bandelier's boys."

McCoy exploded. "Why the hell are you bringing him here?"

Doc was really enjoying himself since he didn't especially like McCoy to begin with. He motioned over his shoulder toward the surrey, following. "He's with them."

McCoy's boiling point was approaching. "Doc, I ain't in any mood for a lot of guff. Who are they?"

"Why don't you ask them? I may not have got it right."

"I'll damn' well do that, since you ain't makin' any more sense than a locoed calf."

He rode back to the other vehicle, saw the ladies, and removed his Stetson. Pretty women were scarce around Dorado and beautiful ones almost never seen. He was tongue-tied for a minute, then recovered and addressed Grut Voerbeck whom he picked as the leader. "Are you folks lost? We don't allow visitors here." His voice was definitely unfriendly.

Voerbeck raised his hat and replaced it. "I appreciate your concern. Perhaps my name will be familiar. I am Grut Voerbeck. I own the Amarillo Grant. Is Lord Ransom here?"

McCoy's face registered several things in rapid order: surprise, consternation, awe, panic, and fawning respect. He thought: *Holy Christ! What a hell of a time for Ransom and Wingfield to be gone.* He didn't know what to do or say.

Voerbeck realized the man's perplexity. "Perhaps you'd be good enough to show us to the house and help us get settled. We will be here for a long stay."

"Yes sir. I can sure do that. Pardon me for looking surprised. Nobody told me you were coming."

Voerbeck said: "Nobody knew I was coming. Where is Lord Ransom?"

"I don't know," replied McCoy. "He left early, according to the man down at the stables, and didn't say where he was going. Maybe somebody up at the house knows."

"Very well, lead the way."

As he rode ahead, McCoy was thinking rapidly and concluded he had better contact Ransom and Wingfield as quickly as he could.

Carmen and Belen Perez were frightened at first over this sudden arrival, then their natural warm natures and concern for the comfort of visitors asserted itself. After some fifteen minutes of confusion the two housekeepers found the newcomers suitable rooms and got a couple of Mexican ranch hands to move in all the baggage.

"Any rooms are all right for now," Mariposa assured them. "We can move around later if we decide to."

Lord Ransom had never told Carmen that he had a woman in Europe, but her instinct told her who Mariposa was. She watched this golden women with awe. The natural jealousy the situation generated made her wonder what her position would be now. This was the way it had always been for women like her, and she accepted that.

McCoy stood around on one foot, getting in the way, and decided to duck out when no one was looking. Unfortunately for him Voerbeck was looking and called to him: "Don't leave yet. I want to talk to you. Where is a good place for us to talk privately?"

McCoy, squirming inwardly, managed to say: "I guess we could use Lord Ransom's office. He and Wingfield both use it."

"That will be fine. Lead the way. Who is Wingfield?" Before the man could answer, he turned to the others who were gathered in the living room. "Mister McCoy and I will be conferring for a while, if you will excuse us."

Voerbeck didn't hesitate to seat himself behind what he assumed was Lord Ransom's desk. The office was a large room with bookcases along all the walls between high, deep windows and on each side of the fireplace. The construction of the entire building suggested to Voerbeck that Ransom had spent lavishly to achieve comfort, expenditures that somehow hadn't shown up on the accounts he'd submitted.

"Sit down," Voerbeck invited. "I assume you are in charge when Lord Ransom is not here. You mentioned his leaving without letting anyone know of his whereabouts. Does he do that often?"

McCoy recognized that he was on the spot and was going to have a very bad time of it, both now and later when he accounted to Wingfield and Ransom for anything he said that he shouldn't have. He took the chair and held his Stetson in his hands, twisting it awkwardly. Voerbeck thought he looked like a schoolboy being confronted by the headmaster and held back a grin.

McCoy decided his best alternative was simply to tell the truth. "Lord Ransom comes and goes pretty much as he pleases without telling anyone . . . least of all me. Maybe he tells Mister Wingfield."

"Ah, yes, Mister Wingfield. I asked who he was?"

"He's the boss right under Lord Ransom."

Grut wondered why he'd never so much as heard the name. He could think of no legitimate reason why he hadn't. "Do you know how many cattle this ranch has on it?"

"Not exactly."

"Are you concerned with the cattle operation, Mister McCoy?"

"Not directly."

"What do you do?"

"I take care of raising hay, irrigating the orchards, and boss the Mexicans who work here at the ranch headquarters."

"How many of them are there?"

"About twenty most of the time."

"What do they do?"

"Lots of stuff. They do the farming under me, keep up the buildings, keep the fires going in the winter, take care of horses, that sort of thing."

"Isn't that quite a large number for that purpose?"

"Well, there's about a dozen play polo mostly."

Voerbeck kept an absolutely straight face. "I see," he said, but he didn't see. He particularly didn't see what he needed a polo team for, much less two. Yet, anyone who knew Lord Ransom would understand why *he* might want a polo team, or even a dozen of them. Voerbeck had a mental vision of Montague Ransom walking a plank, with himself shoving a sharp sword in his buttocks. He changed the subject. "I have heard of a man named Bandelier from Lord Ransom. Do you know him?"

"Not very well. I know who he is. I guess everybody does around here. He was one of the first settlers in the country."

"What does he do?"

"Why, he's a rancher. The biggest one around, next to you."

"A rancher. Does he do anything else besides that?"

"Not that I ever heard."

"Is he the leader of a large outlaw band?"

McCoy looked puzzled. "Not around here, he ain't. He was in the Army before he came here. I never heard about him being an outlaw. Of course, Ransom . . . Lord Ransom, I mean . . . and Wingfield don't have any use for him because he's . . ." — here he paused, not knowing how to proceed without bringing up the contested land grant, but, having gone this far, he didn't see any alternative to taking the bull by the horns — "well, because he's the leader of the people fighting you in court."

Voerbeck nodded. "So I've heard. But he isn't a bandit, so far as you know?"

McCoy had a feeling he'd just put his foot in it, that Ransom may have told a different story. If so, that was too damned bad — if Ransom wanted him to lie for him, he should have let him know more about what was going on.

"You're sure Bandelier isn't like Robin Hood?"

McCoy laughed. He recalled Robin Hood from his school days, when the teacher read to them about Robin Hood and his Merry Men — stealing from the rich and giving to the poor. A small glimmering of light was penetrating his mind, regarding this cross-examination. He knew the ranch was losing cows. He had his own ideas where they were going, and it wasn't to Robin Hood. This old boy smelled a rat and was using him to help ferret it out.

Voerbeck's assumptions went out the window with McCoy's revelations. If what he had seen the day before was not his fearless men, attempting to recover his rustled cattle from the Robin Hood, Bandelier, what had it been? "Tell me this," he asked McCoy, "who in this country would be riding horses and wearing white hoods over their heads and shooting at men who were driving a herd of cattle to market?"

McCoy's heart skipped a beat, then picked up at a more rapid rate. He tried to give a convincing snort of amusement. "There are rumors of people like that, but it's mostly in the newspapers. I never heard of anyone who actually saw that sort of thing." As he said it, he knew he could have taken Voerbeck out to the stables and shown him a locked box full of such hoods.

Voerbeck eyed him severely through his glasses. "You have never met anyone who has seen that sort of thing? You're sure?"

McCoy got a picture of that cowboy of Bandelier's who was now in a room under this very roof and thought he was going to be produced as a witness who'd seen the Whitecaps. He anticipated that. "I wouldn't be inclined to believe anyone who said they did."

"Well, Mister McCoy, I saw that sort of thing yesterday afternoon at a place along the railroad called . . . I believe . . . Tres Huérfanos."

McCoy's jaw dropped.

"You look surprised?"

"I am surprised."

"Do you have any idea who those men were?"

"No sir, I don't."

Voerbeck judged from McCoy's expression that he was lying, although he'd rather not. He turned the line of questioning into a new avenue. "How many riders does Lord Ransom employ here in addition to the twenty who chop wood and play polo?" He was being deliberately droll, but it went over McCoy's head completely.

"At least a dozen cowboys."

"Where are they now? I didn't see a single one."

McCoy shrugged. "They work out on the range, all over."

"Do large numbers of them ever work together?"

"Only during roundup season."

"And when is that?"

"Usually during the spring and fall."

"Well, Mister McCoy, we have a mystery on our hands that you may be able to help me solve. A large group of men, wearing the hoods I described, attacked Mister Bandelier's herd of cattle at Tres Huérfanos yesterday afternoon and shot the young man who's here, recuperating. They would have killed him but for Baron Waterford, interfering with a shotgun. I have been told by Lord Ransom that Mister Bandelier is a bandit. Obviously he is not. Can you imagine why I have been misled in this manner?"

McCoy thought: *If you can't figure that out, I sure can't help you.* He said: "I don't really have any idea. Nobody tells me anything except how much hay they'd like me to grow, or when they want a window or door fixed, or a room painted. That sort of thing." He laughed at his own poor performance.

The laugh was so ingenuous Voerbeck felt sorry for him. Here was a fellow that liked his job, wanted to stay out of trouble, and, in time, might even tell the truth to accomplish that end. Voerbeck decided he couldn't spare him. Nonetheless, he recognized that he wasn't going to get the information he was fishing for just yet. He rose, signaling the end of the meeting. "Thank you. You've been very helpful. If you find out where Lord Ransom went, send someone after him and tell him I want to talk to him. The same goes for Mister Wingfield. I must meet them soon."

McCoy thought: *I'll bet both of them will have a hot time with this old boy. I'd like to be a little mouse, listening in.* He said: "Yes, sir, I'll ask around and see if I can find out where they are. Mister Wingfield took a crew out to work some cows yesterday, so he can't be too far away. Maybe Ransom . . . I mean Lord Ransom . . . is with them."

"Thank you," said Voerbeck. "And, by the way, you don't have to call him Lord Ransom around me . . . unless he's here himself." There was a slight hint of a friendly twinkle in his eye when he said it. Voerbeck sensed he was a fundamentally honest man, perhaps one of the few he was going to find working for him. Experience had taught him they were hard to come by. He intended to remove the pressure that was making McCoy evasive now and question him again sometime soon.

As for McCoy, he liked his job. It was the best one he had ever had, and one he hoped to keep. He figured there was a chance to do that, if played his cards right. After getting the drift of what Voerbeck must suspect, he wouldn't have made the same bet about either Ransom or Wingfield. He'd spotted the man he intended to play to from now on.

Inquiry by McCoy among the Mexicans turned up one who forgot he was supposed to tell McCoy that Ransom had left word he'd be over at the Bandelier ranch. Ransom had even said that he was going there with the sheriff, since there'd apparently been some trouble, involving Wingfield's men. He decided he'd better ride after Ransom himself.

McCoy knew that there was a lot of friction between Bandelier, the other squatters, and the syndicate, but he hadn't thought it would come to the shooting stage so quickly, if at all. He'd hoped to avoid shooting, having been down in Lincoln County a few years before, where he'd pulled out once the shooting started. Anyone who'd been there could read the signs all over the Texans that Wingfield had imported. They were the same hard kind he'd seen drifting into Lincoln County. A large contingent of them had pulled out of the ranch the day before. After hearing from Voerbeck, he suspected they probably had a lot to do with any trouble over at Bandelier's — also at Tres Huérfanos.

McCoy found Ransom at Sheriff Butler's camp and tried to draw him to one side for a private talk, but Ransom was more interested in the arrival of the scout who reported the recovery of the two dead marshals' bodies and tried to brush him off. McCoy decided to get his attention the best way he could think of and loudly said: "I thought you'd like to know that a Mister Voerbeck is over to the ranch."

That got Ransom's attention. "Say that again."

"A Mister Grut Voerbeck asked me to come over here and tell you he wants to see you. Wingfield, too."

"Not so loud!" Ransom cautioned. He quickly looked around to make sure the sheriff hadn't heard. He was afraid of Butler's new independence and recognized the need to prepare

Voerbeck for meeting him. No telling what Butler might tell him. He drew McCoy well aside. "Is Voerbeck alone?"

"Got some more furriners with him. His daughter and some other woman and Baron somebody or other."

"Waterford?" Ransom guessed.

"Sounds like it," McCoy agreed. "And Doc Ewing."

"What's he doing there?"

"They brought in some guy that got shot up at Tres Huérfanos."

"Why would they do that?"

"They way I got it, a bunch of fellows wearing white hoods jumped Bandelier's crew up there and shot one of them."

Ransom looked carefully at McCoy to see if he was being snide, but McCoy, who knew he wasn't intended to know anything about the whitecaps, successfully masked his knowledge. He suspected that to survive in this dangerous situation, his best strategy would be to keep up his pose as a stolid bumpkin.

Wingfield, if he'd overheard McCoy, would have found that extremely disquieting, since he'd managed to keep any information about the affair at Tres Huérfanos from Ransom who now quickly recognized that he'd been hoodwinked. He'd have to talk to Wingfield as soon as possible. The Texan had obviously got the fat in the fire by going off half-cocked.

Ransom had no desire to confront Voerbeck until he talked with Wingfield. "Don't tell Voerbeck you came out here," he told McCoy. "Don't let him know that you know where I am." He took out his purse and passed a twenty dollar gold piece to McCoy. "There's more where that came from, if you keep quiet about this. It's very important. I can't tell you why just now, but believe me it is. Now get out of here fast. I don't want anyone here to know Voerbeck is around, especially the sheriff."

McCoy didn't see any reason not to do as Ransom's asked,

at least for the time being, nor did he see any harm in not mentioning Voerbeck's presence to anyone else. Twenty dollars was a substantial sum, and he was smart enough to know he'd most likely just found a gold mine.

As he rode away, he was mulling over all that he'd learned that morning. He concluded that, if he were either Ransom or Wingfield, he'd probably be packing his bag as soon as possible, before he was invited. Of course, they hadn't yet talked to Voerbeck. He wondered how Ransom, who knew the old man, could have been so stupid as to assume he could pull the wool over his eyes. Wingfield had a wonderful experience in store for him, too, if McCoy was any judge.

Chapter Eighteen

Doc Ewing was called away by a messenger from town and left shortly after the Voerbeck party got settled. As he was leaving, he said: "If he gets worse, send for me. If I ain't in town, they'll know where to reach me, and I'll come as soon as I can."

Grut Voerbeck spent the rest of the morning rummaging in the account books in the ranch office and found the effort highly rewarding. He was not surprised — particularly after his cross examination of Randy McCoy — to find little resemblance between them and the reports that had been made to him. He gained a pretty good idea where things really stood and realized another reason why the enterprise hadn't shown a profit aside from cattle losses. Lord Ransom had been living very well, augmenting his salary by a multiple of at least ten. In addition, he had a large number of men on the payroll at salaries far higher than he had been told were the going wages in the country. He was, as yet, unfamiliar with what were called "fighting wages."

After ransacking the office, Grut had a leisurely lunch with the others and a cigar and coffee in the living room. Then he excused himself. "Time for this old boy's nap."

He was constitutionally suited for one of the congenial amenities of Southwestern existence. He loved his naps and would only have to change the name to *siesta* to conform to local custom.

Mariposa left the baron and Lady Fetherstonhaugh in the large living room, chatting, and wandered away to explore the house. She had placed Johnny in the care of Carmen, who immediately melted at the sight of someone suffering and seated herself beside his bed, feeling his forehead for a fever, then taking one of his hands in hers to transmit her strength to him.

Mariposa had said: "If he gets restless, call me."

Carmen had her own idea about what to do if he got restless, which was take care of him herself as she and her people knew best how to do. She admired Mariposa's blonde beauty, but she didn't feel that anyone so lovely would be able to do much that was practical. On the other hand, Mariposa wasn't sure that an uneducated rustic could nurse anyone seriously injured.

Mariposa was pleased by the *hacienda*'s architecture and furnishings and intrigued by the Navajo rugs and Indian pots that decorated the rooms. Some of the pots were extremely fine, having been skillfully glazed and fired in intricate patterns, a few with subtle pink fire blushes that Mariposa had never seen before. The rugs were tightly woven, obviously made by hand, and cleverly dyed in bright colors.

She returned to the living room. "I'm going to walk around outside. Do you two want to join me?"

Waterford declined. "I'm going to take a leaf out of your father's book and nap. I've been sleepy ever since we reached Denver. The altitude, probably. I get the same way in Switzerland."

"How about you, Daisy?" Mariposa asked.

Lady Fetherstonhaugh shook her head. "Inspecting grounds and livestock isn't my forté. You go ahead. I may take a beauty rest myself. At my age I need it."

Waterford snorted ungallantly and earned a hard look from Daisy. "Don't ask," she said.

"Ask what?"

"What age that is."

"I already know."

As she was leaving, Mariposa heard her say: "I lied." She

called back: "Keep an eye on our patient while I'm gone."

Outside, she examined the trees and plants, many of which were new to her, then strolled to the outbuildings and corrals and was surprised to discover no horses in what was obviously a stable. She examined the strange saddles with high pommels and cantles, wondering who would want to sit on such unwieldy and dangerous-looking things. There were also a good many English saddles and even a couple of ladies' sidesaddles. She recognized Ransom's cavalry saddle as well. She wondered what in the world was the purpose of the horns on the American saddles and, of course, didn't know what they were called.

As she looked around, she became aware of someone observing her and, turning, saw what she assumed was a Mexican servant. Although she wasn't fluent with her school-girl Spanish, she divined that was the language she should use.

"*Buenas días.*"

This brought a big smile to his face. "*Buenas días,*" he replied, and inclined slightly in what she thought was a charming little bow. It put her fully at ease.

She couldn't think of anything more to say, so merely continued with her investigation. Outside, she discovered a corral behind the barn in which there were a half dozen horses. Her new companion followed her. "Can I ride these?" she asked.

He shrugged. She didn't realize that he wasn't sure she knew how to ride anything, much less a ranch-broke mustang.

Finally she said: "Saddle one for me." In her eagerness to be on a horse she forgot her wounded patient in the house.

He hesitated.

Sensing his problem, she said: "I can ride."

She watched as he took a braided leather rope that had been coiled around a corral post and climbed in among the horses, which circled away from him. He threw a loop of the rope from behind his shoulder and snared a small line-back dun. She was fascinated and would have been even more so had she realized that he caught exactly the horse he intended. She expected the horse to fight him, but it became tractable as soon as he jerked the rope tight around its neck.

He led it to the stable, haltered it, and secured the rope to a ring in the stable's masonry wall. He then went inside and returned with one of the sidesaddles, a Navajo saddle blanket, and a silver-mounted bridle with the most villainous-looking bit she'd ever seen. He had the horse ready for her quickly. She'd never had a horse tacked in such short order.

When he finished, he said: "Wait."

He saddled a horse for himself. Finally he went into the stable and returned with a rifle in a scabbard that he fastened to his saddle. He made no explanation and didn't have to. She was fully aware that the country still harbored hostile Indians and dangerous outlaws.

He led her horse to a mounting block and held it while she climbed aboard.

"I will adjust your stirrup," he said, but it was half a question. He was obviously fearful that he might accidentally touch and offend her.

"Please do," she reassured him.

She tested the horse's response to reining as soon as he turned it loose. She was totally unaware that it neck-reined, and her European plow-horse technique, even though she had light hands, made it nervous almost at once.

Her companion had seen dudes try to ride Western horses before and attempted to explain the problem to her. Finally he bounced onto his horse like an uncoiling spring and said: "I will show you."

She watched him, tried what he was doing, and the horse responded immediately, settling down.

They moved out together, with him leading the way, then

drawing slightly behind to watch in case she got in trouble with her mount. He was pleased to observe that she knew how to handle a horse, a fact of which the horse was also quickly aware. After a while she tried a trot, then a lope, gratified to discover that the horse was completely controllable and made no effort to take its head and run away with her. If it had, she was confident she would stay on it and ride it down, provided it didn't fall.

They rode along the stream on which the ranch buildings were located, then up into the juniper-dotted hills. Once her Mexican guardian cautioned: "Not that way. Maybe *los Indios.*"

He led the way along the ridge, overlooking the ranch buildings far below. "Maybe go back now," he finally suggested. "*Señor* Ransom will be unhappy with Domingo." He pointed at his chest when he said Domingo.

"Don't worry," she said.

From their look-out rippling ranges of hills rose in waves to snow-capped peaks. As they climbed, the juniper belt mingled with bigger trees that she would learn were called Apache pines. She made a vow to ride to the far peaks some day, whether anyone wanted her to or not.

A voice spoke inside her. *This is the place. This is home.* Suddenly she knew that this was *her* country, that she'd been born away from her home and had just returned. The incense of junipers and pines filled her lungs and was utterly different, far more heady and pungent than conifers in settled parts of the world. Was it only her imagination, prompted by the strangeness and her knowledge that this was still a savage, only partly civilized land? She felt a powerful urge to ride on and on to the far horizon, so clearly and sharply defined in the dry air, then cross that far ridge, and another, and another, until she'd explored them all. She would take a bodyguard, if need be, but go. . . . She came to her senses with the realization that she'd left without a thought of the wounded man in her charge.

To Domingo she said: "I forgot something. I must go back quickly."

He nodded and led the way at the fastest pace he considered safe. When they hit the flat land, Mariposa urged her horse into a run, Domingo siding her, neck and neck, looking at her once and grinning broadly. She threw back her head and laughed out loud, thrilled by the wind whipping her face, the thundering of hoofs.

This is the place, the voice said again. She was still breathless and glowing when she arrived at the house.

Daisy was on the verandah and met her. "Where in the world have you been? We had started to worry."

"You needn't have. I was out for a ride. How is the patient?"

"Sleeping like a baby. He was awake a while and talked to the girl. She's still with him, holding his hand. She's an angel."

Chapter Nineteen

Pancho Wingfield returned to Butler's camp with the men who brought in the two bodies. He checked with Butler, whose only orders were: "Put them bodies downwind somewhere. I sent for Doc Ewing, but Lord knows when he'll show up."

After talking to McCoy, Ransom motioned to Pancho with a jerk of his head.

"What's eatin' you?" Wingfield asked, rolling a cigarette.

"Voerbeck is over at the ranch."

Pancho paused and looked at Ransom closely, interrupting his cigarette rolling. The news didn't bother him as much as it did his lordship. He didn't have as much to lose, though he wanted to hang onto his soft job with a license to steal as much as Ransom. He turned over the possibilities. The syndicate owner hadn't sent word he was coming, and he probably smelled a rat. Another thought occurred to him — the sightseers who'd interrupted his raid the previous afternoon at Tres Huérfanos were foreigners. He asked: "Do you have any idea how Voerbeck sneaked in?"

"On a private train," Ransom replied. "If I'm any judge, they got a look at some of your handiwork over at Tres Huérfanos on their way in." He watched Pancho closely as he said this.

"How's that?"

"A bunch of men wearing white hoods shot up Bandelier's cowboys, so I hear, and ran off his herd."

Wingfield laughed. "You don't say? I wonder who that was?"

"Why didn't you tell me before now?"

Wingfield laughed again. "I'm trying to keep stuff like that off your conscience . . . especially after the fit you had when you found out about them bear hunters."

"And I'm trying to keep us both out of trouble," Ransom reminded him. "If you'd have kept away from those bear hunters, as you called them, they might have brought Bandelier in by themselves without any trouble."

"That wasn't exactly the idea."

"Well, they'd have got him out of his house and taken care of him. In any case, we wouldn't have the sheriff up here, snooping, and Bandelier might be out of the picture. Did it happen to occur to you that, after you interfered and got those two killed, you might simply have gone away and let Bandelier get rid of the bodies, instead of trying to get the law to do our work? You could have said nothing about it and gone after him again later."

"Word would have leaked out anyhow," Wingfield defended himself.

"And?"

That stumped him. "I don't know." It was said weakly. This cross examination by a man he'd heretofore considered a cipher took him by surprise and didn't sit well. He knew who'd gotten the whole operation off track and could admit it to himself, but he didn't like this Englishman's implying he'd done something stupid. "Blame it on Pringle," he added. "He's the one who got greedy. He wanted Bandelier out of the way because he beat him out of a beef contract at Fort Union."

Ransom hadn't known that. He reflected just how precarious his situation was due to associating with ruthless, unscrupulous people — schemers at cross-purposes with one another and him — while he had to try at the same time to hoodwink Voerbeck. He wondered if Percy Waterford would take him back to manage his farm if this situation went sour. He rather thought he would, and that was a small comfort. He looked forward to seeing Percy again. He'd love the hunting here.

His mind came back to their present dilemma. "Did Pringle ask you to bring a bunch of gunmen out with those two marshals?"

Wingfield's hesitation answered the question.

Ransom continued: "Of course, he didn't. We'll be lucky to get out of this with whole skins. Pringle could ruin us both."

"Yeah, and we can ruin him, too," Pancho insisted.

"In any case, Voerbeck is nobody's fool. He wants to talk to us. I told McCoy not to let him know he'd found me, so we don't have to go right over there."

"I may not go right over there now or any other time," Wingfield declared. "I aim to talk to Pringle before I see the old Dutchman. Maybe I'll quit, and you can blame me for everything the old boy doesn't like. What have I got to lose?"

The suggestion surprised Ransom but made sense. As far as that went, what did he himself have to lose? He had more eggs in Pringle's basket than in Voerbeck's, assuming his marriage plans went out the window. He was half owner with Pringle of a lot of cows somewhere in Wyoming, and he'd heard the grizzly bear hunting up there was outstanding. What he didn't know was that Pringle had no notion of ever delivering to him his half of the cows. If he'd have thought about it, Ransom would have realized he didn't even know where Pringle's Wyoming ranch was — or if he really had one.

Wingfield could see that he'd started Ransom thinking about who was going to take the blame when Voerbeck found out his range had been stripped. He said: "First of all, I aim to stay here and try to put Bandelier out of the way, if I can. As far as we've gone now, that's the only thing to do. We can both blame him for our main problem, and, if he's dead, Voerbeck won't have much choice but to take our word for where his cows went. If Butler gets him, and he stands trial, we might not like what he has to say in court. We're better off if he never gets there."

Ransom nodded. All the same he wondered how he'd got into such a mess and wished he was elsewhere. "I guess I might as well go over and face the music. Get word to me what you're doing. We're in this together."

To himself Wingfield said: *That's what you think.* Aloud he said: "Like I told you, I aim to stay right here until I find out about Bandelier. Then I might go down and have a talk with Pringle before I see Voerbeck . . . if I ever do. Right now, I'm going to get some shut eye. I've been up since yesterday mornin'."

Ransom told no one he was leaving. He simply mounted and rode off. His whole future was wrapped up in this affair. He kept his horse at a walk all the way back to the ranch, postponing as long as possible the inevitable embarrassing interview on which his future depended. It was easy to look back at the preceding three years and recognize his mistakes. Foremost among them was not attending to business. When he'd come, he didn't realize the consequences. As long as one could play and pay the price later, if ever, that was what life was about. So he had his polo teams. He could have spent the time learning the cattle business, but he'd had Wingfield to supply his want of knowledge. That led to the siphoning off of Voerbeck's cattle, which appeared to be a small matter as long as he didn't miss them. Indications now all pointed to the fact that Voerbeck had missed them. Even his last interview in Holland with the man had touched on it.

Blaming the losses on Bandelier had seemed then like a stroke of genius, but it might backfire if Bandelier lived to have his day in court. Wingfield hadn't helped. Pringle, behind Wingfield, was an even greater potential threat. He knew enough to ruin Ransom, whereas Wingfield didn't, so far as he knew.

While Ransom was pondering the future, so was Pancho Wingfield. He was weighing his alternatives carefully. Only a fool would deceive himself into thinking that Voerbeck couldn't find out nearly everything about the local situation. In that light Wingfield saw no way he could retain his position on the Amarillo Grant and had no desire to have a nasty interview with the owner as a preliminary to being fired. In his mind he resigned the moment Ransom departed for the ranch. He had a vision of how it would go for the Englishman and didn't envy him. He also did not pity him. In Ransom's situation he'd have played his cards right and fixed himself for life. Well, that was still possible. He and his brother, thanks to Ransom's pliability, had several thousand head of cattle on a prime range in the Nebraska panhandle. He could still realize his dream of living like a grandee in Santa Fé in his golden years.

He was all the more certain that he wouldn't enjoy a peaceful retirement if Bandelier was alive. It was this line of thought that led him to figuring out ways to get the rancher, and this intention accounted for his being out early the following morning, scouring the hills. By pure chance he ran across Junior Bandelier. For a moment he thought he'd bagged his old man when Harmony Dabney shot the horse out from under Junior. He was further infuriated by Butler's attitude toward the kid. After failing to kill the kid, he thought the least they could do was have him sent to the penitentiary. Even at that, it would be a poor compensation for not getting his father.

While he and Dabney were following Butler back to his camp, Pancho turned over the present possibilities for catching Cleve. He wasn't so sure he was as far away as his son had implied. Maybe he was badly wounded and hidden nearby in some secret place. After all, he lived in this locale and would know of some hide-out that could only be found by the most skilled tracker. Then Pancho remembered a tracker who owed him a favor or, more accurately, whom he could force to do his bidding. The year before he had driven a herd of wet cattle to Tascosa, along with a small herd of stolen horses. It was one sure means of picking up money when he was short. One of his cowboys on the drive, a Jicarilla Apache, had knifed a man in Tascosa and made a successful run for it. All he really owed Pancho was for his lie to the authorities that he'd hired Chunz in Anton Chico and knew nothing of him aside from that, which threw them off the track, but it ought to be enough.

Devil Ed, though, was another problem, given the shape he was in. Wingfield had kept him away from the coroner's hearing, fearful he might babble the truth, since his marbles were still scrambled from the blow on his head. The hearing had been a brief affair in which Wingfield and a couple of others lied appropriately, and the verdict, delivered by a jury composed of Wingfield's toadies, was a surprise to no one. The U. S. deputy marshals, Edward Mason and Daniel Estes, had been shot and killed in the line of duty by one Cleve Bandelier while they were trying to serve a summons on him.

Butler had commented: "We'll put in later all that legal bullshit about 'leaden bullets' and other stuff that keeps lawyers in business."

Directly following the capture of Junior Bandelier, the sheriff had his wagon packed and team harnessed. Then he walked over to Wingfield. "I don't see any reason to stay around here," he said. "I'm goin' back to town."

Wingfield asked: "What do you aim to do with that damned Bandelier kid?"

"If his old man doesn't come back, maybe I'll adopt him."

Uncharacteristically Wingfield realized he was being joshed. "You deserve him." Then he changed the subject. "I ain't as sure as you seem to be that Bandelier has dusted out. I'm gonna hang around here another day or so. You wouldn't care to deputize me, would you?"

Butler eyed him coldly. "You're right, Frank, I wouldn't."

Wingfield returned the cold look in kind. "That's what I thought."

Butler turned and walked away, conscious he'd made an enemy out of man who'd been merely a dissatisfied associate up until this time. When he was several steps away, the sheriff turned and said: "Doc ain't takin' Devil Ed along. I guess he can take care of himself."

"I'll see he gets taken care of," Wingfield responded. In fact, he hoped Devil Ed would recover his memory. If he did, there wasn't a more useful man for what he had planned.

Chapter Twenty

Lord Ransom timed his return to the ranch well after dark, unsaddled his own horse, then slowly walked toward the house. Reluctance to face the music caused his feet to drag, and he stopped once, thinking he might go into town and put up at the Santiago. Getting drunk to forget his troubles for a little while appealed to him, and he actually turned and took a couple of steps back toward the stable before realizing he'd already turned his horse loose.

At the front wall he stopped and lit a cigar, then sat, watching lights go out one after another in the various bedrooms, wishing he knew which bedroom was Voerbeck's. Even the thought of seeing Mariposa held no allure for him. In fact, since his intentions were honorable, he'd never so much as kissed her. That wasn't done until after marriage. Besides, wives weren't meant for passion — except the wives of others, of course. A gentleman married to have children and properly took a mistress to avoid bothering a virtuous wife about a woman's "painful duty" except to assure a male heir.

The dim light in the front *sala,* which was always kept burning, was all that shone outside when he finally went to the door. *Now, if only he could sneak in, light one of the lamps kept in the front hall, and slip down to his quarters unaccosted by anyone.* A lamp was lit in the living room, and he tiptoed to the arch to see if someone were still up. Grut Voerbeck was seated in a chair, looking directly at him, as though he'd expected him. For all he knew, maybe he had. The old man had uncanny premonitions that reminded him of Hindu mystics.

"Come in, Lord Ransom," said Voerbeck. "Sit down and join me in a cognac."

Ransom crossed to him, hand extended, and almost choked saying: "It's good to see you. Why didn't you let us know you were coming, so we could have arranged a proper reception and had things ready for you?"

Voerbeck almost grinned at that, thinking the most likely thing he'd have had ready would have been a pile of ashes formed by burning the account books. The prospect of making Ransom repent for his errant behavior was a happy one. Of course, it would be impossible to retain him in his position, but it wasn't necessary to discharge him at once. He would be more forthcoming with information if he assumed he was still hanging on, even though precariously. The matter of the engagement to Mariposa wasn't so simple to resolve; it would depend on her desires. Grut had no objection to settling a large pension on Ransom to provide a suitable domestic establishment and social existence for Mariposa as Lady Ransom. It would certainly have to be contingent on his lordship's remaining married to her and upon his suitable behavior as a husband, all of which he would have to acknowledge in a legal document. Ransom would have kissed Voerbeck's hand, if he'd known the old man was prepared to be that generous with him, but Grut had no intention of letting him discover it.

Voerbeck indicated the bottle of cognac and glasses on the long center table. "Join me?" he suggested again. "I had a long nap this afternoon and am not sleepy. Besides, I get a lot of thinking done when I'm finally alone."

Ransom grasped at that opening. "If you'd rather we talk in the morning, I'll leave you to your thoughts."

"No, no, I prefer to talk now. It was you I was thinking of. You must have had a hard time in these unfamiliar and rude surroundings. Perhaps we haven't been compensating you adequately."

He displayed no outward evidence of irony or sarcasm in his face or voice, though the implication didn't escape Ransom whose hand wasn't entirely steady as he poured his cognac.

"More for you, sir?"

"Yes, please." Voerbeck offered his glass, and Ransom poured shakily, returning the bottle to the table. "I took the liberty of using your office. I found the surroundings most pleasant."

Ransom's heartbeat accelerated. He searched for something to say and found nothing. The account books in the office were, of course, his main concern. Had Voerbeck examined them?

The older man sat comfortably, legs crossed, offering his cognac glass in a silent toast. Ransom lifted his glass and sipped a little. If this was an interrogation, he'd never experienced one like it. No one who'd been favored with one ever forgot Grut's unique approach to business.

"Perhaps you've had a fatiguing day," Voerbeck suggested, "and we should postpone talking until tomorrow."

"I've been out on the range," Ransom confessed, "but I'm in wonderfully good condition as a result of hard work."

Grut forbore saying: *Such as polo, you mean?* "Good. Has the trouble here worn you down?"

Ransom thought: *Which trouble is he talking about?* Grut didn't elaborate, knowing Ransom would have to select some sort of trouble to talk about, perhaps some he hadn't yet discovered for himself. He wasn't disappointed. Ransom took the bull by the horns. "I was with the sheriff most of the day. Our men got involved in helping two U. S. deputy marshals try to serve a summons on that bandit I told you about, Bandelier. The marshals were killed over at his ranch."

Grut absorbed that calmly. "Who killed them?"

"Bandelier himself."

"You are sure of this?"

"Yes. There's no doubt about it."

"Do they have him in custody?"

"He got away. The sheriff is hunting him. I left some of our men with him to help."

"Is Mister Wingfield with them?"

This was another body blow to Ransom. He'd never told Voerbeck he'd hired such a person. One reason had been that he recognized Wingfield was far more qualified for his job than he was, and that Voerbeck might draw the same conclusion if he came in contact with him even by mail. He fervently hoped that Wingfield would act on his threat to quit and never return. In reply to Voerbeck's question, he said: "He was when I left. Since we didn't know you were going to be here, I agreed that he should see Mister Pringle in Santa Fé. The two men killed were serving papers on Mister Pringle's behalf."

"I will want to meet this Mister Wingfield soon."

"As soon as he returns. He's a valuable man. Knows the cattle business from the ground up. I've learned as much as I could from him."

Grut thought: *I'm not surprised, and I hope to as well. I must ask Mister Wingfield if he's ever seen any men riding around with white hoods over their heads.* This brought him to the first matter he wanted to discuss. "My party came in on the railroad from Colorado. At a place with the poetic name of Tres Huérfanos, which I understand means Three Orphans, we observed a rather dramatic encounter."

Ransom knew what was coming. He listened attentively while Grut explained what they'd seen, trying to appear as though it was news to him.

"I mention this," Grut continued, "partly because we

learned the herd of cattle being driven off belonged to Mister Bandelier."

Ransom said: "Probably stolen from you originally."

Grut nodded. "That occurred to me. Naturally it also occurred to me that the men wearing white hoods were your men." He purposely didn't say *our* men. "Is that true?"

Ransom hadn't expected this question to come up so soon, if ever, but here it was, confronting him. If he lied, he'd likely be found out sooner or later. Telling the truth wasn't a much more pleasing prospect.

His hesitancy caused Grut to repeat the question. "Well, were they your men?"

"I suspect they were."

"What do you mean 'suspect they were?' "

"I suspect Wingfield was there without my knowledge."

"Does he often do things without your knowledge?"

"I didn't think so until lately. This incident, for example."

"If he was responsible, and I have no doubt from what you say that it was your men, we rescued one of Bandelier's riders . . . who was already wounded . . . from being killed in cold blood. Baron Waterford drove off the assassin with his shotgun."

"I have never sanctioned such things."

"Nor have I," Grut said. *"Nor will I!"*

The last three words came in an icy voice Ransom had never before heard. He got a picture of many such past incidents coming to Voerbeck's attention and the uncomfortable consequences. There was no way to explain them and little leeway to plead ignorance of them. He was in deep trouble and sorely regretted having given Wingfield such a free hand. Again he reflected on the desirability of the Texan's acting on his threat and never returning. Maybe he could help firm Wingfield's resolve in that respect with a substantial bribe, or perhaps an accurate report of Voerbeck's attitude might scare him away.

Voerbeck startled him by saying: "I had the wounded man brought here. He is in one of the bedrooms and seems in a fair way to recover." He enjoyed Ransom's wide-eyed reaction to this information.

"Why here, sir, if I may ask?"

"There was no place else for him to go. Besides, Mariposa wanted to nurse him."

That was entirely too much for Ransom to handle. A picture formed in his mind of his beautiful, blonde betrothed, ministering to a dirty, malodorous, and crude cowboy.

"You look startled," Voerbeck said.

"Does Mariposa know anything about nursing?" He really meant: *Has she lost her mind?*

"Obviously you don't know my daughter very well."

"It's true, I haven't seen her much the past few years."

Voerbeck smiled inwardly. With a little luck and more time he would best put an end to this impending blight on Mariposa's life. A frank talk regarding happenings here might now accomplish that. He debated arranging a joint conference between himself, Mariposa as his heir and successor, and his lordship. It seemed like a good idea at first, but he would sleep on it.

It suddenly occurred to Ransom that he hadn't inquired after the health of his beloved. "How is your lovely daughter?"

"First rate. She loves the country." He added to get the needle in completely: "She took a long ride with one of your Mexican hostelers this afternoon."

"Who?" Ransom blurted.

"She didn't get his name but mentioned that he was a perfect gentleman."

Ransom hardly noticed his Mexican employees, except Carmen and her mother, and thought of them, if at all, as chess pieces. He had sincere doubts the men were capable of being gentlemen or at least hadn't given it enough thought to form a conclusion. "That was most unwise."

"Why?"

"These people are little more civilized than the bloody red Indians. In fact, I've been told that most of them are part Indian. They are not to be trusted. Besides, the country is still infested with wild Indians. Mariposa might have been carried off or killed."

"I'll have to mention that to her. In fact, maybe you should. I suggest we all have a conference in the morning. As you know, I have no secrets from Mariposa. She will run my affairs when I'm ready to retire, and she is my heir." He signaled that the meeting was over. "You could probably use a little rest after a long, hard day with the sheriff."

Ransom wondered how Voerbeck knew it had been a long day for him and made a note to cross-examine McCoy regarding what he'd told the old boy. "Right, sir. I am about done up. Are you turning in, too?"

"Directly. You go ahead."

Ransom looked back, as he departed, and saw Voerbeck's nose buried in a penny dreadful about Western badmen and red Indians. He went to his room, wishing he knew where to find Carmen without rousing the suspicions of the Voerbecks. His English friends, Percy Waterford and Lady Fetherstonhaugh, were doubtless certain what his relationship was with Carmen as soon as they beheld her rare, blooming beauty. They'd probably even found time to gossip about it.

If Ransom had suspected his mistress was down in the wounded man's room, keeping a vigil beside his bed, he'd have been even less comforted than he was. Finally he fell asleep and blotted out the dreadful prospect of the morning's continuation of his meeting with Voerbeck. The one bright spot was that he'd see Percy again. They could plan a hunt together. If Voerbeck fired him, perhaps Percy would set him up on a ranch somewhere in this great hunting paradise. He could raise horses in addition and pay his own way.

Grut Voerbeck needed little sleep and arose before sunup, hoping Mariposa would join him so he could talk to her privately. He hadn't been up long when she came into the dining room, looking fresh and eager to explore her new surroundings.

"Good morning, dear," he greeted her. "You look like a million dollars, as these Americans say."

"I feel like a million dollars, if it means what I think it does. I'm also hungry enough to eat a bear, to borrow another American term I've heard."

An aroma of fresh coffee wafted to them from the kitchen, and Belen brought them a tray with coffee, cream, sugar, and a platter of fruit and stuffed Mexican pastries called *empanadas*. She was shy in their presence and anxious to please. They had learned the day before that Lord Ransom had her trained in European-style cooking, and that she got by very well in English. She asked: "Do you want breakfast now?"

Grut nodded to his daughter, and she said: "Why not? No telling when any of the others will be up."

They settled on the traditional English breakfast that Ransom normally had. After Belen left, Grut got to the subject on his mind.

"I had an illuminating talk with Lord Ransom last night."

"When did he get in?"

"Quite late. I suspect by intent. He may have known we were here. He appeared startled to see me, but that may have been only because I was still up."

Mariposa could imagine the scene. Thinking of how ridiculous Monty Ransom could be sometimes, she wasn't surprised to discover she was neutral on the subject of meeting her fiancé again. She seldom thought of him. Her immersion in the Voerbeck empire with her father had been her life since she was a girl, and truly romantic thoughts hadn't yet awakened in her, although she was capable of them. If the right man appeared, she was confident that she'd know him on sight and know what to do, too. If he never came, perhaps it wouldn't be too disappointing. In any case, she knew that right man wasn't Ransom. This conviction had come slowly and proved the wisdom of her father's desire to prolong her engagement.

Voerbeck said: "I'm afraid your man is a very bad manager. He really hasn't much idea how to run an operation like I intended to establish here. In fact, I'm sure he has very little idea what's been going on right under his nose and up until last night, may not have seen that it would make much difference to his future. I don't think he had any notion that I'd actually come and look into things."

Mariposa smiled. "He really doesn't know you very well, Papa."

"I don't think he knows my daughter very well, either. Nor do I, sometimes. Which brings up something I have to know. How would you feel about it if I had to discharge him?"

She thought about that briefly. "If you did that, I suspect I'd do the same thing if I possessed the information on which you based your decision. After all, you trained me well."

He chuckled. "I can see that I did. That lifts a weight from my mind. We must talk to Lord Ransom together soon and decide what we must do with him."

The opportunity to do that had to wait until after their breakfast in which Percy and Lady Fetherstonhaugh joined them. Waterford was anxious to rouse his old friend.

Voerbeck protested. "Don't do that. He had a hard day yesterday and got in late. Let him sleep."

Mariposa said: "Let me show you around. You can ride, if

you want to. I'm sure the man who went with me yesterday would be glad to take you out. I want to see Monty when he gets up, and Father wants to talk to him, so we'll stay here."

Waterford grumbled: "He's a slug-a-bed. Always has been. I want to talk to him about hunting and fishing."

Voerbeck dryly added: "And the two polo teams?." He hadn't told them about McCoy's revelation of the previous day.

Waterford looked blank. "What two polo teams?"

"Lord Ransom's two polo teams."

Mariposa brightened. It was the first intimation she'd had that her nominal fiancé may have done something of which she could approve. Polo had become her passion, and she'd found no place to play except at Percy Waterford's estate. If she had her own teams, she could play anytime she wished. She'd already decided to stay in this wonderful place most of the year.

Waterford said: "You're serious? He has polo teams?"

"Indeed."

When Ransom finally got up, he found Grut in his office, but Mariposa was out furiously playing polo with Waterford and a group of dazed Mexicans who had never seen a woman ride astraddle — and what a woman, what a rider.

"I'll have someone get Mariposa," Grut said. "I have no business secrets from her, and I want her to hear what you told me last night. Then we'll decide on some things."

"Where is she?"

"Out playing polo."

"Great God!" Ransom exclaimed. "The sight of her on a polo pony may be too much for the ny-tives."

"I don't think so," Grut disagreed. "I suspect they may be more adaptable than you suspect."

His opinion was based on observation. He'd gone to the field with the others and stayed long enough to see the initial shock wear off. His daughter thundered after the ball in her typical mad style, scattering the swarthy *caballeros* from her path. His judgment was they had unalloyed respect for this weird phenomenon who had fallen from the sky among them. If he were any judge, they were going to worship Mariposa.

She joined them presently, wearing jodhpurs and cavalry boots, out of breath, eyes still sparkling from the excitement. Her father thought she looked like a fresh pink rose. Ransom dutifully pecked her on the cheek she offered, then formally shook hands with her. "It's good to see you, my dear."

Grut thought: *How different from we Dutch. At his age I'd have given my fiancée a big hug and kiss, regardless of who was watching.* He watched Mariposa closely and realized she was thinking the same thing. From that look alone he was confident wedding bells were not in their future.

She broke the ice. "You've done a wonderful job with the polo teams and ponies."

Ransom smiled. "I have my talents" — then, easing into the unhappy discussion he knew would soon follow, added — "but ranching doesn't seem to be one of them." He looked warily at Grut as he said that.

The old man's face was inscrutable. To Ransom's amazement he said: "Maybe. Maybe not."

Ransom's jaw actually dropped, which Mariposa noted and had a hard time avoiding an unlady-like guffaw. She hadn't expected her father to say that, either, but was used to the fact that he often operated in obscure paths to reach an objective. She wondered what her father was aiming at.

After covering all the ground of the night before, Voerbeck concluded: "I think our big problem has been this man, Wingfield. I would like to talk to him personally."

Ransom had a sinking sensation over that prospect. It wasn't entirely out of the question that Wingfield could yet turn the tables on him. He was slippery and a smooth talker. Moreover, if Voerbeck was ready to forgive his shortcomings, he might do the same with Wingfield. The only bright spot was that the old man seemed genuinely appalled at the violence the Texan had introduced on the local scene. Ransom fervently hoped none of them would ever see Wingfield again.

At the end of their meeting, Voerbeck said: "If you'll excuse us, I want to talk to Mariposa privately, but you can assume you still have a job for the time being."

Ransom left in a daze. This hadn't gone at all the way he'd expected. He went outside to look up Waterford, who was still on the polo field.

Grut looked at his daughter and grinned. "What do you think?"

She appraised his face carefully. "I think you're having a lot of fun. I think you've concluded that we don't have much more to lose by not doing anything, until you learn more about the situation."

"Very astute. As a matter of fact, I'm thinking of going down to Santa Fé to have a long talk with Mister Pringle for the very purpose of finding out more about the situation. I want you to stay here and keep your Monty out of trouble."

She grinned. "Normally I'd insist on seeing Santa Fé and all those scoundrels Mister Carson wrote about in his letter. But with two polo teams and Monty to supervise, how can I object to staying here? This time!"

Part Three

The Amarillo War

Chapter Twenty-One

José harbored a strong presentiment that it had been a mistake to send Junior out on Star to lead away the posse and ride for help. He wanted to mention it to Cleve, but, since he was sleeping peacefully, decided not to. Instead he said to Amy: "I'm goin' out for a little while to check around."

"How long will you be gone?" she asked, not wishing to be left alone to take care of her father in case he got delirious again.

"Maybe an hour, two at the most. I want to follow your brother far enough to make sure he got away. I'll have to go slow to make sure I ain't seen, and that'll take a while."

Amy tried not to show her fear — above all, she didn't want to be an unnecessary burden to this man who was risking his life to protect her father. "Maggie and I can make out, I guess," she said, all the time wondering: *What will we do if he doesn't come back?* to which her little voice answered: *Cross that bridge when we get to it. Don't be a scaredy cat.*

José carefully scanned the area with Cleve's glasses before venturing beyond the screening brush surrounding the entrance to the cave. He listened to see what the birds could tell him and heard no alarm calls from any of them, though that might simply mean there was none near enough for him to hear. Jays and ravens were the best for crying a warning. Magpies ran a close third.

He could easily follow Star's tracks, since Junior had intended them to be seen. Nonetheless, he didn't stay directly on the trail but kept to the brush as much as possible. This slowed his progress as it assured he'd stay out of trouble. He didn't want to leave Amy alone very long with Cleve since he had read the hidden fear in her eyes. She had showed grit in not breaking down under the strain of the past couple of days. Not many girls her age would do as well — as least not white ones.

Due to José's caution he saw the rider ahead without being detected and circled from the trail, moving from one juniper to another to remain out of sight, trying to get close enough to see who the rider might be. He recognized the horse as one of Sam Buchanan's string. He'd normally have been glad at the sight of reinforcement, but Sam's presence suggested some new trouble.

Not forgetting caution for a moment, he moved rapidly to head Sam off. When he was very close, he called in a low voice.

Sam whirled in the saddle, his hand darting for his six-shooter before he recognized the voice. He grinned when he was sure it was José. "Boy, am I glad to see you."

"Same here," said José. "I can use some help."

"So can I," Sam said. "They just captured Junior. What the hell was he doing out here?"

José filled Sam in on all that had happened since they'd separated in the Bandelier ranch yard the day before.

Sam shook his head. "It don't look to me like we can help the kid. The sheriff has him. Good thing, too. Wingfield's man, Dabney, was the one that shot Star, and he'd have killed Junior if the sheriff hadn't showed up."

José said: "Best we go back to the cave till after dark. Then I guess I'd better go for some help. I can have fifty men down here tomorrow. If they want a fight, they can have it."

Amy was alerted to the approach of the two cowboys by Maggie's low growl. She prayed it was José coming back. She didn't know who else could be expected, but in her condition she was prepared for the worst. When she saw Sam, she rushed to him and put her arms around his neck. He squeezed her, then held her tenderly. "It's old Sam, honey," he said. "Everything's gonna be all right."

Sam was her second father, and he'd tried to be her mother, too, especially after she was left without one. Before that, he'd helped her mother with her from the day she was born. After her mother died, if he was at the ranch, he never failed to take part in the cooking, bring in kindling and wood, wash dishes and clothes, water the garden, hoe, look after her horse. He could even iron. The other cowboys never kidded him about all that, either. Of course, he could have pounded the pudding out of any one of them if he'd wanted to, but that had nothing to do with it.

Their arrival roused Cleve. "Who's there? I thought I heard Sam."

Sam crawled up to his bed and crouched down near him. "You heard Sam, all right. Man, am I glad you're O K."

"Who says I'm O K? I hurt like hell. And I've got to get up and go again, and that ain't exactly a picnic."

"I'll bet. Want a hand gettin' up?"

"In the shape I'm in, I'll take all the help I can get. If you could go for me, I'd let you do that, too."

Amy overheard this and grinned, glad that her pa was feeling a little perkier. José waited until Cleve rejoined them and lay down again, before he delivered the bad news. He squatted nearby. "I went out to follow Junior a ways to see if he got away."

"Did he?"

"Sam here can tell you."

The black related what he'd seen.

"Bad luck," Cleve said. "But he seemed to be all right, you said?"

"Good enough to ride double behind one of them."

"And you don't know about Star?"

"Afraid to go close enough to see. He didn't get up."

Tears rushed to Amy's eyes, despite her resolve never to let herself be weak again. First the dogs, then her pa and Junior, now Star. At least her brother had pulled through. Flighty as he sometimes was, she felt she'd die if anything happened to him.

José proposed his plan to Cleve about going for help.

"After it's pitch dark," Cleve agreed, "unless another storm comes up. Can't do much about that. Try to go by and check on Star, if you can. I reckon even Wingfield would put a horse out of its misery, and I'm pretty sure the sheriff would." He looked sadly away, remaining silent for a long while. Finally he added: "I wonder what kind of foal Nellie'll have this time."

He was sure in his heart that there'd never be another horse for him like Star, if he lived to be a hundred. Thinking of Star reminded him the rest of the horses hadn't had a thing to eat for a long while. "I think we should turn the horses out when you leave tonight. They won't do us much good half starved, and, if you get back, we won't need them."

Sam said: "There ain't enough grass, or I'd take them out, picket them after dark, and bring them back in."

Cleve nodded. "They'd leave too much sign around anyhow. They'll work their way back to the ranch in a day or so this way."

After dark José saddled Dave, who was a lot faster than his little horse, and led him from the cave. Amy relaxed a little at the thought that soon they'd be surrounded by friends who could protect them, even from Wingfield's men. She looked forward to going up to the Zamora place, which was literally a stronghold. Dolores would help her nurse her pa.

José had suggested that they set up a convalescent camp in

the hidden cliff dwellings in the high country in case Sheriff Butler came to Zamora Plaza. The sheriff would get nothing out of the people there. No one could match the cleverly assumed blank and dumb look of a Mexican or an Indian when he didn't want to be cooperative. They shrugged and looked amiably helpless, saying with their body and facial expression: *What can I do? I'm only an ignorant peon.*

Amy thought of that, and it made her laugh, because she knew that in the hot blood of the simple-appearing Mexicans still lived the spark that had fired the early Spaniards. The Apaches were equally proud and war-like. These two races had fought each other for centuries until their blood lines were so intermingled that they had become almost brothers in places like this. Such men as José and Jesús were the equal of any in the world in courage and loyalty. They would fight to the death for their friends, their honor, and their *patrón,* if he were a good one like her pa.

She rolled up in her robes, relaxed and confident, and sank into her first real sleep since the gun fight at the ranch. Sam was here, and she was absolutely safe.

Later she woke up groggily, aroused by some noise. Maggie was growling ominously and staring toward the cave's entrance. Sam, on the alert, held his finger to his lips, then moved cautiously toward the edge of the ledge. Suddenly something erupted almost in his face. He rolled away quickly. Amy gasped. Then she recognized what had appeared to attack, as Sam did.

"It's Pedro," she said.

Sam chuckled. "That dang cat o' yer pa's almost scared me to death." He shook his head. "He didn't want to be left alone at the ranch."

Amy said: "He wasn't alone. He should have stayed and helped Emily with the kittens in the barn. They're his as much as hers."

"He don't know that," Sam replied. "He misses sleeping on the *jefe*'s bed."

Amy had heard of cats following their people — sometimes for hundreds of miles — and finding them by some secret sense they had. She watched Pedro go over to Cleve, climb onto his robes, sniff his cheek, and start cleaning himself.

Her father stirred under his robe but didn't awaken. As she dropped back to sleep, she wondered what her pa would think when he woke up and found Pedro there.

Chapter Twenty-Two

José pushed Dave to his limit, stopping only once to let him graze and rest a little. Then he pressed on. It was after midnight when he reached Zamora Plaza and went to the house of Anastacio Zamora, the oldest of the brothers and leader of the clan.

His soft knock wasn't answered at once. He knocked again and heard movement inside, then recognized Anastacio's low voice near the door. "*¿Quién es?*"

No light was lit. José knew the door was strongly barred. These were dangerous times, and the Zamoras were particular targets of the night riders due to their militant resistance to the syndicate.

"It's me. José. I need help. Cleve Bandelier's been shot up."

"Wait," came the voice.

A lamp flickered behind the blanket-draped window. Finally the bar scraped, and the door opened. Anastacio was partially concealed behind it, six-shooter in hand, the lamp across the room barely revealing him.

"Can't be too careful," he said. "I wouldn't put it past Pancho Wingfield to bring somebody up here, holding a gun in their back."

"Not me. I'd die first," José protested, injured by the implication but letting it pass. This wasn't the time for points of honor.

He told Anastacio what had happened in as few words as possible. By then Anastacio's wife, Maria, was up, making something to eat, and Anastacio had sent one of his sons to rouse his brothers. José downed a tortilla, wrapped around beans, then another, before the house began to fill with men.

He knew them all and was glad to see Keg Brownlee and a couple of other Anglos join the group. Shortly, Niño Alonzo, son of the old chief, accompanied by another Jicarilla slipped in quietly. His presence meant important reinforcements, since his men were masters of stealth as well as superb scouts and fighters.

Anastacio said to José: "You tell them."

He related the whole story in a few words. "We need a lot of men to take Cleve out of there safely," José concluded. "Cleve can't ride yet, so we'll have to carry him down to the road, then put him in a wagon. We may have to fight the sheriff, too."

Anastacio glanced around, sensing that everyone looked to him for leadership. "The hell with the sheriff! We can't let our friend, Cleve, down now. The time to fight has come."

He fired orders for the rescue force, sent messengers for more men who brought up horses, and personally supervised arranging the wagon with straw and lots of blankets in the back. He asked: "Who has that stretcher you borrowed from the Army? Bring it." A subdued laugh went up from the Apaches who'd stolen it years before in a raid.

There were as many Jicarilla farmers and small ranchers in the community now as Mexicans, as well as several Anglos, married to Mexican women. Keg Brownlee was the recognized leader of the Anglo element.

Before sunup an army of nearly a hundred men took to the road, with flankers out to detain anyone who might detect them. Almost the entire Anglo contingent had been soldiers, and the Mexicans and Indians were used to fighting with the Army, each other, and, at times in the past, the Anglo settlers. The threat to their land had united them all as brothers, at least for now. Maybe they'd fight each other again some day, maybe not, but this wasn't the time to worry.

Keg Brownlee had been a commissary sergeant at Fort Garland when Cleve was sergeant-major there. "Keg" was his nickname, and there were several stories about how it was earned — because he was built a little like a keg; or it was claimed he'd once drunk a keg of beer overnight (not true, it had been only about half); or because he often demonstrated his strength by picking up a keg of nails and holding it at arm's length in front of him. Whatever the case, he was a good man to have in a fight. He was married to a Zamora, spoke Spanish like a native, spoke a fractured Jicarilla, and fit into both cultures due to his friendly nature. Cleve had helped him consume many a keg of beer over the years, not the least of the reasons they were as close as brothers. As he rode beside Anastacio, Keg was wondering whom he could kill to even the score for what had happened to Cleve Bandelier. A picture of Pancho Wingfield came to mind. He thought: *Shooting is too good for that bastard. I'll break his neck instead.*

Approaching Chief Don Alonzo's cave, Anastacio deployed his army in a fan, carefully feeling out the area ahead and encountering no one.

Pancho Wingfield, who had been in the vicinity of the Bandelier ranch, had withdrawn temporarily to Dorado for those comforts he notoriously appreciated. By the time he returned with the tracker, Antonio Chunz, Anastacio's hidden sentinels were spread in a wide perimeter around the cave. Anastacio and Niño Alonzo had accompanied José inside the cave, and several strong stretcher-bearers were waiting outside, concealed about its entrance.

Chunz, on foot, moved ahead, while Wingfield and Harmony Dabney followed on their horses. Pancho, ever cautious, dropped back a substantial distance behind Dabney. Chunz, sensing an ambush, was prepared to run or fight. He hadn't wished to come along. His sympathies lay with his fellow Jicarillas, and he had a wife and kids at Zamora Plaza (of which Wingfield was ignorant since he'd never cared enough to find out). Chunz suspected who might be concealed in the vicinity of Chief Don Alonzo's hide-out, but saw none of them until one willingly showed himself briefly and gave him the sign of a friend. By equally silent signs Chunz indicated that he was virtually a prisoner.

Suddenly a dozen rifleman rose up, and Keg Brownlee yelled: "Reach, Pancho!"

Brownlee used the insulting name, hoping to goad the Texan into reaching the wrong way — for his six-shooter. Instead, Wingfield dropped along the side of his horse, whirled it, and spurred away at a run. Surprised by this move, none of Brownlee's men hit Pancho with the shots hastily snapped off after him, and he was soon out of sight.

"What the hell?" Dabney yelped, throwing up his hands. He was disarmed and forced to dismount. Brownlee gave him a shove that almost knocked him off his feet.

"That ain't nothin' to what I owe you for shootin' Cleve," Keg told him.

"I didn't," Dabney protested. "Devil Ed did."

"You're the son of a bitch that shot Cleve's horse and tried to beef his kid. Now you came back up here to finish Cleve."

Keg shoved him again, hoping he'd put up his dukes. Dabney wasn't having any. He knew Keg well enough not to fight him that way.

Keg said: "I'll tend to you later."

Dabney held his tongue, believing the threat and realizing that Keg wanted him to make a run for it. He cursed himself again for getting mixed up with Pancho, who always stuck his nose in where it wasn't wanted. Every Mexican and Indian in the country hated Wingfield and with just cause, and because of it these men of Bandelier's might decide to string him up.

Montague Ransom decided he'd better mend his fences by spending as much time as possible with Mariposa. She had always found him good company, perhaps because nothing shocked him, and she was a shocking lady at times. She liked men, but most of them were stiff and formal with women. Ransom was wary around her but not stuffy; moreover, he was fully aware of his shortcomings and comfortable with them. This allowed her to say what she thought without offending him, even to the point of kidding him about his obvious deficiencies in management of the Amarillo Grant.

Percy and Lady Fetherstonhaugh had politely allowed them to have their after breakfast coffee alone, and Mariposa brought up the subject. "Whatever possessed you to hire a man like this Mister Wingfield?"

Ransom gave that some serious thought before replying. "I'm damned if I know, pardon my French."

She laughed. "You are priceless, Monty. You must have some recollection of what went through your mind at the time."

He considered that. "He was so . . . ah . . . available. And he does know the range cattle business."

"And you didn't, so you hired him?"

He looked at her innocently. "I guess so. It seemed like the thing to do."

"When did you find out he was going around killing people, or trying to?"

"A couple of days ago. He wasn't at Bandelier's ranch, paying a social call. In fact, the sheriff thought he went there to kill Bandelier rather than help a couple of lawmen serve papers. I suspect Wingfield was in charge of the men you saw shoot the boy you're nursing in the back bedroom."

"Why didn't you fire Mister Wingfield?"

It was a question he could hardly answer truthfully, so he dodged it. "I thought I'd get him to come here, and we'd confront him together. Come to think of it, I wasn't entirely sure your father wouldn't approve of what he'd done. After all, he was trying to get squatters off your land."

"You thought Papa would condone murder?"

"I didn't know him very well."

She nodded. "I guess that's true. In a way we've been to blame, letting things drift here. We should have come here long before now. Do you have any idea where Mister Wingfield is now?"

Ransom shook his head while he hoped the man was riding fast for somewhere far away.

"You admit you haven't learned this business, so who should we get to replace Mister Wingfield?" Mariposa asked.

Ransom laughed, thinking about it. "Probably the best man for the job is Cleve Bandelier, but I have a notion he's not available."

"You're joking, of course.

"Yes."

"Where do you think Mister Bandelier may be now?"

"I don't know. Probably out of the country. Would you like to ride over and look at his ranch . . . which is to say, one of your ranches?"

Mariposa considered for a moment and made a snap decision. "Why not? I love this country, and that will be a chance for you to show me more of it. Is his ranch in a pretty spot?"

"One of the prettiest in the country."

So it happened that a couple of hours later they innocently rode into Anastacio's hidden sentinels, guarding the area near Chief Don Alonzo's hide-out. Ransom's horse first warned him that something threatening was nearby. He cautioned Mariposa.

"Watch your horse. I think they smell a bear. If one pops out, your horse'll shy and run. Let him, but be ready. I'll shoot the devil, so don't worry about that."

He reached to pull the rifle from his saddle boot when several Mexican and Indian possemen popped up, rifles leveled. The horses spooked and spun, saw men behind them as well, and milled nervously, held in by their riders.

"Steady," Ransom said. "They won't hurt us, if we don't try to run."

He accurately concluded what these men were doing here and reproved himself for coming into the area so soon. He should have known Bandelier had gone to ground, wounded, and his men would come for him as soon as word reached them.

Ordered to dismount, they were marched to where Keg Brownlee had posted himself. Ransom recognized Dabney but said nothing. Above them, on the rocky hillside, several men were carrying down Cleve Bandelier on the stretcher, moving slowly, careful not to slip and drop him.

Ransom said to Mariposa in a low voice: "It looks like you're going to get to see Bandelier."

"Is that he on the stretcher?"

"Unless I miss my guess. I wonder how badly he's hurt."

The stretcher was brought almost to where they were being held and deposited on the ground on its short legs. The man on it was swaddled in blankets but was conscious, his head propped up on a rolled blanket. He was in need of a shave, his beard strikingly black, as were his hair and mustache, and lines of fatigue and pain emphasized his prominent Roman nose. Mariposa couldn't tell what color his eyes were, but they looked black. Perhaps he was part Indian. She didn't think he looked mean or sinister. On the contrary, she believed he'd be quite handsome when shaved and cleaned up. She was watching him curiously when he glanced up and saw her. All her childhood fantasies came back, and she thought: *Rob Roy. It's Rob Roy!* Then a chill ran up her spine. She smiled involuntarily. Cleve stared up at her, then turned to the large, heavy-set man who was in charge of all these others, motioned him down beside him, and said something.

A little girl was following the stretcher, accompanied by a tall black man who occasionally gave her a hand over the jumbled rocks. Amy looked at Mariposa, her mouth open a trifle in surprise at finding a woman here. She knew staring was rude but couldn't help herself. She hoped she would grow up, looking half so good.

Mariposa smiled at her. This could only be Bandelier's daughter who, Monty Ransom had told her earlier, had been in the house when Bandelier killed the two marshals. She was a sturdy little thing, dirty-faced, but pretty under it all. Mariposa's heart went out to her. She must have been terrified all through the past couple of days, probably wondering if her wounded father was going to live. From his appearance, that seemed likely. Nonetheless, she wondered if she should volunteer to examine the wound and professionally clean and rebandage it. This wasn't the time to suggest it, but she vowed to ask about it later.

Cleve asked Keg: "Who's the woman with Ransom?"

"Brace yourself for a surprise," Keg answered. "It's old Voerbeck's daughter."

Cleve kept a passive face, but the information was startling. The sheriff had Junior, so maybe a swap could be negotiated. He announced: "We'll have to take Ransom and the woman with us, so they don't go get the sheriff until we're long gone."

Keg nodded. "How about the other guy?" He meant Harmony.

Sam Buchanan, listening, said: "He was with Wingfield when Star was killed. They probably were shooting at Junior, thinking it was you."

Cleve stared at Dabney and said: "Bring him over here." The man was brought near. "What have you got to say for yourself?"

"About what?" Dabney asked with false bravado.

"You were with Wingfield the other night, weren't you?"

"Where?"

"When you shot up my place."

"What if I was?" Dabney retorted.

Cleve's face hardened. "You shot my horse and might have killed my son. What did we ever do to you?"

Dabney, wisely, didn't reply.

Bandelier knew as well as Dabney did that he was being paid fighting wages in what amounted to a range war. You took your chances and paid with your life if you lost. Cleve realized this man would come at them again, if he were allowed to go free. He was mortally certain there was no way to put him in jail where he belonged. It didn't leave much choice.

Dabney read his mind. "Suppose I cut a deal with you and go back to Texas?"

Cleve stared at him contemptuously. He motioned Keg down to where he wouldn't be heard by Dabney and said something. Keg grinned. He got up and grabbed a handful of Dabney's shirt and jerked him around.

"C'mon with me," he ordered, and motioned several others to come along. "Bring his horse."

As they left, Mariposa asked Ransom: "What are they going to do with him?"

"I have no idea, my dear. Maybe trounce him good and run him off."

But Ransom suspected what they were really going to do

with Dabney, having been in New Mexico three years. It prompted him to wonder what they were going to do with him, a man who had, at least nominally, hired such creatures and sanctioned their conduct.

Out of sight, where there was a growth of Apache pine, Keg halted the cavalcade, took the rope from Dabney's saddle, and tossed one end over a large, low limb.

"No!" Dabney protested. "I'll make a deal. There's a lot you don't know yet about Wingfield."

"Tell Saint Peter," Keg replied.

Dabney tried to run away, but his legs didn't work.

Keg grabbed him and slapped him across the mouth, then backhanded him on the side the head with his huge hand. "Cleve thought you might like to sing. If it's the right song, and you write out a confession, you might save your worthless neck. Can you write?"

Dabney was so relieved, he was crying. "I'll cut any deal you want me to. I got an old ma back in Texas. I'm all she's got to support her."

"Aw, bullshit!" said Keg.

"I really do."

"Well, she should've raised you better." He slapped Dabney again and knocked him down. "Put him on his horse and tie his hands to the saddle horn. We'll take him with us. Pity we didn't catch his pal."

In the meantime Cleve had Ransom and Mariposa brought over to him. To Ransom he said: "I ought to hang you, but I'm not going to . . . at least not yet. We've got to keep you with us for a while. Wingfield probably went for the sheriff, but, if he didn't, I can't afford to let you bring him up here."

Ransom returned Cleve's gaze without fear. "I wouldn't get the sheriff. There's a lot you don't know, but I don't think he'd come out here again."

Cleve's curiosity was aroused. "What makes you say that?"

Ransom shrugged, aware that he couldn't make Cleve understand what had been going on the past couple of days. "It'd take a long while to explain. If you're taking us with you, I might have time. Must you take the lady as well?"

Cleve nodded. "Neither of you will get hurt." He laughed a little. "You might get lice where we have to put you up, but you won't be hurt."

Chapter Twenty-Three

Percy Waterford really wanted to ride out with his best friend, Monty Ransom, but was afraid he might be interfering in his romance with Mariposa. He fidgeted around the ranch, in and out of the house, not inclined to play polo without Monty and Mariposa. He thought of reading, taking down one book after another from the well-stocked shelves around the living room, replacing each without interest, looked at the penny dreadful that Voerbeck had been reading, and tossed it down in disgust after flipping through a few pages. He didn't especially give a damn about the adventures of Jesse James, who, if he recalled correctly, had been sent to his Maker that spring.

Lady Fetherstonhaugh watched for a while, then chided him. "You're pacing like the proverbial lion in a cage. Why don't you go hunting or something? I'm sure one of the polo team would be glad to go along."

He looked her over with a wry expression of distaste on his face. "I don't like to go out with people I don't know. Besides, I'm not sure I can talk to any of the grooms. Why don't you come with me for a ride? You're going to grow to that chair if you don't move around."

"You know I only ride to flirt. I've caught my man, so I don't have to do that any more."

"Voerbeck? Has he proposed?"

"Not in so many words."

"What am I to assume that means?"

She grinned. "It means he never talks about the future without me fitting into his plans."

"At his age he may not have much future."

"You'd be surprised. He must have had quite a past, too."

"That good?"

"None of your business, Percy." She grinned again at some thought and added: "He doesn't have anything to be ashamed of, if that's what you're fishing to find out."

"You ought to know."

"Be nice. A single woman without a fortune has to look out for herself with what assets she has."

"Yes, indeed. But how about riding anyhow just to please an old friend?"

"All right," she acceded, "but we must take along Domingo, if we go. Mariposa rode with him and told me, if I wanted to ride, I should be sure to take him so I didn't get lost."

"I never get lost," Percy protested.

"That's what Doctor Livingstone always said."

"All right. We'll take Domingo, if that's the price of your coming along."

"I'll get a riding habit on. And, Percy . . . you're not planning to take advantage of me in some secluded dell, are you?"

"With the faithful Domingo along? Hardly. Besides, I'm a bed man. Did I ever hustle you out into the bushes?"

She left without answering.

Domingo had their horses saddled and ready and led them on the trail that Ransom and Mariposa had taken earlier. He didn't explain his choice of a route, but wanted to follow Ransom and Mariposa to be sure Mariposa didn't come to any harm. He kept up a rapid pace to get within sight of her and Ransom, if possible. Domingo had no confidence that his lordship had enough navigating ability to find his way out of a big hogshead at high noon. He topped a knoll, riding in the lead, and pulled up, silently halting them with a restraining hand.

"What is it?" Waterford asked, then saw the other riders a

quarter of a mile away down the opposite slope. He took his marine glass from its case and trained it on the group. "By Jove! Someone has captured Monty and Mariposa."

"We must go back and stay out of sight," Domingo said. "I think I know who they are. No harm will come to them. Follow me. *¡Andale!*"

Waterford protested. "Nonsense. We must rescue them."

Domingo's face mirrored disgust. Daisy didn't miss the look, realizing that Percy was over his head in this situation, and that his well-known obstinacy was apt to get them into trouble without helping their friends. She turned back as Domingo directed, calling to Percy: "For heaven's sake, do what he says! At least until we find out what's going on."

He followed the other two, dismounted, and returned to take another look through his glass.

"What is it?" Daisy asked Domingo.

The Mexican made a hasty decision that she could be trusted. He told her: "It is the men of my village, come to rescue their friend, Bandelier."

"How could you know that?" Daisy asked.

He knew he couldn't explain to her that he could see as well without field glasses as most greenhorns could with them nor could he explain the grapevine by which his people knew everything, sometimes even before the Anglos' telegraph told them. Domingo shrugged. "We have ways of knowing. You must believe me. Get your friend and tell him they are in no danger. My people will never hurt them."

"Can you go down alone and get them back?"

He shrugged. "Maybe. Get your friend back here, and I will try."

Daisy called to Percy. "Come back here and listen to what Domingo just told me."

Waterford reluctantly returned, and she had Domingo repeat his story. From his earnestness Waterford had to believe him. "Go ahead and try," he said. "We'll wait here out of sight."

Percy kept his glass on Domingo all the way and watched him follow the group of people they'd seen to a place hidden by trees.

"How do you suppose he knows all that?" Daisy asked.

"People close to the earth know things," Percy told her. "I have seen it in India and Africa over and over. Besides, those are his people down there."

"What will we do if he doesn't come back?"

"He'll come back if they let him. If he doesn't, we'll follow their spoor and find out where they're going, then go for help."

"What's spoor?" Daisy asked.

"In this case the trail of their horses will be all we need. There are a lot of them. It'll be easier than following elephants."

"How in the world can you follow a horse trail?" Daisy asked.

"They make tracks on the ground wherever they go. Haven't you ever noticed?"

"You mean like on the bridle path?"

"Of course."

"Of course, I've noticed. Horses make tracks when they put their feet down. But I never thought of following them that way. They always went 'round and 'round, and you knew where they went. How awfully clever of you."

Time dragged while they waited.

"Where ever can he be?" Daisy asked then.

"Give him time. If he's not back in fifteen minutes, I'm going after him." Percy took out his watch and checked the time.

"I'm going with you, if you do."

"Of course. You'd never find your way back to the ranch,

and the red Indians might get you."

Finally they saw Domingo returning.

"They aren't with him," Daisy said. "What are you going to do?"

"I don't know yet."

Domingo rode to them at a lope, knowing they'd be anxious to find out what the story was. He said: "They are all right. As I said, they won't be hurt. Those men won't turn them loose until they get far enough away that they can't ride for the sheriff."

"What made them think *you* wouldn't go for the sheriff?"

Domingo smiled. "They know me."

"What made them think *we* wouldn't get the sheriff?"

Domingo smiled again. "I didn't tell them you were here."

"But we might get the sheriff," Percy said.

"I ask you not to, until I say. By then, they will be far enough away, and *Señor* Ransom and the lady will be on their way home."

Percy said: "All right. From what I heard, this Bandelier is not really a badman. I'll wait until this afternoon, but, if Lord Ransom and Miss Voerbeck haven't returned, then I'm going to the sheriff."

Domingo shrugged. "Waiting will be the best thing to do. Believe me."

Domingo now rode on ahead. Percy remained far enough behind to talk confidentially with Daisy.

"I don't know if that was the right thing to do or not, but I hope so. This is *terra incognita* for us. We just about have to trust Domingo. He looks honest."

As a matter of fact, Daisy thought he looked a lot more honest than some others they had to deal with here — for example, Montague Ransom. Of course, she'd known Monty for years and was well acquainted with his pliable morals. She wondered how he was making out with his captors, who, according to Domingo, were only local farmers and friends of Mr. Bandelier. She said: "If those men are like Domingo, I don't think we have anything to fear. What else can we do?"

"I could have gone down and demanded their release."

Daisy gave him a look that clearly said she thought he was acting simple, though she was aware that he was perfectly capable of doing something that quixotic. His only weapon was a double-barrel elephant gun, for which she suspected he might have as many as a dozen extra cartridges. Her opinion was that, if he'd gone down there, he'd be a prisoner himself by now. And, of course, she'd have had no alternative but to go with him, so she'd have been in the same predicament. The idea didn't appeal to her. She almost wished they'd stayed home, except, if they had, they'd never have learned what happened to Monty and Mariposa.

After Cleve was driven away in the wagon, Lord Ransom looked over their guards and recognized that many of them were Mexicans, but, even were his life to depend on it, he couldn't have told whether he'd ever seen any of them before. They all looked alike to him, even the men on his polo teams. He was conscious that he couldn't order these men around as he was accustomed to doing and chafed at the restraint, finally coming close to apoplexy when one of them tied his hands to his saddle horn, then proceeded to do the same to Mariposa.

"I say! I say!" he stormed. "Aren't there any gentlemen here?"

"Shut up!" Keg Brownlee told him.

Ransom glared at him. "If I were down off this horse, I'd give you the thrashing you deserve."

"Do tell? Git him down off there."

When Ransom was on his feet and facing him, Keg uncorked

a roundhouse swing and was confounded to discover that Ransom wasn't where he'd last seen him. Worse yet, he'd got a couple of jabs to the head that felt like a horse had kicked him.

"Why you little son of a bitch!" Keg stormed at his little six-foot opponent. "I'll git you for that."

Ransom merely smiled and danced around him. Keg swung another roundhouse with the same result as the last and earned a swift counter-punch that knocked him to his knees. He couldn't take in what was happening. The Mexicans, who had seen him fight before and win easily with a few hard punches, stood flat-footed with their mouths open.

Ransom generously extended a hand to Keg to help him up and was unceremoniously jerked off his feet and into a bear hug. The Mexicans smiled widely, thinking the end was near, but were a little premature. Keg came flying up, like he'd sat on a rattlesnake, while Ransom rolled over and leaped to his feet.

"Learned that in Injah, old boy," he said. "Clever, what?"

Keg glowered at him, then doggedly moved in, planning to deliver a kick where it would do the most good. Ransom knew what he had in mind and let him get close enough to launch one, then grabbed his foot, and threw him, delivering a kick to the back of his neck as he went over backward. Keg lay still, breathing heavily, his eyes open and frozen in an unseeing stare, temporarily paralyzed.

"Learned that in Tokyo," Ransom said.

Keg wasn't interested where he'd learned it. When he regained his senses, he said: "Damn it, I believe you whipped me fair and square."

Ransom smiled and again extended him a hand to help him up. "I dare say," he agreed. "No hard feelings, old boy. Now, will you take a gentleman's word that we won't try to escape, if you don't tie us?"

Keg managed a crooked grin. "I reckon. I gotta respect anybody as slick as you at fightin'."

Mariposa had watched this whole performance with amazement. It occurred to her that there was more to Monty than she'd thought. Thrift and acumen with money weren't everything.

The cavalcade returned, as it had come, scouts and skirmishers fanned out, Cleve's wagon at the front of the procession escorted by Anastacio and Keg, who rode like he had a stiff neck.

Anastacio, who hadn't seen the fight, asked: "Is your rheumatism bothering you, *amigo?* My shoulder was bad last night. It must be the wet weather."

Keg grinned. "You wouldn't believe it, if I told you."

Anastacio looked an inquiry at Keg that clearly said: *Try me?*

Keg continued: "You'll hear about it soon enough, anyhow, so you might as well get it from the horse's mouth, or in this case maybe from the other end, the way it came out." He told Anastacio what Ransom had done to him.

"I can hardly believe it," the Mexican leader responded.

"That makes two of us."

Cleve had been resting easy in the wagon, dozing occasionally. Amy was on the wagon seat beside the driver. She heard Keg's story and had as much trouble believing it as Anastacio had. She didn't think anyone could whip Keg except maybe her pa, and she wasn't too sure about that.

"What're you two coyotes jawin' about?" Cleve asked.

Keg rode alongside and told him.

"Well, I'll be go to hell!" Cleve exclaimed.

A little farther along a jackrabbit jumped up under the wagon team's noses and spooked them. Before the driver could curb the team, the wagon tilted into a ditch and tipped, spilling

Cleve onto the ground under it. Amy screamed as she scrambled out just in time to avoid being crushed. Bruised and scraped, but clear-headed, she ran to the horses' heads, grabbed the cheek straps of both their bridles, and hung on with all her strength to keep them from dragging the wagon away in a scared run with her father under it. They jerked her off the ground, but she still held on grimly, biting her lip and tongue. She choked on the salty blood, but tried to ignore it. Anastacio cut his horse in front of the team and blocked it until others rushed in, grabbed bridles, and settled the horses down with reassuring words. Only then could they pry Amy loose and help her away, gagging and dizzy from the violent shaking the horses had given her.

Keg rushed to the wagon and lifted it by himself. Lord Ransom galloped up, leaped down, and was just a little too late to help. Mariposa followed, dismounted, and went to Cleve's side. He'd been badly shaken by the fall, but she noticed that he was as stoic as she'd heard Indians were, and again wondered if he had Indian ancestors. His wound had broken open; bright blood was staining his shirt. She took charge at once.

"Monty, take off your shirt and tear it up into bandages. It's the only clean piece of rag around, unless we tear up my petticoat."

By then Amy had recovered and was beside her. "Is he all right?" she asked in a frightened voice.

Mariposa put an arm around her shoulders and squeezed her, amazed at how skinny she was. "He's all right," she assured her. "I'm a nurse, and we're going to clean up and bandage his wound again. I want you to help me." Then she noticed Amy's bloody lips and asked: "What happened?" while brushing at the blood with a small white handkerchief.

"I bit my lip. My tongue, too." Amy let out a little hysterical laugh. "But I guess I'm all right now."

Mariposa said: "You were a brave girl. Now you can help me and take your mind off of it."

Mariposa was almost sure there wasn't any disinfectant, so didn't even ask, but suspected there would be plenty of whiskey in this crowd of fighting men. It would work as well as anything for disinfectant.

Cleve tried to read her facial expressions as she skillfully cut away his dirty old clothes. She handed him the whiskey bottle. "Drink some. This might hurt."

He took the bottle and followed orders.

Amy looked at the terrible bloody rip the bullet had made, now black and blue and even a little green and yellow around the ragged edges. She almost fainted. It wasn't easy to believe her eyes when Mariposa put her nose down and sniffed the ugly hole.

"No infection," Mariposa pronounced, not even making a face. "We can thank God for that."

There were maggots in both the entry and exit wounds, which had probably averted gangrene. She brushed them away, wondering how they'd got in there in the first place, amazed as always at nature's ways. She wasn't going to kill the little things that had probably saved Cleve's life. Only then did she wash the wound with whiskey. Once the wound was clean, she had Keg help Cleve sit up while she tied the compress-bandage in place with strips of cloth wrapped securely around his whole body, after which she refastened his belt over it to hold it firmly.

Cleve took another big swig of the whiskey before he handed the bottle to Keg. "Yours?" he asked. "I notice it's your brand."

Keg said: "They're all my brand," and took a big swig.

Cleve said to Mariposa: "Thanks, lady. I owe you."

Close up, she could feel the animal strength radiating from him, even though he was badly hurt. She sensed none of the surrender to fear in him that was frequently the prelude to death in people who were hurt and scared. The thought of Rob Roy came back, and her heart gave a lurch.

He said: "You and Ransom can go back now."

She looked at him silently, directly. The intensity of her eyes struck him deeply inside. He had never seen anyone like her. In his limited experience beautiful women were vain and flighty. This one was something else: obviously very strong, a fighter, modestly unconscious of her female impact, and, in any case, lacking the guile to use such power.

She shook her head. "I'm going to stay with you until I'm sure you won't need me any longer. You will require a few days of good nursing."

Cleve wondered how that would sit with Dolores Zamora. He was somewhat surprised she hadn't insisted on coming with her brothers. He wasn't aware that she was visiting in Antonita, but was thinking that a problem would surely crop up when Dolores found Mariposa nursing him. With that in mind he said: "I can probably make out now, but I sure won't forget you."

She stared at him earnestly. "I'm coming anyhow. We can't be sure you won't need me again."

"I think she's right, Bandelier," Ransom said. "Besides, I'd like to talk to you. I think we should have talked before now."

Cleve looked at him and tried to figure that out. It was true. All the trouble could have been averted if they had. "O K," he agreed. "We're probably long overdue for a talk."

The sun was far down in the west when they reached Zamora Plaza. Mariposa surveyed the adobe and stone buildings, sprawled along a tumbling creek, the whole set in a verdant bowl in the hills. Small garden patches bordered the creek, protected by stone walls from free-roaming cattle, sheep, and horses. Goats were penned, and chickens were fenced in away from coyotes. A pack of mongrels rushed to meet them, barking furiously. Children followed, yelling. Women and old men stayed in the background but, nonetheless, were talking excitedly.

When the wagon stopped, many came up to it, and Cleve tried to sit up to greet old friends and squeeze the many hands offered to him.

"We will carry you into my house, *amigo*," Anastacio said. "It is yours."

Cleve looked at Mariposa and Ransom. "How about them?" he asked.

Anastacio said in his booming voice: "We can take care of them, too. Don't worry." He didn't even give Ransom a dirty look as he said it. What Ransom had done to Keg, while hardly mussing his own hair, had set him up high in the eyes of this fighting man, whatever his past sins were. As for Mariposa, Anastacio had watched her work on Cleve and already had made up his mind he'd die for her, if need be.

Chapter Twenty-Four

Monty and Mariposa, of course, did not return by sundown. Percy had taken charge of the ranch by default, with Voerbeck in Santa Fé and the crew obviously conditioned not to think. He kept a horse saddled and waiting at the house. Both he and Daisy were acutely aware of marking time, waiting for the drama to play out, tension building in them with each passing hour.

"Well," Percy sighed, "it's sundown, and there's only one thing to do."

Daisy said: "I don't like the idea of staying here alone, but I guess I wouldn't be of much help if I came along."

"True. And you're hardly alone with thirty or forty people around."

"You know what I mean."

He gave her a hug and headed out the door. She followed and watched him ride away. He obviously knew which road went toward town, and she recalled his brag that he never got lost. *I hope he doesn't,* she thought. *That would be all I'd need to come unraveled. I wonder how poor Mariposa is making out.*

Percy, who had no idea where to look for the sheriff, was attracted to the lights of the Santiago Hotel, entered the bar, and inquired. His English accent netted him a careful look from the bartender who said: "The tall, skinny feller over there with the mop'll show you for four bits."

"Four bits?" Percy asked, confused.

"Yeah. Fifty cents American, a half dollar."

"Oh."

"Hey, Dick-Dick," the bartender yelled. "How about takin' this gent over to the sheriff's house?"

When they got there, Percy gave him a whole silver dollar, which Dick-Dick recognized even in the dark by its size. "Thanks, thanks a heap," he said. "Just go up and knock on the door. I'll wait, and, if he ain't home, I'll take you down to the jail."

Butler himself answered the knock.

Percy said: "I'm Baron Waterford, a friend of Lord Ransom's, staying at the ranch. He and Mister Voerbeck's daughter have been abducted."

Butler kept a poker face, silently digesting that. Then he said: "I'm just settin' down to supper. Have you et?"

Percy was a little surprised at the calm reaction. If he'd come down to Scotland Yard and told them a wealthy heiress had been kidnapped, they'd hardly have told him they were just having dinner, but this was a different world, as he was discovering. He correctly assumed he was being invited to eat.

"No, I haven't, but I'm not sure I could eat with my best friend and his fiancée being carried off by a band of ruffians." Besides, he wasn't sure he wanted to risk eating this barbarian's fare.

Butler recognized a possible reproof but ignored it. "Come, have a chair anyhow, and tell me about it. There ain't much I can do till morning."

Percy followed the sheriff through the front room into the kitchen where the table was set. Butler introduced him: "This is the missus, and this is Junior who's stayin' with us. This is Baron Waterford. Did I get that right?"

"Yes," he said, surprised to find the sheriff married to a Mexican woman, and one getting pretty hefty at that. The boy had obviously broken a leg recently, judging by the relatively clean plaster cast.

Percy accepted a chair and a cup of coffee. The boy and woman ignored him and went back to eating, but he was aware they were watching him and sizing him up, anxious to hear why he was there.

"Spill it," Butler said, cutting a big piece of steak, forking it into his mouth, and chewing rapidly.

Percy told the story as he had learned it, including what Domingo had told them. He finished by saying: "I guess the outlaw, Bandelier, is holding them."

"That's a damned lie!" the boy said. "My pa ain't no outlaw! If you furrin crooks would stay home, where you belong, we'd all get along a hell of a lot better."

"My word!" Percy gasped, realizing who the boy was. He looked at the sheriff as much as to say: *We don't let little ruffians speak insolently to their betters in England.* Butler had trouble stifling a guffaw.

Percy gave Junior a reproving look and got it back with interest. "Why don't I wait somewhere else until you've finished eating?"

"I'm finished. Let's go in the front room while Junior helps Ma clean up. We can talk there."

Percy was dismayed to see the sheriff roll a cigarette and spill tobacco all over himself and the floor. They sat in rocking chairs, facing each other. Butler said: "I don't see a thing I can do tonight. Those people ain't gonna hurt your friends. They may be holding them because I've got that boy here. Maybe they want to arrange a swap. In that case, there ain't a problem. He isn't under arrest. He can go join his pa anytime he's able."

Unfortunately, Junior wasn't aware of that. He went out the back door, managed to mount Percy's horse on the awkward saddle, and was on his way to tell his pa what was going on. He wondered how to shoot the strange rifle, sticking up high in the scabbard on the right side of the saddle. In the dark he couldn't be sure whether it was actually a rifle or a shotgun. Well, if he had to, he'd figure out how to use it. The horse, at least, was a good one with a ground-covering trot. He couldn't use the right stirrup because of his cast and didn't need the other, having ridden bareback almost from the cradle. With luck, he'd be up at Zamora Plaza long before morning.

Butler told Percy: "I couldn't get up a posse big enough to take that crowd. I'll come by the ranch in the morning and pick you up, and we'll go in there alone and talk to 'em. It'd take an army to whip all those people. I really don't think you have anything to worry about."

He went back out with Percy, and they found the latter's horse missing.

"Great guns!" Percy exploded. "My damn' horse is gone."

Butler asked: "You sure you tied him good?"

"Of course."

"Maybe some kid come along and untied him, just to be ornery."

"In front of the sheriff's house?"

"Sure, *especially* in front of the sheriff's house. They don't mean anything by it."

"I heard they hang people out here for horse stealing."

"Not kids."

Percy inquired: "What sort of country is this?"

"Better'n most. Leastways we don't hang kids."

"Some of them probably need it," Percy observed, thinking of Junior Bandelier. "Damn!" he cursed. "Now, how in the deuce am I going to get back to the ranch?"

"Well," suggested Butler, "we can look around town for your horse, or get you one from the livery. Better yet, why don't you stay down at the hotel for the night? The ranch keeps a room there."

"I might as well stay but is there really any point in my going with you in the morning?"

Butler considered that before he said anything, and an idea that appealed to him came to mind. *Why should anyone go?* He was mortally certain that Anastacio Zamora and his people weren't going to hurt a woman no more than would Bandelier. "No reason for you to go unless you want. Two of us won't do any more good than one. Like I said, it'd take an army to force them into anything."

"I'll be over at the hotel for the night," Percy said and walked away.

Butler's remark about the Army had given Percy an idea. He knew that Voerbeck had the pull in Washington, D. C., to have the Army called out to rescue his kidnapped daughter. He'd send a message out to the ranch so Daisy wouldn't worry about him, then catch the train out in the morning.

What the sheriff didn't know when he told Percy about the ranch's hotel room was that Pancho Wingfield was there, sleeping off a load he'd tied on, trying to forget his troubles, especially his close call with Anastacio's army.

Butler watched Percy's departing figure with relief. He had neglected to inform the Englishman that, since he wasn't coming with him, he saw no reason to go up to Zamora Plaza, either. Let him swear out a complaint first. While he had been talking to Percy, a thought had occurred to him, regarding who may have taken his horse. He went back in the house and asked his wife where Junior was and got a blank look.

"I sent him out with the scraps for the dogs. I thought he stayed out there with you."

A search of the premises turned up nothing. Butler said: "Unless I'm mistaken, the kid just took that Englishman's horse and headed up to Zamora Plaza."

They both laughed. "Good," she said. "I don't like these

Englishmen and their highfalutin manners."

The night clerk at the hotel was also frequently the bartender. There wasn't enough business to keep anyone on duty all the time. Percy had to find that out for himself by going into the bar and asking.

"I reckon you'll want to stay in the ranch's room," the night clerk said. "I'll have Dick-Dick show you the way."

Dick-Dick, too, was unaware that Wingfield was already in the room. He went ahead with a lamp and was surprised to find another one lit in the room when he unlocked and opened the door, and was even more surprised to see Wingfield, sitting on the chamber pot with a six-shooter trained on him. He was scared speechless.

"Oh, it's you," Wingfield said.

Percy looked around Dick-Dick and said: "My word, pardon us." He started to withdraw.

"Who the hell are you?" Wingfield asked, then recognized the fellow that had driven him off with a scatter-gun up at Tres Huérfanos.

Dick-Dick got his voice back. "We didn't know you was up here, Mister Wingfield. This is a friend of Lord Ransom's."

Wingfield grinned. "Come in, then. Any friend of old Monty is a friend of mine." He wanted to have a talk with this fellow, even if it had to be under his current circumstances. He needed more information about what was going on, and how much anyone knew or suspected about him. This man might innocently reveal that.

Percy had no desire to intrude on the situation and no wish to associate with anyone as disheveled as the man on the chamber pot. Besides, the room reeked with stale cigarette smoke, whiskey fumes, and the contents of the pot. However, this was the man that Voerbeck wanted to see and pump, so he braved up to his obvious duty. He said: "I'll get another room, but I'd be happy to buy you a drink downstairs a little later. I think I need one. I'll be in the saloon."

He didn't give the other a chance to say anything, but noted that he was grinning when he and Dick-Dick backed out and closed the door.

"Jesus Christ!" Dick-Dick quavered. "We could've got shot."

"Surely not," Percy disagreed. "We merely surprised the fellow."

"Do you know who that is?"

"Mister Wingfield, I believe you called him."

"Yeah. And he must've killed about a dozen men in his day, maybe some fer less'n we done."

Percy wasn't convinced. This was a strange and obviously violent place, but he couldn't believe that men killed that casually. He hoped Wingfield would accept his invitation to a drink. After getting another room, he went to the saloon, ordered a drink at the bar, and took it to a table. The only other occupants in the place was a group of men, playing poker at the back of the room.

Percy was gratified to see Wingfield poke his head in a little later and called: "Over here." When Pancho joined him, he said: "What would you like, and I'll have that pathetic creature bring it over." He indicated Dick-Dick with a nod.

Wingfield grinned. He'd heard Dick-Dick called a lot of things but had to agree that fit him the best of anything he'd heard so far. "Hey, Dick-Dick," he called, "bring me the usual." He looked Percy over. "Like I said, any friend of old Monty is O K with me."

Percy didn't realize that Pancho also had seen in him a golden opportunity to obtain information. Wingfield raised his glass, eyed it appreciatively, and tossed it off in one gulp. "Hey, Dick-Dick, bring us another one," he yelled.

Percy concluded that the fellow had been on a substantial bat and needed a few bracers to straighten up on. He'd been there many a time himself. Despite Wingfield's rough reputation, Percy decided to butter him up and see if it got him anything. He said: "Monty told me he didn't know what he'd do without you to run the ranch. You must have had many years' experience."

Pancho eyed him for any signs of guile and saw none. "Been in the business ever since the war. Learned it from the ground up. By the way, where is Monty?"

Percy saw no reason to evade the question, though he would have, if he'd known more about Wingfield's current attitude. "He's up at some place called Zamora Plaza."

"What the hell is he doing up there?"

Percy told him the whole story. Wingfield had no trouble omitting the information that he might well be there himself but for a little luck. He figured that Ransom and the girl had run into the same little army that he had.

"Too bad," Pancho said. "If Bandelier has them, there's no telling what he might do to them."

"Is he as bad as they say?"

"Worse."

"How in the world are we going to rescue them?"

Wingfield thought: *Who the hell wants to rescue old Monty? The girl might be something else.* He said: "It'd take an army to go up there, and they'd probably kill Monty and the girl before they gave them up."

Wingfield cocked his feet up on the table and leaned back comfortably. Percy noted the fancy boots, then saw the W near their tops and knew this was the man he'd prevented from killing the boy at Tres Huérfanos. Wingfield must recognize him, yet had made no sign. The man was a lot more sophisticated than he appeared. If Wingfield was the killer that Dick-

Dick claimed, Percy's life could be in danger every moment he was in his presence. It didn't deter him from pressing on with his fishing expedition.

"I'm going down to Santa Fé tomorrow to inform Mister Voerbeck what's happened to his daughter and Monty. I suppose we could wire, but it would be better to give him the details personally, what do you think?"

Wingfield weighed that, wanting to think over its implications for his own situation. Then he said: "It won't hurt to hold off on the news a few hours. There's nothing he can do about it anyhow, unless he can bring in the Army, and they ain't allowed to butt into such affairs any more. Some colonel got his ass into it down in Lincoln County for that. They ain't about to get mixed up in anything like that. Especially General Gryden. They tell me he's tighter'n a bull's ass in fly time about goin' by the book." All the time he talked, he was thinking about his own future moves. "I don't reckon Monty told you, but I'm on my way back home to Texas. I was plannin' to pull out on the train in the A.M."

"Will you stay around a few days to help us rescue Lord Ransom?"

"I don't see how I'd be much help. Besides, I kind've aimed to pack it in around here. Too damn cold in the winter. I told Monty I probably wouldn't be back."

Percy wondered what that signified, correctly thinking it didn't ring true for some reason. Was it possible that this fellow knew that a good thing was over now that Voerbeck was here? Very likely. A thought occurred to him, and he asked Wingfield: "We'll most likely be on the same train tomorrow, won't we? What time does it come through?"

"No tellin'. Supposed to come through at about ten but could be any time. You know, I reckon, it only goes as far as Española? Folks have to take the stage from there."

"No, I didn't. In any case, I'd be happy to buy your breakfast in the morning before we leave."

"You got a customer," Wingfield said. He rose. "I've got to go up the street and visit some friends, so I'll see you in the A.M." He had a perverse notion to drag Percy down to Maud's and thought better of it, since he was planning to pump Percy further on the trip to Santa Fé. He had decided to find out as much as possible, then check in with Pringle.

The only place to get a meal in Dorado was The Railroad Cafe operated by *Tía* Placida. It was open only on mornings when a train was due. Pancho Wingfield found Percy already there and joined him at a table. They had barely ordered when Devil Ed came in, looked around, and hobbled over to Pancho on one of Doc Ewing's gadgets made of a cut up boot with iron side braces, all plastered inside a cast so he could navigate. His bare toes stuck out the front. He scarcely looked at Percy and said to Pancho: "I need a stake."

Pancho fished a purse from his vest, took out a double eagle, and handed it to him without a word. Devil Ed went to the counter and slouched down, not looking back. Pancho figured he must be getting his mind unscrambled, since he sounded normal — or as normal as he ever did, which was good, since he'd been extremely useful and could be again.

"Who in God's name is that astonishing creature?" Percy asked, perplexed as well by the fact that Pancho had shelled out a gold piece without question to a man whose odor still hung in the air.

"He works for the ranch," Pancho said in a low voice. "I'll tell you about him later."

Outside, after breakfast, Percy noted a well-formed paint horse and said: "I wonder who owns that horse . . . surely not that monster inside."

"Naw," Pancho said. "He's mine. I bought him from the ranch."

Percy, horseman to the core, looked the paint over closely. He pointed to the brand. "What are these marks that you Americans put on your horses?"

"Brands, to identify 'em."

"Why do you need to do that?"

Wingfield had trouble not showing his impatience. "We brand 'em so it's harder to get away with stealing 'em. Do the same with cows. We don't have any fences and damn' few barns. It'd be different if we could go out in a little dinky postage-stamp pasture and find them there every morning. Of course, we use the brands on cows to round them up and sort them out."

"How in the world do you get a mark like that to stay on?"

Pancho looked a trifle amazed. "Why, we burn it in with a hot iron."

"My word! It must hurt like fury."

Pancho laughed. "I suppose it does."

Percy changed the subject. "You were going to tell me something about the crude-looking individual inside."

"Oh, yeah. That's Devil Ed Targee. He works for the ranch."

"Doing what?"

"He's a scout. First rate at tracking stolen cows and horses, and tracking men, too. He's aces at doin' it so's they don't know he's trailing 'em."

"If he's good at that, he must have tracked down a lot of the cows that were stolen before the thieves got away."

"Some. The trouble is Bandelier and his crowd have too many men. We can't watch 'em all. When we find out some cattle have been stolen, we go after them and bring them back."

Percy thought of the remark Ransom had made that maybe

the cattle involved in the fight at Tres Huérfanos had been stolen from Voerbeck. That thought led to another: that the mark Wingfield called a brand was the same on this paint horse as on the horse the man with the W on his boots, obviously Wingfield, had ridden when he shot Bandelier's young cowboy. That horse had been a dun. Naturally a fellow up to mischief wouldn't ride a horse as easy to identify as a paint. Percy got a creepy feeling, thinking that perhaps this man, whom Dick-Dick had branded the killer of many men, might divine what he was putting together about him in his mind. He'd taken the precaution of putting his Irish Guards pistol in his back pocket and hoped it didn't show under his coat.

"Is there a name for the brand on your horse?" Percy asked.

"Diamond A."

It never occurred to Pancho that this ignorant Englishman might associate the brand on his horse with one he had seen on the horse Wingfield had been was riding in the raid at Tres Huérfanos. If it had, he wouldn't have cared too much, since Ransom already knew who'd pulled off the raid. Percy reminded Pancho of Ransom, so dense he was entertaining. He was beginning to like him.

Pancho loaded his horse into the stock car that local trains always included for men like him, then joined Percy in the single passenger car. Side by side they presented a marked contrast, the dark, black-eyed Englishman with a carefully trimmed mustache, wearing an English riding habit, and the blond, blue-eyed Texan with a long, shaggy handlebar, both possessed of jutting chins typical of fighting men the world over. Pancho wore cow-country dress, Levi's tucked into his tall high-heeled boots, checked flannel shirt, worn vest, and a weathered, floppy-brimmed Stetson.

Percy offered Pancho a cigar and was happy to see him light it, rather than cut it up for a pipe as the doctor had done. He lit his own, then said: "I'd like to know more about this man, Bandelier. Is he really as bad as I've heard?"

"Like I told you last night, maybe worse."

"What do you mean by that?"

"He used to be in the Army. I heard he was thrown out for being too hard on the men, may have killed one or two of his own detail. He's drygulched some around here since he came in and started a ranch. His ranch has grown so fast it's a sure thing that he's stealin' his neighbors blind all the time, particularly us."

"What is 'drygulched?' " Percy asked.

"Killed. When you get shot by somebody hidin' on your trail, or when they sneak up on you, especially at night. He's dragged men outside of their own houses at night, took them away, and hung them or shot them, and even shot them through their windows. People keep blankets over their windows at night on account of him and his men."

"Great heavens! Do very many get shot like that?"

"Plenty. Some we don't even hear about if they live alone. They just disappear. Lots of widows have packed out of the country with a tribe of orphans on account of Bandelier."

Percy was watching Pancho's face while he told all this and thought: *He looks so earnest and truthful, I can hardly doubt what he's saying. Voerbeck has to have a chance to talk to this man. Maybe he can't afford to lose him. He could be exactly the medicine to fight Bandelier, if what he's saying is true.* "Does Bandelier do this all himself?"

"He's got a lot of cutthroats to back him, mostly Mexicans and Indians. Life's cheap to them."

"What you've been telling me is certainly interesting." Percy watched Pancho very closely as he added: "On the way down here we ran across a fight where some men, wearing white hoods, were stealing Bandelier's cattle and shooting at his men.

Do you have any idea who they were?"

Pancho hadn't expected this question, certainly not directly. He flushed, searching for a suitable answer. "I didn't hear about that. It was probably some of the small ranchers trying to get their cows back. They wear masks because they're afraid Bandelier and his gang will find out who they are."

Percy thought: *Bravo! Not a bad lie for having to think it up on the spur of the moment.*

When they parted in Española, Percy wasn't sure that he didn't believe Wingfield, or at least wasn't sure what he should believe. He was certain that Voerbeck should have a chance to talk to him if at all possible. Accordingly, as they shook hands and parted, Percy said: "I think you should wait for me in Santa Fé and go talk to Mister Voerbeck and tell him what you've told me. I think he'll be very interested."

Percy had been troubled at the time over Domingo's and Sheriff Butler's comfortable assumptions that the kidnapped pair would be back alive and well. Domingo had said they'd be back the same night they were captured, but they weren't. Domingo could well be Bandelier's spy on the ranch. He certainly didn't want his best friend hurt and possibly killed, and, needless to say, one didn't kidnap ladies, especially beautiful ones. Suppose they ravished her?

Wingfield was certain now he shouldn't leave New Mexico just yet. He congratulated himself for a fine job of acting — and lying. He saddled up and rode out of Española at once, not even stopping for a drink, intending to reach Santa Fé well ahead of the stagecoach and confer with Pringle. He wondered how much it would be wise to tell Pringle, regarding recent events up on the ranch. He was sure he'd already heard of the twin killings of his U. S. deputy marshals. He wasn't looking forward to hearing about his horning into that. Nonetheless, he felt elated. His lies to Waterford would have a beneficial effect, since the baron would give Voerbeck a good report, and maybe he could salvage his soft spot here yet — provided he could muzzle Ransom. All the more reason to see Pringle as soon as possible and get his new marching orders straight. If anyone could muzzle Ransom, it was Pringle. He had even more on him than Pancho did, enough to put him in prison.

Chapter Twenty-Five

Grut Voerbeck carried a letter of introduction to General Gryden. It was the sort of introduction that guaranteed a cordial reception, even from usually gruff Army officers, unless they didn't want to live and do well in their profession. Gryden did. He was one of the former Civil War generals, every one of whom hoped to wear stars again someday. All they'd salvaged of their glory was the right to be addressed as general, regardless of their actual rank.

In contrast the orderly, who was self-importantly guarding the door of the colonel's office, did not expect to make general someday and, in fact, never expected a better job than he had. Furthermore, he wasn't kindly disposed toward little, bespectacled civilians with foreign accents. He accepted the sealed envelope that Voerbeck handed him, offered him a chair, but showed no disposition to do much else in a hurry. Then he glanced at the return address on the envelope:

Chester A. Arthur
President of the United States
The White House
Washington, D. C.

One of the reasons the orderly was holding his job was that he could read. What he read animated him as though he were sitting on something uncomfortably hot. He shot into the vestibule of the colonel's office where Voerbeck heard him knocking as peremptorily as he suspected an orderly was allowed to knock on his commander's door, and the old Dutchman smiled. America might boast of a classless society, but some things were the same the world over.

Shortly Gryden came out and extended his hand. "It's a pleasure to have you visiting us, sir. Come into my office where we can talk."

He led the way, offered Voerbeck a chair, then a cigar from a humidor on his desk. Voerbeck, estimating the quality of cigars that colonels smoked, reached into his coat, and withdrew his leather cigar case. "Let me offer you a prime Havana, sir."

Gryden accepted the cigar, said "Thank you," bit off the end without preliminary, and lit it, the beatific look of the *true* cigar smoker with a *true* cigar infusing his expression.

Voerbeck joined him, blowing smoke at the ceiling.

"A fine cigar. Thanks again. It's hard to get fresh ones out here," Gryden said. "Now sir, I am at your service."

Voerbeck thought: *Obviously.* Nonetheless, he liked Gryden's looks, a tall, thin man with a horseman's narrow hips and long legs. Not the usual heavy-handed professional cavalryman, he possessed the face of a scholar and wore a Van Dyke beard and mustache, all set off by twinkly, intelligent brown eyes. Even Voerbeck had heard of Gryden's famous raid that pulled General Grant's chestnuts out of the fire and made Gryden a general.

Voerbeck said: "I am not familiar with what Chester wrote to you, but my immediate needs are limited." The *Chester* naturally sunk in as intended. Not everyone addressed the President by his first name or even thought of him that way. Voerbeck continued: "I am looking into the condition of a property I purchased a few years ago, with which you may be familiar. The Amarillo Grant."

Gryden nodded. Everyone was familiar with the grant, and

anyone who read the territorial newspapers was familiar with the name Voerbeck, either as the foreign schemer who had done honest Americans out of their land, or the benefactor who was going to bring prosperity and civilization into the hinterlands. Gryden was probably more familiar than most with the affair.

He said: "Perhaps you should read what the President wrote?" and handed him Arthur's letter.

My Dear General Gryden:

The gentleman who will present you with this letter, Grut Voerbeck, is an old and dear friend. Your attention to his needs, which he will make known to you, will be appreciated. I am sure you will provide every lawful assistance to him.

Sincerely,
Chester A. Arthur
President of the United States
Commander in Chief

It was clear to Voerbeck that this was no simple request but an order, made clear by the words "I am sure you *will* provide" rather than "I would be gratified if you would" and the addition of the title, Commander in Chief. Chester was a man who didn't forget past favors and friends, or one who was unconscious of the possible need for future favors after he was out of office. This could be a very useful piece of paper. Of course, the word *lawful* provided the colonel with a "protect your rear" escape clause in case Voerbeck's requests were too risky.

"You must know the President well?" Gryden hazarded.

Voerbeck nodded, not volunteering that he'd bribed him often when he was collector of the New York Port Authority, as had anyone else with a lick of sense. Arthur's reputation wasn't the best, and he was snidely known as "His Accidency," due to the fact that he held office only because of the assassination of President Garfield. Nonetheless, the key point was that he *did* hold office, would for another three years, and might even be reëlected.

Voerbeck puffed on his cigar for a while without answering the implied question. Finally he said: "I am a sort of orphan in a strange land, especially out here in your Wild West. I think I need some advice to avoid the wolves, but I hardly know where to turn."

Gryden nodded again but couldn't think of anything to say until he found out more about what was being implied, so he waited, happily puffing his cigar, his eyes attentively on Voerbeck.

"That's one reason I'm here. You are in a position to be more objective than most of the people I deal with. I've come here to talk with Mister Pringle, who I'm sure you know. A few years ago he helped me acquire the grant. I have corresponded with him on a few occasions but have never met him. I was concerned to discover that the grant was involved in heavy legal troubles even when I purchased it, which have become more extensive since. It is not a large investment, and I have not devoted the attention to it that I should have. I'm here partly to make up for that, but I'm afraid it's a case of figuratively locking the barn after the horse is stolen . . . in this case a lot of cattle. Several thousand, as a matter of fact. But that's not all. I find that hundreds of small landholders, who thought they held legal titles to homesteads and small ranches, have been dispossessed by the courts and the land commissioners, but they are not willing to vacate the land without a fight. I have been told that the leader of this resistance is a man named Bandelier, who is either an outlaw, depending on who one listens to, or a Robin Hood. Do you happen to know him?"

"No, sir. Naturally, I have heard of him."

"And what have you heard?"

"I suspect about the same thing you have."

"And what is that?"

Gryden smiled, impressed with Voerbeck's bulldog pursuit of information. "He comes across either as an angel or a devil."

Voerbeck nodded. "Exactly. Have you any opinion?"

"Well, he's an ex-Army man who had a very good record. He never served under me, but since these troubles I have made it a point to ask officers under whom he served for an opinion."

"And?"

"He panned out pretty much pure gold."

"That's what I'm beginning to suspect. I was told he was a bandit and that most of my cattle losses were due to the rustling, as I believe it's called, of Bandelier and his followers. Coming down here on the train from Colorado, we became embroiled in the middle of a shooting that involved the theft of Bandelier's cattle, not mine, and one of our party saved one of his men from being killed. I have the man, who was seriously wounded, at the ranch now, recuperating." He laughed at the thought of why the invalid was probably there and explained: "My daughter is a compulsive nurse. Besides, there's no hospital up in Dorado."

Gryden, who had an effective intelligence network, knew of the affair already, as he did of almost everything of significance that happened in the territory. He'd already heard as well of the two marshals allegedly killed by Bandelier. He wondered if Voerbeck had yet heard of those. No doubt he'd mention it sooner or later, if he had.

Voerbeck rose, hauled out his gold watch, consulted it, and said: "Well, I mustn't take up more of your time, General. I am staying at La Fonda and value my naps, so I think I'll go over there for a lunch, then nap a while. I have an appointment with Mister Pringle later."

"I wish we had known you were coming, sir, because I'd have put you up in my quarters. There's lots of room, since the wife is back home visiting, and I'd have appreciated the company . . . especially of a man that keeps a supply of these cigars." He chuckled and lovingly appraised his half-smoked cigar.

Voerbeck hastily reached for his case and offered it to Gryden. "Here. Please accept this as a gift. You may earn it, but it's my pleasure to gratify a fellow cigar smoker in any case."

Gryden protested: "I couldn't, really. But I will accept another one." He took one and returned the case.

"Maybe later, when we know each other better," Voerbeck said. "Oh, one last thing you might favor me with."

"If I can."

"What is your opinion of Mister Pringle?"

Gryden eyed him carefully, trying to judge how far he could carry the truth. He liked this generous and intelligent old fellow and wanted to help him.

Sensing what was behind Gryden's hesitation, Voerbeck prompted: "I don't know the man at all. What you say won't go beyond this room. But I do need an honest appraisal of him for the sake of my future dealings in the territory, which I hope may rectify any injustices that have been done in the past."

Gryden thought: *I wonder if he believes, as I do, that Pringle is actually at the root of a lot of those injustices?* He decided to gamble on the man. He said: "My frank opinion is that Mister Pringle and, for that matter, most of his associates in what they call the Santa Fé Ring are so crooked they'll have to be screwed in the ground when they die." He laughed dryly. Voerbeck joined in the laugh.

"Ah, General," he said, "I suspected you were going to be

a man after my own heart when I discovered you were a judge of good cigars."

As Voerbeck was leaving, Gryden debated telling him something else he'd recently learned about Pringle, but decided it would keep.

Voerbeck was already aware of the delightful addiction of the country to the Spanish custom of *siestas*. He allowed himself until three P.M. before making his way to Tomás Pringle's office. He was surprised to find Pringle just leaving. Pringle gave him a glance and said: "Come back tomorrow."

Voerbeck called after him: "I'd just like a second to thank you for a past favor. . . ."

Pringle paused and turned partly, tilting his head to observe Voerbeck more closely, and waited.

"Years ago you helped me purchase a piece of land. . . ." Pringle started to turn away, when the old man slyly added: "My name is Grut Voerbeck. You may remember me."

Pringle turned like he'd been spun by an invisible hand, his whole mien changed, and he came back, extended his hand, and said: "Indeed, I do! It's a pleasure to meet you, sir. You should have let us know you were coming."

Pringle made a note to have someone's head if they knew Voerbeck was in the country and hadn't informed him. Ransom came to mind as the most likely culpable party. The old man must have been to the ranch, and he surmised how he'd come there. Why hadn't Ransom wired him? "Please come into my office . . . I was headed out on an errand, but it can wait."

The fact was he'd have passed up a front seat at the Second Coming to talk to Voerbeck. His curiosity over the Dutchman's presence practically stuck out of his ears.

Observing Pringle's appearance, the first thought that occurred to Voerbeck was: *This man has something he wants very badly to conceal from me.*

Pringle's pop-eyed baby face made an instantly bad impression on the old man. The signs of what General Gryden had mentioned showed all over him. Moreover, he had a high, piping voice of the variety that had always suggested questionable manhood to Voerbeck.

"Well, Mister Voerbeck," Pringle launched his inquiry, "what can I do for you?"

Voerbeck smiled blandly. "I'm not sure you can do anything for me. I dropped by to thank you for your earlier efforts on my behalf. I really came to town to get acquainted with the people I've heard about all these years from Frank Carson and, of course, to see Frank. He's been most useful."

Pringle said to himself: *Well, what the hell do you know about that? Carson has been holding out on us.* If he'd read Carson's letter, which was in Voerbeck's pocket, he'd have swooned.

Pringle was unsure how to continue, and Voerbeck let him fidget. The ring's leader finally took out one of his cigars and went about getting it ready to light, taking his time. He hoped he was going to get off pretty light. He'd anticipated being reproved, in that he'd obviously been well aware in advance of the pending litigation regarding the grant that had landed in Voerbeck's lap as a surprise. Such impending complications had made no difference to Pringle at the time because, in effect, he'd been desperate to find a suitable interim holding party until he could finance a purchase himself. He hadn't changed his outlook about Voerbeck's rôle in his plans. Getting ownership of the grant had become an obsession.

Finally Voerbeck said: "There are a few small matters about which you might inform me."

Pringle looked interested. "Anything I know."

"For one thing, I had the impression that the grant was rather smaller than I've since discovered. Of course, that's nothing to complain about, or wouldn't be normally, but it seems that a lot of other people had the same impression."

"Oh, I wasn't aware of that. Who might they be?"

"A few hundred settlers who have homesteaded on the land under the U. S. Homestead Act, which I have had looked into."

"Well, that's their problem, as I see it. They should have known better."

"I have discovered that the U. S. Land Commissioners held the same view at the time. Should they have known better?"

"They've been replaced."

"So I understand."

This wasn't going the way Pringle had hoped. This man knew too much for comfort, and he wondered how much more he'd found out.

Voerbeck continued: "I don't see where there would have been any particular problem except for those ignorant people. If there is no other problem, they can probably be bought out. Are there any other problems?"

"None that I'm aware of." The prospect of Voerbeck's buying out the settlers and, in effect, solving a future problem for Pringle pleased him immensely.

Voerbeck sunk his harpoon with a seemingly innocent remark. "I assume, then, that you haven't heard of the beatings and killings up on the grant. How is that?"

Pringle hoped his jaw hadn't dropped, but it was a vain hope, and Voerbeck had been watching him like a hawk for reaction. "Those are rather isolated instances. There haven't been any that I've heard of for a long while."

"Odd that the news hasn't reached here that a man named Bandelier allegedly killed two U. S. deputy marshals at his ranch the other night, delivering papers on your behalf, especially since the sheriff was out there, and there is a telegraph between here and there."

Pringle took that solar plexus punch very well, though he

was astonished at how much this shrewd Dutchman had found out in a short while. "That isn't supposed to be public knowledge yet."

"What will your notoriously hostile American newspapers say about it?"

Pringle almost said — "I don't give a damn!" — which was the fact of the matter. Another fact was that the U. S. Attorney was preparing murder warrants on Bandelier and planned to pull him in for a preliminary hearing before the U. S. Commissioner. "We are in a rather touchy situation right now," Pringle conceded.

This appeared fairly obvious to Voerbeck, though he wasn't sure to which situation Pringle was referring. He merely raised his eyebrows to show his interest.

"We are trying to get permission from Washington for the Army to help us go up into that country after the murderer."

"Why is that a problem?" Voerbeck asked.

"The situation is very involved as far as technicalities of the law are concerned and their history, but it's illegal for the Army to be used to assist civil authorities in executing warrants or even in suppressing riots, if it comes down to that. The U. S. marshal doesn't have the manpower to go after Bandelier. In the meantime we don't want him to get wind of what we're up to."

"You refer to what *we* are up to. What is your official position in this?"

"Well, actually none. But my close friends are all concerned."

"And they would be . . . ?"

"The chief justice, the U. S. attorney, the U. S. marshal whose men were killed."

Voerbeck knew that those officials amounted to Pringle's pawns in this territory but didn't comment. "So you're playing a waiting game?"

"We have no choice."

"I can see that. Before I leave, there is one small favor I'd like of you. I'm a stranger here and have heard conflicting stories about this man, Bandelier. Has he ever been apprehended actually committing the crimes of which he's accused? I understand from Lord Ransom, who was at the scene of the killings, that it's not even certain that Bandelier was home the night the two men were shot."

"Nonsense!" Pringle exploded.

"Why do you say nonsense?"

Pringle laughed. "Maybe that was wishful thinking. Anyhow, the man will get his day in court." To which he silently added: *Over my dead body.* If Bandelier talked, he could sink them all. The Pinkerton investigation Bandelier had set afoot might sink them whether Bandelier was dead or alive, but Pringle wanted him dead, if for no other reason than that he'd interfered with plans that obsessed him. Besides, if the dust settled and he got his hands on the grant — and he'd never wavered in the belief that he would — he didn't want a man of Bandelier's caliber up there, providing leadership to the settlers. "What else can I do for you?" he inquired. "And, I might add, that I have a huge, practically empty house where I'd be pleased to put you up."

Voerbeck said: "No thanks. General Gryden made the same offer. You people are all too kind. But I like to come and go at my own pace."

He slyly watched, certain a suspicious man like Pringle would desperately want to know why he'd seen General Gryden. He gave him high marks for taking that blow with a poker face and not asking a question he'd obviously have liked to ask.

"I will be in touch," Voerbeck said, rising to leave. "I plan to be in town for a few days."

Pringle escorted him to the door and shook hands as he left.

Chapter Twenty-Six

Mariposa dozed in her chair beside Cleve Bandelier's bed. She woke up in a shadowy, lamplit room, confused, and said aloud: "Where am I?"

She didn't recognize Cleve in the dim light, propped up on pillows, looking at her. He smiled, but at first his haggard face appeared threatening, and she started.

"You're all right," he reassured her. "You were dreaming."

Then she remembered. She was in the house of Anastacio Zamora and had met the whole family the evening before, brothers, so many she couldn't remember their names, children, all bright-eyed, smiling shyly, and curious about the pink lady with the long golden hair.

Maria, Anastacio's wife, unlike most of the women she'd seen when they drove into the village, was not fat but thin, wiry, and quick as a bird. They liked each other at once, and she had even been allowed to help Maria make a late supper which all except Cleve had eaten. He fell asleep almost as soon as they helped him into bed. It was then she realized what a terrible strain he must have been under since he'd been shot.

"Sleep is the best medicine for him now," Maria had said.

Mariposa wondered if Maria had had many gunshot cases, convalescing in her house, and would have been surprised at the number. It was a violent land, and many were shot, some not so lucky as Cleve, as the cemetery on the hill, bristling with crosses, attested. Among the grandmothers and grandfathers were many who had been cheated of life.

All the people she had met, and there had been many,

were delighted at Mariposa's hesitant Spanish, happy that someone tried to get on in their language, everyone eager to help when she stumbled. There had been a lot of laughing over that.

While they had been talking over supper, Cleve had yelled out from the bedroom: "What are you coyotes howling about?" They had all gone back to see him. His voice had been surprisingly strong, which had pleased her. She had felt his forehead, and he had no fever, but you never knew in such cases.

Later, after he'd downed the broth Maria had made for him and beans in a tortilla, Mariposa had said: "I will sit up with him."

"Me, too," Amy had said. "I won't be able to sleep."

But she had, with a pillow and blanket on a thick mat on the floor, with Cleve's terrier, Maggie, curled up in the curve of her body. She had snored, as exhausted people often do, which had awakened Mariposa. When she realized what it was, she said to Cleve: "The poor thing is worn out. Do you know how much she loves you?"

He nodded. Their voices woke up Cleve's cat, Pedro, who yawned, stretched, and settled back down next to him on the bed.

Mariposa impulsively reached out and took Cleve's hand in both of hers and pressed it gently. Their eyes met and held, and she thought he looked like a sick little boy whose mother had come into the room, where he'd been battling alone, and had given him the great lift he needed. In that instant she knew she loved him. She didn't care if he had killed a dozen men, his eyes told her he was a good person and a real man, the brave, wild clan leader she'd dreamed of since she'd first read of Rob Roy.

She held his hand until he leaned back on the pillow. "I'm so sleepy all the time," he sighed.

"It's nature's way of helping you get your strength back. Go to sleep."

She watched his face a long while, then dozed off once more herself. Light was filtering into the room when she woke up again, while Maria was taking the blanket down from the window. Maria said in a low voice: "You need some sound sleep."

Mariposa nodded. "I dozed a little, but, yes, I am tired."

Maria led her by the hand to another room and put her into bed, gently covering her. "It gets cold here at night even in the summer," she said, pulled the blankets over Mariposa, then left.

Mariposa went to sleep smiling, exhausted from the worry and strangeness but happy, wondering if the man she'd suddenly and surprisingly chosen would ever feel for her what she did for him. She was wise enough in the perplexing prejudices of the world to know that her background, so different from his, might daunt him.

Zamora Plaza was awakened *en masse* by an outburst of dogs' barking, soon joined by braying burros and bleating goats. Anastacio had posted guards on the road south, and they intercepted a strange rider just at first light: Junior mounted on Percy's stolen horse. He was escorted to Anastacio's by Refugio Zamora, youngest of the brothers. By the time they reached there, Anastacio was up and outside to see what the uproar was about.

"Look what I dragged in," Refugio crowed.

Anastacio helped Junior down and supported him while he got his legs working. He hugged the boy, whom he considered one of his own.

At eighteen, Refugio was young enough to have bonded with Junior as his best boyhood companion, and he took over from Anastacio, giving Junior a supporting arm into the house. "I'll bet you're starved," he said.

"Close," Junior said. "And damn' near worn out. This leg hurts like hell. But I want to see Pa before I do anything."

Cleve, awakened by the hubbub, heard them help Junior inside. Amy was up before Junior was off his horse, went to see what was happening, and ran back and told Cleve: "It's Junior!" then scurried back out and hugged her brother. He hugged her back fiercely, then remembered his manhood, and shoved her away, a move she understood perfectly. "Don't push me away, you ninny," she whispered. "I hugged you because I love you." She looked at him and realized he was fighting back tears. "C'mon in," she said. "Pa's awake." She gave him her arm on the other side, and she and Refugio helped him to the bedroom.

Junior hobbled to Cleve under his own power and stood awkwardly, looking at the emaciated man that he scarcely would have recognized if he'd run across him somewhere else. "Well, I finally made it up here . . . a little late, I guess."

Cleve laughed, reached out, grabbed his arm, pulled him over, and squeezed his shoulders. Junior was surprised at how strong his pa was despite what had happened to him. He thought: *He's gonna get better, thank Christ!* The tears came. He wiped them away. "I can't help it, Pa." He didn't give a damn who knew he was crying. "I got Star killed, Pa. I'm sorry."

Cleve had a hard time to keep from bawling with him. He'd never been so proud of him in his life. "I know. It couldn't be helped, son. We'll all get over it in time."

Keg Brownlee had taken it upon himself to solve the housing problem for Lord Ransom and Sam Buchanan by setting up Army cots outside, behind his stone house, and giving them blankets. "If it rains, drag 'em in the kitchen. We ain't exactly set up for company."

Harmony Dabney hadn't done quite so well. Keg had padlocked a chain around one of his ankles, padlocked the other end around a large pine tree, and had tossed him an old, threadbare Army blanket. "This'll have to do for you," he had told Dabney. "I hope you freeze. It'll save us the trouble of hangin' you."

In the morning, when he called Ransom and Sam in to eat, he passed Dabney a cold tortilla. "It's better'n you deserve."

Dabney didn't say a word and wolfed it down. "What do I do if I have to go?" he asked as Keg walked away.

"Do it in your pants for all I care. You probably will anyhow before we're done with you."

Ransom had awakened early and had thought over his situation. He had no doubt he'd be in real trouble if Pringle ever sang, but that wasn't likely. That left the question of how much he could tell Cleve Bandelier, if anything. At breakfast he said to Keg: "If Mister Bandelier feels up to it, I'd like to talk to him."

Keg said: "Go over and see after you're finished. We ain't keepin' you under guard."

Ransom walked to Anastacio's house immediately after he ate and knocked. Anastacio himself answered the door. "Come in. Have you eaten? We are just finished and having coffee and a smoke."

Ransom was surprised to see Cleve, bundled in blankets, leaning back in a deep arm chair made of broad leather thongs, smoking a cigarette. Mariposa, beside him on a stool, held his coffee cup for him.

Ransom shook Cleve's hand. "You must be feeling better."

"Doctor's orders," Cleve replied. "She says my insides may grow together if I don't move around."

Mariposa interjected: "What I said was you might get adhesions, and you might."

Cleve laughed. "And I asked you what adhesions were, and you told me, and I just told him."

"It's true," Ransom affirmed. "Lots of gunshot wounds do that. Your guts grow to the wound, even if they aren't punctured, and a damned doctor has to cut you open again and cut them loose. We don't want that to happen."

Cleve thought: *He's mighty concerned about me all of a sudden. I wish he'd got that way a few years sooner and I wouldn't be in this shape.*

Cautiously Ransom got around to what was on his mind. "Is there somewhere we won't bother anybody? Maybe outside, since you can navigate a little?"

"I got nothing to say that all these people can't hear," Cleve told him.

Mariposa said: "My father has no secrets from me. I can represent him, since he can't be here himself. He already knows a lot has been going on here of which he doesn't approve and wants to correct it. That's why he went to Santa Fé."

Anastacio looked pleased. Maria spoke no English, and he said to her: *"Tarde te diré todo."*

Ransom leaned forward in his chair. "First of all, I had nothing to do with the attack on your ranch the other night. I didn't know it was afoot, and I would have forbidden it, if I'd known what Wingfield was up to."

Cleve's eyes were cold and steady. "How about whoever jumped my herd at Tres Huérfanos . . . nobody but Wingfield would pull off something like that?"

"I knew nothing of that in advance, either, but I presume you're right. It was Wingfield. He's obviously taken a lot onto himself lately, which is my fault."

Mariposa said: "If we had known this sort of thing was going on, we'd have come here sooner. You can be sure that Mister Wingfield is no longer in our employ."

It was music to Ransom's ears. He wondered where Pancho was and sincerely hoped he'd skipped the country. He continued: "A lot of things have happened that wouldn't have, if I hadn't left things up to Mister Wingfield. I didn't suspect him of double-dealing until these last two raw blunders of his." He turned to Mariposa. "I think we'd better get back to the ranch before they panic and think we've met with foul play. We can definitely discharge Mister Wingfield, if he shows up there, and I want to lay all my cards on the table with your father to make amends for letting you down."

Cleve was ready to forgive this rather pathetic yet likable Englishman. He thought: *Talk about a pound of cure. Well, better late than never.*

Mariposa felt the same, but told Monty: "You go back to the ranch. Father will be in Santa Fé by now, so he isn't apt to hear we've disappeared and do something rash before you can get word to him that we're all right. I'm going to stay and keep an eye on my patient. I think you should send Doctor Ewing here to examine him, too."

Ransom looked uncertain. "Are you sure you want to stay?"

"Of course, I'm sure.

Ransom shrugged and turned back to Cleve. "I hope we've cleared the air, and I intend to see more of you in the future. After all, we're neighbors." He rose and gave Mariposa a pecking kiss on her cheek. "I'll be pulling out in a little while. Don't worry about anything."

After he left, Cleve said: "I'm going to take a little *siesta,* then I think we should have Dabney in for a talk."

Anastacio grinned, anticipating the possibility that he'd get to use persuasion to oil the Texan's tongue. He related to Maria all that had been said and then went out to see to his daily chores.

When the women were alone, Maria said in Spanish: "You

should see our village, and I want you to meet Anastacio's mother and father and some other people. You will want to see *Padre* Maldonado, if he is here . . . a very interesting man and a legend among my people and the Indians."

They went out shortly. Amy spotted them and tagged along.

"Where's your brother?" Mariposa asked Amy.

"Some men are getting ready to go grizzly hunting, and he and Refugio are talking with them." She pointed up the street. Mariposa looked where she pointed and could see that Monty Ransom was up there, too. He'd learned that Junior had stolen Percy's horse and thought it was extremely funny. Junior had heard how Ransom beat the tar out of Keg and had a new respect for him, especially after he showed him how the stolen rifle worked, although he cautioned him to return it some day.

"Somebody found a crutch for Junior," Amy said. Like the stretcher they'd used for her father, the crutch also had been appropriated from the Army by the Jicarillas.

Rosa and Euphemio Zamora were sitting in front of their house under an arbor, arguing, when Maria brought Mariposa to meet them.

Mariposa asked Maria: "Hadn't we better come back some other time?"

"Why?"

"Because they seem to be having an argument."

"They're *always* having an argument."

Amy didn't want to listen to adults' fussing. "I'm going to see Junior."

Maria led Mariposa up to the old folks. "This is Mariposa, and she is a nurse, staying with us, taking care of Cleve Bandelier."

They knew all about Mariposa — the whole village did. At

first everyone had been horrified when they discovered she was the daughter of the great *diablo,* Grut Voerbeck, who owned the syndicate. Then they learned the truth, that Voerbeck was not the *diablo* they'd heard he was, that it was bad men working for him who had deceived him, and that surely this bright creature, his daughter, was an angel. Wasn't she taking care of the wounded Cleve Bandelier? And hadn't he been their protector for years? Now, everything would be all right, and the trouble would be over.

The elder Zamoras had always felt that someday *Padre* Maldonado would marry their only daughter, Dolores, to Cleve Bandelier. This had been the subject of their argument when Maria and Mariposa arrived. Dolores was not visiting in Antonito, as they had heard. A messenger had just arrived with news of her whereabouts.

"We have very bad news," Euphemio said. "We have just heard from Dolores."

"Is she sick?" Maria asked.

"Worse," said Rosa.

"Not dead?"

"She might as well be," said Euphemio. "She ran off and married that wind bag, Polocarpio Baca."

"I knew no good would come from him teaching her to read and write . . . especially English," said Rosa.

Euphemio objected. "That isn't the truth. You thought it was wonderful, because it would be a surprise for Cleve Bandelier, and he would be happy with her . . . maybe marry her himself."

"I always knew her cousin was no good. Someone else could have taught her."

"Well, it's too late now," Euphemio said. "How will we tell *Señor* Cleve?"

Rosa looked very sad. "Dolores and Polocarpio are in Denver. An evil place. A big city."

Maria looked at Mariposa. "We always thought that Cleve would marry Dolores some day. But he never asked, and she is getting old."

"How old is she?"

"I don't know, but she should be married by now." She turned to Rosa. "How old is Dolores?"

"Nineteen. And you are right. We must make the best of it. She needed to be married." Then she thought of Polocarpio, living in Santa Fé, and she was angry again. "*¡Aiee!* He will take my baby away, and we'll never see her."

"She will visit," Maria tried to comfort her. "They should have told us, though. *Padre* Maldonado won't be happy, either." She shook her head. "Probably, if they'd told us, Anastacio would have killed Polo."

They all nodded.

Euphemio said: "I never would have given my permission."

"Nor I," Rosa added, looking solemn. "How could that girl do this to us?"

Mariposa was beginning to get the drift and thought it was funny. Actually, they'd been thinking more of themselves than poor Dolores, regardless of what she did, or what they said about it. It was even funnier that they thought nineteen was way too old to remain single.

They left the old people, who resumed their argument. Maria said: "I must tell Anastacio. He will be furious. He wanted her to marry Cleve."

Mariposa wondered why these women were so willing to let men run their affairs and make the decisions about their lives. Obviously Dolores hadn't been one of them. She might have made a suitable wife for Cleve, but Mariposa was glad this unexpected event had occurred, for her own sake. She would make a far better wife for him. And she had already decided she wanted to live here before she'd set eyes on the "bandit chieftain." She smiled inwardly. She was very happy, but she wondered how Cleve would receive the news.

Chapter Twenty-Seven

Tomàs Pringle's boiling point had been reached before Grut Voerbeck left his office. He sat at his desk, viciously chewing an unlit cigar and staring at the wall. He was in this state when his secretary, George Hall, came in and said: "Mister Wingfield is outside."

"Send the son of a bitch in," Pringle said. The fact that he allowed himself to be seen with Wingfield in broad daylight testified to his state. "Where the hell have you been?" he asked once he entered.

Pancho was in no frame of mind to take much guff himself. "What do you mean, where the hell have I been? I've been up north, having a damned bad time of it, trying to rake our chestnuts."

"Did you get my wires?"

"No. When did you send them?"

"Every damn' day of the last three."

"Well, I didn't get a one of them. Where did you send them?"

"To Dorado with instructions to try to find you at the hotel or ranch."

"Well, I still didn't get a one of 'em. What did you want?"

"I wanted to know what the hell was going on, and what the hell you were trying to do."

"I was trying to get Cleve Bandelier killed, which is what I thought you wanted."

"God damn it to hell, if you'd left those two killers I sent up there alone, he'd be dead by now."

Pancho wondered how Pringle knew about that, but then Pringle heard about almost everything that happened in the territory. He was all too aware that what Pringle alleged was true, and it put him on the defensive.

Pringle continued: "If you'd left well enough alone and just scattered that herd, I'd have been satisfied."

"I sure as hell did that."

"And that's about the size of it." Pringle looked at Wingfield balefully. "Do you know who just left here about ten minutes ago?"

Pancho shrugged. "How the hell would I know? So, who just left here?"

"Grut Voerbeck. And he's nobody's fool. He's onto just about everything that's been going on."

Now Wingfield shrugged. "I heard he was here. I was thinkin' of goin' back to Texas, anyhow. I told Ransom before I left."

That ran Pringle's blood pressure up again. "Where is that English idiot? Why didn't either one of you bastards warn me Voerbeck was in the territory?"

"I was way the hell out in the country when Ransom told me. I thought he told you. As for where that idiot is, this will kill you. He's up at Zamora Plaza."

"Zamora Plaza! What the hell is he doing up there?"

"I ain't sure, but I'd guess he didn't go up there on purpose."

"I don't have time for guessing games. We have to do something damned quick, or we might end up in the pen."

Pancho thought: *You might. I kinda like Mexico, if it comes down to it . . . especially the gals.* He said: "Keep your shirt on. Ransom had a little bad luck. He was out, riding around with Voerbeck's daughter, and ran into about a hundred or so of the Zamora crowd that came down to rescue Bandelier."

"From what?"

"Devil Ed shot him. We thought he'd just pinked him, and he got out of the country. He was hiding out, bad hit, I guess. I thought he might be and snooped around up there with Harmony Dabney and almost got took in myself. I ran for it with a few lead pills whistling around my ears, or I wouldn't be here talkin' about it."

"How about Dabney?"

"I reckon they netted the damned fool. He should've run for it like I did."

"Just how much does he know?"

It was a question that had also occurred to Wingfield. A truthful answer would have been — *A lot. Enough to get us all hung.* — but Pancho didn't think this was a good time to tell Pringle, especially since he was at fault. "I never told Dabney much," he lied.

"Thank God for that! So they got Ransom and the Voerbeck girl?"

"Of course."

"How do you know?"

Pancho repeated what he'd learned from Percy Waterford on the train. That set Pringle thinking, staring at the wall, during which time Pancho rolled a cigarette and watched Pringle's face, but he could read nothing from it.

Then Pringle said: "If this is all true, then we may be able to get Voerbeck on our side, after all. Let's see, when will the stage be in?" He consulted his watch. "About seven. It's four now. When he gets in, Waterford undoubtedly will look up Voerbeck. Give them another hour or two after that, and I can talk to them. Voerbeck is going to be hot as hell to get his daughter back."

"Hell, she's probably on her way back by now, and Monty with her."

"Maybe so. But we don't want Voerbeck to hear that. His

connections are just what we need to get Washington to turn the Army loose on Zamora Plaza. They'll be hiding Bandelier, and they won't give him up, not even to the Army. A big shooting with the Army on our side is what we need. It'll get us everything we want in the long run. What judge in his right mind is going to rule for a crowd that's shot it out with the Army? It'll put an end to that bullshit about carving a Jicarilla agency out of the grant, too."

Wingfield decided it might be a good idea to hang around New Mexico. It was obvious the meeting was over, and he got up. "I'll be staying at the usual place, if you want me."

Once Wingfield had gone, Pringle called in Hall. "I want you to round up Laxelt, Norton, and Hank Ball and get them down here as soon as possible." They were the U. S. attorney, chief justice of the Territorial Supreme Court, and the U. S. marshal, and he held them all in the palm of his hand. The first two had survived as New Mexico politicos through several Republican administrations in Washington, holding one post or another, Norton actually having been fired as governor, then re-appointed later as chief justice.

When all three were present, Pringle said: "I just had a couple of interesting visitors. First of all, Grut Voerbeck, old Midas himself. He's a little shrimp with glasses and not too impressive until he starts cross-examining you. He should have been a criminal lawyer. The son of a bitch knows too much, and what he doesn't know, he suspects."

Laxelt said: "I don't see how we can do much about that."

"I didn't, either, till my second visitor came in." Pringle paused like a good storyteller, biting off the end of a cigar.

"So? Who was that?" Laxelt asked.

"Pancho Wingfield."

That brought unhappy looks to the faces of all three visitors.

"Yeah, I know. He's trouble. But this time he had some

good news. Get this. Bandelier and that crowd up at Zamora Plaza have kidnapped Voerbeck's daughter."

"The hell you say?" Laxelt said.

"You know what this means?" Pringle asked.

The U. S. marshal had visions of it meaning he'd have to do something he'd rather not, but held his tongue.

"I'm telling you this, so it won't be a surprise when Voerbeck calls on us later, probably this evening, to organize a rescue of his darling daughter. We'll need some more warrants, most likely."

The U. S. marshal finally put in his oar. "It'll take more than warrants. Where the hell would I find the manpower to go up into the Zamora hornet's nest and pluck the girl out?"

"Pancho Wingfield can put in a dozen real tough gunslingers," Pringle said, "but you aren't going to need them. A little bird told me that old Voerbeck and His Accidency in the White House are thick as thieves. This is our chance to get the Army out against that crowd. Voerbeck has the influence to get just about anything he wants out of the President. I'm going to wire Slinkard as soon as we break up here and have him standing by for a telegram. I want him to wake up His Accidency in the middle of the night, if need be, and get a wire back here to the Army. By tomorrow Gryden can be on the way up there with half a regiment."

Chief Justice Sam Norton asked: "What about Bandelier? You mentioned rescuing Voerbeck's daughter. I presume we'll be up there to pull in Bandelier, too."

Pringle laughed. "Of course. We'll bring him down here and put him in a nice, cozy cell. Provided something doesn't happen to him on the way down."

U. S. Attorney Laxelt asked: "Are you going over and tell Voerbeck what happened to the girl? He'll want to know how come you found out?"

"I won't have to. One of Voerbeck's foreign toadies is on his way down here to take care of that for us."

"How the hell did you find that out?" Laxelt wondered.

"Wingfield rode as far as Española on the train with him."

The stage deposited Percy Waterford at La Fonda, and he saw Grut Voerbeck as soon as he entered the lobby, seated in earnest conversation with another man. He went up to him immediately. "Good evening."

Voerbeck looked at him. "Percy. What brings you here?"

"Pardon the interruption, but I need a word with you in private."

Frank Carson, the man with Voerbeck, said: "I can see you some other time, Mister Voerbeck."

"No, stay around. I have a few other things to go over. I'll only be a minute."

He drew Percy aside. "What is it?"

"Your daughter and Monty have been kidnapped by Bandelier."

Voerbeck's improved opinion of Bandelier practically flew out the window with those few words. However, he seldom leaped to conclusions. "Are you sure?"

"As sure as I can be. I'm embarrassed to tell you the details, but I saw it happening. I was misled into believing they were being temporarily detained after having accidentally encountered a group of men who came to rescue Bandelier. I was told that they simply wanted to get away far enough so your daughter and Monty wouldn't come back and alert the sheriff before they escaped, after which they would release them."

Voerbeck nodded. "That would have made sense to me. Who told you that they would be released?"

Percy explained the entire situation as it had occurred. "I expected them back at the ranch before dark. Naturally, when they didn't return, I went to the sheriff."

"Has he gone after them?"

"I doubt it. People keep saying it would take the Army to go up into the country where Bandelier's followers live."

Voerbeck said: "I'm sure we can arrange to have the Army help us, if that's what's required. I think Frank, here, should hear about this. He can advise us how to go about that. The United States has some strange law, making that sort of thing difficult."

He led Percy back with him to where he'd left Carson and introduced them. "Percy has just brought some bad news. It seems my daughter and Lord Ransom have been kidnapped by the man we were talking about."

Voerbeck had Percy relate his story again.

Carson said: "I think we should talk to the territorial officers before we go after the Army. I know they had their heads together earlier about this very thing, not necessarily the kidnapping, which they probably don't know about, but the matter of how to apprehend Bandelier and bring him to trial. If you want, I can have them over here in a half hour or so."

"Please do," Voerbeck said. He turned over the possibilities. He still was not ready to believe that this situation was necessarily as it appeared. He hadn't forgotten what General Gryden had said about Pringle and the others who would be coming to confer with him. Frank Carson had told him practically the same thing, and they were his associates.

Nonetheless, Mariposa had been kidnapped and was being detained. The thought occurred to him that perhaps the settlers were going to try to use her as a pawn to get him to settle their land claims. He did not believe that she would be hurt in the long run, although he wasn't as sanguine about Ransom's chances in the hands of the people who saw him as the instrument of their oppression. The question in his mind was whether moving on these people with the Army wouldn't even more endanger their lives.

When Carson brought the group back with him, they went over all the ground that had been covered individually by Percy and Wingfield, by Pringle and Voerbeck earlier, and by the ring that afternoon. Nothing was entirely certain except that Mariposa and Ransom were, indeed, being held by people who had no reason to love Voerbeck and the syndicate. Voerbeck concluded with the key question: "Will my daughter be murdered if we come with the Army?"

Pringle said: "These people are not irrational. In fact, they are warm-hearted and chivalrous." He wanted to be sure that Voerbeck would not scotch the idea of the Army, which would serve his own purposes so admirably. "I would say that there is no possibility they would hurt a woman. My feeling is that they will be forced to release her if the Army demands it. That will leave us free to deal with the outlaw, Bandelier, and do it with the Army's backing."

As a result of that meeting, a wire was drafted and sent to Senator Slinkard in Washington, D. C., for delivery to the White House that night. It read:

His Excellency
Chester A. Arthur
President of the United States
Washington, D. C.

Dear President Arthur:

From Grut Voerbeck — stop — My daughter has been abducted by a combination of lawless citizens who are defying the civil authorities and are in such numbers as to intimidate them and render them ineffective — stop — She is being held in a place known as Zamora Plaza

— comma — not a recognized town but an assemblage of Mexican and Indian people living by illegal pursuits for the most part — stop — I urgently appeal to you to authorize forces of the U. S. Army to support civil authorities in an effort to gain my daughter's freedom and to suppress this lawless combination which has been in a state of practical insurrection for a number of years — stop — Their leader — comma — Cleve Bandelier — comma — has killed two deputy U. S. marshals and is himself wounded and being protected from arrest by his followers at Zamora Plaza — stop — It would also be expedient to authorize the Army to assist in his arrest after my daughter is liberated — stop — Haste in this matter will be appreciated — stop — Your Friend — comma — Grut Voerbeck — end

A return wire to General Gryden was on the way within an hour of receipt of the above at the White House, re-transmitting the foregoing wire, and advising him to contact the civil authorities and Grut Voerbeck upon receipt as well as to ready an immediate force to proceed to Zamora Plaza.

It is possible that this operation could have been aborted had Monty Ransom hurried back to the ranch and wired Grut Voerbeck regarding the actual state of affairs to allay his concern for Mariposa. Unfortunately, he was so captivated by the preparations for the grizzly bear hunt from Zamora Plaza that he joined the hunting party. If Mariposa had been aware of his typically irresponsible conduct, she would have made certain that such a wire was sent to her father.

Chapter Twenty-Eight

Pringle's optimistic forecast that half a regiment would be on the road to Zamora Plaza by the next day was overtaken by reality in the person of General Gryden. He knew that troops didn't materialize out of barracks in an instant, hung down with field equipment, and that horses weren't always in a newly shod state. Railroad cars had to be requisitioned, ammunition and rations must be issued to men, with reserves packed in wagons, and a hundred other minor details needed attention.

At the fort the next morning Voerbeck merely shrugged when Gryden enumerated the reasons for delay. "I understand," he said, remembering his own experiences around the world, dating to the Crimean War which had been a disaster due to lack of preparation.

The general knew how he must feel and reassured him. "I'm not aware of what happened or why, but I feel sure that no harm will come to your daughter at the hands of Bandelier. Time will tell, of course."

"I have that feeling myself, although I don't know why."

"There is something you should know. Perhaps I should have told you yesterday. Bandelier has placed in the hands of the Army information regarding a vast cattle-stealing operation which we are investigating. At the center of this operation is our crooked friend, Pringle. He is probably aware he's on the spot. In fact, I'm sure he is . . . also who put him there. Anything he says about Bandelier will be tinged with a desire for revenge."

"Are you saying that the thousands of cattle I apparently have lost were stolen by Pringle or men in his employ?"

Gryden nodded. "That's about the size of it."

"And Bandelier was portrayed as the guilty party . . . as a scapegoat?"

"Yes. Almost certainly."

"How about his outlaw band?"

"A myth."

Voerbeck nodded. "I have suspected as much. Nonetheless, I think you should go ahead with your operation. We can't be sure that Bandelier controls all those people. If he isn't the rustler I've been led to believe, and he isn't the leader of a band of lawless people, either, he may have little control over them. I want my daughter back, or I want some heads on spikes as a lesson." The general saw tears in Voerbeck's eyes as the man paused. "I don't know what I'll do if I lose Mariposa. She is my whole life. I lost my wife . . . I can't bear the thought of losing her."

For a moment Grut Voerbeck was simply a vulnerable old man. The general rose and put a sympathetic hand on his shoulder.

"I am going to move heaven and earth to get her back safely for you, sir. Unfortunately, I can't simply turn on a spigot to get the force into the field."

Voerbeck smiled wearily. "I know, General. I know. I'll try to be patient. And I won't get in your way. I am going to return to the ranch and keep tabs on things from there. I would appreciate your allowing me to accompany you when you get into that part of the country."

"I will arrange for you to join us when the train goes through Dorado. We will detrain at Tres Huérfanos and ride in from there."

"I can't ask for more, General. By the time you arrive, I will have had time to interview the sheriff at Dorado. Perhaps my daughter and Lord Ransom will have returned by then, and it will turn out you will be going on a wild goose chase."

"If so, do you intend to ask the President to call off the Army?"

Voerbeck considered a moment. "I wonder. Perhaps it would be best to try to get this Bandelier in custody, as much for his protection as not. I feel that he would come out all right in an honest court."

The general snorted. "There is no such thing in this territory. Pringle calls the turn in all of them."

"What do you think would be best?"

"I think we should go ahead for now and play it by ear."

Percy Waterford accompanied Voerbeck back to Dorado. When they detrained, Voerbeck said: "I think I will look up Sheriff Butler. Would you care to come with me?"

"Indeed, I would. Maybe he's found my horse or, more accurately, your horse." He'd told Voerbeck of that singular occurrence.

Voerbeck chuckled. "This is, indeed, a fascinating country. I almost wish I'd come here when I was young."

Percy understood that. He hadn't been able to hunt or fish, or even ride in the wilderness, except for that one unhappy occasion, but he fully intended to. He had a half-formed plan to buy a ranch here. Maybe Monty would run it for him. He anticipated that his friend would need to look for a new situation when all of the facts were in. Monty would serve well enough for what he had in mind — a play ranch, with a little horse breeding and a base for hunting forays into the wilderness. Monty could employ his chambermaid to do the housekeeping, which would be an added inducement for him to accept the isolation. If things got dull, he could ride over to the Voerbeck's and play polo, provided Grut didn't discharge the Mexican cowboys who seemed to have been employed mainly for that purpose.

He was walking beside Voerbeck on the way to Butler's as he ruminated about his plan when a group of horsemen rode into the main street with Wingfield at their head. The Texan spotted him and swerved his horse over.

"Howdy," he said. "I see you got back."

Percy nodded and felt decidedly uncomfortable. He wondered if Wingfield knew, or suspected, the identity of the man with him.

Voerbeck took the bull by the horns. He asked: "I have a feeling that you are Mister Wingfield, is that true?"

Pancho looked him over coolly. He nodded. "You got the right man."

"I am Grut Voerbeck, your *former* employer," he said and lifted his hat politely, locking eyes with the Texan. "If I owe you money, let me know."

He resumed his pace down the street, never looking back. Percy paused a moment, watching Wingfield for some hostile motion, then followed. Pancho simply grinned crookedly at Percy, then turned, and followed his men up the street. His instructions from Pringle were explicit. No more forays into trouble-making. He was to stand by and wait to join the Army procession up to Zamora Plaza, which Pringle himself intended to accompany in the guise of one of Hank Ball's deputies.

Wingfield had observed to Pringle: "I can't very well take the boys back to the ranch, because I suspect Papa doesn't live there any more. Where the hell do you suggest we stay?"

Pringle had thought about that for half a second. "Why don't you move into Bandelier's place? I have a notion he won't be needing it for a while."

Pancho had snorted. "A good idea, unless his boys are back there by now."

"I leave that up to you. We don't need *them* in that part of the country any more than we need old Cleve."

Wingfield was on his way to carry out that suggestion and was in a hurry, since he wanted to get to the Bandelier ranch before Bandelier's cowboys returned, if possible. He didn't fancy trying to shoot his way into that stone-walled fortress.

Sheriff Butler was curious to know who this unpretentious old fellow was accompanying Percy Waterford to his door.

"I didn't find ary sign of your horse," he informed Percy. "I have a pretty good idea where he went, though."

"I didn't come about that. This is Mister Voerbeck who wants to talk to you about the kidnapping of his daughter. I judge you weren't able to get her back."

Butler extended his hand to Voerbeck. "Howdy. Come in and we'll talk."

He seated them in the parlor and rolled a cigarette in the same messy fashion that Percy had observed with distaste on his prior visit. "Smoke if you want to," Butler invited. "The missus don't mind."

Voerbeck withdrew a cigar and carefully prepared it for lighting, meanwhile observing Butler. He decided to break the ice lightly. "As a matter of curiosity, where did Percy's horse go, in your opinion?"

"Well, I had a feisty kid here, as your friend may have told you, Cleve Bandelier's boy, as a matter of fact, and I suspect he stole the horse to go join his pa as soon as he found out where he was. If he did, he got on the critter with a cast on his foot, and that couldn't have been easy."

Percy said: "The boy needs a good birching."

Butler grinned. "Most boys do. My pa like to wore out an orchard of switches on me, and I needed it 'most every time."

Voerbeck then got to the point. "What is your opinion of my daughter's chances of being freed by those people?"

"Absolutely one hundred percent. I can think of only one reason she hasn't come back before now."

Voerbeck straightened up. "And what would that be?"

"She doesn't want to."

"Why do you say that?" The idea hadn't occurred to him, and he was surprised it hadn't, since he usually canvassed even wild possibilities when he studied a problem. Knowing her, it was possible.

Butler shrugged. "The people up there are really very friendly, but she ain't stayin' just to visit. She's a nurse, I understand, and Bandelier needs one."

"By Jove!" Percy exclaimed. "I wouldn't put it past her. And Monty is staying to look after her among the barbarians, I suppose."

Voerbeck said: "I'd think she'd have sent back a message so we knew she was all right. In any case, I hope you're right. Sheriff, would you take us up to this Zamora Plaza? It might avert a lot of trouble for everyone." He explained that he had obtained the assistance of the Army, which might lead to an unnecessary confrontation.

"It's quite a ride."

"I can manage it," Voerbeck insisted. "I'm sturdier than I look. How long will it take us?"

"It's pretty much an all-day ride unless you want to wear out a horse."

"It is getting late. We will go to the ranch and start early in the morning, if that's agreeable to you."

"Suits me," Butler said. "I might take Doc Ewing along."

When Voerbeck and Percy reached the ranch a little later, Daisy met them at the door, threw her arms around Grut's neck, and hugged him. "Thank God you're back! I was going out of my mind."

Percy remembered then that he'd forgotten to send a messenger back to tell her he was going to Santa Fé. He would have been the first to forgive Monty for wandering off on a hunting expedition when he was supposed to be carrying a similar message to the ranch.

Cleve, Anastacio, and Sam Buchanan, along with Keg and Niño Alonzo, had grilled Harmony Dabney thoroughly. He knew what would happen to him if he wasn't cooperative, and he sang like a good fellow. What Cleve learned was little more than he already knew, until Dabney said: "You could probably get some of them cows back from Wingfield's place up in Nebraska."

Cleve's ears pricked up at that. Rather than directly asking where the ranch was, he inquired: "Have you ever been up there?"

"With a cattle drive last year."

Cleve said: "It's a pretty cold place for a Texan like you."

Dabney agreed. "I wouldn't go up there in the winter on a bet. It's bad enough around here." He was beginning to think he might get out of this with a whole skin. Cleve certainly hadn't shown hatred toward him, though he didn't care for the malevolent way Anastacio and Niño eyed him. Nor had he forgotten what Keg had threatened earlier. He hoped Keg had been bluffing, but, in any case, Cleve was his hope for skinning out alive. He went on: "I should never have left Texas, with Ma down there alone."

Cleve eyed him seriously, seeing in him a young fellow like he'd once been in his early days in the Army with his life ahead of him. He could just as easily have gone bad. Some of what he'd had to do was brutalizing, and Lord knew he'd been wild enough. But the influences around him had been good for the most part, and, when he landed in trouble a time or two, there'd always been someone to let him up easy. He weighed Dabney's case in his mind. On the bad side was the fact that this fellow had shot his favorite horse, an animal the likes of which he'd probably never own again, but Dabney was only doing what Cleve's own cowboys would do for him, being loyal to the outfit for which he worked. Dabney was playing to the hilt the rôle of the young fellow gone bad who would go straight if given another chance.

"I almost forgot, just where is Wingfield's ranch up in Nebraska?" Cleve asked.

"In the sand hills up around Fort Robinson. He sells a lot of beef to the fort."

Cleve looked around at the rest of them. "Anybody else got something to say?"

"Yeah," Keg put in. "Let's take the bastard out, hang him, and get it over with."

Anastacio didn't have to say what he was thinking, and it was obvious Niño would have cut the *Tejano*'s throat on the spot, if Cleve suggested it. Niño, of course, usually looked like he'd slit someone's throat. Nature had built him that way. One of his black eyes had a slight cast, and the lid drooped as did the eyebrow on that side. This, coupled with a face that seemed chiseled from stone, deeply fissured, added to his sinister appearance. His broad, squat body seemed shorter than his true six feet and was strong as a bull's, with huge, gnarled hands that he frequently flexed, cracking his knuckles as he did. He cracked them now as he malevolently glared at Dabney. The latter's insides turned to water, looking at the chief.

He was glad to hear Cleve say to Keg: "Chain him back up." To Dabney he said: "We'll have to think on your case a while."

Cleve read the fear in Dabney's eyes and pitied him, but wanted him to be scared. It might teach him a lesson he needed to learn.

Junior, who had been a silent observer to all this, said: "I didn't hear him squawkin' when it looked to me like Pancho was gonna plug me."

"You didn't tell me that," Cleve said.

"I forgot. Why don't you turn him loose and let me try that double-barrel rifle on him. It shoots a mile. I'd be willing to give him a head start about as far away as I was when he killed Star." Cleve looked away, not liking the expression on his son's face.

Anastacio said: "My friend, I think this *Tejano* is a bad one."

"Let me sleep on it," Cleve counseled. "I'm about wore out again. Keep him out of here while I have a private word with Keg."

When he came out of Cleve's bedroom, Keg called back through the door: "Don't make any decisions till I get back." He dragged Dabney away. To Junior he said as he went out: "Your pa wants to talk to you."

The Texan didn't like the sound of any of it. He yelled back to Cleve as Keg dragged him away: "I told you everything you wanted to know and then some . . . ." Whatever else he said was muffled by distance as Keg herded him out of hearing.

Cleve said: "Let the bastard sweat a while. Maybe the Almighty will take his case out of our hands. He could get struck by lightning out there under that tree Keg keeps him chained to."

Anastacio read the signs of Cleve's forgiving nature coming to the surface, but knew there was nothing he could do to talk him out of his folly. He led Niño outside where they wouldn't be overheard by Cleve or Sam. "Let's go down to Keg's and have a little talk together," he said.

They arrived as Keg was padlocking Dabney to his tree again. Junior followed a little later, Refugio with him. Dabney saw this delegation coming, and his stomach started to churn.

He felt his bowels turn to water and wondered if he'd shame himself right in front of them.

Keg left Dabney and conferred with the others, out of hearing. Dabney fearfully watched them, imagining what they were saying. They talked earnestly a while, then gathered around Dabney silently, hostile eyes staring at him. Finally Anastacio spoke for the group. "Did you ever hear of running the gauntlet?" he asked.

Dabney, who'd made it through fourth grade in a Texas country school, hadn't heard of it. He shook his head.

Anastacio said: "It's an old Indian custom. Captives are run between two lines of men with clubs and get the shit knocked out of them. If they make it to the end, they can run away, provided they can run faster than all the guys who did it to them."

Dabney could read no sign in Anastacio's eyes that he was bluffing. He suspected he was going to die before the sun went down and hated the idea. Bile rose in his throat; his face turned yellow, and he gagged. He managed to say: "Bandelier didn't tell you to do this, did he?"

Keg said: "Old Cleve is a leetle too soft-hearted for his own good. If it wasn't fer him, we'd have run you bastards out of the territory before now."

Anastacio said to Junior: "Go get that cannon you stole from the Englishman." He turned back to Dabney, "The kid gave me a great idea. We're gonna let you get about as far away as he was when you shot his horse, before he starts shooting at you. You can run anywhere you want to after that. The kid is a dead shot, by the way."

Dabney wanted to plead some more but could think of nothing to say. It had never occurred to him until then how it must hurt to have a big bullet tear into your body, how it feels just before you die. Now he thought of the big, black horse, lying dead. He'd been close enough to hear its last pitiful cry, when it was terrified by the final realization that it had to leave the world it had loved. He was going to experience the same thing. He'd never been a very fast runner and didn't expect to get away. He pleaded: "At least give me a horse. The kid had one when I shot at him. I ain't no runner."

Niño spoke for the first time. "I think we should give him a horse." He winked at them and left, returning in a moment with a sawhorse that Keg had left sitting alongside his house. "Here," he said. "If the kid misses you and shoots the horse, it won't hurt anything." He laughed.

Dabney thought dismally: *I never knew Injuns laughed.* Then: *Why am I wasting my time thinking stuff like this . . . I oughta be praying?* He tried to think of a prayer, and the only one he could remember was: *Now I lay me down to sleep . . . . Aw, hell, I'm going to die.* "Please," he said, "I told you everything you wanted and more. My poor old maw needs me."

"Tough," said Keg. "Here comes the kid with his rifle. We're gonna take you a long ways off, so no one will hear the shooting. On the way you'll have a lot of time to think about how you should have been good, so's your old maw wouldn't have to wonder what happened to her little boy. Sheeit! You never had a maw . . . your kind crawls out from under rocks."

"Christ!" Dabney said. His knees were so weak he could hardly walk.

They escorted him out of the village, many eyes following the procession, but no one saying anything to them or trying to follow. Downhill, there was a long meadow that suited the purpose of the game. Keg asked: "You up to shootin' this bastard down, kid?"

"Hell, yes!" said Junior. "Star was worth ten of him. I told him I'd get him for doin' it. Besides, he wasn't tryin' to shoot Star. He missed me and hit Star by accident . . . . You got any special flowers you'd like on your grave, mister? We're gonna plant you proper so you won't stink up the place any worse than you do right now."

Keg drew him aside and let the others go ahead. He said: "Don't forget your pa will disown you if you actually shoot this bastard. He just wants him scared out of his wits."

"I know," Junior said. "I wouldn't do it for anybody but Pa. He'll probably be sorry some day." He had half a notion to shoot him anyhow, but he'd seen the sad look on his father's face earlier at his eagerness to kill. His pa had had to kill a lot and wished he hadn't. Now that Junior had cooled down, shooting a man in cold blood without giving him a chance to fight didn't appeal to him.

Refugio was standing by with a .45-70 Winchester. He said: "Just in case you miss with those two rounds."

"I ain't gonna miss. Hell, I ain't missed a deer runnin' in the last ten tries, and they run a hell of a lot faster than this son of a bitch. Get ready, mister. At least you know ahead of time somebody's tryin' to plug you, and you can dodge. It's more'n I got to do."

Keg gave Dabney a shove, and he fell down, got back up, and ran faster than he ever had in his life, wronging himself both ways as he went. The first shot whizzed by his ear. He dodged and almost lost his footing, then a second followed. He thought: *The kid missed. Maybe I got a chance!*

More shots followed. Refugio had given Junior his Winchester to do the actual shooting, because he only had a dozen rounds for the big English double barrel and didn't want to waste a one of them. He sent a few more shots after Dabney until he dodged out of sight in the trees across the meadow.

"I can smell him on the breeze," Keg laughed. "I'll bet he don't slow down till he crosses the Texas line."

Junior thought: *I wouldn't count on that.*

Chapter Twenty-Nine

Antonio Chunz depended on his job at the Amarillo Ranch to support his family in Zamora Plaza. As the last of six brothers, when it was his turn, there was no family land left to divide, and, although most years with a small garden and some chickens and goats you could feed a family enough to stay alive, there was no cash income to buy a little sugar and coffee, a few ready-made clothes, cloth and thread, an occasional ribbon, or some candy. So he'd welcomed his job at the ranch and actually loved the polo playing, once he got the hang of the strange saddle and Pelham bridle. Unfortunately, his wife wouldn't agree to leave her family and live at the ranch.

He'd returned to the plaza with Anastacio's rescue party, fearing that Wingfield would suspect him of treachery in letting him ride into an ambush, but he wished he could go back to his job on the Amarillo. It didn't make sense to him that whites were all too ready to believe Indians had second sight and could invariably detect the presence of their own stealthy kind or track over bare rock where there was absolutely nothing to track. He was confident that Wingfield would never believe he hadn't been aware of the ambush until they rode into it.

Chunz heard from Niño Alonzo what had happened to Harmony Dabney and asked his chief's permission to do what he might to salvage his job. It made sense to the chief. So, riding his own horse and leading another loaned to him by Niño, Chunz followed Dabney's trail, overtaking a very sore-footed Texan before dark. Dabney had been struggling along, alternating between a half trot and a fast walk, imagining that someone who hadn't agreed with Bandelier's generous decision to turn him loose might be trailing him, intending to finish him off. His noisy passage and labored breathing prevented him from hearing Chunz approach until he was almost upon him. He whirled and put up a fending arm, involuntarily crying: "No!"

Chunz reassured him. "I am here to help not harm you, *amigo.*"

Dabney's pathetic expression of relief disgusted Chunz, who'd rather have died than show fear or appear to grovel. "Thank God!" he gasped. He waited a while to get his breath, then mounted. "You don't happen to have the makin's, do you? I need a smoke."

Chunz passed over his tobacco and papers, elated that he'd accomplished his purpose. Dabney would put in a good word with Wingfield, and Antonio would still have a job. They reached the Amarillo that night and discovered from the Mexican hands that Wingfield was no longer employed there, over which circumstance there had been much rejoicing.

Dabney read the handwriting on the wall, got together his possibles, and pulled out on a stolen horse. He sought the comfort of Maud's, where he knew he'd run into Wingfield sooner or later. He was absolutely correct in that guess. When Pancho came in and saw him, he asked: "How the hell did you get away?"

Dabney told him.

Pancho said: "Well, I'll be go to hell. I thought the damn' Injun led us into a trap."

"No way. He's ashamed as hell. Says he really owes us."

"Maybe we'll collect one of these days."

The next morning Dabney rode with Pancho's crew to Cleve's ranch. He had never intended to pull out for Texas, unless forced to it, and had no little old mother living anywhere.

Bandelier would play hell getting his hands on him again. He felt no gratitude for Cleve's generosity and was inclined to pity anyone who was sap enough to turn loose an enemy at his mercy.

Sheriff Butler arrived early at the Amarillo, bringing both Doc Ewing and Undersheriff Dave Ralls. Voerbeck invited them in.

"We're just having breakfast. Why don't you join us? I seem to have trouble getting used to this early-bird country. In Europe the business day starts later."

Butler said: "We could just as easy wait out here and smoke."

"You can smoke inside," Voerbeck said. "At least have some coffee with us."

Doc Ewing, hoping he'd get another cigar for his corncob, thought that was an outstanding idea. He'd finished the other and considered it the best pipe tobacco he'd ever had. Percy eyed him warily, determined he wasn't going to sacrifice another good Havana to a villainous pipe. Ewing hinted: "I believe I left my tobacco home," feeling around in all his pockets. Percy declined the bait. Voerbeck braved up to the obvious demand of hospitality and offered a cigar. "Have you ever tried cutting off a piece of one of these and smoking it in your pipe?" He eyed Percy as he said it. If Ewing recognized the sarcasm, he didn't let on, nor did he waste any time in murdering the Havana to stoke his corncob.

After breakfast, Daisy accompanied them to the barn while they readied horses. Percy said: "I'm going to try one of these confounded American saddles. You can tie more stuff on it." He had a .45-70 Winchester in a scabbard, a canteen of brandy so big everyone assumed it was water, and a lunch that Carmen had packed for him, carried in a canvas haversack. Noting this,

Domingo, who was saddling their horses, added a large pair of saddlebags behind Percy's saddle.

"My, word," Percy said. "How deucedly clever. I could have used one of these in Injah."

Ewing said: "In a groundhog case, you can fill 'em with dirt and make a breastwork . . . leastaways with ones that big." Percy eyed him, not sure he was serious. Noting Percy's skeptical look, Ewing continued: "Word of honor. If Custer had 'em, he'd prob'ly still be up there standin' off old Sittin' Bull."

Percy was sure his leg was being pulled. "You don't say?"

Grut kissed Daisy good bye like they were twenty-year-olds. Then, unassisted, he mounted the biggest horse on the place, a sixteen-two, buckskin broomtail named Tonto that danced around like he intended to bog his head, until he recognized that, every time he got set to do something ornery, his rider kept him off balance. He settled down and moved out with the rest, and to the practiced eye of Sheriff Butler, who was certain horses wore facial expressions if you knew how to read them, the animal looked as disgruntled as a horse can look.

Daisy waved after them until they were out of sight. Domingo risked saying: "The *señorita* looks like she'd like to go with them."

She agreed. "I would. I don't see why women always get left behind."

Domingo regarded her approvingly, an unmistakably sympathetic look in his eye, which she read.

Impulsively she asked: "Would you take me after them?"

He nodded and roped two more horses from the corral.

"I'll be back," she told him. "I've got to get on my riding habit."

Domingo was careful to assure that they didn't overtake the Voerbeck party until afternoon, when they were so far out that they wouldn't send Daisy back. Grut said nothing when Daisy rode up.

"Are you angry with me?" she asked.

"No. I was wondering why I didn't invite you to come in the first place."

Butler wasn't quite as enthusiastic, but figured Voerbeck as a damned good judge of people who didn't seem concerned by Daisy's joining them. She had a shotgun hung on her saddle which suggested that she could shoot, a good sign in the sheriff's book. He thought all women should know how to shoot for their own protection. His wife was a crack shot.

Anastacio's look-outs saw this strange cavalcade approaching when they were far off and sent for the *jefe*. Anastacio brought Niño with him and then studied the approaching cavalcade a long while through field glasses. Niño Alonzo said: "Six men and a woman. The sheriff and his *segundo,* Domingo from the Amarillo, Doc Ewing, and the woman and two others."

Anastacio could finally make that out himself but wasn't surprised that his friend had been right. He'd seen him count antelope correctly with his naked eye as far away as he could make them out with glasses. Doc Ewing had once told him: "It's probably because they never waste their time reading, like we do." He said, half to himself: "I wonder what the hell they want. Maybe they'd like their *cojones* cut off . . ." — then, as it occurred to him this would be impossible in the woman's case, added — "or something."

He went to meet them alone, stopping in their path and sitting his horse silently. Sheriff Butler came on alone, then stopped, and said: "*Buenas días,* Anastacio."

"*Buenas días.*" He eyed the sheriff suspiciously, didn't ask his purpose, and didn't exactly bar his way, though Butler knew that's what he was doing.

Voerbeck pulled abreast of Butler, sized up the situation, and with a past score of similar confrontations with Afghan tribesmen, Zulus, and an assortment of other inhospitable people to guide him, stated: "I am Grut Voerbeck." He removed his hat and replaced it. "I have come to get my daughter, Mariposa, who I am told is visiting you. The sheriff has been kind enough to show me the route."

Butler looked at Voerbeck, detected no signs of fear, and told himself: *This son of a bitch has sand.*

That's what Anastacio thought, and he defused the situation as soon as he found out who this little man was. "Ah, you are the father of the golden angel who has honored us with a visit. *Bienvenido.*" He smiled broadly, showing big even white teeth. "I will take you to our village as soon as I have a word with my men."

He galloped toward the hills and disappeared into the trees. To his brother, Emiliano, he said: "It is the *Señorita* Mariposa's father. The sheriff is with him. Go up and make sure Bandelier stays out of sight. Maybe we should take him farther away now."

"I don't think so," said Emiliano. "Wait till we have to and he will have more strength."

Anastacio nodded. "We will keep the sheriff away from him for sure. I think that he will want to talk to the girl's father. It may benefit all of us." He rode back and motioned Voerbeck's party to follow him, slowing to let them come abreast of him. He told Voerbeck: "Your daughter has made herself a favorite of everyone, especially *Jefe* Niño Alonzo, who is wondering how many ponies you would accept in exchange for her." He held up his hand. "It is an honor, *señor,*" he assured him.

Voerbeck said: "I felt sure it was. I once had an emperor inquire if I'd sell my wife to him."

Anastacio laughed. "Ah, the world is the same all over."

Everyone in the village knew who was coming. Mariposa was waiting beside the road. Her father saw her, dismounted. She ran into his arms and kissed his cheek. He hugged her tightly, tears coming to his eyes. He brushed them away after releasing her.

"I hope I haven't worried you too much," Mariposa told him. "I sent Monty to assure you I was all right."

Voerbeck looked puzzled. "Monty didn't reach us."

She looked equally puzzled, then concerned. "But I sent him. . . . Something must have happened to him."

Overhearing this conversation, Anastacio said: "Your friend, Ransom, went grizzly bear hunting with some of my people. I thought you knew. I wasn't aware he was to deliver a message, or I would have sent someone else for you."

Mariposa looked at her father, shrugged, and they both laughed. He said: "It is how I lost ten thousand cattle. Lucky it wasn't more."

Mariposa wanted to get her father alone to tell him that Bandelier was there, and that she had been nursing him. She was happy to see Dr. Ewing, all the same. She said to Anastacio, avoiding mention of Cleve, since she wasn't sure if the sheriff knew he was there: "I think you should ask the doctor if he wants to stay here and look at the children who have a cough."

Ewing missed that but said: "Glad to. I'm gettin' too old to be ridin' so far. I could stand to bed down for the night right here."

"Mi casa su casa." Anastacio assured the doctor.

Butler interjected: "I don't think you people need me. I reckon maybe me and Dave can pull out for home."

Voerbeck turned to him. "I appreciate you bringing me up here, Sheriff. You may suit yourself about leaving. I don't think I will be going for a while, and, when I do, I am sure these people will provide us with a guide."

Percy spoke for the first time. "We won't need a guide. I know the way."

Voerbeck eyed him. "Fine, Percy. Thank you. It's a great relief to know that."

Daisy said: "That's right. Percy never gets lost. Sometimes he's a little forgetful, though, about keeping people informed. Anyhow he can keep Domingo on the right trail."

Percy gave her a severe look and humphed.

The sheriff touched his hat in a salute to the ladies, turned his horse, and departed with Dave following. He said to the undersheriff: "It's what I thought. They got Bandelier in the village, sure as hell, and the girl has been taking care of him. Doc Ewing can stay and look him over. Nobody's gonna bother Doc, if he has to ride back alone."

"Do you think Bandelier will decide to come in?"

"I wouldn't. The Army ain't gonna get the job done, either. By the time they get here, Bandelier will be long gone, probably up in the old cliff dwellings somewhere."

"Pringle won't like that, I reckon."

"I have a notion there's lots of things Pringle won't like that're in store for him. Maybe you can run for sheriff, when I quit, without having to play his game."

"If I lose my marbles and decide to run, I sure as hell hope so. I've watched it make an old man of you before your time."

Butler eyed him. "About how old do you mean?"

"Older'n me, at least."

When she was finally alone with her father, Mariposa said: "You should talk to Cleve Bandelier."

He thought: *So, it's Cleve, is it?* He said: "I hoped to. I think we can settle just about all the trouble around here between the two of us."

"That's what I told him."

He raised an eyebrow. "I guess I have to back up what these

people would call my *segunda.*"

"Leave the arrangements to me," she said. "We will probably eat with Anastacio. You will meet Cleve there."

Voerbeck didn't know what he expected Bandelier to look like, but he didn't expect the emaciated figure, sitting in a leather-thong chair — a rangy man with an Indian complexion and very dark eyes, heavy black handlebar mustache, and needing a shave. By contrast, his hair was neatly combed. His eyes met Voerbeck's impassively, as if to say: *So you're the foreign devil that caused all the misery up here for years.*

Grut offered his hand, and Bandelier accepted it. An uncomfortable silence followed before Voerbeck said: "I am sorry to find you like this. If I had come here sooner to find out what was going on, this would not have happened to you. Please accept my apology."

Mariposa had prepared Cleve to expect her father to be reasonable, but he hadn't expected this. He thought: *Boy, did we get the wrong picture of him . . . and I guess he thought we were skunks.*

Anastacio was listening closely, his eyes moving between them. Maybe a great thing was going to happen. He wasn't sure how it had come about, but he was thankful.

Anastacio had a long plank table set up for all of the people who should be a part of a feast of thanksgiving. Even Junior and Amy had places at the table. Others were Mariposa, Daisy, Percy, Doc Ewing, Keg, Sam, and Maria — who bustled around preparing food, with help from her mother, Mariposa, and Amy. Anastacio's parents, brothers, and their wives were all there, and also expected was *Padre* Maldonado who had been out of the village on one of his wedding, Mass, and baptizing circuits. Niño Alonzo brought his wife. Children wandered in and out, not wanting to miss anything. Good wine flowed, and outside were secreted bottles of *aguardiente* for the men to sample when the mood struck them. The big front room overflowed with people.

Doc Ewing interrupted by announcing: "I think I'd better take the patient back and look over his wound before he passes out for lack of air. I guess you can walk, eh?"

"Give me a hand out of this chair and I can."

They disappeared for a few minutes into the bedroom, Mariposa with them. Doc looked over her handiwork and grunted. "Its coming along fine. Too late to stitch it now. I couldn't have done any better, keeping it clean, and that's all you need to do with a wound like this," He smiled at Mariposa while he put on fresh bandages. "If you ever need a job, let me know."

"I will," she said, not sure if he was being droll or not.

The high point of the affair was the late arrival of *Padre* Maldonado. Mariposa had heard a great deal about him, but no one had told her he was six foot seven. He was dressed as a typical priest, in black, wearing a broad-brimmed, low-crowned black hat, his pants tucked into riding boots on which he wore silver-roweled spurs with little bells that tinkled when he walked. She was surprised to see him take off an ivory-handled six-shooter, held in a carved black scabbard with a matching cartridge belt, and hand it to Maria to hang up on the wall pegs that held a lot more of them.

After supper her father and *Padre* Maldonado talked for a while and found something to laugh about together. She wondered what it was and later asked her father. "I told him smoking cigars stunted my growth, and he said having to fight off women, because he was so blindingly handsome, had probably stunted his . . . or maybe associating with Jesuits."

It was impossible for Cleve and Grut to get down to business in the cheerful, noisy house, and, by the time the gathering started to split up, Cleve was bone tired. Mariposa helped him to bed. Before he left, he assured Grut: "We'll talk in the morning. I reckon we got a lot to straighten out."

On impulse, after she tucked him in, Mariposa kissed Cleve's lips gently and received a startled, almost frightened look from him. She sensed that he had a great hunger for a woman but would have been surprised to know he hadn't kissed one since his wife had died. His lips had met hers willingly, and his eyes held hers for a long while, questioning, but he remained silent, finally sighing and closing his eyes. She had hoped he might ask her why she'd done it, in which case she would have told him the absolute truth. He was the man she'd picked, and she intended to have him.

Grut Voerbeck slept on the mattress in the straw-filled wagon that had brought Cleve to the village, Doc Ewing sharing it with him. Percy put up on the cot down at Keg's that Ransom had used a couple of nights before. Sam's bedroom was the hayloft of Anastacio's small stone barn, which suited him since he wanted to stay close to Cleve.

A great silence descended after all the kids were in bed. Occasionally a dog barked, was joined in a chorus by others, scolding a coyote that serenaded them from the mountainside downwind of the village, probably circling to find an unwary cat or a chicken that had somehow got out. Voerbeck went to sleep quickly, tired out by his long ride and soothed by the fragrant balsam that scented the chilly mountain air.

Chapter Thirty

Jesús had been making a short-handed roundup of Cleve's scattered herd and finally realized it was too big a job for four men. He decided to circle back by the home ranch with his three-man crew before heading up to Zamora Plaza to recruit extra help. He was pins and needles all the way back, scouting every ridge before they crossed it, not knowing what they might run into. It bothered him that neither Cleve, José, nor Sam had come out to join them. He had a feeling that things had somehow gone badly amiss, and he was anxious to know what had happened.

He timed their arrival at the Bandelier ranch for the late afternoon, thinking that, if they ran into trouble, they could make a run for it and count on getting away in the dark. He left the crew hidden within a half mile of the buildings, moving forward alone to the ridge above the barn. The first thing he saw was Pancho Wingfield's paint horse in the corral behind the barn. "Uh, oh," he said under his breath. "Bad news. Good thing we didn't ride in like a bunch of ninnies."

He decided to stay and watch a while, moved back, tied his horse, then returned, and saw Pancho's men moving around the place. Using his field glasses, he counted seven men and figured there were probably a good many others inside, since it was supper time. The remuda was loose, grazing near the ranch, which gave him an idea. He got his horse and went back to the crew.

"I'm gonna run off their horses," he said. "When I start yelling and shooting, I want you birds up on the ridge with your Winchesters to work over everybody that moves. This is our chance to even things up a little. When I get the herd out of sight, you guys run for it. I'll meet you at Zamoras', if I don't find you sooner."

Jeff Mill's stomach crawled. He'd been shot at by this crew a few days before and had dirtied his pants, which he'd kept from the others. He hadn't tried to shoot back — had been too scared. This was the first time he'd ever been expected to shoot at anyone. He asked: "You want us to try to kill them?"

Jesús gave him a hard stare. "God damn right I do! What the hell you think they've been trying to do to us? Grow up, kid!"

Jeff gulped and couldn't say a word. He followed the others as they moved up and tied their horses out of sight. His knees were weak, his stomach still crawling.

In a few minutes Jesús broke into sight, hollering the indescribable war whoop of those master horse thieves, the Comanches. The horses threw up their heads, saw the screaming apparition thundering toward them, swinging a slicker and shooting, and spun away in a frantic run for their lives. Skillfully he bunched them while he kept up his blood-curdling racket. He had the herd almost beyond gunshot range before any resistance was organized.

Jeff saw a man run out of the barn and quickly slip a hackamore on the paint horse, open the gate, leap on bareback, and thunder after Jesús. Lawrence, the best shot in his regiment during the war, carefully tracked the horse, squeezed off, and watched it go end over end. The rider fell heavily and didn't get up. Dabney ran toward the fallen man, flinched as a Winchester slug whined past and veered away into a small depression, hugging the ground.

Jeff tried to draw a bead on any one of the running men who poured out of the house and couldn't, instead spraying the general area. He forgot to be scared in the excitement, encouraged by the barrage that his pals were pouring at Wingfield's men. He saw a man drop and wondered if he'd killed his first man. Another fell with his leg cut out from under him. Then the first return shots were fired.

"O K," Lawrence said. "Let's haul it before they settle down and start aimin'. Jesús is out of sight."

They withdrew behind the hill, mounted, and cut out at a run, not stopping till they'd reached the chop hills a mile away. Lawrence pulled up and looked at their back trail, realizing there could have been other horses out of sight in the barn. "Best reload now, while we got the chance," he said.

Jeff was surprised to discover he felt good, instead of scared. Lawrence looked him over with the eye of a combat veteran. He'd wondered what kind of a trooper this kid was going to make, read the signs, and was satisfied. He clapped him on the shoulder and said: "You done real good, kid."

Jeff wondered if one of his shots had hit someone and felt no qualms. It could have been the guy that shot his buddy, Johnny. He wasn't aware he'd just graduated from his first course in becoming a fighting man.

Dabney crawled out of the ditch when he was sure the shooting was over and ran to where Pancho lay. The paint horse was dead, but Pancho was stirring. Finally he sat up, shook his head, and looked around.

"Give me a hand up," he said.

"You O K?" Dabney asked.

Pancho moved his various parts slowly. "Nothing broke . . . just shook up. He was going full tilt when he was shot." He went to his dead horse and patted it. "Some son of a bitch is going to pay for this!" he vowed. "That was some of Bandelier's crew for sure, and I'm goin' to get old Cleve in a gun sight if it's the last thing I do."

"Well, I can tell you for sure he wasn't with 'em," Dabney said. "He ain't gettin' around too good yet. Can hardly get out of bed."

"I don't give a damn! I want his scalp first of all, anyhow. There ain't gonna be any peace in this country while he's alive."

Anastacio, *Padre* Maldonado, and Niño Alonzo were having a hard time overcoming lifelong prejudices about women in decision-making capacities when they met with Grut Voerbeck and Cleve and discovered that the Dutchman insisted on his daughter's presence. Voerbeck understood. "It may seem unusual to you gentlemen to have my daughter here with me, but I have no secrets from her. She is going to take over and run my affairs when I am too old, and certainly after I die. So I ask your understanding. If I died today, you'd have to deal with her regarding the Amarillo Grant, and you all have a great stake in its future. I intend to see that all past injustices committed in my name against you and your people are corrected, and we can iron that out today, if you are willing. We can handle the legal technicalities later."

Cleve certainly had no reservations concerning Mariposa's presence and neither did Keg Brownlee who was representing the Anglos on the grant who lived in Zamora Plaza. Cleve wasn't sure what he felt about this unusual, foreign woman, but he knew he liked to have her around. He wondered if he'd dreamed that she kissed him the night before and convinced himself it had really happened because it had been a long while before he went to sleep afterward, thinking of her. He was sure she wasn't thinking of him romantically but was overwhelmed with pity for his helplessness. Whatever the case, it had been wonderful.

Voerbeck thought he knew what all of these people wanted. Niño desired a reservation for his people where whites wouldn't constantly encroach and force them to move on. Anastacio wanted the Spanish grants of his people confirmed, so they could be sure they really owned what they had always thought of as theirs. Keg wanted the homesteads, from which he and his Anglo friends had been driven by the courts, reconfirmed as legal. He'd taken refuge in the plaza after being driven from his small ranch, as had many other Anglos. *Padre* Maldonado was the supporter of these small people and wanted justice for them all. Cleve had always felt the same as their nominal leader and, for himself, wanted the ranch he'd built on a desert homestead proved up on. There was plenty of open range for grazing and would be for many years.

Voerbeck voiced his understanding and concluded: "I can see that you all get what you want. I have had people looking into it for me for quite a while. These court cases have been pushed without my detailed knowledge of what was going on. It's true, I put up the money, but I've been misled regarding the rights of the people involved. Lord Ransom was greatly at fault for not paying attention to business, though at heart he is a good man, simply foolish. I know that now and will have him replaced. In addition, I discovered that I was grossly misled by Mister Pringle in Santa Fé. I will deal with him separately, but, I can assure you, he won't bother you any more as far as your property rights are concerned."

A babble of voices followed this announcement, all thanking him and assuring him that, if what he said was true, they would never resist any just laws that applied to them. Cleve looked at Mariposa, as he often did, and she caught his glance and smiled.

Voerbeck added: "Unfortunately, the Army is headed up here to support the U. S. marshal in arresting Mister Bandelier. That's the last thing I have to take care of for you."

Anastacio said: "He won't be here when they come, I can tell you that."

"They won't come now," Voerbeck assured them. "I thought you had kidnapped my daughter, which is why I supported their coming in the first place . . . in fact, that's the only reason the President allowed them to come. He is an old friend. I have only to send him a telegram, and he will order the Army to go back, and I intend to do that. And I am going to meet General Gryden and stop him until I can wire the President and get an answer."

Mariposa helped Cleve back to bed after the meeting. She was glad to see that he was steadier on his feet. As he turned to get into bed, he found her close to him, the invitation in her eyes unmistakable, and he put his arms around her, waiting to judge her reaction before he made a fool of himself. When she pressed against him and put her arms around his neck, he kissed her, gently at first, then demandingly. A surge of passion overwhelmed him. He'd waited years for the right woman to come along, and now she was in his arms. They held to each other for a long while, both overwhelmed by discovery, she of her first experience of true physical passion, he of its reawakening.

They heard the door opening, and she quickly made as though she was helping him into bed. It was Amy. "Pa, when do we go home?"

He got into bed and covered up, too unnerved to answer her right away. After Mariposa fluffed his pillows, he said: "I don't know, honey. As soon as we can." But he knew he might never be able to return.

Before they could discuss it further, the village erupted in the typical hubbub regarding something unusual afoot. Jesús and the ranch hands arrived. Amy went to see what was happening. Mariposa took the opportunity to lean down and kiss Cleve hard again. "I love you," she said.

"I love you, too," he whispered, still stunned by what had

happened. "Very much . . . but I don't know what can come of it."

Before she could answer, Amy returned. "It's Jesús and our cowboys," she told them.

Jesús was behind her, his face wreathed in a broad smile as he and Cleve exchanged an *abrazo*. "Emiliano told me what happened to you," he said. "It's good to see you getting better."

Cleve returned the smile and *abrazo* as best he could. He was glad to see his *segundo* since he had things to arrange. A plan had been forming in his mind as he lay awake at night. He had been about to mention it to Mariposa when they were interrupted.

It was clear to him that as long as Pringle and the ring ran the territory, he could not stay here. There was no way that he could expect to be acquitted in a trial for the double killing at the ranch, especially since the victims were at least nominally federal officers. And, if he were acquitted, he was sure Pringle's gunmen would be after him until they finally got him.

Voerbeck knocked on the door. Entering, he said to Cleve: "I'm leaving to head off the Army. Mariposa is staying here. She has developed a great liking for this part of the country, she tells me, and doesn't want to leave just yet. I can appreciate that. There is something about the air and water."

Mariposa interjected: "What he says is true. Besides, you need the ministrations of a skilled nurse."

The recollection of her warm, soft lips reminded him of the ministrations he was most likely to need in his opinion, since he seemed to be recovering from his wound without complications, except stiffness and pain when he used the muscles on that side.

As soon as they'd gone, Jesús turned back to Cleve. "That bastard, Wingfield, has taken over the ranch." He told the story of his attack on Wingfield's crew.

"That's the only kind of medicine he understands," Cleve observed. "But I may not be going back to the ranch. I'm thinking of hiding out until the heat dies down. I may sell or lease the place."

Jesús' face fell. "You can count on me and the boys to run it while you're on the dodge."

Cleve shook his head. "I may always be on the dodge. I've been thinking of going to Argentina. I have a friend there who skipped out a jump ahead of a rope for something he didn't do. He says it's great ranching country."

Jesús protested: "If you go there and ranch, me and the boys will come along." Then he thought of Cleve's children. "What are you going to do with the kids?"

"Bring them along, naturally."

"Do you have the money? We didn't get the herd rounded up again. We need some help."

Cleve said: "You may not have to round them up. We can sell lock, stock, and barrel, book count."

Jesús laughed. "If you find a damn' fool. . . . Englishmen are best."

"It happens that I know an Englishman who isn't exactly a damn' fool but wants to buy the ranch. In fact, I had a long talk with him about it."

Jesús waited to find out who that might be.

"Baron Waterford wants a ranch."

"I don't know him."

"I'll see that you meet him. He's a friend of Voerbeck's and Lord Ransom's."

Jesús looked pained at the mention of Ransom. He hadn't yet heard the details of his rehabilitation by besting Keg in a fight. "He'll have a helluva job taking over the ranch if we can't get Wingfield out of there."

"I have a notion Pancho hasn't got too long to run in this

territory. Without Voerbeck or Pringle behind him, Wingfield will have to pull out. We've got enough on Pringle to put him in the pen for a few years. He'll be willing to play our game. In fact, he won't have any choice."

Jesús shook his head. "Pancho isn't going to go without trying to get even. I know his type. We'll probably have to kill him."

Jesús brought in the crew to see Cleve and have a small reunion of their own. Jeff was just getting over the shock of discovering Mariposa there, since he'd last seen her heading for Dorado on a train, nursing his wounded buddy, Johnny. He hardly knew how to approach any woman, much less a beautiful one, but managed it, hat in hand, without falling down. She restrained a laugh and reassured him that Johnny was doing just fine and had been stitched up by Doc Ewing. "The doctor is here to look at Mister Bandelier, and you can ask him yourself," she told him. Jeff was beaming from ear to ear when he came in to see Cleve.

Cleve filled them in on his plans to sell the ranch and got the expected unhappy reaction until he said: "You can all stay and work for Baron Waterford. If that doesn't suit you, when I get settled in Argentina, or wherever, you can come down there and work."

"I always wanted to travel," Jeff said. "How about you guys?"

The consensus was that Cleve would have a ready-made crew wherever he went into ranching.

Anastacio provided Grut Voerbeck an escort to Dorado where he expected to meet the Army column under General Gryden. Prominent in the bodyguard was the tall figure of *Padre* Maldonado, mounted on a large mule. He rode beside Voerbeck, smoking one of his cigars, and dilating on the damned Jesuits. "They always overmanage everything. Never satisfied to let sleeping dogs lie." At the root of this complaint was the fact that it had been a visiting Jesuit who had brought to the attention of Archbishop Lamy the rumors that Maldonado wasn't a model of celibacy. Lamy had called him to Santa Fé for an accounting, but he hadn't yet condescended to go, since it had only been three years since he was invited. *Padre* Martínez had never paid much attention to Lamy, either, and had been excommunicated for his independence. As a result, Martínez had organized his own church, like a peddler, setting up a shop across the street from a competitor who has irked him. Maldonado would have no trouble doing the same. His flock was loyal to him, not some jackleg, distant authority in Santa Fé or Rome, spouting incomprehensible theology rather than something that made sense, like seed corn or sheep and goats — to say nothing of love-making. Thinking of his personal authority, he waved a long arm over his head, to test his arrangements for Voerbeck's protection, and a line of horsemen materialized along the hills on both sides of them and paralleled their progress, until he waved again, and they seemingly evaporated, like smoke.

Voerbeck didn't have to go as far as Dorado to meet the Army. It was ahead of schedule, due to General Gryden's admirable efficiency, and had already detrained at Tres Huérfanos. A patrol came out to discover who was approaching and carried word back to General Gryden who personally rode out to greet Voerbeck. They shook hands warmly.

"It's good to see you, General. You are ahead of schedule."

"Yes, and it's good to see you."

"I have found my daughter well and safe," Voerbeck said. "She sent word that she was all right, but the message went astray. I have put you to a great deal of trouble for nothing."

"My men need the training," Gryden rejoined. "Besides, I still must help the U. S. marshal."

Voerbeck looked embarrassed. "I want to discuss that with

you. I don't really think that's such a good idea. I've met this fellow, Bandelier, and he is, as you say, pure gold. I think, if he is taken into custody, he may be killed by his enemies."

Gryden agreed. "The same thought has occurred to me. Can you get your *friend in Washington* to call off my dogs?"

"I will need to get through a telegram. It may take time."

"There is a telegraph office at Tres Huérfanos. I can camp here and stall until you get the proper orders for me."

"Good. Good. That's what I'd hoped you'd agree to do."

Gryden laughed. "Pringle will probably have apoplexy."

"Ah, we all have our health problems," Voerbeck chuckled.

Seeing Gryden start to set up a camp, Pringle came over and asked: "What are you doing?"

Gryden feigned surprise. "Why, I'm setting up camp."

Pringle spotted Voerbeck and pointed at him. "Did he have something to do with changing your plans?"

"I hadn't been aware that I told you what my plans were."

"Well, I assumed. . . ."

"Yes," Gryden prompted, but he didn't make clear what he was saying yes about.

Pringle went over to Voerbeck, who was sided by *Padre* Maldonado, gave the latter a poisonous look, and said: "Did you recover your daughter?"

"Yes," Voerbeck said blandly. "I discovered she had sent me a message that miscarried. She wasn't being held against her will at all."

"So, where is she?"

"I'm not sure, right at the moment, but I assume she's still up at Zamora Plaza."

Pringle couldn't stifle the natural question. "Doing what, for heaven's sake?"

"She likes the people. She thinks it's quaint. As I told you, she's a great tourist."

"My God! Those people are close to barbarians." Then he remembered that Maldonado was within hearing. He felt a large, strong hand on his shoulder, and it turned him around.

Maldonado smiled at him without the slightest mirth in his eyes. "I had a dream about you, Tómas," he said. "I dreamed the Almighty gathered you to his bosom for being a bigot." He gave him a shove. Pringle turned and left in a hurry.

Ever since Wingfield hadn't shown up to meet him at Dorado, Pringle had been irritated. Of course, he arrived early, but Pancho should have been there, waiting. He'd left a message for him, and he still hadn't shown up. Pringle waited his chance to talk further to Voerbeck without Maldonado's presence and approached him again when he saw he was alone.

"Is the bandit, Bandelier, in Zamora Plaza?"

"I meant to talk to you about that. I found Mister Bandelier grossly misrepresented. I was thinking of arranging a meeting between you two. I feel sure you'd agree with me. Someone has been slandering him." It was a calculated irony, since they both knew that *someone* was Pringle.

Pringle said: "It's too late now. He's killed two lawmen and has to answer for that. I hope you aren't thinking of having the Army recalled now that your daughter is safe. The marshal still needs all the help he can get to apprehend Bandelier."

"If the Army should go up there, only trouble would follow. These people would fight the Army to protect Mister Bandelier. He was planning to leave there to avoid a fight when he heard the Army was coming."

"The Army should give those people a lesson. It's time someone made them law-abiding. They have resisted court orders issued on your behalf for years. What do I have to do to convince you of that?"

"Nothing," Voerbeck said. "If I had known what was really going on, there would have been no court orders. But that's neither here nor there. I have a proposition for you. I don't need any more of the kind of trouble I'm having here. I have more important and lucrative things to do with my time."

Pringle's heart leaped, anticipating what this man was about to propose to him.

Voerbeck went on: "Before I make my proposition, I want to say that you have played me false from the beginning, and I know it. I shouldn't even talk to you. But I am a businessman, not a moralist. How much would you buy me out for?"

"You paid fifty thousand dollars. I can give you that."

Voerbeck laughed at him. "I paid fifty thousand dollars, thinking I was buying forty-two thousand acres. Thanks to my money and your men, the grant now is over two million acres, legally or otherwise. That's what you'll be buying. And whether you wish to admit it or not, your people have succeeded in stealing cattle from me worth as much as I am asking for the grant. Don't talk to me about fifty thousand dollars. It's three hundred thousand dollars, take it or leave it."

Pringle didn't bat an eye. He had $300,000.00. It was the exact amount he was willing to go as his top figure. He quickly said: "You've got a deal," and extended his hand to shake on it.

Voerbeck said: "There will be a few minor hold-outs for my friends, unavoidably, but not over a hundred thousand acres, all told."

"I'm sure that can be arranged between our attorneys."

"Good," Voerbeck said. "It will be a great load off my mind."

Pringle thought: *You just think it's a great load off* your *mind.* He could hardly keep himself from dancing a jig.

Chapter Thirty-One

Tomás Pringle finally found Pancho Wingfield in the Santiago Hotel saloon in Dorado and marched over to the table where he was seated, holding a water glass half full of whiskey.

"Where the hell have you been?" he demanded.

Wingfield, unaware of what had transpired between Pringle and Voerbeck, which boded well for his own future, wasn't in a mood to take a lot of lip. He eyed Pringle insolently, half drunk, laughed nastily, and said: "You wouldn't believe me if I told you."

"Try me."

"Me and the boys been out on a long walk."

Pringle's bulgy eyes indicated that he, indeed, didn't believe him. "A walk?"

"Yeah, a walk. We went over to Bandelier's and took over all right. Then some son of a bitch ran off the remuda and killed my paint horse in the bargain. We had to round the hosses up on foot . . . there wasn't a nag left on the place."

Pringle strangled a laugh. He could afford to see the humor in the situation since Wingfield's absence hadn't really affected him. His plans for the future were a different proposition, and Wingfield was prominent in them. He debated how much he could safely reveal to his treacherous cohort. After getting a drink and firing up a cigar, he said: "We got a new deal coming up."

Wingfield absorbed that news without displaying any great interest. He'd heard the same story before, only to see Pringle's plans fall flat.

"I just bought the grant off Voerbeck," Pringle said, satisfied to see a complete change come over Pancho at the receipt of that information.

"The hell you say?" The Texan got an instant picture of his ambition to own a ranch materializing from that development. "How did you manage that?"

"The old bastard is tired of the trouble it's caused him. He wanted to unload it. There's a string or two attached. He wants to hang onto small parts of it for some friends."

"That ain't apt to be a problem, is it?"

"Not unless one of the friends is Bandelier."

"How in the hell would Bandelier get to be Voerbeck's friend? The old boy ought to hate him."

"They spent a couple of days together up at Zamora Plaza, and I think maybe Bandelier convinced him of what's really been going on."

"If Voerbeck knew what's really been going on, he sure as hell wouldn't have been willing to sell out to you, would he?"

"I think he would. As a matter of fact, he said he's into money, not morals, which gave me the notion he's onto our game and doesn't give a damn."

Wingfield considered that. "Bandelier can still be a big fly in your ointment if he stays around. Even if he gets hung, or goes over the hill, his trial will get you a lot of bad publicity."

"Don't think that hasn't occurred to me."

Pringle definitely wanted to avoid the black eye that adverse publicity would get him. Politics and politicians have long memories. He knew he'd never achieve his long-range political objective of becoming one of New Mexico's first senators if some other contender could harp on that sort of record.

He said: "Your number one job is to get Bandelier out of the way once and for all."

"That's the kind of job I like. But I'll never get close to him while he's still up with the Zamoras."

"I don't think he's there any more."

"Where is he?"

"Voerbeck said when Bandelier heard the Army was coming to help the marshal pull him in, he dragged his freight to avoid putting his friends in a bind."

"Did he say where he went?"

"No, but he isn't apt to go far till he gets on his feet. He's probably hiding out somewhere up in that country."

Wingfield's mind flashed to an immediate picture of the many cliff dwellings that would admirably suit such a purpose.

Pringle asked: "You got any idea where a man would be apt to hole up around there?"

Pancho nodded. "Not only that, but I've got the ideal man to sniff him out."

"Devil Ed?"

"Better'n him. I got one of the Jicarillas who owes me."

Pringle held up his hand. "I don't want to know any more about it. Just get him. From then on, we'll have clear sailing."

Grut Voerbeck returned to Zamora Plaza, intending to pick up his daughter and return to the peace and quiet of the Amarillo ranch. It was one of the properties he intended to hold out of the sale to Pringle. Bandelier's ranch was another, since he knew Percy wanted to buy it. The other hold-outs were the many homesteads of small settlers in addition to the ancient, small Spanish grants of native landholders.

He learned that Cleve had departed, escorted by his cowboys as well as reinforcements provided by Anastacio, and that Mariposa had gone with him. He thought: *Ah, my compulsive little nurse. I might have known.* Suspicions were forming that it was more than that. He would have to consider that possibility carefully — this could involve complications like her previous choice, Lord Ransom.

He asked Anastacio: "Can you take me to them?"

Anastacio nodded. "*Mañana.* It's too late today . . . we'd be stumbling around in the dark, and they might be nervous."

The place to which Refugio Zamora led Cleve's party was on the north side of a broad canyon where the ancient Indians had built their pueblos beneath rock shelves that shielded them from mountain cloudbursts, shaded them in the summer, and admitted rays of the low winter sun while avoiding icy north winds. They transported Cleve on a stretcher, supported by poles slung to the sides of two old, steady mules. He found it comfortable, except when the slope was too steep, and he had to hang on to stay in. He was weary and ready for a long *siesta* by the time they reached their destination.

"You will have all the comforts of home here," Refugio told Cleve. "There are enough of these little houses so everyone can have their own."

They got Cleve located in his house, where Mariposa insisted she would also stay. "We can hang blankets for privacy," she said.

Amy had counted on being Cleve's special nurse but deferred to Mariposa, whom she adored. Her wise little voice told her: *Your pa thinks she's special . . . leave him alone with her. She's good for him.*

Emiliano Zamora had accompanied them for the purpose of setting up security arrangements. He was joined by Jesús and Sam Buchanan. Emiliano said: "This place is easy to guard. There are only two trails in . . . a man on each end, day and night, if they don't go to sleep, will let you know if anyone is coming and can keep out of sight in the bargain."

Jesús, accompanied by Sam and Emiliano, inspected the entire area before the sun went down. They posted guards, then went back to the big bonfire in front of Cleve's house. Lawrence had appointed himself chief cook, and he was a good one. Amy helped him, the two fussing at each other over who got to do what, and how it should be done. They laughed a lot while they were at it. Cleve woke up, heard them, and smiled. It was almost like home again. But it also saddened him when he reflected that they'd probably never be able to go back to the ranch again. He wondered what would have happened if he hadn't shot those two men and become a fugitive. *The hell with it,* he told himself. *It's over and done. It's all working out for the best, and I can go away and take the kids. We'll be rich if Percy gives me half what he said he'd pay, and we can use it to start over in Argentina.*

What saddened him most was leaving Mariposa right after he'd found her. He could see no way that her father would let her run off to a place like Argentina, even if she were willing to go. He recognized and admitted the soundness of all the reservations Grut would have, particularly his own lack of education and polish. *Well,* he concluded his reflections, *nobody ever said life would be a bed of roses. At least I'll have the kids.*

Mariposa came in to check on him. "You're awake." She leaned down and kissed him gently. A tight pain gripped his chest, knowing that he loved her and had to give her up. She was young and probably hadn't thought beyond their immediate bliss. In time she would recognize how impossible it all was.

She helped him walk outside to eat. Refugio hadn't exaggerated about the comforts of home. The pack train had brought up an assortment of convenient camping equipment that had been absorbed from the Army over the years. The folding canvas officers' chairs and folding tables were a blessing to a man in his condition. If he sat on the ground, he might need a lot of help getting up.

After eating, they sat around the fire, hypnotized by the

flickering, many-hued flames, each wrapped in private thoughts. A hunting owl hooted somewhere. Mariposa, seated next to Cleve, found his hand, squeezed it, and held on. Amy noticed this and thought: *I wonder if Pa is falling in love?* She thought a lot about love because of the novels owned by Gloria Peabody that she'd read — behind Gloria's back, of course. She wasn't sure what all it involved, but this looked like the kind she'd read about in novels. It would be nice if her father married this beautiful lady, whom she wanted to grow up to be like, even if she could never look like her.

The others slipped off to bed one by one, leaving Mariposa and Cleve. They watched the moon rise over the trees and light the mountainside opposite them.

"It's almost as light as day," Mariposa marveled.

"It gets like this in the high country," he said. "And you can see a lot more stars here than anywhere else."

She leaned back, looked at the millions of stars, and felt how little humans actually were in this vast universe. *Little and happy,* she told herself. The universe might be endless, but only a minuscule part of it could feel and experience love.

They watched the night and listened to its muted sounds, till the fire burned to ashes, then went inside.

"I'm cold," she said.

He took her in his arms and kissed her, feeling her warm response as she pressed tightly against him. He wanted it never to end.

Later, Mariposa lay awake on her cot, staring up in the darkness and wondered what it would be like to experience love to its fullest. She speculated on how long Cleve would be incapacitated, and where they might be when he got well. She didn't know but was certain she was going to be with him for the rest of her life. Notions of being manager of her father's empire had evaporated. She suspected that had been something to divert her energies till the right man came along. The volcano she'd discovered inside overwhelmed her completely.

After breakfast, Refugio showed them the way to the hot mineral spring. It bubbled up in a narrow, rock-walled gulch and fell into successive pools, each a little cooler. "Feel them," Refugio said. "You can pick your own temperature. Take your clothes off and get in, Cleve. It's what you need now."

"I won't look," Mariposa said.

"I don't care if you do," Cleve said. "I'm gonna dunk myself. It'll be the first good bath I've had in ages."

Refugio grinned. The male-female thing was what really made life worth living, and Mexicans all knew it. The toil was necessary to feed the body, but love fed the soul. "I'll leave you two," he said. "Don't worry about anyone peeking. We've got scouts out to keep anyone from getting in here without our knowing about it." He left, smiling.

When he was gone, Mariposa said: "What he meant was that I can go in, too. He knows about us. His people are very understanding, and they see things we don't."

She was taking her clothes off as she talked, and Cleve watched her tall, slim body emerge from fashionable layers of underthings, holding his breath at the beauty that emerged as the dress went over her head, the camisole fell, exposing generous, perfectly formed, pink-nippled breasts. Finally she stood naked, with the lovely triangle of golden hair fully exposed, framed by thighs that were a sculptor's dream. She stood very still, knowing he was looking at her, and that she had aroused him.

Then she came to him in the warmth of the pool, her body meeting a man's fully unclothed for the first time. They came together, thrusting and demanding, and she forgot about his injury, as he did. He led her to the grassy bank and carefully let himself down beside her, then experimented to see if he could do what he needed so badly. He told himself: *I will, if it kills me.* His terrible, long loneliness ended as he urgently sought her lips while streaming inside of her and felt her meeting him in her first devastating realization of passion. Then they lay exhausted, side by side.

She recovered first. "Did I hurt you?"

"If you did, I survived. Let's look."

His wound hadn't broken open, and he wouldn't have cared if it had.

"Thank goodness for that," she said, and sought his lips again. "I love you so much."

His eyes told her all she needed to know about his feelings.

From a considerable distance, Refugio yelled: "Hey, Cleve! Somebody to see you two in camp." Considerate, he never came closer but gave them a knowing smirk as they joined him on the path after getting dressed.

Her father had arrived and was smoking a cigar, sitting in a camp chair, looking across the valley. "I wonder if I own this?" he mused aloud. "If I do, I'll have to make sure to hang onto this part."

"Of course, you own it," Mariposa said. "You own everything all the way to Colorado."

"But not for long."

"How is that?" she asked, alarmed at the possibilities.

"I'm selling it," he said.

"Selling. To whom?"

"Pringle."

"Pringle?" It came out as a gasp.

"Hold your shirt on, as these Americans say. There's more to it than that." He explained his arrangements, leaving out a few details. "What worries me is what we should do for Mister Bandelier here."

Cleve said: "You don't have to do anything for me. I'm

sellin' out to Percy and goin' to a healthier climate."

Voerbeck nodded his approval. "A wise move. At least for now. If you were tried and convicted, I'm sure I could get you a Presidential pardon, but I'm not sure we could keep you alive long enough to be tried, or even after you were acquitted, if that's possible in one of Mister Pringle's courts."

"Likely it isn't," Cleve conceded. "I can't risk it, for the kids' sake."

Mariposa gave him a look that said — *How about for my sake?* — but he didn't notice.

"I've been thinking about how to get you out of here when you're able to travel," Voerbeck continued. "How do you feel?"

Cleve glanced at Mariposa and grinned. "A little tired, but I could travel right now if I had to."

"Good. In a few days I'll let you know where you can come, and I will slip you out of this country. If you want to go to Argentina, I can get you to New York without anyone finding out. I own a steamship or two you can get on without papers."

Mariposa debated telling her father that she was going with Cleve, but decided it could wait. After *Padre* Maldonado married them would be time enough. Now she had to figure out how to get Cleve to propose.

"Are you coming with me?" Voerbeck asked his daughter as he prepared to leave.

"Not yet," she said. "I've never had so much fun in my life. Let me stay a little longer. Besides, my patient may need me."

Voerbeck eyed her closely, and what he saw satisfied him that his suspicions were correct. He discovered he rather savored the prospect. He told himself: *Cleve Bandelier has done something that my daughter liked very much.* The signs were evident to an old *roué*. He wasn't sure how much he'd done, or was capable of doing yet, but he knew what a woman in love looked like. He liked her pick this time a lot better than the last. The only sound reason to marry was for love.

Antonio Chunz had spent two days reconnoitering the vicinity of Cleve's hide-out before he brought in Wingfield and his men. He posted them at night and hoped they'd stay in place until the right time, without giving themselves away. The sun was fairly high when Pancho observed Cleve and Mariposa leave their camp. His strong glasses brought them close enough to recognize, though they were almost beyond rifle shot. He followed their progress to the pool, and his jaw dropped as he watched them disrobe. This was too good a show to let anyone else in on it, and he hoped his accelerated breathing wasn't apparent to Dabney, who was close by. Chunz's return irritated him.

"Come," Chunz said, beckoning. "I will lead you by a secret path."

Wingfield thought: *This is rare. I want that girl alive.* He already imagined himself in some remote hide-out with her in his power. He had four riflemen with him, besides Dabney and Chunz, and figured that was more than enough. His practice was to have as few witnesses as possible. As they moved forward, he could hear Cleve and Mariposa laughing and splashing in the pool. He thought: *That son of a bitch won't be laughing in a little while.*

He rounded a turn in the narrow path and walked straight into a double-barrel shotgun. "Hands up!" The command was repeated all around them. He knew when not to reach for a six-shooter. "Drop those rifles and stick 'em high!" The bushes bristled with shotguns and rifles, trained on his men.

"Keep your shirts on," he said. "We're just up here hunting."

Anastacio stepped forward. "Bullshit, Pancho! We know

what you're hunting. Chunz told us."

"That son of a bitch! I knew I should have killed him."

Chief Niño stepped in front of him and glared, not speaking. He dragged his finger across his throat. "You ain't gonna kill anyone any more, *gringo cabrón.*"

Wingfield felt the sand running out of him as he was marched up the path toward the cliff dwellings above. The defenders held him and his men in a tight group just beyond the pueblos, then prodded them forward.

Cleve was seated alone, like a judge, with a folding table as his bench. He gave Pancho a stony look. "You should have accepted my invitation to come in and talk the other night. I had to put these people to a lot of trouble to get a-hold of you." To Dabney he said: "I see you didn't go back to your old mother in Texas. What a shame."

Dabney was silent, suspecting where they were all headed.

Cleve said: "You birds have anything to say for yourselves? We know why you were up here. Chunz told us."

They were a scared-looking bunch, except for Devil Ed, who didn't have sense enough to be scared. He spotted Amy and Junior in the background and snarled: "You're the ones!" He felt the knot on his head that still hadn't gone down entirely.

Junior laughed and called: "She brained you with a big rock. I didn't."

Devil Ed glared at Amy, and she was glad he wasn't loose. She wondered what her pa would do to the man who had shot him.

Cleve said: "Take them down to their horses."

He struggled onto a horse for the first time since he'd been shot and followed. By now, the guard force had grown to thirty or more, as men came in from the perimeter where they'd been posted, hearing that they'd captured their quarry.

"We'll use their own ropes," Cleve decided.

That was too much for Dabney. "Please," he quavered. "They caught me and made me come with them."

Pancho gave him a disgusted look, then turned to Cleve. "That's a damn' lie."

Cleve said: "I don't especially give a damn whether it is or not."

At that point they were interrupted by the arrival of more men with Monty Ransom as their prisoner.

"I was out bear hunting," he said to Cleve.

Bandelier responded: "Pity you should show up when I'm not in a specially good mood." He called Anastacio to one side and conferred with him. When he came back, he said to Monty: "I got a special rope for you."

The Englishman didn't understand what was about to happen. "What do you mean?"

Wingfield said: "He means he's gonna hang you along with us, you dumb son of a bitch!"

"Hang me? For what?"

"For bein' a damn' nuisance," Cleve said.

They lined up the seven on their horses under several Ponderosas with convenient stout limbs, hands tied behind them, a man holding each horse until they affixed the ropes. Dabney pleaded all the while, but the rest of them were taking it like men.

"Where's Junior?" Cleve asked. "I want him here while we swing off the son of a bitch that shot my horse tryin' to beef him."

"Here I am, Pa. I had to shoo Amy back."

Cleve showed Monty his special rope before they affixed it about his neck. It had a red bandanna tied around it above the noose. "I figure you deserved a little extra attention," Cleve told him. "If I had a Union Jack, I'd have used it. I know you're a gentleman, so we won't even tie your hands behind you."

Ransom was accepting his fate like a true warrior and officer of Her Majesty's forces — with a stiff upper lip. He hadn't expected to meet death this morning, but he'd known he would sooner or later and had resolved, years before, to meet it like a man.

At a signal from Cleve a man quirted each horse smartly, and they leaped forward, leaving their riders swinging behind — except Monty. His rope parted and he left with the noose still around his neck as his horse bolted. In a while he got it under control, turned, waved, and yelled: "You only get one chance!" He whirled the horse and spurred off. He was a mile away before he removed the rope from his neck and saw that the end had been cleanly cut. He muttered to himself: "The bloody *bastard,* he was pulling a prank on me. What a tale to tell the grandkids, if I ever have any."

Mariposa met Cleve when he came back to the cliff dwellings, curious about what he'd done. He was silent a while, took out a cigar her father had given him, spent his time getting it going to his satisfaction before he said: "What are we going to do about us? I'm leaving as soon as your father can make the arrangements."

"And I am going with you."

He frowned. "I don't think I'm exactly someone you want to have around the rest of your life. I'm not much more than an ignorant cow hand."

She came to him, pushed the cigar out of the way, and kissed him. "You're the man I'm going to marry. If you won't ask me, I guess I'll have to ask you." She saw that he was going to protest further and put her hand over his mouth. "If you have no honor, I will point out that *gentlemen* always make honest women of their conquests."

He laughed. "I guess that'll be your first success at making me into a gentleman."

"Besides, I might be pregnant."

The thought hadn't occurred to him. He was too dazed in his aura of happiness. He looked straight at her, watching her pupils dilate as she divined what he was thinking. "I hope you are. I'd like a little girl just like you. I'm not sure about another boy like Junior."

They both laughed. "If I'm not pregnant, I'm sure we can do something about it soon."

Mariposa regretted that her father couldn't be present when *Padre* Maldonado tied the knot for her and Cleve, but it was a formality they would repeat for his benefit.

Epilogue

A strange entourage emerged from a palace car in New York City a few weeks later: Cleve, looking like he'd been shoehorned into a dude suit, Mariposa on his arm; his two kids, Junior and Amy, wide-eyed; Sam Buchanan and Jesús Sandoval; and last, Grut Voerbeck and Daisy.

Voerbeck said: "I have a special place up the Hudson, that I've borrowed from a friend, where we can stay till our steamship gets in."

He didn't explain why they couldn't stay at a hotel, but the reason was that he knew they'd have trouble getting a good hotel to allow Sam Buchanan to stay there.

A historic formal photo was taken of the party in a New York City gallery. In the center are Grut and Daisy, seated, Mariposa also seated, with Cleve standing, hand on her shoulder, with his other hand thrust into the breast of his coat, Amy and Junior bracketing them, and Sam and Jesús at the very ends. Years later it would be a perennial in outlaw-lawman photo albums compiled by authorities who knew as little about the people about whom they pontificated as they did of Swahili grammar. The photo always appeared in a discrete section titled: **The Amarillo War**.

Another photo exists that never became public, taken of the wedding of Grut and Daisy, when Cleve and Mariposa joined them in a second wedding for Grut's sake. He put the final touch on the affair by inquiring: "How can I give the bride away when I'm the *victim,* standing next to her with my own bride in a double wedding?"

"Mind your tongue, old fellow," Daisy cautioned him.

A clipping from the files of the Santa Fé *New Mexican*, dated August 13, 1882, reads:

> News reaches us from Dorado that the night train from Colorado was stopped just south of the line where two armed and masked men entered the cab and took charge, while others loaded horses onto the usual live-stock car. The men, masked in long sheets with eye holes, remained in control of the train until it reached Dorado, where they ordered it stopped. The horses were unloaded, and supposed accomplices rode forward after some delay and picked up the two bandits who had held the trainmen under their guns, then all galloped off into the night. The engineer pulled out immediately, for fear the men might return, and raced, full-throttle, for Española. At daylight, early risers in Dorado noticed bulky objects lying at the side of the right of way, which investigation revealed to be the bodies of six men. Two were well known in that town, being Frank Wingfield and Harmony Dabney, formerly employed by the Amarillo Grant. An autopsy performed on those two by local coroner, Dr. Ewing, disclosed that they had both died of suffocation. Dr. Ewing, noted for his pithy findings, stated it was his opinion that they, as well as the other four, may had died of emphysema, which has symptoms similar to suffocation and sometimes occurs in high altitudes. Sheriff Butler of Dorado is investigating the deaths.

March 14, 1883
Mr. Grut Voerbeck
Leyden, Holland
Dear Mr. Voerbeck:

I urgently solicit your assistance in regard to the legal maneuvering in which the boundaries of the Amarillo Grant have been drastically reduced due to preposterous new legal decisions which have determined that the original grant was only 42,000 acres, as the squatters who preyed on your herds always maintained, and that intervening decisions to the contrary were in error.

This request is made because I know that you will want to see the right thing done. It may be necessary for you to return to America and appear in several hearings.

Haste is necessary since the U. S. Land Office is again opening the land to homestead entries, and Congress has set aside a reservation on it for the lawless Jicarilla Apaches.

I look forward to an early reply.

Very truly yours,

s/Tomás Pringle

The reply was written on a ship *en route* to Argentina and posted from Rio De Janeiro.

April 1, 1883
Tomás Pringle, Esq.
Santa Fé, New Mexico, USA
Dear Mr. Pringle:

You are absolutely correct in your opinion that I

want to see the right thing done. Before I left your country, I conferred with Justices Bradley and Field, who have always been the most supportive toward entrepreneurs, and thought I had secured that end. I am sorry that you do not concur in their decisions, but I did the best I could.

My health does not permit my traveling. I'm afraid the troubled state of affairs when I was in New Mexico has completely broken down my nerves.

Sincerely yours,

s/Grut Voerbeck

New Mexico
June, 1930

The Packard touring car stopped in front of the two-story stone building with the gas pump out front. The faded sign on the porch read: **Mills and Evans, General Store**. Another touring car followed, filled with movie cameras and tripods.

Two men got out of the first car and went back to join two others who climbed out from the second. The rider from the first car, obviously the leader of the group, said: "This is the place, I guess. It doesn't look like much."

One of the others said: "We'll have to take down that sign. Do you suppose they'll let us do that?"

"This don't look like the world's most prosperous operation. Of course, they'll let you take it down. Money talks."

A short, very old Mexican man came out, followed by a tall, stooped Anglo. They were staying at the Amarillo ranch. Both seated themselves on the porch bench, watching the new arrivals.

The leader went up to them. "Do you fellows run this place?"

"Inside," the Anglo said. "Johnny Evans." He motioned with his thumb.

"Come on," the man called to his followers. "Maybe we can get something cold to drink."

He looked around the dim interior, spied a Nehi cooler, and went over to it. He found it full, but the pop was all warm, and he looked around in disgust.

From somewhere deep inside a voice asked: "Can I help you?"

"Got anything cold to drink?"

"I'm afraid not. The ice truck from Dorado broke down last week and ain't fixed yet. Pretty good water from the pump in the yard. There's a tin cup out there."

The four men exchanged looks. The leader said: "We're from Hollywood, and we're gonna make a movie about the famous outlaw leader, Cleve Bandelier, and the Amarillo Range War. Come to get some still shots and a little footage, then we'll shoot the rest in the San Fernando Valley, most likely. Anyone around here that might know anything about the war?"

The man looked at him a while and made a decision that amounted to strike three for Hollywood. "I don't reckon. Leastaways, I never heard of any war up here."

"Ain't this the house where it all started? Used to be outlaw headquarters for Bandelier and his gang?"

"I never heard that Bandelier was an outlaw. I guess he used to live here, all right. His name is the first one on the deed. But he was just a rancher."

"I read it different in a book."

The storekeeper looked disgusted. "A book! By who?"

"By the world's foremost authority on Bandelier and the Amarillo War."

"You might ask them two old-timers out front. They was around here then, I reckon."

The four went outside and looked over the old-timers, who ignored them. The leader shook his head and walked away to the pump, the others following. The leader said: "Anybody got a cup in the cars? I ain't gonna drink out of a community cup in a place like this."

Before they left, they sneaked a couple of free still shots of the building, knowing they could airbrush out the sign and two loafers on the porch. One of the troupe went back in and asked the storekeeper the way to Zamora Plaza, assuming the two on the porch might be too dense to know.

"Maybe we should have talked to those two old-timers," the driver said to the director, riding beside him as they drove away. "You can never tell."

The director said: "They'd turn out to be a couple of old windbags. I've heard it all before. It's all in the book. We wasted our money coming up here."

The storekeeper cranked the phone and raised Zamora Plaza. "That you, Refugio? A couple of big touring cars full of dudes are headed up your way. Get this! They said they're gonna make a movie about the *outlaw,* Cleve Bandelier, and the Amarillo Range War. Know all about it from a book. Charge 'em ten bucks a shot if they want to take pictures. I didn't think of it in time. They might even stand still for twenty."

In response to what was obviously a question from Refugio, Johnny Evans replied: "They wouldn't have to go over to the Amarillo Ranch to talk to him, he's sittin' on the front porch with Jesús. Ain't that a leg slapper? And don't you dare tell 'em he's in the country. If he wanterd to talk to 'em, he'd have spoke up."

The man on the porch to whom Evans referred turned to

his Mexican companion. "What do you make of that, Jesús? You hear what they called me."

"*Sí,* an outlaw."

"Wait'll I tell Mariposa that."

Glenn G. Boyer was born in a log cabin in Wood County, Wisconsin. He spent twenty-two years in the U. S. Air Force and retired as a command pilot with the rank of lieutenant colonel. While an Aviation Cadet in Santa Ana, California, Boyer met members of the Earp family and went on to become the doyen of historians of Wyatt Earp and his brothers, amassing a vast research collection that became the basis for numerous publications. Among the most notable of these have been *The Suppressed Murder Of Wyatt Earp* (1967), concerned with the development of the Wyatt Earp mythology, publication of the memoirs of Josephine Earp as *I Married Wyatt Earp* (1976) that also served as the basis for a motion picture for television, and more recently *Wyatt Earp's Tombstone Vendetta* (1993). He is currently at work on a definitive book collecting his numerous articles and essays about the Earps, Doc Holliday, and other historical personalities involved in the Earps years in Arizona. With *The Guns Of Morgette* (1982) Boyer launched a second career as a novelist of the American West. In his series about the adventures of Dolf Morgette and together with the novel, *Dorn* (1986), he readily established himself as one of the finest authors of the Western story, with fiction as notable for its sharp and penetrating characters and grippingly suspenseful plots as for the authenticity and accuracy of the historical backgrounds and settings.